To Love and to Cherish

KELLY IRVIN

HARVEST HOUSE PUBLISHERS

EUGENE, OREGON

Unless otherwise indicated, all Scripture quotations are taken from the King James Version of the Bible.

Cover by Garborg Design Works, Savage, Minnesota

This is a work of fiction. Names, characters, places, and incidents are products of the author's imagination or are used fictitiously. Any resemblance to actual persons, living or dead, or to events or locales, is entirely coincidental.

TO LOVE AND TO CHERISH
Copyright © 2012 by Kelly Irvin
Published by Harvest House Publishers
Eugene, Oregon 97402
www.harvesthousepublishers.com

Library of Congress Cataloging-in-Publication Data
  Irvin, Kelly.
  To love and to cherish / Kelly Irvin.
    p. cm.—(The Bliss Creek Amish ; book 1)
  ISBN 978-0-7369-4371-0 (pbk.)
  ISBN 978-0-7369-4372-7 (eBook)
  1. Amish—Fiction.   2. Abandoned wives—Fiction.   3. Widowers—Fiction.   4. Kansas—Fiction.
  5. Domestic fiction. I. Title.
  PS3609.R82T6 2011
  813'.6—dc22
                                                                  2011016288

Printed in the United States of America

12 13 14 15 16 17 18 19 20 / LB-NI / 10 9 8 7 6 5 4 3 2

To Tim, Erin, and Nicholas
Love always

Acknowledgments

As always, I'm awed by the people God puts in my life to guide, direct, and encourage me in my writing journey. This book would not exist if it weren't for the encouragement and persistent nudging of my agent, Mary Sue Seymour. Thank you, Mary Sue, for challenging me to try something outside my comfort zone. My thanks also to Kim Moore of Harvest House Publishing for taking a chance on me, and to my editor, Kathleen Kerr, for her discernment and care in helping me to shape the story into a true romance.

My path to publication would have veered into the wilderness long ago if it weren't for my writing buddies in the Alamo City Christian Fiction Writers group. Their prayers, fellowship, and encouragement mean so much to me. Eileen Key, Valerie Goree, Roxanne Sherwood, Donna Robertson, Heather Tipton, and Allison Pittman, I treasure the time I spend with you at those "board" meetings. A special thanks to Eileen for her eagle-eyed proofreading and for reminding me I'm not allowed to quit—not today.

My gratitude to my husband, Tim, and my children, Erin and Nicholas, for not only putting up with me, but for loving me for who I am.

Thank you, God, for the privilege of knowing each one of these people.

Chapter 1

The ripe aroma of wet earth filling the air around her, Emma Shirack shifted the basket of tomatoes on her hip and picked up her pace on the dirt road. Her bare feet sank down as the mud oozed between her toes.

The sky was dark overhead as rain clouds gathered in the distance. She should've taken the buggy, but hitching the horse seemed a waste of time when it was such a short walk to the produce stand on the highway. "Come on, girls. We have to get these tomatoes to Catherine at the stand quickly or we're going to get wet walking home."

Giggles met her urging. She glanced back to see the twins squatting in the middle of the road. Lillie had a small rock in her hand, and the two of them peered at it as if they'd found a great treasure. "Girls! Now!"

She used her schoolteacher voice. At five her sisters hadn't been to her school yet, but they recognized the authority in her tone. Lillie hopped to her feet, Mary right behind her. "See, it's a pretty rock, *schweschder*."

"*Jah*, very pretty, but right now we have work to do." A fat drop of rain plopped right between Emma's eyes. "As soon as we give the tomatoes to Catherine we'll go back to the house to start the chicken and dumplings for tonight."

Mary dropped the rock and clapped her tiny hands. "Dumplings!"

Her braids bouncing in glee, Lillie did the same. "Dumplings!"

Two peas in a pod. Emma smiled and focused on the road ahead. The smile faded. It would be so easy to pretend the twins were hers. But that would be wrong. They were her little sisters. At twenty-three, she alone among her friends had no babies of her own. As *Mudder* liked to say, "In God's time, not yours." Emma clung to that thought.

One more curve and they would be at the highway.

"Schweschder, where do the clouds—"

The shrieking of rubber on asphalt drowned out Lillie's question. Emma stopped dead in her tracks. The sound of ripping metal tore the air. A horse's fearful whinnies screamed and echoed against the glowering sky.

Emma's basket hit the ground. She'd spent enough time at the produce stand to know that sound. She lifted her long skirt, leaped across the spilled tomatoes, and ran. "Girls, go to the side of the road and sit down. Don't move! I'll send someone for you!" she shouted, not looking back. "Do as I say!"

The sound of their childish voices whipped in the wind around her. If she was right about that sound she couldn't let them see what lay ahead. For a few minutes, they were better off on the side of the less-traveled farm road with each other for company.

Oh, God, let me be wrong. Let it be a near miss. Let it be an empty wagon. Let it be…anything but the worst. She stumbled on the rutted road and her heavy dress tangled around her legs. Sweat mingled with splashing raindrops. She fought to breathe in the heavy, humid air.

The road straightened. Emma blinked against a sudden gust of moist, hot wind. Where dirt road met asphalt, where their way met the *Englisch* way, a buggy sprawled on its side, its metal wheels twisted and broken, the orange triangle-shaped symbol for *slow* still dangling from the back. A mammoth wheat truck, the black tarp that covered its load flapping in the wind, dwarfed the spindly remains.

Emma jerked to a stop. No air filled her lungs, and black and purple dots danced on the periphery of her vision. She bent, hands on her knees, and gasped for oxygen. Nothing. Her lungs ached. Her heart pounded.

The horse reared and screamed, its nostrils flaring, eyes frozen wide open, frantic with fear. Her sister Catherine had two hands on the reins, trying to calm the flailing horse. "Easy, girl, easy!" Catherine's words didn't match the heart-wrenching anguish of her tone as she fumbled with the harness. "Down, girl. It's over. Easy!"

Catherine. What was she doing here? Their horse. Their gray mare. Emma forced herself to think. Their horse. Her sister. Her gaze dropped to the figure on the dark, wet pavement. *No. No. No.*

Her neighbor Thomas Brennaman knelt next to a twisted figure that lay motionless. Her brother Luke crouched down next to him, bending over the still, white face. Mudder's face. Thomas raised his head and his fingers touched Mudder's throat. Emma swallowed the bile in her throat. She tore her gaze from the picture, her heart pounding.

A man in overalls and a John Deere hat held a cell phone to his ear. "Hurry. Tell them to hurry. They're hurt bad," he bellowed. "It's them Amish people with their buggies. I think I…I think I killed them!"

Killed them. *No.* Suddenly adrenaline overcame the paralyzing dread. She dashed forward. "Mudder! *Daed!*"

With all the strength he could muster, Luke staggered to his feet. "Emma, help Catherine with the horse! Let it loose before it hurts someone."

What was Luke doing here? Why wasn't he at his shop? She shook off her questions and his command and dropped to her knees next to her mother's still body.

But Thomas grabbed her arms and pulled her to her feet again. His broad frame served as a formidable barrier between Emma and her mother. "No, Emma. Do as Luke says."

"I can help her!"

Thomas's grip kept her from sinking to the ground again. Eyes the color of maple syrup held her tight in their gaze. Thomas, of all people, knew this kind of pain. "Your mudder is gone, Emma."

Still, she struggled. "Daed!"

Luke's strangled sob spoke for him. "No, Daed." She ripped away from Thomas and dashed around the broken buggy. "Please!"

Luke held up two bloody hands, palms flat in the air. Emma slammed to a halt. Her brother's raw agony radiated from his sweet, plain features. His lips trembled over his long beard. "No. Don't look. Don't! I tried, but nothing." His voice cracked. "He was already gone. Help Catherine. Help her!"

Sirens, their shrill cry an alien sound in this Kansas farmland, cut the air. Emma backed away from Luke. The rough asphalt scraped her feet, but she welcomed pain—the only thing that could penetrate this kind of numbness. She shook her head. "No. No!"

Catherine's cries forced her back into the moment. Here was something Emma could do, something to ease the horrible, enormous sense that she should be doing something. She ran to Catherine's side and together they loosened the horse's restraints and led her to the grassy shoulder of the road. The mare, sides lathered with sweat, snorted and pranced but didn't bolt. "Easy, girl, easy." Emma patted her long, graceful neck. "It's all right."

Words of comfort murmured where there was none.

Catherine threw herself into Emma's arms. "It was horrible. I saw the whole thing from the produce stand. Mudder waved to me and smiled as they slowed down to make the turn. Then the truck came…"

Catherine's voice faded. Her knees buckled.

Emma struggled to hold her up. "I'm sorry. I'm so sorry."

Her poor sister would have the images burned on her brain forever. Catherine didn't need to see any more of this horrific scene. Emma grasped her sister's trembling shoulders. "I need you to do something for me."

Catherine's face was white and wet with rain and tears. "I couldn't help them. I can't help anyone."

"Yes, you can." Emma hugged her and then gave a gentle shove. "Lillie and Mary are down the road. Go get them. Take them home."

Catherine shook her head and sobbed. "I don't want to tell them—"

"Don't. Don't tell them anything."

Catherine wiped at her face with a sodden sleeve. "Are you sure you don't want me to stay with you?"

"Go. Make sure they're safe. Take them home. Luke and I will come when we can."

"What about Annie and Mark? They'll wonder why Mudder hasn't come home from town yet."

"Tell them there's been an accident. Then wait for Luke and me."

Catherine took off, her stride unsteady at first, then she picked up speed. Faster and faster, as if those horrifying images pursued her.

Emma wanted to run after her, surpass her, and keep on running forever.

"Miss? Miss!"

She forced herself to turn and face the wreckage.

"It was an accident." The farmer, his craggy, sun-ravaged face wet—whether from rain or tears Emma couldn't tell—moved closer. He crumpled the green John Deere cap in his huge hand, smoothed it, crumpled it again. "I'm sorry, so sorry. I was in a hurry to get to the mill in Bliss Creek before the rain came. I drove up over the bluff and they were right there. I guess they slowed down to make the turn. I tried to stop. I did, but the truck skidded into them." He wiped his face with the backs of his stubby fingers. "It was an accident."

Luke strode toward them, his long legs eating up the road. Her bear-sized brother usually walked the road the way he walked life—in a calm, deliberate manner. Now the world had tilted, taking everything familiar with it. "I know, Mr. Cramer. Don't worry. We forgive you."

The man's mouth gaped wide, exposing crooked teeth. After a second, it closed. "Thank you," he whispered. "Thank you."

Emma raised her head to the spattering of raindrops. Maybe they would wash away the anger in her heart. When Carl had left, she'd thought the worst thing that could ever happen to her was done. Over. Now this. Not an intentional abandoning, but an accidental one. In the end, the effect was the same.

Luke was right to forgive. But sometimes right was too hard.

Chapter 2

Thomas longed to help her. Them. He longed to help them. He forced his gaze from Emma to Luke. They huddled by the side of the road, waiting in the misting rain. Their gazes strayed now and then to the yellow tarps the paramedics had used to cover the bodies. Their pain gathered like a shroud around them. It was so familiar. When cancer had finally taken his Joanna, she'd been a paper-thin replica of her former round self. Thomas gently laid her memory aside and focused on Luke. "I'll stay here until the medical examiner comes," he said. "You should go tell the others." He cleared his throat. "Annie and Mark will know something is wrong. You shouldn't keep them waiting."

"I can't leave them. Not here. Not on the road." Luke's voice cracked, but determination made his features sharp and noble. "I must deal with the officers and…the arrangements…for after they're finished here."

The screeching of tires on damp payment and the squeal of brakes interrupted the exchange. A truck with a microwave dish on top of it and TV station call letters splashed across the side skidded to a stop behind the police barricade. A man jumped from the driver's side and pulled a camera from the back.

The media loved to tell stories about the Plain people. The curiosity of the Englisch didn't bother Thomas, but it pained him to think of

Emma and Luke's grief displayed on a box in the living room of people who didn't know them or thought of them as an oddity that provided entertainment. "At least take Emma home. I'll stay with them until you come back."

Luke's gaze whipped from the photographer to the tarps. He wiped his eyes with a white handkerchief. "Could you walk her back?"

Luke's look was blank, unseeing, caught up as he was in his grief. Thomas wondered if he knew. Knew that Thomas wanted to be more than Emma's friend. Had William Shirack spoken of it? William had been a good man, a fair man, a dedicated father and husband. He had said Thomas was too old, too many years separated him from Emma. As much as every fiber of his being said William was wrong, Thomas had honored his wishes. "Of course—"

"You don't need to trouble yourself. I'll be fine." Emma's tone belonged to one bewildered, trying hard to fathom the unspeakable.

"No, but you will need someone to stand with you and Catherine when you tell Annie, Mark, and the twins." Thomas moved closer. "I would be honored to do that for you."

They began walking. She didn't speak. Silence cloaked them, but he knew thoughts ran rampant and loud in her head. The last time she'd seen her parents, what they'd said, all the insignificant moments that had become so enormously important. Enormously painful.

"Why were your parents together?" It didn't really matter, in the end, but the question filled the silence. "Why wasn't your father in the fields today?"

"Mudder finally convinced Daed to go to the doctor." Emma's voice was high, tight. "For the pains in his stomach."

She stumbled. He grabbed her elbow until she could right herself. She glanced at him, her eyes bright with pain. "*Danki* for being a good friend."

A good friend. He swallowed and let his hand drop. When he looked at Emma, he saw a beautiful girl with eyes the color of summer sky and white skin that would be soft under his farmer hands. She was sturdy, yet somehow the way the folds of her dress draped across her body hinted of a womanliness that caused him to look away in deference to propriety. Emma had a sweet disposition. She was intelligent. And faithful. Everything a man could want in a *fraa*. He saw in her the possibility of a fresh start with someone who would be a good wife and a mother for his two children. It was obvious that when she looked at him she saw a neighbor, her students' father, and an old family friend—with an emphasis on the *old*.

If a good friend was all she saw, that was what he must try to be.

Chapter 3

Emma shifted in the sofa. The nightmarish images in her head of the mangled buggy and her parents' lifeless bodies on the dark asphalt made the serenity of their home seem surreal. The weight of the twins, one on each side, seemed so much more when they were asleep. They looked so peaceful. What a blessing sleep must be. She remembered when they were born. The midwife had clapped her hands and said, "A double blessing."

In those days, Emma had been anticipating a life in which she would have many babies. She had been caught up in the preparations, trying to learn for when her time came. It had been a day of great joy. Mudder had thought herself done with childbearing, but the twins had been a welcome addition to their big family. The more the merrier, Daed had said. Mudder had been so happy with her little bundle on each arm.

Now they were gone and the twins' infectious laughter had turned to tears.

Of course, they hadn't really understood. They reacted more to the suffering of their big sisters and brother than to any realization of the meaning of Emma's words. They would grow up with loving sisters and brothers and aunts and uncles, but not parents. No one to call Mudder and Daed.

Catherine and Annie huddled on a long bench, Mark between them. Only a year apart in age, the girls could've been another set of twins, except Annie was taller. In this painful moment, she seemed intent on the role of older sister, her arm tight around Mark's shoulder. Their eyes and noses were red, but the sobs had subsided. Thomas stood at the window, the green blind lifted, staring out. Although he hadn't spoken a word, as was usual with his reserved character, his tall frame gave her a strange sense of comfort, as if his being there kept them safe from more bad news.

"Why was Luke at the stand?" The question kept her from thinking of other things, other questions yet to be answered. "Why wasn't he at his shop?"

"One of my horses threw a shoe. He was making a house call—my mother offered to feed him for his trouble." Thomas turned, his face creased with a sad smile. "They're coming."

Soon the house would be crowded with the men of the family. The women would come next. Emma breathed in and out. "Then we must prepare supper."

"Wait until your aunts arrive. They'll bring more food and they'll help." Thomas lifted Lillie from her lap. When the little girl opened her eyes, he smiled. "Time to wake up. You have company."

Lillie wiggled from his grasp and poked at Mary, then ran to the window. "The uncles are coming. And Luke. Is he staying for supper? Are William and Joseph coming, too?"

Luke's sons most likely would come later, but this would be a time of discussion for the adults. Emma stood and smoothed her apron. "Catherine, Annie, make some lemonade. And heat up that chicken casserole. Mark, after the twins eat take them to their room so they can get ready for bed. I'll be up to say prayers later."

"I want to see Luke! I want to play with Joseph!" Lillie's face scrunched up in a frown. Mary's quickly matched it.

Before she could add to the refrain, Emma pointed at the door. "Not tonight. Go."

The children went, their faces downcast.

Catherine hadn't moved. "How can you think of food right now?"

"Not for us. For them."

Her lips drawn in a tight line, Catherine sprang from the sofa and stomped toward the kitchen, her long skirts flouncing. Annie followed, but paused in the doorway. "Don't worry, Emma," she said. "We know what to do. You talk to Luke. Ask him…ask him what we'll do now."

What would they do now? Annie had asked the question Emma had been trying to ignore. Without Daed, who would run the farm? Who would harvest the corn and alfalfa and wheat and take care of the livestock? She and the girls could handle the vegetable garden, but an entire farm? With three children who needed supervision?

The house filled with men, each one greeting her with simple words of condolences. After greeting them, Thomas turned to go, but Luke stopped him with one big hand on his arm. "Stay."

"You have talking to do. Plans to make—"

"You're a good friend. A wise one."

Thomas inclined his head and settled back on the bench next to Mark. The boy scooted a little closer and Thomas laid a hand on his shoulder. Luke turned to Emma. "The arrangements are made. They'll bring the…bring them here tomorrow morning. The funeral will be the day after."

"I'll get the clothes." Mudder would need her white apron and Daed his Sunday suit.

Luke's jaw twitched. "Uncle Noah will take them to the funeral home."

She nodded. The furniture would need to be rearranged. The wake would begin as soon as Mudder and Daed arrived.

Luke sank into a chair. "We need to talk about what happens… after."

"I'll stop teaching." The words were out before the thought was fully formed. "Mark and the twins will need me."

"The school needs you. And we need your income."

"They'll understand and we'll make do. The family comes first."

"I'll take care of the children." Annie stood in the doorway. The nineteen-year-old's gaze fell on the deacon. Then Uncle Noah. Uncle Peter. Uncle Timothy. She turned to Emma. "I'm old enough to care for them and the house. And the garden. With Catherine's help."

"But what about Robert? Aren't you and he—"

Annie shook her head hard. Her beseeching expression made Emma close her mouth. "Or I could take the teaching job, if you prefer to oversee the household."

"I have no doubt you're capable of taking over the teaching duties." Luke's tone was gentle. "But your income from the pies and cakes you sell at the produce stand is more than we can afford to lose. As are Catherine's earnings from cleaning the Englisch homes. We need everyone to work, and I don't believe you can bake and sell all those desserts with two five-year-olds underfoot. Even if Mark helps." He let out a heavy sigh. "But that doesn't address how we'll keep the farm going."

"Then what do you suggest?" Emma struggled to keep her tone civil. It wasn't Luke's fault he'd suddenly become head of two households. "We can't lose the farm, and we have to take care of the children."

"Either we sell this farm and you all move in with Leah and me, or I sell the shop and our home and we move here."

Live with Leah. Emma tried to imagine that. Leah had been ahead of her at school. They'd never been close. When Luke and Leah married Emma had tried to be friendly, but her advances had been met with a reserve that she couldn't seem to penetrate. Her brother's wife was a taciturn woman who'd grown up in a family even more conservative than Emma's. She always seemed to be frowning at Emma's light-hearted approach to life. Emma couldn't remember ever hearing her laugh, not even at the wedding.

Emma glanced at Deacon Pierce and the uncles. Daed's brothers. Mudder's brothers. It surprised her that none had joined the discussion. She studied their faces. They were all looking at Luke. He was the head of the family now. The eldest son. The decision would be his. And she would have to live with it, even if that meant learning to live with Leah.

She opened her mouth, then shut it. This was her home. All of them, including Luke, had grown up here. His home was small, too small for their combined broods. Luke cherished the home he'd made with Leah, too. He'd worked hard as an apprentice blacksmith. Now he owned the only place in town where horses could be shod. The brisk business supported his family. The decision should be his. "Luke, I don't want to lose the farm, but I don't want you to lose your shop, either. Whatever you decide, that's what we'll do."

Catherine inched into the room. "What about Josiah?"

At seventeen, Josiah wasn't old enough to run a farm by himself, but another set of hands and feet would help. Emma met Luke's gaze. He nodded. "He'll have to be told," Luke said. "He'll need to come home. Maybe this will…"

Luke didn't finish the sentence, but Emma finished his thought in her head. Maybe this would make Josiah see how important it was to end his *rumspringa* and be baptized. When the first year passed and he made no move to go to the baptism classes, they'd all been surprised. When he'd taken up with a New Order Mennonite family in Wichita, Emma's parents had been devastated. Now they were gone and Josiah would never be able to make it right with them.

Thomas shifted in his chair, his long legs sticking out almost to the sofa. "Josiah must be told. Now." His brow furrowed. "Tonight. If the things I hear are true, he's far into the fancy ways. He could see the story on the television. That's no way for him to learn of your parents' passing."

Luke stood. "I'll make the decision on the…other matters…when I return." He brushed past Emma and headed to the door. "I have to get him back here in time for the funeral."

"I'm going with you." Emma couldn't let Luke bear this burden alone. "He's my brother, too."

Chapter 4

Luke hired his Englisch friend Michael to drive them to Wichita. Emma sank down into the soft upholstery of the backseat. It felt like a cocoon that kept her safe from the world streaking outside the windows. Darkness cloaked the car so she couldn't see the passing scenery, but the rushing of the air outside made her feel as if she were flying.

As a child, she'd loved the outings her parents had planned that involved hiring a car. The trip to the Wichita zoo. Visits to friends who'd left to start new districts. Eating chicken fried steak and French fries in a restaurant. And now this new memory, riding into unfamiliar territory to tell her little brother their parents were gone.

And what would Josiah say? A conversation with Mudder replayed in Emma's head. Her mother had blamed herself for Josiah's prolonged running around. He should never have been allowed to go to Wichita. Of all the Shirack children, his will had been hardest to break from the time he was small and refused to sit still for the prayer before meals. At seventeen, he chose to stay with a Mennonite family that had abandoned many of the Plain ways in favor of the more relaxed New Order. She had worried he would find those ways alluring.

Emma's mind whirled round and around. Josiah would find his way back. He tested boundaries, but he had a passion for his faith. His heart was good. Miriam Yonkers, the girl he had courted before moving away, still waited patiently for him. The image of Miriam's bright face, with its freckles and brown eyes, warmed Emma's heart. The girl came from a conservative family. She worked hard at her father's harness shop, was steadfast in her faith, and committed in her feelings for Josiah. And she had a lovely laugh. He would want to come back to her.

A small sniff in the darkness broke the silence. Ragged breathing told her Luke was trying to stifle the tears. "Luke?"

"I'm fine."

She let her hand creep toward his. He grasped it, held tight for a second, then let go.

She swallowed the hard lump in her throat. "Did you mean what you said to the farmer?"

"I always mean what I say." His hoarse voice quivered. "It was an accident."

She knew that. Still, bitterness and anger wrapped around her heart. She didn't know how to make it dissolve into the lovely grace of sweet Jesus that she'd been brought up to believe in. "Knowing the right thing to do or say is different from being able to believe it."

"You don't believe Mr. Cramer deserves our forgiveness just as we've been forgiven?"

She closed her eyes, put both hands to her face, and listened to the rushing air. "Jah, but I can't find it in my heart."

"Look harder."

Luke was disappointed in her. The thought rankled. She dropped her hands. "When Carl left, I was so angry. It's been four years and sometimes, I'm still angry," she whispered. "I think I have a hard heart."

"You have a generous, loving heart. Carl made a choice that hurt you, but more than that, it hurt him. Do you ever think of what his life is like away from his family and our community?"

"Jah. I also think of what we would've had. A marriage. Children." She bit her lip and focused on the dark windows through which she could see nothing except an occasionally bouncing light. "This morning, I was listening to the twins laugh and I caught myself wishing they were my children, pretending they were mine. You don't think...I mean, now I will raise them."

The painful confession hung in the air. She waited, eyes closed, listening to her brother's jerky breathing. Finally, he cleared his throat. "I'm a simple man, not the smartest man, but I think God is a loving God. He is far too wise to do that. You'll keep teaching. Leah and I will raise the girls."

The words inside her head ached to get out. That wasn't fair. They had two boys already. She had no children of her own. She stayed quiet. Giving the girls a good and faithful home and family life—that was the goal. Not being fair.

Teaching made her happy. Maybe that was God's plan all along.

She couldn't help it. "Now the happiness is gone again," she whispered.

Her brother sighed. "We will be happy again."

"It doesn't feel that way." She nibbled at her bottom lip, trying not to cry. "I don't understand. Our family has been faithful to God all our lives. Mudder and Daed were faithful. Why didn't He protect them?"

Luke didn't answer for a long time. "Like I said, I'm not that wise. Daed would have been able to answer."

"Daed would've said it's not up to us to know God's plan, only to believe that He has one. His will be done, not ours."

"See, you already knew the answer."

Feeling like a small, stubborn child, Emma folded her arms. "The problem is I don't like the answer."

This time Luke didn't respond. She was making him feel worse with her rebellious attitude. "I'm sorry, *bruder*," she whispered.

Sorry she couldn't be stronger in her faith.

"Me, too." His whisper matched her trembling tone.

The car stopped at a flashing red light.

"We're almost there." Michael's voice rasped with fatigue. "I just wanted to give you some forewarning, so you might think about what you'll say."

Luke shifted on the seat next to her. "I know what I'll say."

His callused hand patted hers and withdrew. The small gesture almost undid her. He might be disappointed by her difficulty with forgiveness, but his love remained unconditional. She drew strength from the thought.

Several minutes later, Michael pulled up next to the curb. He turned off the car. Sudden silence broken only by the *tick, tick* of the hot engine enveloped them. A stark streetlight threw rays that bounced against an oak tree in the front yard of a red brick house. Michael turned in the seat. "I'll wait here for you."

Determined to get it over with, Emma beat Luke to the door. She knocked with a sharp rap. Luke shook his head and pointed. A doorbell. "Oh." She pressed and a muffled melody rippled on the other side of the door.

A few seconds passed, each one longer than the last. Finally, the door opened. Sarah Kauffman, her face full of surprise, stood there staring. Emma stared, too. The girl wore shorts, a sleeveless T-shirt, and purple plastic flip-flops. Only the *kapp* that slid halfway down her head, long hair spilling out of it, suggested she wasn't entirely Englisch. "Emma, Luke, what are you doing here? Joe didn't say you were coming."

Joe? "We need to speak to Josiah."

Emma saw the moment when the teenager realized their presence could only mean something bad had happened. Her smile crumpled and she hurriedly backed away from the door. "Right. I'm sorry. Come in. Please come in." She gestured to the living room. "I'll get him."

Emma followed Luke into the room and immediately moved to the sofa, but Luke remained standing, his big hands slack at his side. From time to time they curled into fists. He immediately shook his fingers out again. "Luke, do you want me—"

He shook his head, his gaze still on the hallway through which Sarah had disappeared.

The slam of a door and feet pounding on the wooden floor told Emma that Josiah had received the message. His face red under a mop of unruly brown hair, he stomped into the room. He wore shorts and a white T-shirt and carried a shiny, flat box in his hand that had wires that went to his ear. Emma barely recognized him as her little brother. Not so little. He'd grown in the six months since he'd turned seventeen. "I'm not going home."

Even his voice had changed. Deeper with a slight edge that said Josiah intended to fight.

Tugging the wire from one ear, he halted at the edge of the huge braided rug as if it were a fence between them. "I don't know what you've heard, but I'm not going back."

"Josiah…" Luke moved toward the sofa. "Sit down."

"Why is Emma here? Why did Daed send you? Why didn't he come?"

Luke's face broke Emma's heart. He cleared his throat. "There was an accident."

After that Emma ceased to hear his words. She could only see Josiah's face as the would-be man crumbled, leaving behind a little boy too shocked to speak. He shook his head. She knew exactly the feeling in the pit of his stomach and the throbbing ache where his heart had been. She stood and went to him and held out her arms. He walked into the hug, but his wiry body didn't relax against her. He stepped back, brown eyes wet with unshed tears. "I'll pack."

"Good. We have to get back. Tomorrow there will be so much to do."

Josiah nodded and whirled to go. At the doorway, he turned back again. "I'll go, but I'm not staying."

Chapter 5

Mudder and Daed had spent their last night in their family home. Emma's back ached from sitting up straight on the crowded bench, and her fingers hurt from twisting them in her lap. The bishop had been speaking for almost an hour. It would be over soon. Annie's soft sniff told Emma her sister had given in to the tears. Catherine, seated on the other side, hadn't made a sound through the entire funeral service. The twins looked half asleep. Emma nudged Catherine, who immediately tapped Lillie's arm. The little girl straightened and giggled, the sound light in the heavy air.

Frowning, Leah leaned past Miriam, who sat between them, tilted her head toward Emma, and shook it vigorously. As if Emma needed to have Luke's wife tell her that Lillie should behave herself. She lifted the girl into her lap and put her lips to her ears. "*Shhh*. Hush up and say a prayer."

The bishop went on as if he'd heard nothing. Emma hoped he hadn't. It was her job now to make sure the children behaved. So as not to embarass Luke.

The bishop intoned the verses of the Gospel of John that spoke of everlasting life. Emma blinked back tears. When he closed the Bible, everyone knelt. It was a relief to be on her knees. To allow the bishop to speak for her what she couldn't say to God herself.

Annie's hand on her arm jerked her back to this place in time where her parents were making their final journey. She realized the bishop had begun the benediction. She stood on trembling legs, Lillie's tiny hand in hers.

"William and Ruth Shirack were married twenty-seven years. They had eight children." He'd moved on to the obituaries. The simple summing up of two lives full of love, hard work, and faithfulness to the *Ordnung*.

As the bishop finished they rose simultaneously. Miriam squeezed between Catherine and Annie. "Emma, I'm so sorry. Is there anything I can do?"

Emma swallowed tears that threatened her determination to remain steadfast in this time of darkness. She cleared her throat. "You can find Josiah, make sure he's all right."

The expression on Miriam's freckled face looked uncertain. Her eyes were wet with tears. She had such a heart for others' pain. "Of course. I looked for him earlier, but I couldn't find him. He hasn't come to see me. I know he must need time to mourn, but I thought I might offer some small comfort."

Emma patted her arm. "People mourn in different ways. Especially men. There will come a time when he will need you."

Miriam nodded. Her cheeks blushing pink, she sighed. "I'll go to him."

After admonishing Catherine to keep a tight rein on Lillie and Mary, Emma followed Miriam from the room. She rushed down the hallway toward the bedroom where the simple wooden caskets sat on trestles her uncles had built. The men and women began to move the benches for the viewing. Aunt Rachel and Aunt Bertha would take care of serving the refreshments.

She rounded the corner, intent on the tasks at hand. Josiah leaned against the wall, his hand to his ear. Miriam whirled at her approach. "Oh, Emma, I don't know…he's talking on a cellular phone!"

Emma halted. "Josiah, is that a phone?"

He straightened and his hand dropped to his pants, but not before

Emma saw the compact black phone. She'd seen many like it in town where the Englischers seemed to delight in having loud conversations as they perused the items on the grocery store shelves or bought muffins at Sadie Plank's bakery.

Defiance radiating from his face, Josiah crossed his arms. "So what if it is?"

"At your parents' funeral?" Emma turned to Miriam. "I'm so sorry you're in the middle of this. Please…could you help in the kitchen? I'll take care of it."

Her expression stricken, Miriam looked back at Josiah. "I want to help. If you need to talk, you can talk to me. You don't need that phone."

Josiah had the good grace to look embarrassed. He took a step closer to Miriam, pointedly ignoring Emma. "I'm sorry. I know you expected something from me, but I don't think I'll be able to give it to you. I'm sorry, really I am."

Her cheeks blazing, Miriam stepped back and turned to Emma. "I won't say anything. I know you'll make it right."

She fled without looking back.

Glancing around to make sure Luke and her uncles were nowhere in sight, Emma grabbed Josiah's arm and ushered him into the boys' bedroom. She managed to keep her voice at a furious whisper. "Have you no shame? You just hurt a person who cares deeply for you. And you've shamed us all by bringing this phone into our home! Do you realize what could happen? Who could you be calling at a time like this?"

"Maybe at a time like this I need to talk to my friends." His voice wavered between harsh and tearful tones. She could see the little boy inside busting to get out. "And I didn't call. I texted and I listened to a voicemail."

"Texted?"

"Yeah, you know, typed messages."

"Splitting hairs. You have friends here. People like Miriam. She's been waiting for you to approach her."

"I don't know what to say to her. Things have changed."

"Her feelings for you haven't."

"I can't help that."

"You're not trying."

Josiah smacked his fist against his open palm. "You of all people should understand. You saw how Carl needed to leave."

"And I know what Miriam will go through if you don't mend your ways. You have to get rid of that thing. Now, before Luke finds out. Before Leah finds out."

"What do you want me to do?" Josiah shrugged. "Throw it in the trash? I'm not doing that. It belongs to Sarah."

"Why did she give it to you, then? She knows it's forbidden. The bishop doesn't allow it."

"She knows, but she couldn't stand the thought of not being able to talk to me."

The significance of what he was saying hit Emma like an enormous boulder shaken loose in an avalanche. "You and Sarah are…"

He nodded. "We are."

"It has to stop. No more." The dark, gaping tunnel that Miriam would face opened in front of Emma. The sight was all too familiar. Emma had walked through it alone, and the memories still haunted her. "Please don't do this to Miriam. She's been waiting patiently since you went to Wichita. She doesn't deserve this."

The belligerence drained from Josiah's face. He ducked his head. "I'm sorry about Miriam. I didn't plan this. Sarah and I became friends and then we realized it was more than that. Miriam is a good person, but my feelings are for Sarah now." His hoarse voice dropped to a whisper. "You're not my mother. And anyway, the decision is mine. Mudder and Daed would tell you that if they were here."

He held the phone close to his heart as if she might try to snatch it away. "I'm only doing what you didn't have the strength to do. You wanted to go with Carl, but you were too afraid of what Daed would say. So now you're stuck here all alone, no husband, no children. An old maid."

The cruel words sliced through her like the molten poker Luke used when he made the horseshoes. The truth at the center of Josiah's malice dared her to deny it. She had missed the opportunity for her own children because of Carl's decision, but she'd never considered going with him. No matter what it cost, it wasn't worth her faith. "You don't know what you're talking about. Carl never asked me to go with him. If there was one good thing about him, it was that. He never asked me to abandon my family or my faith."

"Because he figured you were too scared. Too weak."

"No, too strong."

They glared at each other. The air around them seemed to quiver with animosity. It was more than Emma could bear. On this day of all days, she needed her brothers and sisters to be close. "Throw the phone away. Get rid of it. Now. Go find Miriam and apologize."

"I can't." He punched buttons on the phone and held it to his ear, a look of pain mixed with bravado plastered across his face. "Daed and Mudder are gone now. Life is short. I have to do what makes me happy."

"You're not an adult. You're only seventeen. You don't get to decide—not yet." She snapped forward and tried to snatch the phone away. He danced back, leaving her hand dangling in empty air. "Give it to me."

"No."

If she couldn't discipline Josiah over a phone, how would she make him see reason on other, bigger things? She stood still and breathed. After a few seconds, she looked him in the eye and spoke very softly, so softly he had to lean forward to hear. "Then take it to the barn for now. I want you to have Sarah come and get it. Immediately."

The emotion faded from his face. He shoved the phone in his pocket and headed toward the door. A snippet of wire hung from his waistline. "What is that?"

He glanced down. "Oh, that." His face reddened again. He snatched the wire up and the flat box he'd carried in his hand at the Kauffmans' appeared. "It's an iPod. You are so out of it, sister."

She'd heard of iPods. She wasn't so *out-of-it* that she didn't know what it was. But she'd never seen the little electronic box that allowed people to listen to all those songs like they played on the radio at the restaurant in town. "You can't listen to music on that thing. It's forbidden."

Josiah shook his head, his expression full of disbelief. "It's only music."

"It's worldly. It's obvious that it has led to feelings you shouldn't be having, thoughts that are taking you to places you shouldn't go. Take it to the barn with the phone." She pointed at the door. "Now."

Muttering under his breath, Josiah shuffled toward the front door. His hand reached for the knob, then dropped. He turned back. "You know that verse that says, *This is the day which the Lord hath made; we will rejoice and be glad in it?*"

She nodded, even though she knew where the question was headed. "How's that working out for you?"

He disappeared through the door before she could answer. Thankfully. She had no answer. It seemed God had forsaken her. And now Josiah had chosen a road that could take him far, far away. Who could rejoice on a day like this?

The enormity of Josiah's actions stunned her. Luke couldn't know. The elders couldn't find out. Did her brother understand the kind of trouble he could get into? And the trouble he brought on her by putting her in the position of knowing about his sin? Miriam stood to lose the most. Would she be able to keep her promise to remain silent? Emma would understand if she didn't. A broken heart and a violation of the Ordnung at the same time. It had to be wrenching for her.

Emma bent over for a second, fighting lightheadedness. Josiah's words had cut deeply. She had no husband or children because she'd been unwilling to leave her family and her faith. She'd done the right thing. Still, it seemed as if she were the one being punished, not Carl. She was stuck, unable to move forward because of his betrayal.

"Are you all right?" Thomas stood in the hallway, his sharp features dark with worry. "Do you need to sit down?"

Emma straightened and smoothed her apron. "I'm fine. I need to prepare for the viewing."

Thomas drew her toward the kitchen. "Your face is white. Sit—I'll bring you a glass of water. The men are placing the caskets. You have a few minutes."

He dodged Aunt Bertha, who carried some sort of casserole, and grabbed a glass from the open shelves. Emma took a quick look around. No Miriam. She was probably too overwrought to help in the kitchen. Emma prayed she had a friend she could confide in. Someone to help her through her pain, as Annie and Catherine and the cousins had done for Emma.

Thomas handed the water to her without speaking. The lump in her throat might not allow her to drink it. The quiet in the kitchen permitted her to breathe in and out without fearing someone would know she was falling apart inside. She sipped the cool water and the lump eased a little. "Danki, Thomas."

He nodded, then shuffled from one foot to the other. His gaze dropped to the floor. He was never a big talker, at least not in her presence. She set the glass on the table. "I should help with the viewing."

"Jah." He ducked his head. "I baked two loaves of bread and a lemon cake…"

The image of Thomas in an apron, kneading dough, lightened her mood for a moment. "I didn't know you baked."

"I do many things I had no need to do before." Before Joanna died. His matter-of-fact tone made Emma's heart ache for him. He gave her a rueful smile. "I want Rebecca to learn. My mother and sisters help, but it's not the same as having a mother at home. I can't teach her to sew and do all the womanly things Joanna would've wanted her to know."

Joanna had been a lovely person with a gentle spirit. Emma recalled her as a woman who never had an unkind word for anyone—just the right person to bring a shy, awkward man out of his shell. Thomas knew about loss. "I don't know how you do it." She straightened her kapp. "I don't know if I can. Luke has decided he will sell his home and move his family back here. Leah and the children and us all under one roof."

Thomas wiped his hands on a towel. "I know. He told me." His gaze caught hers. "That worries you. Living with Leah."

He was an observant man. It shamed Emma to admit her misgivings.

She hadn't told anyone, not even Catherine or Annie. "Jah," she whispered. "Does that make me ungrateful? It is a sacrifice for them."

"Change that comes from tragedy is bound to be hard." This time his smile didn't reach his eyes. "You'll learn to get along with Leah—"

"Do what with me?" Leah stood in the doorway, her round face frowning once again. She glanced from Thomas to Emma. "Are you talking about me?"

"No. Yes. I mean…" Emma stuttered. "I was just telling Thomas that you and Luke are moving here to help with the farm and the children."

Leah's frown deepened. "You should be helping instead of chattering with Thomas. The twins are racing around like little vermin and Luke is looking for you. The viewing line is forming. You should be there."

Emma jumped to her feet. "I'm coming."

Leah whirled and disappeared down the hallway, leaving Emma biting her tongue to keep from saying something ugly. To her surprise, Thomas chuckled. "God strengthens our characters in ways we may not appreciate, but like the Father He is, He knows what is best for us."

Emma squared her shoulders and started for the door. "Does that mean we have to like it?"

She made it halfway down the hallway when a solid rap at the front door drew her away from the viewing area. Probably a latecomer. Emma hoped it wasn't more food. The tables were practically groaning under the weight of the dishes. The cabinets in the kitchen were crowded with pots, platters, and bowls. They'd have to start putting dishes on the floor.

She opened the door. Bob Cramer, his John Deere hat shoved back on his sun-wrinkled face, stood there, looking like he wished he were anywhere else in the world. A chubby woman in a black dress stood next to him. He held a casserole dish in two meaty hands while the woman clutched a pie tin in hers.

"Mr. Cramer." Emma's throat closed up. The last person she wanted to see on the day of her parents' funeral was the man who killed them. "What are you doing here?"

He thrust the casserole at her. "Sorry to intrude on your day of mourning, ma'am." Not knowing what else to do, Emma took the dish. Mr. Cramer jerked his head toward the woman. "This here's the missus, Lois Cramer. She made the lasagna. And the pie."

Mrs. Cramer craned her head as if to look over Emma's shoulder. "It's cherry. Made it myself this morning."

Emma's feet were cemented to the floor. She cleared her throat. Duty dictated that she should let them in. They'd come to mourn with her. She cleared her throat again and took two steps back so they could pass. "It's nice of you to come."

"Don't worry, we're not staying." Mr. Cramer shifted, but he didn't enter. "I just wanted to say again how sorry I am for what happened." His voice choked. His eyes reddened. "Worst thing that ever happened to me."

To him? Worst thing that ever happened to Emma and her family. She choked back the words. "Do you need a glass of water?" she asked.

"You're so sweet, dear." Mrs. Cramer whipped past Emma and set the pie on the nearest chair. She immediately returned to her husband's side. "What my husband means to say is if we can do anything for you, anything at all, please call—I mean come by…You know what I mean. Just ask."

Emma opened her mouth. Closed it. The sound of steps behind her gave her a reprieve. Luke appeared at her side. "There you are. The twins need your attention." His words trailed off. "Mr. Cramer. How kind of you to come. Would you like to come in?" He frowned at Emma but didn't remark on her lack of hospitality. "The viewing is almost over. We'll be leaving for the cemetery soon, but you're welcome to join us."

"No, no." Mr. Cramer's face turned a red so dark it looked purple. "I was just telling your sister if there's anything you need, you just holler. I noticed you still got wheat out there. You need help harvesting, you let me know. I've got equipment and farmhands. We'll get you taken care of in a jiffy."

"I'll keep that in mind." Luke smiled, nothing in his response reflecting the fact that they could never use the farmer's equipment. "I appreciate the offer, sir."

"Least I can do." Mr. Cramer ducked his head. "If it weren't for me—"

"Everything is as God planned it." Luke held out his hand. "I told you. You're forgiven."

How could he do it? How could he be so forgiving? Shame coursed through Emma. She framed the words, but nothing came out. Her voice was locked in a painful battle with her heart.

Mr. Cramer grabbed Luke's hand and pumped it. Luke winced, but managed a smile.

"We won't keep you." Mr. Cramer doffed his hat at Emma. He and his wife walked down the steps toward an old green truck. They held hands.

The wind caught Mrs. Cramer's high voice and whipped her words in the air. "See, that wasn't so bad, was it?"

The line of buggies stretched as far back as Thomas could see. He reined in the roan a little. She kept trying to pick up the pace as the funeral procession moved slowly behind the wagon carrying the caskets. Thomas, too, would have liked to hurry—hurry to find a way to be close to Emma. To provide her with support, if nothing else. Finally they made the turn and entered the cemetery. Eli and Rebecca fidgeted on the seat behind him. "We're here."

"Finally." Eli leaped down.

"Son, behave yourself. This is a sad occasion. Children are not to be heard."

"Jah, Daed." Eli threw the words back as he trotted away, probably looking for Mark and the twins. Knowing Eli's kind nature, he would try to make them feel better with a little story or the pretty, smooth pebbles he'd picked up along the creek.

Thomas tied the reins to the hitching post and swung Rebecca to the ground. Without a word she put her hand in his, and together they made their way through the gathering crowd. She'd been quiet since he'd told her about the deaths of their neighbors. Ruth Shirack had always been so nice to his children, treating them like they belonged to her brood. At six, Rebecca was too young to remember her own mother. "Are you all right, Rebecca?"

She nodded, her face solemn. "Is this where my mudder is?"

Even after four years, his heart twisted. "Jah."

She stared up at him, so like Joanna with her blue eyes and the dark hair that wreathed her head under her kapp. "Can I see her?"

He cleared his throat. "You can see her gravestone."

"Will William and Ruth see her in heaven?"

"Jah, I believe they will."

Her small fingers tightened around his. "Good."

They reached the spot where the Shiracks would be buried next to William's parents and the baby they'd lost many years ago. Thomas wanted to stand close to Emma. She looked pale, worn-out, and surprisingly fragile for a woman who had always struck him as solidly planted on the ground. He wanted to put an arm around her, or at least hold her small hand in his big one. Give her comfort. Let her lean on him a little. He wanted to be the one she turned to in both sadness and in celebration. He wanted small, private moments shared only by the two of them.

Stop. Thinking along those lines when she had shown not a sliver of interest in him was dangerous. Wanting something he could not have would only lead to discontent and hurt. Even so, he found himself seeking her face in the group of women on the other side of the bishop. She stood in a row with her sisters. William and Ruth could be proud. Their daughters stood tall, shoulder to shoulder, with quiet dignity. Emma's face was still, her wet eyes averted, and she made no sound as the pallbearers lowered the caskets into the ground. The dull thud of the clods of dirt on the wood filled the silence.

Thomas bowed his head as the midday sun beat down on them. Flies buzzed in the breathless heat. The bishop's voice carried across the rows upon rows of plain, white headstones. The cemetery offered a nice place to rest. Thomas always took comfort in that thought. Joanna rested in good company here.

The bishop's voice encouraged them to pray silently. Then his voice ceased. The service had ended.

Rebecca tugged at his hand. "Now, Daed, now can we see Mudder?"

He nodded and turned toward the west. "As soon as we pay our respects."

Rebecca in tow and Eli not far behind, he threaded his way through the crowd until he was close enough to get Emma's attention. Her smile encompassed all three of them. "Thank you for all your help, Thomas." She rested a hand on Rebecca's shoulder. "Thank you for coming. I hope you'll join us for the meal back at the house."

"We're going to see my mudder's grave first," Rebecca replied. "She's visiting with your mother in heaven now."

Emma met Thomas' gaze over the little girl's head. "That's a nice thought—"

Her already pale face blanched and her eyes opened wide. Thinking she might faint, Thomas started forward, hands outstretched. She shook her head. "It's…it's him."

Thomas swiveled to follow her gaze. An oddly familiar figure stood several yards from the crowd now dispersing. Thomas peered at the man, whose tilted head allowed the shadow of his hat to obscure his face. As if he knew they'd spotted him, the man stepped from the shade of a huge oak tree.

It couldn't be. He'd been gone for four years.

Carl Freiling had returned.

Chapter 6

Emma plucked a shirt from the laundry basket and shook it out harder than necessary. It felt good to do ordinary tasks, to leave behind the wrenching duties involved in burying loved ones. The sun shone on her face. She soaked it up, along with the smell of freshly cut grass that Annie had mowed that morning.

She hung the shirt on the clothesline and smoothed it out. Work soothed her. It helped her think of something besides Carl standing in the cemetery. How could he show up at her parents' burial? Because of his decision to leave the Plain way of life he couldn't approach the gathering, and she had fled without speaking to him. A week had gone by and there'd been no further sign of him.

Why had he come back? Would the bishop let him stay? The questions swirled in her head, no answers to be had. It didn't matter, really. He probably wouldn't stay. Even if he did intend to ask the bishop to allow him to return to the Plain ways, that didn't mean anything still existed between them. Absolutely not. Of course not.

Yet, her heart hurt. Seeing him had brought back all the memories—and with them the pain—of his abandonment. He'd arrived at the house in the early morning, odd in itself. He wore no hat and a belt adorned his pressed slacks instead of suspenders. The world tilted even before he began to speak.

"I'm sorry," he'd said. Those first words slammed the door shut on their future. After a while, the words didn't register anymore. He was leaving. Not just her, his family, and the community. After being baptized, he had changed his mind about being Amish. She managed to choke out one question. "Why?"

His answer baffled her. "I have to see what's out there. I'm suffocating here."

She wasn't enough to keep him here. His *faith* wasn't enough to keep him here. He'd left, taking with him her ability to trust. For four years, she'd avoided getting close to anyone. There had been a few men along the way who'd tried. More than one offer of a ride home after a singing. Even an occasional flashlight in the window. She'd found herself unable to return these overtures for fear of suffering the awful hurt and sense of betrayal again. She couldn't go through it again. So she'd rebuffed the advances. Kindly. Carefully. Not wanting to hurt the way she'd been hurt. No one had persisted. And that was fine with her. Just fine.

Emma swept the memories under a mental rug. No sense in dwelling on the past yet again. She turned to pick up another shirt and caught a glimpse of someone walking toward the road. She straightened and put her hand to her eyes to block the sun. It was Josiah, trudging toward the highway. They'd barely spoken since the incident at the viewing. She'd seen the Kauffman pickup truck in the driveway the next day, but none of them had entered the house, not even to offer condolences.

"Josiah? Josiah! Where are you going?"

He glanced back but kept walking, his long, skinny legs eating up the yards. "To town."

"It's a long walk. Why don't you wait until you can get a ride with Luke?" None of them had broached the subject of getting the old buggy out of the barn. Not yet. "He's coming by later."

Josiah's pace slowed. Then he stopped and turned back to face her. "I'd rather not. Luke always wants to talk about what I will do next. He wants me to take over the blacksmith shop."

She strode toward him, wanting to close the gap between them.

"It's a good job and Luke loves that shop. It would allow us to keep it open and in the family."

Josiah shook his head. "I don't want to be inside all day. I need to work outdoors. I'm a farmer. Like Daed."

Emma could understand that. "Then that's what you should tell Luke, instead of avoiding him."

"It's not just that. I want to study farming. There are better ways to do this. Ways that will make us more self-sufficient. I need more education."

More education. The teacher in Emma struggled to tame a shameful pride. Her scholar thirsted for knowledge. She cast her pride aside. "What you need to know about farming you have learned here, in the fields, with Daed and Luke. If you want to learn more you can read books from the library."

Josiah smiled for a second. "You are forever faithful, schweschder, I respect that."

"I have days when I'm not sure."

Josiah looked beyond her to the fields. "I have to go."

"Where?"

"To the harness shop."

"You'll talk to Miriam, then." A flicker of hope flamed inside Emma. Perhaps he would find his way home after all. "She'll be pleased to see you."

"Not when she hears what I have to say."

The flame died. "Are you sure, Josiah?"

"Very sure."

"Give it time!"

He'd already turned to walk away.

The pain awaiting Miriam bruised Emma's heart. "Think of her."

Still, he walked away.

She sighed and went back to hanging up the clothes. She needed Luke's help with Josiah, and her older brother had his hands full with the farm and trying to sell his house and keep the business running. They would have to talk—soon—but she hated to add to his burden.

"More clothes. You're getting behind."

Emma glanced back. Annie traipsed across the yard and plopped another laundry basket in the grass. Emma grabbed the last dress from the first load and pushed the basket toward Annie. "I'm getting there."

"Good, because there's more where this one came from." Annie smiled. She seemed better today, her natural resilience obvious in the way she'd fussed over the biscuits at breakfast, bickered with Catherine about who would wash and who would dry the dishes, and teased Mark about the size of his growing feet. "You sure have been lost in thought today. What are you dreaming about?"

Emma wished she could be as light-hearted as her younger sister. Josiah's problems confounded her, but even more the death of Mudder and Daed hung over her in a shroud of anger and inability to forgive. Why couldn't she forgive? She shoved the thought into the far corner with other thoughts too hard to bear. Emma considered her sister's question. What could she tell her? "Did you know Carl is back?"

Annie eased onto a huge stump that had once been an elm tree felled by tornado-force winds a few summers earlier. "Jah."

"Why didn't you tell me?"

"I didn't want to stir up old hurts."

Instead she'd let Emma find out the hard way. Emma grabbed a dress from her basket and shook it out. "You knew I'd run into him sooner rather than later."

"There's been much going on here in the last few days. Your old beau wasn't at the forefront of my thoughts." Annie's tone had turned sharp, unusual for someone with her kindness of spirit. "Surely you don't still pine for him...or do you?"

Emma turned toward the clothesline and let her face bathe in the sun—that way Annie couldn't see it. She didn't pine for Carl. As far as she could tell, God's will for her didn't involve him. So why did he fill her thoughts every waking moment? "No, of course not."

"Good."

How could feeling like this—so full of conflicting emotions—be good? She grabbed a shirt from the top of the new basket and shook out its wrinkles. "Why is it good?"

Annie laughed, a lovely, clean sound. "Because of Thomas, of course."

What about Thomas? "Thomas?"

"Oh, surely you can't be that naïve." Annie clapped her hands together, her face alight with good humor. "Thomas has courting written all over his face every time he looks at you. Everyone knows it. Even Luke, and he's as dense as this old stump when it comes to matters of the heart."

Stunned, Emma searched her memories. Attentive, kind, thoughtful. Handsome in a rough-hewn sort of way with tufts of his thick brown hair sticking out from under his hat, dark, intent eyes, and full mouth. Not that she'd studied these things. One simply couldn't help but notice. A tall man—one you couldn't miss in a crowd. Truly, it had never seemed to her that he might be interested. It never showed. Thomas was Luke's friend, like the older brother he would never have. He was definitely older. Several years older than Luke even. Annie suffered from what Daed would call a flight of fancy. "You're just trying to take my mind off Carl."

"Actually, it was Mudder who mentioned it." Annie's voice trailed off. The light died in her face. She sighed. "She knew Thomas had an interest in you, but Daed said he was too old—"

"He talked to Daed about me?" Emma tackled the new basket of laundry like it might try to fly away. Work was much easier, much simpler than these affairs of the heart. "Why didn't he say anything to me? Why didn't anyone mention this to me?"

"Because Thomas is an honorable man. He suspected Daed would object and he would never come between a daughter and her father." Annie clasped her hands around one knee and rocked back on her stump-turned-chair. "Mudder didn't want to tell you because she thought it would only make you feel worse. You went through so much with Carl."

Well. Emma sputtered, unable to think of an adequate response. Daed should have discussed it with her. Mudder should've told her. And Thomas. How many times had she looked at her brother's friend and wondered whether his attempts at conversation—if one could call the frugal three-word sentences conversation—were meant to signal some kind of interest in her? Thomas was easy on the eyes with a deep voice that he only used when he truly had something to say. He was so steady, so sure. He might have been the one man she could trust with her scarred heart. The fact that he hadn't persisted in trying to convince Daed stung. If he were truly interested, he would've kept their private matters private in the beginning. Courting should be done in private. Only he'd chosen not to court. He hadn't been interested enough to come to her. Seek her out.

Emma slapped another shirt on the line. This conversation had gone far enough. Their words wasted time, considering Thomas had chosen to take *no* for an answer. She felt peculiarly disappointed. Like she'd lost something she'd never even known she'd had.

Besides, who was Annie to talk? "What happened between you and Robert?" Emma asked. "Why did you say you would teach when you know Robert is going to ask you—"

"No, he's not." Annie jumped to her feet. She picked up the empty basket. "He's not, I promise. I need to get back to the sewing before Catherine comes looking for me. She's in a mood today."

Catherine had been in a mood since the accident. The circumstances entitled her to a bit of an adjustment period. After all, she'd witnessed an event horrific beyond comprehension. "Don't change the subject. Catherine is grieving. It'll take time for her to recover, but she will. Why isn't Robert going to ask you? You two have been going to the singings together for more than a year."

Annie started walking toward the house.

"Annie, wait! Are you all right? Was he respectful?"

Annie stopped, but she didn't turn around. The tears in her voice told the story. "Very respectful, when he came to tell me he was in love with another."

With those tearful words she escaped back into the house.

In love with another. Emma stooped to pick up the dress she'd allowed to drop back into the basket. Poor Annie. Were the Shirack sisters destined to be alone?

At least she had her teaching. She had her students. The thought lifted her heart. Another month and she could have the school cleaned and begin preparing for the new year. There would be a meeting of teachers from the nearby districts to talk about curriculum. Lesson plans to prepare. It was something to look forward—

"Emma."

She froze, her hands still on the dress she'd thrown over the taut line. His voice hadn't changed. The way he said her name as if the two syllables rolled from his tongue hadn't changed.

God, this is not what I meant. I didn't mean to improve my affairs of the heart by bringing him back. Not him.

"Emma, please. I'd like to talk to you."

She closed her eyes. *Put your arms down. Don't just stand here.* Slowly, she turned and faced him. "How are you, Carl?"

"I'm getting there." He stood half a dozen feet away, long, thin fingers loose at his side. Like always, his curly blond hair stuck out from under his hat, as unruly as the man could be. He wore Plain clothes again, not the slacks and button-down collar shirt he'd worn the day he came to tell her he'd made a decision. A decision that did not involve her. His pants were wrinkled. He was doing his own laundry, then. His parents were right to keep a distance until he proved himself. Otherwise they would only get hurt again, just as she would.

She turned around and picked up a shirt. No sense in wasting time. The laundry had to be hung while there was time for the sun to dry it. "Why are you here?"

Footsteps sounded. His shadow touched hers. She inhaled the clean scent of his soap and fought the urge to run into the house. Catherine and Annie were in there, sewing new dresses for the twins, the *thump-thump* of the foot pedal on the treadle machine drowning out the songs they sang as they worked. The little ones would be learning to mend. Her sisters couldn't protect her from reliving a painful past.

"Emma, look at me, please. I need to tell you how sorry I am."

She smoothed the wet cloth with a trembling hand and forced herself to meet his gaze. "Don't be sorry for me. Be sorry for yourself and all that you missed."

He frowned. Lines that hadn't been there before crinkled around his eyes. He had the pale skin of a man who worked indoors. "You're still angry with me."

"No. I'm sad for you."

"Don't be sad. Be happy for me. I'm coming back. I've met with the bishop. He's giving me a chance to prove I can return to our ways."

That didn't surprise Emma. The elders wanted the wayward sons and daughters to come home. They wanted the community to remain strong. But they also set a high standard. Carl would have to work hard to show them he was sincere and committed to the Ordnung. In the meantime, she should be supportive. That would be her role. Nothing more. She swallowed against the lump in her throat. "I *am* happy for you." She picked up the basket. "I'm happy for your family. Your parents must be so pleased."

"I'm staying in the *Groossdaadi Haus* until it's determined that I will be successful in returning. Now that *Groossdaadi* and *Groossmammi* have passed on, it stands empty until Mudder and Daed's turn. I'll have regular sessions with Deacon Pierce and the bishop." He stepped into her path. "What about you? Does it make *you* happy that I'm back—happy for you?"

She sidestepped him. *Happy* wasn't a part of the swirling emotions inside her. Only *confused* and *uncertain*. "That is neither here nor there."

"Don't you want to know why I came back?"

She balanced the basket between them. "I would hope you came back to be reunited with your family and your community, to return to our ways instead of the world's."

"I did." His eyes full of entreaty, he paused as if searching for words. "I also came back because of you. I couldn't forget about you. I thought of you often over the years. I even wrote you letters. I could never bring myself to send them, but I wrote them."

If he had sent the letters, would things have been different? She couldn't fathom how. The distance between them would remain the same. Yet those letters would've meant everything to her. She worked to keep her voice steady for one syllable. "Why?"

"What do you mean, why?"

"You didn't think about me when you made your decision to leave." Good, her voice held no hint of tears. She lifted her chin and sought his gaze directly. "Why would you think of me later? You abandoned what we had. You made your choice."

"I know. That's why I couldn't send the letters. I knew it would only make it harder for you. But I thought you would forgive me."

Forgiveness. There it was again. She hung her head. *God, forgive me, please.* "I try. Every day I try. I truly do. I know I must." Even if she forgave him, Emma couldn't imagine how she would come to trust him again. As much as a certain part of her—the part in her heart—wanted to trust. "That doesn't mean we can pick up where we left off. I'm older. So are you and who knows—"

"Who knows what worldly things I did out there?" He finished the sentence for her just as he had in the days when they'd gone to the singings together and he'd driven her home in his buggy, still laughing at the antics of their friends.

"I didn't mean it that way."

He had the audacity to smile. "Yes, you did. You are still my innocent, imaginative girl."

Anger flooded her. He had been gone a long time, and she had grown up in his absence. He could not presume to know her. "No, I'm not—"

"Emma, I went to community college. I worked on computers." He took the basket from her hands. To her surprise, she let him. He stepped closer to her. Close enough for her to smell the soapy scent of his clothes. "I worked for a grocery store chain as an accountant. I went to a Mennonite church. Nothing I did shames me or you. I'm still me. I'm still Carl."

His hand came up. Emma took two steps back. Carl had always been a little more forward than gave her comfort. Keeping herself chaste from his touch had been a challenge. Four years out there in the Englisch world hadn't changed that. "Did you own a car? Did you live in a house with electricity? Did you watch television and go to the movies? Did you fly in an airplane? Did you drink beer and dance in a club? Did you play war games on a computer? Did you court an Englisch woman? I'm not your girl anymore."

She stopped, her breathing ragged. So much pent up for so long. She'd been so sure she'd managed to forgive him. But she was no better. Her inability to forgive him, to forgive the truck driver, to forgive period, showed that. And what did it matter if Carl had done those things? If he had embraced the Englisch world it was no concern of hers. She hastened her steps toward the house.

He fell into step next to her, his presence like a splinter driven deep into the palm of her hand. "I did some of those things, not all, and none of them turned me into someone you can't know and like. The deacons are giving me a chance to prove myself. Can't you do the same? Let me do this for you. Let me prove myself."

Emma was almost to the back door. She hesitated, then turned to face him. "If those things were so wonderful, why did you forsake them to come back?"

His long, thin nose wrinkled. "It's hard to explain." His gaze roved over the fields across the road instead of meeting hers head-on. "It was the noise."

The blaring of horns? The screaming of electric guitars? The babble of voices on a television? Were those things enough to bring a man back to his faith and family? "The noise?"

"There's so much noise in the Englisch world. I missed the blessed assurance I always found in the quiet. I missed being able to hear God, to feel His presence in the rustling sounds of the leaves on the trees when even the slightest breeze picks them up." He averted his gaze. "I missed the nicker of the horses and the lowing of the cattle. Can you understand that?"

Emma gripped the basket tightly. He'd always had a way with words. Unlike Thomas. That stray thought brought her up short. What did Thomas have to do with this? Annie's silly meddling had opened a door Emma had always thought of as nonexistent. Thanks to Annie, she now knew her silent admiration and her unspoken wondering were shared. But what to do with that knowledge—that was an entirely different ball of tangled yarn. She forced herself to focus on the man in front of her. Carl looked so repentant. He looked…tired and world-weary.

Older and wiser. They were all older and wiser. With each passing day. He had been so easy to love once. Now she feared the pain that emotion might bring. "There is one thing you can do for me."

His face lit up with that broad smile that once had turned her heart to mush. "Anything."

She forced her gaze over his shoulder. "I need you to talk to Josiah. Share with him why you came back. Maybe that will help him make the decision he needs to make."

The smile died. His gaze flitted back to the fields of alfalfa, corn, and wheat. Then his emerald eyes held hers, filled with a meaning she couldn't interpret. "For you, gladly. With all my heart, I'll try."

She forced herself to break the mesmerizing hold his gaze had on hers. "Let's keep our hearts out of it, shall we?"

Chapter 7

Thomas tugged gently on the reins and brought the horses to a stop in front of the Shirack home. Tossing her regal head, the roan snorted and stomped. She seemed as agitated as Thomas felt. The oppressive July heat didn't help. His shirt was soaked with sweat and stuck to his back. Beads of perspiration ran from under his hat into his eyes.

Shirack family members, along with their neighbors, swarmed the back end of the wagon and pulled off boxes of Luke and Leah's belongings. Annie and Catherine trotted down the front steps, the twins right behind them. No Emma, though. Good. That was good. Really, it was.

Maybe Thomas wouldn't have to get down. With all these hands, maybe they really didn't need his help to carry the table and chairs into the house where surely Emma was waiting to tell them where she wanted the furniture placed.

It would be unneighborly not to at least offer to help, he chided himself silently. In the two weeks since he'd seen Emma's reaction to Carl Freiling's appearance at the cemetery, Thomas had been careful to avoid her. Prayer service was easy, with the men on one side and the women on the other. When she took her turn at the produce stand, he toiled in the fields. This time of year there was no shortage of work to be done. The soybeans were planted, but he still had milo to harvest and alfalfa that needed baling. He wished he were in the fields now. Hard labor had its own rewards. Exhaustion numbed the feelings he wrestled with in the wee hours of the morning.

Luke had managed to sell his house. Luke needed Thomas to be there to help him move his family back home. It was a bittersweet time for his friend. Thomas realized that. He wanted to tell him that he respected his choice to give up the home he'd made with Leah and the boys and return to the family farm. But Thomas had no words for things like that.

Slapping at flies that buzzed his ears, Thomas lowered himself to the ground and stomped toward the back of the wagon. At the corner stood Emma, directing traffic. She'd slipped into the crowd of helpers without his noticing. Her eyes made brighter blue by her indigo dress, she looked cool and unfazed by the moist heat. She had a box of dishes in her arms.

"That's too heavy for you." Ignoring the desire to run the other direction, Thomas held out his hands. He was no coward. "Let me take it."

A deep, red blush darkened her cheeks and raced all the way to the roots of her blonde hair just below her kapp. "I've got it."

He tugged at the box. She didn't release it. "Let me, please."

"If you want—"

"If you want—"

They let go at the same time. The box smashed to the ground, with a crash that told Thomas not all the carefully wrapped dishes were going to survive.

"Oh, no! Oh, no!" Emma sank to the ground. "How clumsy of me."

"It's my fault. I'm sorry." His neck and face burning with embarrassment, Thomas squatted next to her. "I'll get it."

"I think that's how this whole thing started," she snapped.

"My fault." Embarrassment melded into a knot of misery in his midsection. Her reaction to his presence was obvious. She didn't want him around. After all, Carl Freiling had returned. "I'll get out of your way."

Emma didn't answer. Her head was bent, her fingers busy picking up a few shards of china that had escaped their wrappings. Every tiny piece had to be found so the children playing in the yard wouldn't cut their feet.

He stood and backed away. His first instinct had been correct. He shouldn't have come.

∗∗

Talk about cutting off her nose to spite her face. The box had been heavy. Why hadn't she let Thomas carry it? What possessed her to act like that? Ever since her conversation with Annie over the laundry basket, Emma had been unable to think of Thomas without a needle prick of anger and a greater sense of loss at what he'd forfeited—for both of them. He hadn't given them a chance. She hadn't realized how much that chance might have meant to her until Annie had given voice to it.

Shaking her head as if that would clear the confused thoughts away, Emma dragged the box into the kitchen and hefted it onto the table. Most of the pieces had made it, thanks to Leah's careful wrapping. Unfortunately, a platter and a gravy dish were victims of the crash. Mudder and Daed had given Luke and Leah the extra set of dishes after their marriage. She touched the platter. No use crying over spilt milk. Another useful maxim. She seemed to be full of them today.

"Is that platter broken?" Leah set a box of pans on the counter next to the gas stove. "How did that happen?"

"I…it…the box slipped." Emma quickly laid the broken dish aside and rummaged through the other packages. "Only two broke. The rest are fine."

Leah folded her hands over her expanding waist. It had become apparent in recent weeks that Luke and Leah were expecting another child. Emma tried hard to be happy for them. It was mean and small of her to feel that pinch of envy. She swatted the dark thoughts away. Joy came from knowing life was renewed even in the darkest days of loss.

Leah's peeved expression erased the thought. "Your mother gave those to me. They can't be replaced. How could you be so careless?"

"I—"

"Never mind. Let the others carry the boxes. You may unpack them."

"I…you…" Did Leah think she was stepping into Mudder's place?

Apparently so. She thought she would direct Emma now, like a mother or an older sister. She was neither. "This is not your—"

Thomas stuck his head through the door. He didn't make eye contact, but something in the way he held his body told Emma he'd heard the exchange. "Leah, I just came to tell you again how sorry I am about dropping the box."

Leah's face suffused with color. "Thomas. Your apology's accepted. They're just plates." A quick smile—barely qualifying as a smile—came and went. "We have plenty, with two households' worth."

Emma waited for an apology directed at her. None came. Leah went back to unpacking the pots and pans.

Thomas turned to Emma. "Could you please come tell us how you'd like the table and chairs placed?"

Leah's head came up, but Thomas gave her no opportunity to intervene. He turned and slipped through the door. Surprised at his insight and pleased at how easily he made the point, Emma followed him into the dining room. They would have to place the two tables parallel, side by side, in order to have room for everyone to eat together. The men quickly arranged the furniture. Emma stood by and watched, unable to keep her gaze from sliding to Thomas. It was strange knowing something about him she shouldn't. Annie shouldn't have told her. It made things so awkward.

He moved quickly, lifting the tables and benches with little effort. He worked hard. He wasn't so very old, really only a few years older than Luke. *Stop it.* The power of suggestion. That was all.

He looked up at her then glanced away, his ruddy complexion suddenly even ruddier. He turned to go. She scurried after him. "Thomas, wait."

He did as she asked, but his gaze still didn't meet hers. She hugged her arms to her waist. She hated this. Why had Annie said anything? "Danki."

He looked over her shoulder as if seeking escape. "Ask yourself why Leah is the way she is. There's always a reason." His voice sounded oddly harsh. "A loving heart can overcome anything."

He touched the brim of his straw hat and slipped past her. At the door, he glanced back. "Just about anything."

She opened her mouth, but he bolted without waiting for her response.

Emma clutched a tablecloth to her chest. His words resounded in her ears.

Just about anything.

Chapter 8

E mma whipped through the kitchen, one arm wrapped around an enormous bowl of mashed potatoes. She needed a serving spoon. Where had it gone? She'd laid it on the cabinet only a minute before. Everyone sat in the other room, waiting for their midday meal, and she had lost a spoon. She turned to check the preparation table and nearly plowed into Leah.

"Careful! You almost made me drop the plate." Her sister-in-law swerved to the right, a platter of fried chicken balanced between them. The serving spoon dangled from her other hand. "Why don't you serve the potatoes before you spill them? The men must get back into the field as soon as they eat."

Emma sputtered, then closed her mouth. The kitchen used to seem so big and airy with room for all of them to cook together, laugh, talk, and share their little secrets. In the days since taking up residence here, Leah had somehow shrunk it. "Sorry. I just needed a spoon."

"I brought enough spoons to feed half the families in the district when we moved in." Leah's voice got louder as she marched from the kitchen. "Maybe you need to get the kitchen more organized. Come along, before the food gets cold."

Emma tossed a glance at Annie, who was busy wrapping hot rolls in a clean towel and depositing them in a basket. "*I* need to get the kitchen organized?" Emma whispered. "I unpacked almost everything!"

"Remember, she's expecting. It probably makes her a little cranky. Especially when it's so hot." Even though her words were wise and true, Annie made a face and crossed her eyes. "Chin up. It will take a while for us to get used to living together, but we will."

Emma couldn't help but laugh at Annie's funny face, just as her younger sister intended. Annie let things roll off her, like rain rolled from the leaves of an oak tree during a spring deluge. And she went out of her way to give people the benefit of the doubt. Emma needed to learn to do the same. *Thank you.* She framed the words without making a sound.

Annie grinned. "We'd better get in there."

The tables were already laden with food—fried okra, corn on the cob, stewed tomatoes, cole slaw—a veritable feast. Most of it had been raised right there on the farm. It looked and smelled like home. They were blessed. Emma tried to remember that as Leah cleared a space, set the chicken down, and gave Emma a pointed look. She quickly added the potatoes.

"Are we ready?" Luke had his hands folded. "Time's wasting. We've heard from a farmer down the road that a storm is expected. We need to bring the rest of the wheat in today. Helping the others harvest first has put us behind."

Leah sank onto the bench next to Luke, then gave Emma and Annie another look. They scurried to their places and bowed their heads in silent prayer. After a moment, Luke cleared his throat and muttered, "Amen."

Leah immediately popped up and began serving the children.

Emma sneaked a look at her brother. His skin glowed a burnt, ruddy hue from days spent in the blazing sun. He and the other men were taking turns bringing in the wheat crop. Yesterday they'd spent all day in Thomas's fields, working late into the evening. This morning they'd risen before dawn to start on their wheat. Luke looked exhausted. But even as he chewed on a piece of chicken, his gaze followed Leah's every move. She *tsked* toward the children's table. "Slow down. You're not pigs, are you?"

Josiah made a tiny oinking sound. Mary and Lillie tittered. Leah's face darkened. She clutched the bowl of okra to her apron and bore down on Josiah. "You can leave the table if you can't set a better example for the children."

Josiah chomped on an ear of corn, chewed, and swallowed. Butter left a greasy sheen around his lips. "You're not my mother. You can't tell me what to do."

"Josiah!" The anger in Luke's voice cut the air like a finely honed ax. "Don't be disrespectful to your sister-in-law."

"Sister-in-law, not mother." Josiah wiped his hands on his napkin and laid it on the table. His voice remained soft, almost monotonous. "Just like you're not Daed."

"There's apple pie for dessert." Emma laid her drumstick down, her hunger turning to a sick despair in the pit of her stomach. Meals had always been a happy time when Mudder and Daed were there. A time for sharing their days. Now the tension in the room enveloped them like a dark, dank fog. "Eat up before the food gets cold."

Josiah slid off the bench and stood. "I'm not hungry anymore."

"Sit. You're not eighteen yet. Nor too old to be taken to the shed for a whipping." Luke rose. He had four inches and twenty pounds on his brother. Always the mild-mannered one, now he seemed to seethe with anger at the slightest provocation. "You and I have things to talk about after we finish eating."

His gaze swept over Annie, Catherine, and Emma. "Eat, all of you. Then you may go back to your chores."

Josiah seemed to hesitate for a second, but finally sat down.

The fury in Luke's eyes dissipated and he returned to his seat. He inclined his head toward Leah and she slipped back into her spot next to him. He picked up his fork and began to eat. The others did the same. No chatter. No giggling from the twins. No recounting of the morning's work.

Emma fought the urge to lay her head on the pine table and cry. She took a bite of the hot, buttery roll. It tasted like sawdust in her mouth. How could they go on like this? Would this be their life from now on?

The minutes dragged by until finally Luke wiped his mouth, drank the last of his water, and cleared his throat. "Cousin Caleb has agreed to take over the operation of the blacksmith shop."

Emma looked up with a bright smile. Good news. For once, good news. "That's wonderful. That means it'll stay open and in the family."

Luke straightened the dirty knife and fork on his plate, then crisscrossed them. "The district needs the shop. Caleb apprenticed with me before he decided he was needed on his father's farm. Now that his brothers are older, he can get away. He can handle the shop until Josiah takes over. He's willing to apprentice Josiah and give him a small salary."

"Me?" Josiah's fork, loaded with mashed potatoes, stopped halfway to his mouth. "I told you I want to farm!"

"You'll start your apprenticeship as soon as we finish with the harvest." Luke pushed his plate away. "Until you turn eighteen, I'll be making the decisions. Daed left me in charge. I'm your legal guardian now."

Disbelief danced with anger across Josiah's face. Tendrils of empathy grew and wrapped themselves around Emma's heart. Josiah was only seventeen and so sure that what he sought could only be found elsewhere.

If Carl had talked to him about his time away, Josiah hadn't mentioned it to her. What was Carl waiting for? "It's only for a while, Josiah, not forever. If you want to do something else later—"

"Don't fill his head with silly dreams." Leah intervened. "It's time he grew up and carried his share of the burden around here."

"He's worked hard during the harvest." Emma wanted to say something to wipe the look of despair from her younger brother's face. "He's carried his weight."

"You don't have to defend me." His expression mutinous, Josiah slammed his fork on his plate. "If you think I'm not doing my part, I'll go."

"No, you won't. Everyone needs to do more if this farm is going to sustain the family." Leah patted her stomach. "It's a growing family, and the economy is bad. If we don't have a good harvest, we could lose—"

"That's enough, Leah."

A look passed between Luke and his wife. A look that demanded her acquiescence. Leah's gaze dropped to her plate. Fear made a hard lump in Emma's throat. "What is it? Are we going to lose the farm?"

Luke shook his head. "No. You know our family and friends wouldn't allow that to happen. The money Josiah will earn at the shop will help cover the cost of running the farm, that's all. I don't want to be a burden to the others."

Catherine's face crumpled, showing emotion for the first time in a long time. Emma reached for her hand, but her sister quickly withdrew it. "The farm's losing money?"

"The price of wheat is down." Luke's expression said he didn't want to talk about this anymore. "All our costs are up."

The screen door slammed. A second later, Thomas rushed into the room. "Beg pardon for the interruption." His gaze caught Emma's, and his face turned red as a radish. He ducked his head. "We need to get the rest of your wheat in. The storm is close. An Englisch man from near Pottersville stopped by the produce stand. He said it's been raining up there since yesterday."

"Josiah, Mark, let's go." Luke stood. "Bring supper to the field this evening, Leah. We'll stay out until we're done or it storms—whichever comes first."

His gaze traveled around the table, stopping at Emma. "Everything is fine."

Emma forced herself to nod.

The men tromped from the room. Josiah trailed after them, his head down.

Fine was indeed a relative term.

Chapter 9

Emma hefted the cooler into the backseat of the buggy, then added the baskets. The men were having roast beef sandwiches for supper, along with fried potatoes, pickled cabbage, and thick oatmeal raisin cookies, her favorite. She and Leah had made enough to feed half the district since their uncles and cousins were helping bring in the wheat in hopes of beating the storm. A fat, wet drop of rain plopped on her face, telling her their efforts might be in vain. After Leah's dire words at the dinner table, the thought made Emma's heart beat faster. They needed this harvest. *Please, God, hold off the storm a little longer.*

She glanced up. A sky that had been partly cloudy only a few hours earlier when she hung sheets on the line had turned dark and threatening. The sheets made a *flap-flap* sound as a hot wind filled them like sails that billowed in white patches against a black horizon. She should've brought them in before she loaded the supper. Now they would have to wait. The men had been toiling in the field all afternoon. They needed to nourish their hungry, tired bodies.

She should let Leah or Catherine or Annie take the meal so she could finish the task she'd started. That would be the right thing to do. Still, she climbed into the buggy. Hanging clothes on the line only reminded her of her conversation with Carl. She didn't want to think about Carl and his wish to return to something long lost. Those thoughts only filled her with uncertainty.

Besides, Leah looked tired. And Annie was playing games with the twins and Leah's boys, keeping them from being underfoot. Emma should deliver the food. Maybe she would see Thomas. *Stop being silly.* She hated that Annie had planted that seed. Thomas hadn't spoken two consecutive words to her since the day Luke moved his family into the house. If Carl suffered from an endless medley of words, Thomas practiced frugality with his. Not that one had anything to do with the other.

The image of Thomas's long, tanned fingers shoving his straw hat back to reveal a sunburned face in the kitchen earlier in the day popped into Emma's head. Despite herself, she let the image linger. His big, callused hands were gentle every time he lifted his daughter into their buggy after prayer service. Emma had seen his hands at work hundreds of times. Why did the thought of those hands send a shiver through her now?

"Giddyup, come on, Carmel, let's go." Irritated with her own thoughts, Emma shook the reins. Silliness. Pure silliness. Thomas was still Thomas. Nine years older and a lifetime wiser. The horse snorted and took off at a brisk trot. Emma vowed to deliver the food and make a speedy exit. Plenty of work waited for her at the house. Plenty. "Good girl. You'll get us there in no time."

Thunder rolled in the distance, competing with her encouraging chatter. Lightning sizzled across the darkened expanse above her and the rain began to pelt her with increasing ferocity. She bit her lip and wiped at her face with her sleeve. Turn around or keep going? She didn't mind getting wet, but the buggy wouldn't do well if the wind strengthened.

As if he'd heard the argument inside her head, Thomas appeared in the distance, his horse moving at a gallop. He waved toward the house. "Go back!" he shouted. "We're coming in!"

Behind him the clouds dipped and writhed as if they were about to give birth to an enormous storm. She tore her gaze from the sky. "What about Luke and the boys?" she yelled over gusting wind that drove the rain like hard pellets against her cheeks.

"Josiah went into town for a replacement part." Thomas clamped his free hand on his straw hat to keep the wind from capturing it. "Luke and your uncles are moving the equipment. He and Mark will be in soon."

Emma tugged on the reins and turned the buggy. Carmel's nicker sounded anxious. "It's all right, girl." She had to shout to make herself heard over the wind. "Let's go home, let's go."

Thomas in the lead, they made their way back toward the barn. "Drive it inside. I'll unhook the horse there."

She followed his instructions, glad to get out of the wind.

Thomas moved quickly, efficiently, a man at home with horses. Intent on keeping her gaze from his hands, Emma studied his damp face. His eyes were dark, focused on the task. He looked so...strong, so sure. Yes, his skin was toughened by years in the sun, but the lines around his mouth came from years of smiles. His gaze lifted. He'd caught her staring. Emma's cheeks burned. "I should get back to the house and make sure everyone's all right. You'll join us for supper?"

He nodded and smiled. It transformed his face. He looked younger and...very handsome. "I would like that. I'll carry the cooler; you get the baskets."

He shoved open the barn door and waited for her to slip by. Together they tugged the cooler through and he managed to close the door, straining against the wind. They started across the yard. There didn't seem much point in hurrying now—they were already soaked. Except now that they walked side by side it seemed she should say something. For the life of her, she couldn't think of a thing. She shifted the basket handles to one arm and studied her straw and mud caked shoes. Why was it suddenly so awkward to talk to a man who'd been a family friend for as long as she could remember? His silence didn't help. He could at least try to make conversation.

She quickened her pace. Something about the dank air felt oppressive. She shivered and grasped for some elusive memory. She'd felt this before. As a child, rustled from her bed by Mudder. Big storms left murky memories of nights spent huddled half-asleep in the root cellar listening to the wind ravage their house. It had been a long time since the last trip to the cellar.

The wind howled and whistled through the porch eaves and then died, leaving a sudden, eerie silence. The rain stopped. The air quivered around them. A yellowish green haze of clouds heaved across the flat Kansas plains. A dark massive swirl descended from the heavens in a twisting, dancing rope, like a lasso in the hands of a cowboy. Her heart thumping painfully in her chest, Emma pointed with her free hand. "Thomas."

His gaze followed her finger.

He dropped the cooler and grabbed her hand in a painful grip. "Run!"

"We have to get the others!"

"I'll get them." He let go and gave her shoulder a sharp nudge. "You go to the cellar."

"No, we go together."

They sprinted to the house. With his long legs, he quickly outpaced her. The wind tore at her kapp. Emma struggled to keep up, but her wet dress tangled around her legs. She lifted the skirt. Her foot caught on the hem and she stumbled. She fell flat and smacked her chin and nose on the ground. She tasted dirt and blood.

Thomas jerked her upright. "Hurry!"

The front door flew open just as they hit the porch steps. Her hands around her belly in a protective gesture, Leah leaned out. "What is it? Where's Luke?"

"Gather the children! Tell Annie and Catherine." Emma gasped for breath. "We need to go to the cellar. A tornado is coming."

Leah didn't move. "Where's Luke?"

"He's fine; he's with the other men." Thomas took her arm and gently moved her aside. "We must go quickly!"

Leah's face changed. She charged ahead, leading the way as they scattered through the house, gathering startled children. It gave new meaning to the word *herding*. The errant thought whirled in Emma's head. Time seemed to stand still and then rush ahead of its own accord.

Outside the wind took her breath away and forced her to double over at the waist in an effort to make any forward progress. Thomas, a twin hoisted under each arm, reached the cellar door first.

Lowering the girls to the ground, he tugged open the heavy wooden door. "Go! Go!" The children scrambled in, then the women. Thomas followed and fought the wind until the door slammed behind them. The screaming of the wind became a duller, muffled sound, but screaming nonetheless.

With a muddy, shaking hand, Emma felt along the ledge until she found the matches. She lit the kerosene lamp that hung from a wooden dowel above her head.

Thomas took the lantern and dangled it close to Emma's face. His free hand came up. For a second she thought he might touch her. She swallowed hard, caught between the sudden hope that he would and the certainty that he shouldn't. Their gazes met. He looked away first and his hand dropped. "Your lip is bleeding."

Her face as hot as if she'd been standing in the blazing afternoon sun, she touched her mouth. Her fingers came away bloody. "I bit it when I fell."

Thomas produced a white handkerchief. "It's clean."

"Danki."

Their gazes held for a long second. He smiled. "Keep it."

Emma felt as if she still stood in the buffeting wind, breathless. "Danki," she said again, even though he'd already turned away.

Then he clomped through the cellar, his muddy boots leaving tracks on the cement floor. The dancing flames reflected on row upon row of mason jars filled with tomatoes, pickles, chowchow, beets, jams, jellies, and other bounty stored away for use during the winter months. He glanced back. "Amazing how quickly the weather changes. It was an unremarkable rain a few minutes ago."

Emma drew a trembling breath, thankful for Thomas's effort to focus on the weather. How could she be thinking about him at a time like this? She couldn't help it. His presence gave her comfort and an off-kilter sensation that she might lose her balance at the same time. But what about Luke and Mark and the uncles and cousins? What about Josiah? What about Carl? Was he in a safe place? She didn't ask those questions aloud. Another thought pierced her heart. "What about your children? Where are Rebecca and Eli?"

"They're with my mother. She'll have the whole family in the cellar." Thomas held the lantern up so it shone in the dark corners. They were clean and dry, as always. "They know what to do. And the Lord will protect them."

He stood, a calm, sturdy island in the midst of swirling turmoil, so sure of his faith. Emma wanted that assurance. She missed it.

"Joseph, be still, son. Stop wiggling." Leah's voice teetered on the brink of anger. Her youngest son didn't like storms, and he especially didn't like the cellar. "Sit still and be quiet."

Tearing her thoughts away from Thomas, Emma walked over to her sister-in-law. "May I help?"

Leah's gaze met hers. "Pray."

Emma nodded and bowed her head. She didn't want to pray. Praying had become increasingly difficult with the rancor in her heart over Mudder and Daed's deaths. She found their absence impossible to forgive. Now this. *We need Luke. We need Josiah. Please protect the house and the barn, the horses and the other livestock. They are our livelihood, Lord. Please.*

No doubt the storm would take what was left of the wheat. But her brothers? A sob burbled in her throat. Thomas shook his head. She followed his nod toward the girls huddled on a blanket on the floor. Lillie snuggled against Annie, and Catherine held Mary. The twins took turns sniffling. "I want Mudder." Mary burrowed against Catherine, her voice a tiny whisper. "I want Daed."

"Me, too." Lillie's lower lip curled under. "I miss them."

Poor things. Poor little things. They never complained. They coped. Better than Emma did. Of course, they were children who could laugh and play one minute, cry the next. "We all miss them, but they're with

God, and they would want us to be brave." She cleared her throat and forced a smile. "Let's play a game while we wait."

Her tears forgotten, Lillie grinned. "Oh, a game, a game!"

Mary didn't look as enthralled at the idea. A massive crack of thunder made her clutch her sister's arm. The four girls squeezed closer together. "Like what?"

Emma wracked her brain. Blank. She had a blank brain in her head. She glanced around the cellar. No paper, no crayons. No building blocks. Mudder used to stock the cellar for occasions just such as this one. Emma would have to learn to step into that role now. "Let me see…"

Thomas saved her. "How about I start a story and then the next person has to pick up where I left off?" He plopped down on a stool near the bottom of the steps. "And we keep going until everyone has told part of it."

"What kind of story?" Mary asked, her sweet face puzzled.

"Well, that remains to be seen, doesn't it?" Thomas smoothed his beard with callused fingers. "Let's see. Once there was a little boy—"

"I want it to be a little girl." Lillie frowned. "Two little girls, twins."

Thomas chuckled. "Ah, but this is my story. When you have your turn, you may add little girls, if you like."

Emma eased on to a box in the corner and leaned against the wall, watching as Thomas spun the simple story of a little boy walking in the woods who came upon a wounded bear. Even William, trying so hard to be all grown-up at six, crept closer to hear Thomas's rhapsodic spinning of a simple tale.

As a schoolteacher who spent all day eight months a year with children, Emma should've been able to come up with a simple game. She sneaked a covert peek at Thomas. He used both hands as he talked, waving them about, measuring how high the bear stood and how short the boy was. So quiet and reserved in adult company, he had an easy way with children, as if more comfortable with them. A quality that made for a good father. Of course, Thomas had proven that already with Rebecca and Eli. It was something else that drew Emma to him.

He didn't have to show off or spout words. He simply stood firm in his own quiet assurance. He didn't need to seek adventures in faraway places; he found contentment in simply being who he was.

"And the boy—take it away, Emma!"

Grinning, Thomas leaned back on the stool and folded his arms.

Emma opened her mouth and closed it. She'd been so busy studying Thomas, she hadn't given any thought to participating in his little story. "I...I..."

"Come on, teacher. Surely you should be the best storyteller of all."

Thomas grinned at her, his eyes alight with good humor. She couldn't help but smile back. He looked like a mischievous boy.

The twins clapped their hands and giggled. "Emma can't do it. Let me go next, Thomas, me!" Lillie crowed.

"No, me, please!" Mary pouted. "I have a story. Can I be next?"

Thomas shook his head, a pretend mournful look on his face. "Come on, Emma, the girls are going to make you look bad."

Emma threw her hands up in the air. "And the little boy gave the bear a roast beef sandwich."

The children roared with laughter so loud it almost covered the sound of the storm overhead.

"What?" Thomas's exaggerated tone only made them laugh harder.

"It's my story." Emma shot back. "And I'm hungry. Take it away, William!"

The little boy wiggled with delight at being singled out to go next. When she was sure the children were caught up in the raucous storytelling, Emma let her own amusement subside. She used the opportunity to lean toward Thomas. "Do you think Josiah is all right?" She kept her voice soft, aware of little children with big ears.

"When they activated the sirens, he surely took cover at the hardware store."

"And Luke and Mark?"

Thomas held up a hand. He stood and moved up the stairs. "The tornado has passed," he called back.

Suddenly even more afraid, Emma grabbed Annie's hand and

squeezed. Her sister squeezed back. Time to see what destruction the tornado had wrought on their home. She wanted to stay in the cellar a little longer. Leah's face said she too feared what they would find.

"We haven't finished the story," Mary pointed out. "What about the story?"

Thomas pounded down the stairs and grabbed her around the waist. He swung the little girl up to the third step with no effort at all. "Nothing says you can't finish the story topside, little one."

Together they marched up the stairs and climbed onto the wet grass. Leah took off across the yard. Thomas strode after her. "I'll look for him, Leah. You stay here with your boys."

Leah stumbled. Emma caught her arm. "Let Thomas do it. Let him go."

Leah shook her head, the fear in her eyes swallowing Emma whole. "I have to know."

"I'll go with him."

Leah nodded, but her hand gripped Emma's arm. "Hurry, please."

Emma gently shook loose and trotted after Thomas. Her shoes stuck in the mud, making it hard to pick up speed. *Luke. Luke. Luke.* His name sang like a refrain in her head. *Give me a sign, God, that You're still there, give me a sign.*

"There! There they are!" Thomas shouted. "Luke!"

In the distance, she saw the blue patch of his shirt. Her brother ran toward them, Mark stumbling behind him. Whole. Solid. "Luke. Mark!" She fell to her knees. "How? How? Where did you weather the storm?"

Luke helped her up. "We climbed into a drainage ditch along the road and hid in the pipe." He looked exhilarated. "I've never seen a storm like that."

"What about the others?"

Luke started toward the house. "They're headed back to check on their own homes and families."

Mark's white face told Emma the experience had been frightening for him, but he didn't say a word. Head held high, he marched alongside his big brother, his arms swinging.

Luke clapped his shoulder. "Good work, bruder. You were very brave and helpful today."

Mark grinned. Luke wiped mud from his cheeks with his handkerchief. A few seconds later the intensity drained from his face. "Everyone all right here? And the house? Still standing?"

"The house seemed all right, but we shall see." Emma fought the urge to close her eyes and never open them. From their vantage point, the house looked untouched. She moved forward, each step slower. They rounded the corner. The front porch remained intact. The house looked fine. Emma let her gaze roam from the house toward the barn.

Or what used to be the barn.

Chapter 10

Thomas hopped down from the buggy and stretched both arms over his head. His muscles ached from the hard labor of the previous day. Removing the debris and preparing the site for the barn raising had taken a full week. Several more days had passed in cutting the lumber to size at another nearby barn and hauling it in, along with the other supplies. Not only would the barn have to be replaced, but the buggy, and most of the livestock. It would be the Shiracks' second buggy in two months. And three horses were missing. Thankfully, the bishop and the deacons had agreed that the Shiracks' situation warranted a community barn-raising with everyone donating their labor.

Thomas's own farm had been spared, other than a few loose shingles and some downed tree limbs. He sighed. The Shiracks had much to overcome. Emma had much to overcome. He wanted to say something, do something for her, but he could never find the right words.

He was better at showing than telling. Maybe building a barn would speak to her. Of course, every man in the community plus those from several nearby towns would be building that same barn today. With a grunt, he helped Eli down and swung Rebecca to the ground behind her brother. His daughter smiled up at him. "It's a beautiful day, isn't it, Daed?"

From the mouths of babes. Instead of being discontented, he should be thankful. The sun slipped above the horizon, spilling pink and orange rays across wisps of lingering clouds, in a glorious display of heavenly beauty. This was the best part of the day, before the temperatures climbed toward a hundred and the still, oppressive heat soaked them in sweat. As was his habit, he said a quick prayer of gratitude for the blessing of being allowed to enjoy another sunrise. "Every day the Lord makes is beautiful."

The buggies already lined the road that led to the Shiracks' homestead. Deep voices filtered through the dawn air. Hearty shouts of "Good Morning" and "How are you?" were like a melody in Thomas's ears. The mouth-watering aroma of frying bacon and sausage mingled with the clean scent of freshly cut wood.

Thomas unhitched the horse and tied him close to the hay stanchions. Then he slid his tool box from the back of the buggy. With his free hand he grabbed Eli's arm before the boy could scamper away. "Remember, you're here to help with the barn raising. Be ready to fetch tools and lumber as they are needed. Jeb Steubing is the foreman. He will give out the assignments."

The boy's forehead wrinkled in a miniature imitation of an irritated adult. "Why can't I help raise the frame?"

"When you're older and bigger, you will."

"I'm eight. How old do I have to be?"

"Sixteen."

"That's..."

Thomas watched in amusement as the boy did the math in his head. "How many years? What is Emma teaching you?"

"It's eight years. That's a long time. I'm big and strong *now*."

"Is that backtalk I hear?" Thomas smiled to show he wasn't angry. The boy's enthusiasm for the job warmed Thomas's weary bones. "Best behavior, son."

With a quick, not-quite-impatient nod, Eli trotted toward a cluster of young boys who sat at a table wolfing down biscuits and gravy. Thomas turned to Rebecca. "And you, my girl, may help in the kitchen. I imagine you'll be carrying things, too."

"But I want to make pies." Her nose wrinkled in disappointment.

She and her brother were two peas in a pod. They were good workers. "I want to show Teacher I know how to make a pie."

Emma would find it hard to say no to the little girl. She had a kind heart. That was what made her a fine teacher. "I imagine the pies have already been made for today, but you can help carry them out later."

Rebecca skipped happily toward the house, a tiny replica of Joanna. He watched until she disappeared through the front door. Time for a quick breakfast and then to work. Tables and benches had been set up nearby and the women were already carrying out the food. He cranked his head, looking for Emma. Her slim figure and shining face didn't appear to be among the masses of women streaming to and from the house.

"Looking for someone?"

He turned. Carl Freiling propped both arms on the buggy. His face had a sort of amused looked on it, as if he'd just heard some private joke that no one else would understand.

Thomas ducked his head and picked up his toolbox.

Carl laughed. A very funny private joke, apparently. "It's okay. The deacon gave me permission to be here."

"I'm sure your parents are very happy." Thomas started toward the work site. "The whole community is glad to see you rejoin us."

"I know you're a friend of Emma's." Carl whipped around the buggy and fell into step next to him. "I just want you to know I'm not going to hurt her again."

The man had brought his Englisch ways with him. These weren't things Thomas wanted to discuss. Things of the heart were private. Besides, Carl would never get a chance to hurt Emma again. Thomas would see to that. The thoughts swirled and seethed inside him. He'd been too reserved with her. He had to find a way to be more forward before it was too late. Thomas faced the other man. "If you're here to work, then you need to find Jeb Steubing. He's the foreman. He'll have an assignment for you."

Carl stood his ground. He scratched at his neck, his blue eyes hard. "And leave Emma out of it?"

"Yes."

Carl smiled and let his hand drop. "That's what I thought."

"What do you mean?"

"I saw the way you looked at her at the cemetery."

Thomas started walking again. "Why are you here?"

"Emma asked me to talk to Josiah." Carl kept pace. He was like a horsefly, persistent and annoying. "To encourage him to stay. She thought with my…travels…I would be a good person to do that."

It was so like Emma to take pity on the man and allow him to have contact with Josiah. It was foolish, though. Carl Freiling had too many experiences with worldliness—exactly what Josiah sought. Still, Thomas would do well to learn from Emma's forgiving spirit. "So do it."

"Actually, I have. Twice."

Thomas let his gaze rove over the crowd, looking for Josiah. No sign of Emma's troubled younger brother. Thomas hoped he planned to do his share today. It would lighten Luke's load. "Is it helping?"

Carl shrugged. "He seems more interested in my so-called adventures than why I came back."

Exactly as he suspected. Thomas stifled a sigh. "So you're actually making it worse?"

"I wouldn't say—"

"Good morning, gentlemen."

Thomas looked up at the sound of that voice. Emma's voice. She strode toward them, an enormous platter of scrambled eggs in her hands. Mary and Lillie walked on either side of her, like matching bookends, carrying platters of bacon and sausage. Her expression quizzical, Emma's gaze traveled from Carl to Thomas and back. Thomas struggled to find words that suddenly disappeared into a mystifying fog. "Emma…the food…the food smells good."

"The eggs are from the chickens Lillie and I are raising," Mary piped up. "We gathered the eggs ourselves from the chicken coop."

"As is your job. You shouldn't expect praise for it." Emma's smile softened the words. "Go put the platters on the serving table."

"Good job, girls." Thomas called after them. A bit of praise now and then for the little ones didn't hurt. As long as it wasn't overdone. He glanced at Emma. "You, too."

Her smile came and went in a fleeting way that left him wondering if she understood his compliment. She was doing a good job with the girls, a job she'd been thrust into by circumstances.

He opened his mouth to explain, but she spoke first. "Sit and eat. Luke will want to get started as soon as possible."

"The weather looks to be good for it." Reduced to talking about the weather. Thomas kicked himself mentally. "We should be able to finish by dusk without a problem."

"When you have a chance, Emma, I'd like to talk with you about Josiah." Carl took a step closer to her. "We've had some interesting discussions. I'd like to give you a progress report."

Her expression lightened. "Oh, you've been talking to him. That's good."

"I won't keep you from your work." Carl took the platter from her and set it on the closest table. "We can walk and talk."

Emma glanced back at Thomas, but didn't speak.

He touched the brim of his hat with one finger. She nodded and turned her attention to the man walking next to her. Too close to her. Thomas watched them stroll away. What else could he do? She hadn't assigned to him this important task of saving Josiah from himself. She hadn't loved him once.

His appetite suddenly gone, Thomas went to find Jeb. Time to swing a hammer. Constructive, clean, honest work. That should be his focus. Even if it meant he would be alone at the end of the day. Like he had been every day for the last four years.

❈

Emma eased farther away from Carl. His stroll at her side seemed too comfortable. There was something too familiar about it. Luke wouldn't be happy to see them talking, but Carl wouldn't be here if he didn't have permission. Annie had heard from Carl's sister that he'd been meeting with the deacon regularly. He now attended the prayer service on Sundays.

None of that took away what he'd done to her, but it was a beginning. She needed to be supportive of his efforts and happy for his family. They needed their son back. The community needed every one of its members. Plus, she'd asked him for his help and he was trying. She smiled up at him, hoping he would see her gratitude in her face. "So you talked with Josiah. How did it go?"

Carl opened the front door for her, pausing to let her enter first. "It seemed to go well. He asked many questions about where I'd been and what it was like being out there on my own. I answered them as honestly as I could."

"But you told him it was a mistake, right? You told him that leaving was a mistake."

Carl's hand touched her dress sleeve. She pulled her arm away and stopped. His sad face confounded her, touching her in a way she wouldn't have thought possible. If he had been so sad before he left, she'd never noticed it. Shouldn't being back make him happy? His smile never reached his eyes. "I never said it was a mistake to leave."

"But…then why did you come back?"

"Because I realized this is where I want to be." His jaw worked and his eyes seemed suspiciously bright. "You are the one I want to be with. I had to go out there in order to understand that. Without my time away, I could never settle down and be satisfied with my life here. Maybe the same is true with Josiah."

Emma couldn't help herself. His sadness touched her heart. The icy shell around it started to melt. She shook her head and backed away from him. Carl was a grown man. He had to deal with the consequences of his actions. This concerned Josiah. "What did you tell Josiah?"

"I told him the truth: that he has to embrace this life and be satisfied with it. Or leave it. In between, there's only discontent, bitterness, and the certainty that you've missed something. Something big. He should not be baptized until he knows for sure. Once he's baptized, he's committed himself to being Amish for the rest of his life. Life is fleeting, Emma. You of all people should know that."

Emma's heart beat in an aching, painful rhythm. How could he do this again? Carl's face swam in front of her. She brushed away the traitorous tears. "And I, of all people, know that's why you must hold your family close, closer than anything else in the world. You hang on to them. You don't fill their heads with fantasies that can only take them far from God and everything that is godly. You're not helping Josiah."

Carl blew out air in a mournful sigh. "Yes, I am helping him. He's seeing the price I still pay for my transgressions. He knows about my feelings for you and how much I miss you. How what I did caused me to lose you. The problem is he hasn't found a girl here in this community who makes him feel that way. The girl he cares for is out there in the world."

"There is a girl who cares for him and he knows it. Don't let him tell you otherwise. He's hurting her just as you…" Emma backed away. "I have to help with breakfast."

She whirled and rushed down the hallway to the kitchen. Annie stood at the stove, stirring more gravy to go with the mounds of biscuits piled high in a long row of baskets. Emma poured a glass of water and drank until the lump in her throat washed away. How could she let that man get to her again? Because her heart still held a place for him? Had she been holding it all this time? How could that be?

She slapped the glass on the cabinet and surveyed the scene. Time to work. Work would steady her. A group of young girls giggled as they picked up the baskets and carried them toward the door. Thomas's daughter gave Emma a shy smile. "I was going to show you how I bake pie, but Daed said you probably already made them so I should carry things."

Emma returned the smile and patted the girl's shoulder. She looked so much like her mother, but she also favored Thomas with her maple-colored eyes and dimpled cheeks. "Your father is very wise, but come see me another day and I'll help you make a pie."

"Really?" Rebecca danced around the kitchen, nearly endangering the basket of biscuits she clasped to her chest.

"Really. Now go deliver those biscuits. The men will be ready to get to work any second."

Rebecca skipped away. Emma watched her go, squelching the desire to skip out with her. Thomas had beautiful children. She had a hole the size of Kansas where her own babies should be. Thanks to Carl. Best to remember that. She heaved a deep breath, composed herself, and turned to Annie. "Is everything under control?"

Annie added a dash of salt and pepper to the gravy. She smiled, a blissful look on her face. "Doesn't it smell good in here? When good food is cooking, it's almost impossible to be sad, isn't it?" She stopped stirring. "Do you think Luke would let me work in the kitchen at Louella's restaurant? I might earn more than I do making pies, and I could cook all kinds of things for people all day long, not just desserts."

Emma had no idea her sister dreamed of more than making pies, cookies, and cakes. She seemed so content. "I don't know. If you were in the kitchen, you wouldn't be exposed to too much of the outside influences he worries about. But they do use all those electrical appliances. And they have the radio on. And a telephone. I don't know what Luke would say to that. Maybe you should ask him."

Annie gave her a sideways glance, her lips turned up in a mischievous grin that made her look twelve instead of eighteen. "Maybe you could ask him for me."

Emma crossed her arms. "Why? You're a big girl. Besides, you get along with him better."

Annie laughed. "Because you like to argue. Like right now."

"I'm not arguing. I never argue." Emma snagged a biscuit and slathered it with butter. "What else needs to be done before we start the noon meal?"

Her face thoughtful, Annie surveyed the kitchen. "Breakfast is taken care of unless they ask for more milk or juice. You could find Catherine, though. She went to get some onions from the garden for the roast we're making for lunch. She never came back."

Emma took a bite and chewed. The biscuit melted in her mouth. Annie really was meant to cook. "This is so good—"

A shriek cut her words short.

"You know better than that, you naughty little girls." Leah marched through the door, dragging Lillie and Mary with her. "I'm taking you out to the shed. You'll have a whipping, both of you."

Emma laid the biscuit on a napkin. "What happened? What did they do?"

"Nothing, we didn't do anything!" Lillie cried. She struggled in Leah's grip. "We just wanted to take the pies outside."

"We don't have pie for breakfast. You know that. You're lying—adding to your transgressions." Leah dragged them toward the back door. "You were eating the pie and it fell on the floor, didn't it?"

"No, no! We already had breakfast," Mary sobbed. "I don't even like pie."

Emma brushed crumbs from her hands and stuck them on her hips. "Let them go."

"What?"

"Let them go. They've explained what happened. I'm sure it was an accident. They'll clean up the mess and spend the rest of the morning scrubbing the floor."

"They must have a whipping."

"Only if they deserve it. And then Luke is the one who will deliver their punishment. That's how it's done in our house."

Emma and Leah stood nose to nose. "They're lying. One is lying for the other. That's what twins do. I should know—I have twin brothers."

"Twins or not, my sisters don't lie. My parents raised us right."

"Spare the rod and spoil the child."

"Loving compassion makes kind people. Let go of my sisters."

"I won't have them setting a bad example for my boys."

"Your boys are outside dumping nails on the ground and using them to play pick-up-sticks."

Leah gave Lillie and Mary a slight shove toward Emma. "Fine. They'll be your problems."

"They're not problems, they're children."

Leah whirled and disappeared through the door.

Annie chuckled.

"It's not funny."

She grinned. "Playing pick-up sticks with nails. You made that up."

"I may have embellished a bit, but I did see them with a box of nails. Luke was getting after them."

Emma turned to Lillie and Mary. "Did you drop a pie?"

Her little chin trembling, Lillie nodded. "We wanted to carry it out to Luke so he could see what we'd made."

"And now it's all over the floor. The pie we made!" Mary sniffed. "It's ruined."

"Then you will clean it up and scrub the floor."

"Yes, schweschder."

"And then you'll make another pie, an even better one." Emma smiled at them. "Annie will help you. Won't you, Annie?"

"Of course." Annie waved a ladle at the girls. "Go clean it up, quickly, before the ants carry away the pie tin."

The girls ran.

Annie turned back to the stove. "It probably wasn't a good idea to question Leah's authority. She'll tell Luke, you know."

"I know." Emma sighed. "But she isn't their mother. I can't stand by and let her treat the girls as if she were."

"Poor babies. They need a mother."

"They have us."

Annie stirred the gravy harder. "Yes, and we have each other."

"Speaking of which, have you noticed how Catherine has been behaving lately?" If anyone knew what was going on with Catherine, it would be Annie. "She doesn't seem to be eating. She's lost weight."

Annie laid down her ladle and faced Emma. "She won't tell me what's wrong. I've asked." She smoothed a tangled curl that had escaped from her kapp. "Haven't you heard her crying at night? She tries to muffle it with the pillow, but it wakes me up."

Emma's own dreams often left her exhausted in the morning, but she rarely awoke from them during the night. "I guess I'm too tired to hear her."

"And you don't share a bed so her tossing and turning doesn't bother you." Annie didn't sound as if she were complaining, only trying to figure something out. "When I try to comfort her, she says it's nothing, to go back to sleep."

It wasn't nothing. "I'll talk to her."

Annie nodded and went back to the gravy.

Emma headed for the back door. Catherine had taken on two more houses to clean since Mudder and Daed's death. She had dark circles around her eyes and her round face had become increasingly angular. Her intentions were good, but she worked too hard.

No one occupied the garden except for a small brown rabbit that took off when Emma startled it from its hiding place in the carrots. "Catherine? Catherine!"

She listened for a reply. Nothing. She stooped and plucked some tomatoes that were plump and ripe. Any longer and they'd be overripe. The wrenching sound of a sob brought her upright.

More muffled sobbing followed. The sound wafted from behind the chicken coop, mingling with the squawk of the chickens. She wanted to run. Emma forced herself to move toward it. The sobs plucked at the ends of her nerves and caused pinpoints of pain from her fingertips down to her toes. "Catherine?" She whispered the name. "Is that you?"

She rounded the corner. Catherine sat hunched against the wall. Her head hung between her arms. Her shoulders rose and fell with each shuddering sob. Emma sank to her knees. "What is it? Please tell me what's wrong."

Catherine shrank away from her touch. "It's nothing. Go away."

Emma threw an arm around her. "I'm not leaving. Tell me why you're crying."

Catherine stiffened, then sank against Emma's shoulder. "It's so awful."

Emma rubbed her back in the same circular motion Mudder used to use to calm her after a night terror as a child. "It'll help to talk about it, I promise."

Catherine raised a tear-soaked face. "Every time I close my eyes, I see it."

Emma tightened her grip on her sister. "You see it." She knew now what was coming. She should've known the trauma wouldn't fade so quickly. "You see the accident."

"Yes." The sob that shook Catherine made Emma's body tremble with the same awful anguish. "I see the buggy topple over. I see their bodies fly through the air. I hear the screeching brakes. I hear the horse screaming. I see their blood soaking into the ground. Over and over again. If I do manage to sleep, I dream about it. It's horrible, horrible."

Emma hugged Catherine and rocked her shaking body. "Shhh, shhh. It'll be all right. I promise it'll be all right."

Somehow, it had to be all right.

Chapter 11

Emma tried to relax, but Doctor Miller's stern expression didn't help. She glanced at Luke, wanting his support. He didn't look back. He sat stiffly in the straight-back chair, a look on his face like a piece of clothing must be chafing him. Only Catherine appeared more relaxed, lighter, than she had when they'd first arrived. Doctor Miller spoke with her privately for almost thirty minutes before they returned to the outer office. Emma could only imagine how that conversation had gone.

After Catherine's crying bout in the garden, Emma had been forced to wait until the barn-raising ended to speak to Luke. His face radish-red, his words halting, he beat around the bush for a full five minutes before Emma figured out his response. He thought it was a womanly problem. Her brother was such a man.

Doctor Miller leaned forward and put his elbows on his knees, his hands clasped in front of him. "You've all been through a traumatic experience. Luke and Catherine, you saw it happen. There couldn't be anything more traumatic, short of war itself." His faded blue eyes were kind behind silver-rimmed glasses. "I suspect Catherine's not the only one having trouble sleeping. What about you, Luke? Any bad dreams? Loss of appetite? Depression?"

Luke crossed his arms. "I'm blessed with a large family and a farm to operate. I don't have time to be depressed, nor reason to be."

"What about you, Emma?"

Emma followed Luke's lead. She would be as brave as he. "I'm fine."

"What about Josiah? And the little ones—Mark, Lillie, and Mary?"

Doctor Miller had provided medical care for all the Shiracks. Daed had been of the opinion that Plain people should be good stewards of their physical bodies—gifts from God, he said—as well as their spiritual life. Doctor Miller knew each child, so he knew how different each of them was. Emma struggled for a response that reflected both the truth and their faith. "They're doing the best they can, all things considered. They miss their parents, but they know they're in heaven with God."

Rubbing a hand over his bald head, Doctor Miller leaned back in his leather chair. "Look, I have great respect for your Amish ways. You take it on the chin, and you keep on going. You're made of tough material that doesn't rip or tear. But I also know your hearts are tender. You don't build up those thick layers of scar tissue that make the rest of us so cynical and distrusting. When something like this happens, you lean on your faith and you keep putting one foot in front of the other, believing it's God's will. I respect that."

He stood and picked up a card from a desk cluttered with files and medical supply catalogues. "But sometimes your hearts hurt. I'm just a small town doc who treats broken arms and strep throat." He held the card out to Catherine. She stared at it like it might be a rattlesnake preparing to strike her. "You need help I can't give you. I suspect all three of you need it. But especially you, Catherine. You're suffering from post-traumatic stress disorder. I'm afraid it won't go away on its own. Doctor Baker specializes in this kind of problem. I've sent a few vets with PTSD her way over the years."

Her hand shaking, Catherine finally took the card and handed it to Emma. *Doctor Sheila Baker.* The word "psychologist" jumped out at Emma. The doctor's office was in Wichita. They'd have to go there to get help for Catherine.

Luke slapped his huge hand on his pant leg. "So you're saying there's nothing physically wrong with Catherine?"

"Technically, I could find nothing wrong, but my diagnosis is she is an eighteen-year-old girl with a broken heart." Doctor Miller's tone was sharp. "That's not an ailment to be taken lightly. It's manifesting itself in physical ways. She's not eating. She's losing weight. She's not sleeping. If this keeps up, she'll start to have physical problems and she won't be able to get on with her life. You must deal with it."

Tears burned Emma's eyes. Her sister suffered from a broken heart. Emma knew exactly how that felt, even if for different reasons.

Luke stood and strode to the door. His hand on the knob, he looked back. "We'll take care of her, Doctor."

Out on the sidewalk, Emma scurried to keep up with Luke's long-legged gait. Catherine, who was even shorter, practically had to run. Finally, Emma plucked at his sleeve. "Slow down, please!"

He slammed to a halt. Catherine nearly plowed in to him. "Are you angry with me?" Catherine's mouth quivered. "I'm sorry. I'll try to do better. I'll be fine."

"I'm not mad." Luke's gaze swung beyond them. "Not at you."

Emma turned to see what he was looking at. Miriam stood in front of the harness shop. Josiah, one hand around the waist of Sarah Kauffman, turned away from her and walked down the sidewalk toward the Home Town Restaurant.

Her head down, Miriam disappeared into her father's shop. Emma didn't know where to go first—the shop or after Josiah. Luke made the decision for her. He started across the street. A car honked. Another swerved, then whizzed by.

Emma scampered after him, Catherine on her heels. "Careful, Luke!"

"He's supposed to be at the blacksmith shop."

"It's lunchtime," Emma offered. "He's getting something to eat."

"We agreed that he would take his lunch to save money." Luke jerked open the door. "And what is Sarah doing, coming all the way from Wichita to be seen in public with him? To flaunt herself in front of a good Plain woman?"

Emma couldn't argue with either point. She'd made the sandwiches and packed the cooler with pickled cabbage and shoo-fly pie. She knew about Josiah's interest in Sarah and hadn't told Luke, fearing his reaction. Obviously for good reason. Poor Miriam. Had it been pure chance or had Josiah made it a point for Miriam to see him with Sarah? "Maybe he didn't know Sarah was coming."

"Maybe." Luke muttered. "Or maybe he's deceitful and can't be trusted to do the right thing. Either way, I intend to find out."

Inside the restaurant, the aroma of frying chicken, sizzling steaks, and onions on the grill would've made Emma's stomach rumble if it weren't already tied up in knots about what would happen next. She tried to keep up as Luke dodged a waitress with a heavy tray laden with steaming chicken fried steak, mashed potatoes, and gravy. Luke wouldn't make a scene. It wasn't their way. But this was new territory for Luke. Thrust into the position of leading their household.

Shaking her head at the waitress who wanted to seat them, Emma threaded her way through the packed tables, nodding at several familiar faces. *Please, God, don't let this blow up into a big scene. Please help Luke find his way. Help Josiah find his way. Let us find it together. Please.*

"Josiah." Luke could pack so much disapproval into three syllables. "What are you doing?"

Josiah looked up. He and Sarah were seated on the same side of a scarred vinyl booth, sharing a menu. Sarah's smile froze. She leaned away from Josiah. He grabbed her hand and held it on the table. "What are you doing in town?"

"That's it, isn't it?" Luke eased into the seat across from them. "You figured I wouldn't come into town so I'd never know about these dates."

Emma debated. Should she and Catherine keep standing or sit? It would be more obvious if they continued to stand. She slid in next to Luke and lifted her eyebrows at Catherine, who immediately sat down beside her.

Josiah shrugged. "Plain people always court privately. No one is to know until it's time to announce the nuptials. It's tradition."

Emma gripped her hands together, trying to keep her temper in check. Josiah was baiting Luke. She waded into the foray in hopes of finding a way to mediate that didn't end badly for anyone. "Sarah's not Plain. And since you haven't been baptized, neither are you."

Sarah's cheeks stained red. "I'm sorry—"

"Don't, Sarah. Don't apologize. You're not sorry." Josiah glared at Emma. "No kidding, Emma. Glad you straightened that out."

"There's no need to be disrespectful to your sister." Luke's voice was low, but Emma heard the steel in it. "Have you made a decision about your baptism?"

Josiah studied the menu for several seconds. Emma couldn't breathe. Finally, he raised his head. "Yes. It's not for me."

"You're only seventeen years old. You still have time to change your mind. Until then, at the end of the day, I expect you home to do your chores."

Emma breathed. Luke hadn't moved into the realm of ultimatums, and he hadn't raised his voice.

"I plan to be there." Josiah's knuckles whitened as he gripped Sarah's hand. The girl winced, and Josiah's fingers uncurled a little. "I'm sorry, Luke. I'm not doing this to make you mad. I'm just trying to figure out how to be happy."

"What about Miriam's happiness? You led her to believe—"

"I led her to believe nothing. We sang. We laughed. We're friends."

"I don't believe she saw it that way. She forsakes others to wait for you."

"I've spoken with her. She understands."

"I doubt she understands anything." Luke moved a salt shaker to the corner of the table. "I want what is best for you and that's to be with your own kind. To be baptized in your faith."

A tear trailed down Sarah's face. "How can that be the only way when we—"

Josiah shook his head. "There's no point in arguing with him. Luke is even more conservative than my parents."

"I'm sorry for you, Josiah. You wouldn't be in this predicament if they had been stricter with you." Luke's voice cracked a little. His Adam's apple bobbed. "I don't mean to speak ill of them, but they shouldn't have allowed you to go to Wichita."

His eyes shiny with tears, Josiah sighed and released Sarah's hand. "Mudder knew I was different from you."

"All the more reason."

"She had a heart."

"So do I, Josiah. That's why I want to do what is best for you." His expression bleak, Luke nudged Emma. "Let's go."

"But—"

"Up."

Catherine slid out and Emma followed suit. Luke stood and leaned close to Josiah's ear. His voice was soft. "Say your good-byes. You'll not be seeing each other again. I'll go to Wichita to speak to Sarah's father myself."

Josiah flinched as if Luke had struck him. "Luke, no—"

Luke backed away. "Let's go."

Her heart a stone in her throat, Emma glanced back at Josiah. "I'm sorry."

He put his arm around Sarah and smiled, a sweet, little boy smile. "Don't be, schweschder. It's not over yet."

Then why did it feel like everything was ending?

Chapter 12

The babble of many women's voices met Thomas at his parents' door. He smiled at the familiar sound. When he was growing up, quilting frolics were regular events at his house. It brought him comfort to think that some things never changed. Now Rebecca would learn to quilt, just as his sisters had. Just as Joanna had. The thought tasted bittersweet in his mouth.

"Daed, what are you waiting for? I get to cut the squares today, Groossmammi said." Rebecca wiggled past him and pushed the door open. "Groossmammi, we're here! Where are the scissors? Is there pie? Are the *aentis* here?"

Thomas chuckled. His daughter loved social occasions, just like her mother. She loved a good crowd, and the women loved her. They couldn't resist her freckled nose, dimpled cheeks, and sunny disposition. His sisters took turns teaching her the things she needed to know. God provided what Thomas couldn't.

He hesitated. Emma and her sisters might be there. He hadn't thought to ask his mother if they were coming. With all that had been going on at the Shirack homestead, it seemed unlikely. He couldn't decide if he would be disappointed if she weren't in the room or relieved. *Stop procrastinating.* Thomas plunged into a room so filled with women, material, scissors, and his mother's treadle sewing machine, he could barely move. He quickly reconnoitered the room. No Emma. But Annie Shirack sat across from his Aunt Sophie, her head bent over a strip of multicolored squares.

"Thomas." His mother bustled across the room, her hands fluttering. "Come say hello to everyone before you rush off."

"I'm on my way into town for the horse sale." He settled his hat on his head. He knew exactly what his mother was doing. "There's a roan that looks good to replace Doc."

"Two minutes." She held up a plate of brownies. "I know you can't pass up my apple brownies."

She had a point. He selected the largest piece and let her take his arm and guide him through the room. Annie gave him a curious look.

"Annie, it's good to see you out and about." He glanced around. "Did Emma and Catherine come?"

Just the right touch of casual inquiry. And he'd remembered to include Catherine in the question. Just making conversation.

Annie shook her head. "Emma said she had too much work to do, but I think she was feeling blue today. I wish she would've come. The company would do her good. She needs to get out more."

Something in the way she looked at him made Thomas examine her words for some inner message. What was she saying? Why didn't women just say what they had on their mind? It would make life so much simpler. "I hope she feels better."

His mother tugged on his arm. He started to move away. Annie inclined her head over her work. "I'll tell her you asked after her." Her words wafted after him.

Thomas tried to think what that meant. Nothing. Anything.

His sisters Molly, Elizabeth, and Delia had an assembly line going. One measuring squares, one cutting, and the other starting to pin them together. They were so similar in looks and nature, they could've been triplets. "You remember Helen Crouch, don't you?"

Next to Molly sat Helen, a short, rather roly-poly woman he'd known since he was knee-high to his father's breeches. As his mother knew. He'd grown up with Helen, just as he had all the women in the room. Bliss Creek was a small town and the Plain people's community even smaller. He inclined his head and greeted her. "How are you?"

Helen dropped her strip of squares and smiled. "Fine. I can't complain when it's God's will for me. And yourself?"

He understood exactly what she meant. Her husband had died of a heart attack while pushing a plow three years earlier. Helen had four children to raise. She'd moved back into her parents' home without a word of complaint. "Keeping busy."

"That's my motto. Keeping busy is the best medicine, that's what George used to say."

Thomas had worked side-by-side with George on more than one barn raising. Close in age, they'd played baseball as youngsters and fished at the river on many long summer nights. Thomas had attended their wedding. He remembered Helen as a bride, with the sparkle in her eye directed at her husband and no one else. "George was right about a lot of things. I know he felt very fortunate to be married to you."

Helen's eyes teared up. "That is very nice of you to say."

"I only speak the truth."

"Helen brought a cherry pie. It's delicious." Molly patted the woman's arm. "You're such a great cook. Try it, Thomas, it's excellent."

He held up the brownie. "Some other time, but thank you."

Helen looked disappointed. She picked up several blocks of material, her head bent. "We'll be having a hog butchering frolic soon. Be sure to come. My father is experimenting with some new feed for the pigs. He says they're putting on weight faster. You should come by and talk to him some afternoon." She ran the words together in a sudden rush. She stuck a pin in a blue patch of material. "*Ach*, got my finger." Her cheeks tomato-red, she sucked on the tip for a second, then shook it in the air. "I suppose I better pay attention to what I'm doing."

Thomas caught the tiny smile that played across Annie's face. He stifled his own. "Yes, I guess you'd better." He backed away, ignoring the triple threat stares of his sisters. They were always doing this. They meant well, and Helen Crouch struck him as a very nice woman. For some reason, he couldn't bring himself to find her interesting. He wished he could, but she wasn't...Emma Shirack.

He headed toward the door. *Horses. Think horses.* His mother planted herself in front of him before he could get his hand on the doorknob. "Going already?"

She need not give him that look. Affairs of the heart should be private. "I'm short a horse since Doc died. I don't want to miss that sale. I'll swing by and pick up Rebecca on my way home. Don't let her eat too much pie—it gives her a stomachache."

Mudder grabbed his arm and accompanied him onto the porch. "Give Helen a chance," she whispered. "She likes you. She said as much to Molly the other day."

Thomas closed his eyes and summoned all his patience. "I'm a grown man. I don't need a matchmaker."

"You're a grown man. You need a wife. Rebecca and Eli need a mother."

"Helen Crouch will never be their mother."

"I realize that."

"I—"

Thomas stopped. Helen Crouch stood in the doorway. "Don't let me interrupt. I left a piece of batting in the buggy." Her face stricken, she slipped past them and clomped down the steps.

"Now look what you did." His mother slapped both hands on her ample hips. "You hurt her feelings."

"I did? You were the one..." He didn't bother to finish the sentence. His mother flounced into the house without a backward glance.

Women.

Chapter 13

Emma jumped down from the buggy. She felt lighter already, just seeing Aenti Louise's wrinkled, smiling face. She perched on the step looking like a small sparrow in her brown dress. Maybe Luke was right. Maybe Aenti Louise served a much greater purpose than any school-educated psychologist in the big city. *Please God, let that be true.*

Even though it had meant missing the quilting frolic at Thomas's mother's house, it had been easy to convince Catherine to come on this visit if it meant no more doctors. Catherine loved Aenti Louise as much as Emma did, and as little girls they'd always thought of Aenti Louise as a doctor of sorts. For years, she delivered all the babies in the community. In fact, she'd delivered Catherine and Emma. Her midwifing days were over, but not all the caring she did for her babies, now grown.

Emma took the basket of bread and sweets from the floorboard. Together, she and Catherine strolled up to the porch of the Groossdaadi Haus Aenti Louise had occupied since Daed's parents passed. It was a neat little cottage dwarfed by their Uncle Noah's rambling wood frame house, added on to half a dozen times over the years as Daed's brothers and sisters kept coming. Aenti Louise was the oldest of nine children, while Daed had been the youngest.

"I'm so glad to see you, dearies." Beaming, Aenti Louise set the book in her gnarled hands aside and clamped them together with the sweet enthusiasm of a child. "You brought me goodies. How thoughtful!"

Emma wouldn't dream of visiting her favorite aunt without treats. Aenti Louise's sweet tooth had taken on legendary proportions in recent years. No matter how much she ate, her tiny frame continued to shrink until she looked like a little girl—a wrinkled, gray little girl. Emma held up the basket. "Your favorites. Apple muffins, oatmeal-raisin cookies, and cinnamon rolls."

Aenti Louise squealed. "The tea is cold. Come on in, girls. We're having a feast."

Catherine laughed, another sound too long missing around the Shirack house. Emma relaxed a little. This would be all right. She wouldn't have to convince Luke to take Catherine into the city to tell her darkest thoughts and fears to a stranger.

Aenti Louise stood and picked up her book. She hugged it to her chest.

"What are you reading?" Emma took her arm and helped her hobble up the steps.

"The Good Book."

Emma read the gold letters on the front. Aenti Louise's Deitsch translation of the Bible. Emma was thankful her community allowed study of the Bible. It gave Aenti Louise such comfort. She was one of the few people Emma knew who read frequently and for pleasure as Emma liked to do. That was part of the reason she was such a good storyteller.

Aenti Louise hugged the Bible to her. "I've a lot of free time these days. My fingers are too bent to sew and I don't have the strength to help with the laundry or the cooking anymore. So I draw a different kind of strength from reading."

Emma nodded. She understood that. She'd grown up listening to her aunt tell stories she'd read in the Bible. It gave her a sense of peace to know some things hadn't changed.

Inside, they sat around the small pine table in the kitchen, sipping tea. Aenti Louise was so short, her tiny feet barely touched the floor.

"So." She sank her teeth into a cinnamon roll. She chewed and sighed deeply. "Annie made this, didn't she? Tell her it's a little piece of heaven on earth."

Emma smiled and nibbled at her apple muffin. "At the risk of making her big head bigger, I'll mention to her you liked it."

"So. You're mourning. The grief seems greater today than it did yesterday. Or last week. It's growing so large, you're afraid your heart will explode and tear open your chest." Aenti Louise never spent much time on small talk. She rubbed the spot on her chest where her heart must be. "That's it, isn't it? That's why you've paid old Aenti Louise a visit."

She had an uncanny way about her.

"Something like that." Catherine spoke in a halting voice. "Not just my heart, but my head. I feel as if every part of me will collapse in a heap of worthless pieces."

"Catherine!" Emma reached across the table.

Catherine held up both hands. "Don't comfort me, please, I'm sick of comforting words. Meaningless comforting words."

Aenti Louise rocked back and forth in her chair, nodding her head. "Uh-huh, uh-huh. She's right, Emma. In order for her to get better she must confront her grief. Let it out. Rage against it."

"But isn't it wrong to be angry about Mudder and Daed's death?" Pain and fear made Catherine look far older than her years. "Isn't that questioning God's will? Deacon Pierce says God has a plan for us and we have to accept that."

"God understands your pain. His innocent Son suffered terribly and then died. Think about how that must have hurt God's heart to let that happen. But He did. For us." Aenti Louise rocked some more. "When your Uncle Samuel died, I was truly bereft. When they told me what had happened, I ran out to the barn and threw myself down on the ground next to his poor, broken body after the fall from the loft. I thought I'd just stay there until I died, too. I held my breath, thinking I'd starve my brain of oxygen until I was gone. But you know what? After a while I got up and went about my business."

Tears slipped down Catherine's face. To her surprise, Emma realized her own face was wet. "How? How did you do it, Aenti?" She brushed tears from her cheek with the back of her sleeve. "How did you get that image of his broken body out of your head?"

Catherine nodded. "That's the problem. The nightmares. Every time I close my eyes…"

Aenti Louise hopped down from the chair. Her knees popped and creaked as she shuffled around the table. One arm encircled Emma, the other went around Catherine. "It will take time. You will let it go. You will move on. I promise. Right now what you need is peace. Let's take a walk, dearies."

So they walked, a slow, leisurely pace that allowed Aenti Louise to keep up. She held Catherine's hand. No one said anything for a while. Emma breathed in the warm air of the July day. She didn't mind the heat. It might melt the hard lump of anger in her chest.

When they reached a small stand of trees, Aenti Louise trotted over to a fallen trunk and plopped down on it. "Sit a spell." She fanned her face with her fingers. "Heat feels good to these old, achy bones."

With a sigh, Emma sat. Dabbing at her face with a hankie, Catherine joined them. Her face seemed as tranquil as Emma had seen it since the accident. A delicate breeze rustled the leaves. Soft shafts of light filtered through the tree branches.

Aenti Louise took her hand. "Do you feel it?"

"Feel what?"

"God's presence."

Emma swallowed the knot in her throat. She closed her eyes and listened to the coo of a mourning dove. "Yes."

"Forgive."

She opened her eyes, startled. "How did you know?"

"Don't you think I rail against the circumstances? I loved my brother, your father. I loved your mother too, like a little sister." Aenti Louise plucked at her apron. "A person gets to be my age and she's been through this a few times."

"How do you do it? Forgive." Emma so wanted the answer to that

Kelly Irvin

question. She didn't want this poison coursing through her veins anymore. It separated her from her family. It separated her from her faith. "Luke forgave Mr. Cramer in an instant. It's been weeks, and I still feel anger every time I think about it."

"Luke is a smart man." Aenti Louise squeezed her hand. "He started by simply saying it. Whether he felt it or not. He knew that he had to commit to forgiving. So he did. Because that's what we do."

A bitter taste in her mouth, Emma shook her head. "It's not just Mr. Cramer." She swallowed. Dare she say this aloud...even to Aenti Louise? "I'm not just angry at Mr. Cramer."

"You're angry at God."

A statement, not a question. Aenti Louise didn't even sound shocked.

Emma ducked her head and nodded hard.

"He understands."

"How can He?"

"He had a Son."

Of course.

Emma clutched her arms to her waist, head still lowered. If she didn't start trying now, she might never be able to move forward. "I forgive Mr. Cramer."

She waited. Nothing felt different. Not yet. And she didn't feel better. Honestly, she didn't forgive. She couldn't. Not Mr. Cramer. And not God.

Her wrinkled face sad, Aenti Louise patted her shoulder. "You must forgive yourself first."

Emma forced herself to look up into her aunt's sweet face. "What do you mean?"

Aenti Louise smiled. "You're not perfect, Emma, as hard as you try. You're forgiven. God forgives you for not being perfect. He knows what's in your heart."

"If He does, He knows I don't deserve His forgiveness. He knows my heart is hardened against Him."

"It will soften, dearie, in time. It will soften. The Lord knows what He's doing."

Emma slapped her shaking hands to her face. The tears began to fall. They might never stop.

Chapter 14

E mma shoved open the window. The schoolhouse had been closed up for two and a half months. The hot, stale air smelled dusty. She couldn't wait to get the place clean and fresh, ready for another school year. Since her visit to Aenti Louise, Emma had worked hard to help Catherine—and herself—put the tragic events of the summer behind them. Getting back to school would serve as another step on that journey.

Chattering and laughing, the mothers of her scholars bustled about, wiping down desks and scrubbing the blackboard. With this much help the annual cleaning would take no time at all. Then Emma could review her curriculum and her record books. Having taught for three years now, she knew the name of every child. There would be a new batch of first graders, but in this small community, she would know them anyway. It would be nice if they could afford some newer, more updated textbooks, but the district's parents preferred to put their resources into the farms where their children were getting on-the-job training for their life's work. They didn't need advanced subjects for that.

She tugged open a second window. She still had two weeks before class actually began, but the school cleanup frolic signaled the beginning of a new year full of learning for a group of children she loved. She thirsted for knowledge and some of them did, too. She could see it in the way they touched the pages of the books with careful, gentle fingers. The way they read and reread passages.

She mentally shook a finger at herself. *Be content. These are your children. The ones God has given you to be their steward of learning.* The third window seemed to be stuck. She gritted her teeth and tugged harder. It didn't budge.

"May I help you with that?"

Thomas's voice. It had been two weeks since the last time she'd seen him. He'd kept his distance at the hog butchering, where Emma couldn't help but notice Helen Crouch had her eye on him. Which was just fine with Emma. She smoothed her apron, turned, and nearly bumped into him. "Jah."

He leaned into the job, his broad shoulders tensing with the effort. He had a solid, muscular build. Emma dropped her gaze to the floor. A squeaking sound told her when the task was completed.

She looked up. He brushed his hands together and smiled. "You loosened it for me. Rebecca and her friends can dust the windowsills."

"Danki."

He shifted from one foot to the other.

Emma cleared her throat.

"I—"

"I—"

Emma closed her mouth. Men first.

Thomas's cheeks had red spots that hadn't been there a second earlier. "I noticed the board on the second step is loose. I'll take a hammer to it."

"Good. Danki." Was that all she could say? Thank you? He would think she was trying to be fancy. "How have you been? You haven't been to the house since the barn raising. Luke was just commenting on that last night."

He crossed his arms, uncrossed them. "You know how it is this time of year. Everything happens at once. Always work to be done."

She nodded.

Another pause.

Thomas adjusted his hat again. "I'd better take care of that step. The tree branches also need to be trimmed back from the road in front."

He strode away, looking relieved.

"He's a hard worker, that Thomas Brennaman."

Emma jumped despite herself. She turned to face Helen Crouch. "Yes, he is."

Helen wiped at a puddle of water near the bucket Emma had filled for mopping the floor. "A good father, too."

Uncertain where Helen would have her go with this conversation, Emma picked up her scrubbing brush. "Yes. His children are well mannered and good scholars."

The other woman seemed very interested in the wet rag in her hand. Then she looked Emma in the eye. "My husband has been gone three years now. I still miss him terribly. So do the children." She faltered. "A good man not already yoked to another is difficult for a woman such as myself, with four children, to find."

"I'm sure that is true." Emma knelt and dunked the brush in the bucket. "But I know God has a plan for you, Helen. Time will show it."

Just as He had a plan for Emma. She clung to that thought. Mudder always said to wait quietly for God's plan to unfold.

"I've had four children. I'm not young or…noticeable." The doubt and shame in Helen's voice hit Emma like a two-by-four. "Men don't… they think of me as someone else's wife and mother."

Dumbfounded, Emma sat back on her haunches. She had shared many casual conversations with Helen, but never one of such a personal nature. These doubts were unfounded and a bit untoward, but a testament to how far down Helen had sunk in the muck and mire of loneliness.

"A Plain man wants a woman who is a good mother and a hard worker. A good wife. Such a woman is beautiful in his eyes. You are both. No Plain man would have it otherwise."

Emma bent over the bucket to hide her embarrassment at the frank nature of the conversation. "Will you make sure we have enough markers? I can't remember what I had left at the end of the school year.

I'll make a trip to town next week for supplies." Her stomach heaving, she began to scrub.

"I'll do that right now." Helen's voice trembled. "I'll start a list for you."

Another heart that ached from loneliness. A heart that had much in common with Thomas. Both were hard workers. Both were good parents. Both had lost spouses in their primes. Both suffered from loneliness. Perhaps they were meant to be together.

Emma scrubbed harder. Her fingers, her shoulders, and her back ached. Still, she scrubbed harder.

⌇

Thomas smacked the nail. Why, every time he saw that woman, did all sensible thought flee? He smacked the nail again.

"You'll break the board, you keep that up."

He straightened and slid his hat back so he could see. Luke stood over him, the sun a halo behind his head. Thomas put a hand to his forehead to shade his eyes. "Just making sure it's not a tripping hazard or going to hurt the children's feet when they come barefoot."

Luke nodded, but he didn't look convinced. "Instead of pounding on a nail, maybe you should find out what's what."

Thomas froze. He tried to think of a correct response. None came.

Luke tugged at a shirt soaked with sweat. He frowned. "Wait too long and someone else will step in."

He clomped down the stairs and walked away.

Grunting, Thomas swung the hammer again. Everyone seemed to need a say in his personal business these days. It was private. Between him and Emma. Only there was nothing happening between them. Not yet, anyway. Thomas fished his handkerchief from his back pocket and wiped sweat from his face. He was too old for this. Eli dashed past him. "We're going to play baseball, Daed, as soon as the chores are done."

Rebecca followed, three little girls her exact size skipping alongside her. Lillie and Mary trailed behind them, ever the tagalongs. "We want to play, too," Rebecca called, without slowing. "Is that all right, Daed?"

"When the chores are done and we've eaten." He tapped the hammer on the nail, even though it was so securely in place, it would never move again. "Eli, sweep the porch. Rebecca, there are jobs to be done inside. Take Lillie and Mary with you. They can help dust the windowsills and the desks."

Eli ran a wide circle and looped around to the broom that leaned against the side of the building. Rebecca screeched to a halt. In a more sedate manner, she trudged up the steps. The other girls followed, still giggling, their bare feet making a slapping sound on the rough wood.

He might be old, but Eli and Rebecca weren't. Thomas laid the hammer in his box, practiced breathing for a minute, then followed them inside.

Emma knelt scrubbing the floor, a bucket of soapy water, now dark with dirt, next to her.

Thomas moved toward her. Helen Crouch bustled in front of him, her chubby hands flapping. "Thomas, more wood will be needed for the stove." As usual, she said the words so quickly they ran together. "Will you bring some in and stack it in the wood box? That will save Emma time and effort when winter finally does come."

"That is a good thought, Helen. You're always thinking ahead." Thomas smiled at her. On more than one occasion, she'd shown herself to be a caring, thoughtful person. He wished he felt more inclined toward her. Her load was heavy. "I would be happy to do that."

"I try to be helpful. My husband…well, George used to say I was the most organized person he'd ever known." Her gaze dropped. "Of course, now that I'm raising the children on my own, I have to be even more organized. I'm sure that's something you and I have in common—among other things."

"My sisters and my mother make sure I stay organized when it comes to the children. I'm blessed in that way."

"Yes, but they do have broods of their own. I know how that is with my sisters and brothers."

"True."

He shifted awkwardly. Helen was a sweet-natured woman. A hard worker. A good mother. His gaze strayed to Emma. She was still scrubbing, head bent. She moved the brush in a circular motion so fierce he suspected she might remove varnish from the floor. "I'll take care of the wood in a few minutes."

Helen's gaze shifted to Emma's bent head. Pink crept across the older woman's cheeks. "I'm sure the *teacher* will appreciate it." She ducked her head and hustled away, her long skirt swaying.

The teacher didn't look up, but Thomas felt certain she scrubbed even harder. He eyed the other women. They all seemed well occupied with the tasks at hand. Emma kept scrubbing. Surely she'd heard the exchange with Helen. She knew he stood there. He adjusted his straw hat. Now or never. He squatted a discreet distance from her. "May I ask you something?" he whispered.

She leaned back on her knees and swished the brush in the bucket. Her chin lifted, eyes wary, she tilted her head. "Are you speaking to me?"

He glanced around. No one else lurked in the vicinity. Not even Helen. "May I ask you something?"

She wiped at her forehead with the back of her hand. "Of course."

"Outside."

Her forehead wrinkled. She dropped the brush in the bucket and stood.

The pulse in his temple pounding, he waited for her to pass through the door first, then followed her down the steps. "This way," he said, pointing to the back of the building.

When they were out of sight of the men working on the front yard, he stopped.

"What is it, Thomas?" She crossed her arms. "What did you want to ask me?"

"Do you...I mean...would you..." He threw his hands up in the air. "I'm not a teenager."

"Neither am I." Her tone was tart. "And I have work to do inside. I have students running about who'll wonder what I'm doing behind the building talking to a parent. You know Eli will think he's in trouble, and the school year hasn't even started."

"Eli is busy working." Thomas adjusted his hat again. "The thing is…I will not go to singings with a group of sixteen-year-olds. I'm too old to shine flashlights in windows. I have two young children, so I can't just hop in a buggy and go courting after dark."

Her eyebrows lifted over beautiful blue eyes. "I don't believe anyone asked you to do that—or anything else."

"But if I did—I mean, if I wanted to and I could arrange something… would you?"

"Why?"

"Why what?"

"Why court me now? You never did before. Do you feel sorry for me?"

Thomas's brain felt as if it would explode as he tried to decipher this woman's line of thinking. "No, no, I don't—"

"Just because you're friends with Luke and you want to help him out, don't think it's necessary to court his sister—to take me off his hands, so to speak." She stared at the ground. "I won't be pitied. Not by you, Thomas Brennaman."

He didn't remember courting being this hard, but then it *had* been a long time. "That's not it at all."

"Then what?"

"Do I have to spell it out?"

She put her hands on her hips. "I think so, considering you let my father say no without so much as a word to me. Courting is a private thing between two people. Approval comes later, when serious commitment is involved."

His face burned. "So you know about that."

"Yes, I know about that."

"It wasn't that I let your father make the decision for me. After I mentioned it to him, I realized I wasn't ready."

Her frown softened. "You weren't ready…because of Joanna."

"Yes, but now I am. It's been four years, Emma, and I…I…well…"

He couldn't say it. Not aloud. It would sound unmanly to admit to a loneliness that ate at his very core each day when he arose and each night when he went to bed. He should be content with his children and his work. Yet the feeling of emptiness overwhelmed him in quiet moments. He sucked in air. "I like you."

The frown disappeared from her pretty face. She laughed aloud, a sound sweeter than the birds singing on a fine spring morning. What was she laughing about? "Well, it would be important to like the woman you court."

Nonplussed, he tugged at his hat. "Are you making fun of me?"

"Jah."

A sense of relief assailed him, so acute his legs felt weak. He managed a chuckle. Humor was one of Joanna's qualities he missed the most. "I'm glad I can make you smile."

"Me too."

He looked at his shoes for a minute. "Do you like me?"

She crossed her arms and swung her gaze toward the tree branches swaying in a soft breeze. The silence stretched. Maybe he'd been too forward. Maybe he was wrong.

Finally, she smiled. "That's an awfully forward question."

"And that's no answer."

She sighed. Her gaze didn't meet his. "I made a bad choice once, and it cost me dearly. I don't trust my judgment when it comes to affairs of the heart. Besides, I'm...not a nice person."

So he could blame Carl Freiling for her hesitation. The man's actions continued to hurt Emma, even after all this time. He'd made her doubt herself. The second part of her statement sunk in. What was she talking about, not a nice person? She happened to be one of the nicest people Thomas had ever had the honor to know. "Of course you are."

"Not perfect, then."

What a relief. "*Gut*, because neither am I."

"You might find I'm not what you are looking for." Her gaze finally met his. "You might find I'm not suitable at all."

"We won't know until we try."

She crossed her arms, uncrossed them, then tugged at her apron. "I'm willing to try."

He tucked his hat back a little. "Then I'll figure it out—I mean with the children and all. It might take a while."

"All right, then."

A quick smile and she slipped away.

He stood there for a few seconds longer, thanking God he'd survived. Then he went back to work.

※

Emma's shoes thudded against the steps leading to the schoolhouse porch. The sound surprised her. Surely she walked on air, she felt so light. Thomas might come courting some night. It might take a while. He might figure something out. His bumbling attempt at conversation a moment ago had touched her. His nervousness matched hers. That struck her as sweet, considering he'd done this before. Of course, he'd taken his time getting to this point. Doubt lingered in the pit of her stomach. Maybe he really did feel sorry for her. Maybe he wanted to help Luke. Ridiculous. He said he liked her and he did.

The conversation also told her Helen Crouch's less than subtle attempts to attract his attention had failed. She nibbled at her lower lip. Helen did have more in common with Thomas. They had both lost spouses. They had children. They were closer in age. Helen had a sweet disposition, too, unlike hard-headed Emma. Why had he decided to court Emma? *Because he really does like me?* The thought made her heart contract in a sudden hiccup of emotion.

That didn't even begin to cover the question of how she would compare to Joanna. Sweet Joanna who never had a bad word to say about anyone and who never complained, not even when the cancer gave her terrible pain. Would Thomas compare them and find Emma wanting because of her hard, unforgiving heart? A heart that might still belong to another? That thought brought her up short. Doubts assailed her. She didn't want to hurt Thomas. He had suffered enough. And then she had to think about the effect on Eli and Rebecca.

Enough. Work. They'd never finish if she continued to lolly-gag about, as Mudder used to say. The thought of Mudder didn't bring the usual engulfing wave of pain intertwined with sadness. Emma turned that thought over in her mind. Sad, but not desperately so. That could be called progress of sorts.

Contemplating the tasks that remained to be completed, she hesitated in the doorway. Annie had gone to retrieve a basket of cleaning rags from the buggy and never returned, an act most unlike her sister. Annie not only worked with single-minded determination until a task was done, but she enjoyed it. She loved the camaraderie of the other women during all the work frolics, which was why she organized so many of them. Next week would be the canning frolic at the Shirack house.

So where did her sister go? Emma wrinkled her nose. Maybe she decided to take on the least favorite task: cleaning the boys' and girls' outhouses. That would be like Annie. If that were the case, then Emma didn't mind fetching the cleaning rags from the buggy herself. Now was as good a time as any.

Still replaying the conversation with Thomas in her head, she strode past a long line of buggies. Would he come to the house this week? Surely Mrs. Brennaman would be willing to keep her grandchildren for an evening in the interest of seeing him finally leave behind his extended mourning period.

She inhaled the scent of summer. Dirt and leaves, it was—

A laugh floated on the air. A familiar laugh. Emma slowed her pace, scanning the buggies. There. Annie, her laughing face bright under her kapp, stood next to a buggy—not the Shiracks' buggy. A straw hat blocked Emma's view of the face of the man who stood next to her.

Then he threw back his head and laughed, a deep, hoarse laugh. Emma froze. That sound echoed in her head late at night sometimes, when she awoke from fleeting dreams of buggy rides and singings and sweet murmurs on dark country roads.

She whirled to leave.

"Emma? Emma! Wait, don't go!"

She refused to stop. She had no desire to know why Annie stood outside talking to Carl Freiling.

Chapter 15

"E mma, Emma! Wait, it's not what you think."
Emma ignored Annie's voice wafting on a humid breeze that did nothing to cool her burning face. She picked up her pace until she trotted toward the schoolhouse. Rocks bit into the thin soles of her shoes. Dust from the dirt road clung to her sweaty face. The breeze that had stirred the humid air around her dissipated, leaving behind a dank stillness that reverberated in her ears. What was Carl doing with Annie? Annie had been on the periphery of the storm when Carl left, caught up in the billowing waves of Emma's hurt and disbelief.

Annie's hand caught her elbow and tugged. "Please, schweschder, stop."

Emma breathed in and out. She slowed her pace, then ground to a halt. "You don't have to explain. It's not for me to know."

Except they had chosen to do their courting in broad daylight on a dirt road filled with buggies.

Annie pushed strands of hair back under her kapp. Perspiration covered her rosy face in a light sheen. "It's not what you think. He wanted to talk to me about you! He wanted my help to convince you to give him another chance."

Emma walked faster.

"I told him to give you time. He argued that he couldn't afford to wait. That someone else has his eye on you. And he's right, you know. You'll have to make a decision."

A twinge in Emma's side forced her to slow a little. She put one foot in front of the other. She eyed the schoolhouse. Her secure, safe place. She glanced back. Carl leaned against the buggy, as if he didn't have a care in the world. At least he hadn't dared interject himself in the discussion. "Why is he talking to you now? Why did he come to the school?"

Annie dabbed perspiration from her forehead with a hankie. "He only just arrived with his nieces, Josephina and May. They'll be your students this year. His sister is expecting and not feeling well. We ran into each other quite on accident. He asked me for advice. Emma, I think you should talk to him."

"How can you say that, after what he did to me?"

"Because he loves you, and I think you still have feelings for him. You've been mooning around the house ever since he returned to Bliss Creek."

"I'm not mooning; I'm mourning."

"I know, I know." Annie stopped at the steps to the school. She glanced around, then lowered her voice. "It's hard, but we must go forward. Part of going forward for you is to find a partner. Maybe that's why God brought Carl back into your life at this time."

Emma groaned inwardly. She cared too much for him. There, she'd admitted it. Her feelings for Carl were complicated by a past where joy, love, pain, and betrayal had mingled until one was indistinguishable from the other. "I can't. I have all these feelings for him, but I'm afraid to trust him."

"He's made amends. He's returned to his faith. His family has forgiven him. With forgiveness, the slate is wiped clean and trust follows."

Emma's throat constricted. She couldn't speak. The ache traveled from her lips down her throat into her lungs so that the very act of breathing hurt. How could Annie have any inkling of the pain it caused Emma to think about what Carl had done? The burden weighed on her. Not because of Carl, but because God expected her to forgive just as He'd forgiven her. *How, God? I've tried and tried.*

Say it and in time, you'll learn to feel it. Aenti Louise's voice sounded in Emma's head. She opened her mouth, closed it again. The words echoed inside her head, still unspoken. She couldn't forgive him until she learned to see him as a friend only. To assign those feelings to their proper place. Then she would get her fresh new beginning. Only then.

Emma leaned toward Annie and whispered. "You were the one who said I should consider Thomas."

"Has he...showed an interest?"

Luke and another man walked by. Neither appeared interested in the conversation. Emma waited for them to pass. "We can't talk about this here. There's work to do."

Annie scowled. Emma scowled back. "Jah," she said finally.

"Then you have a choice to make." Annie's frown disappeared. She looked exceedingly pleased with herself.

Emma inhaled, exhaled. They should finish up and get home. Leah needed their help with the laundry, the sewing, and preparing supper. Courting could not be allowed to get in the way of duty. She straightened her shoulders and lifted her chin. "Perhaps, since you're already outside here, you can finish what you started at the outhouses."

Annie frowned and didn't budge. "At least give Carl a chance to speak his piece."

Emma bunched up her apron with both hands. "I have work to do."

"It will only take him a moment or two."

"Fine."

She walked on leaden feet back to the buggy, one hand on her aching side.

Carl straightened and touched the bill of his hat. "Hello, Emma."

She inclined her head. "I have work to do."

"Then I'll talk fast. I know you don't trust me, but I'm...I'm begging you to give me another chance. I can do better. I will do better this time. I promise you."

Emma thrust her hands in the air. "How do I know you can keep that promise? Promises were made before and broken."

"Then promise me one thing."

"I don't know if I can, Carl."

"Promise me you'll keep an open mind. We'll start from scratch." He bowed slightly. "I'm Carl Freiling. What's your name?"

Feeling faintly ridiculous, Emma bowed back. "I'm Emma Shirack."

"It is an honor to meet you. I wonder if I might call on you sometime."

Her heart beat so hard, Emma feared it might explode in her chest. What about Thomas? Thomas deserved better than she could offer, and he had much more in common with Helen. He deserved someone with no reservations, someone with no boulders from the past weighing her down. Besides, he had been so tentative, chances were good he would change his mind, too. She bowed her head. "Sometime."

A smile spread across Carl's sunburned face. "You'll see. You won't regret it."

She already did.

Chapter 16

E mma adjusted the flame on the gas stove in the crowded kitchen. Steam billowed from the pots of boiling water, making her feel as if she were swimming in a sweaty bowl of soup. Perspiration slid down her forehead and dripped on her cheeks. Using tongs, she lowered the first of several mason jars into the bath to sterilize them. Despite the heat, she loved canning. It meant making the garden's bounty available all winter long. Besides, it kept her mind off her problem.

She'd said yes to two men. Two men who claimed to care about her. One had broken her heart. The other hadn't. It was a simple choice. No choice at all. Yes she struggled with the unknown. She struggled with the unforgiven. If she chose Thomas, did that mean she hadn't truly forgiven Carl? If she chose Thomas, how could she be sure he wouldn't break her heart, too? To make matters worse, neither had shown up on her doorstep in the three nights since the school cleaning, and the suspense kept her awake long past dusk each evening.

Enough. She would set those thoughts aside and enjoy the day. Today they would put up the vegetables, ensuring the children would eat well this winter. Emma turned to check on Annie's progress with the tomatoes. Her sister removed skins from blanched tomatoes with a deft touch.

Emma wiped at her own face with the back of her sleeve. "What about the cucumbers? Are they ready?"

Catherine, whose natural ebullience seemed to have gradually crept back over the last few weeks, held up a large pan. "Ready. Aunt Martha and Aunt Bertha have the beets ready, too."

"Don't forget us!" Lillie piped up. She and Mary and their three young nephews were having a fine time snapping green beans. "We're helping."

"Yes, you are very big helpers. *Hmm*, cucumbers first. Bread and butter pickles. I do so like them." Emma smacked her lips. Dill pickles, sweet pickles, chowchow. They were blessed with an abundance of choices. "Do we have plenty of cucumbers and green tomatoes?"

Her cousins Ruth and Cindy laughed. "I don't know, cousin." Ruth puckered up. "You're pretty sour sometimes. Maybe you should have the dill instead of the bread and butter pickles."

"Very funny!" Emma tossed an onion at the girl. "The sour ones are for Leah."

Ruth caught the onion, and the girls whooped with laughter. Even Annie grinned. Aunt Bertha and Aunt Martha exchanged quick, amused glances before fixing Emma with twin stern stares. They were right. Emma slapped a damp hand to her mouth. *God forgive me.* She'd never thought of herself as a mean or snide person. "I'm sorry. I shouldn't have said that. Poor Leah has had a very hard time with this baby. We shouldn't make fun."

"Yes, poor Leah."

Emma knew without turning. Her sister-in-law stood in the doorway. She'd heard. Emma sighed and wiped her hands on a dishtowel. She faced Leah. "We were just being silly. I'm sorry. Are you feeling better?"

Leah shook her head. "I don't believe I'll feel better until this baby arrives. I thought a glass of cool water might help. I'm so parched. Then I'll get out of the way."

"You're not in the way. Sit with us a while."

Leah's gaze swept the room. "It's very crowded in here."

She turned and disappeared from sight.

No one was laughing now. Emma could almost hear Luke's voice.

He would be disappointed in her lack of effort. In the time that they'd shared the house, it still didn't seem like a home for everyone. She grabbed a glass and filled it with water. "I'll be right back."

She rushed through the dining room to the hallway that led to the front bedrooms. Leah spent a great deal of time in the room she shared with Luke. Resting or making clothes for the baby. Beautiful baby blankets and little quilts. She was quite a good seamstress. Emma should try to learn from her.

"What is that? Give that to me. Now."

Leah's angry voice, high and tight, carried down the hall. What was going on?

Emma picked up her pace and rounded the corner. Leah and Josiah stood in the hallway, both of them with glowering faces. Leah held out her hand. "I want it now."

Josiah clutched a cell phone to his chest. "No. It's mine."

"Josiah, what are you doing here?" Emma stepped between them. "You're supposed to be at the blacksmith shop."

The anger in his face faded, replaced with something that looked like shame. "Caleb sent me home. He says I...he says I daydream too much." Josiah snorted. "He says I'll hurt myself or a horse if I don't pay more attention."

"So you decide to come home and talk on the telephone?" Leah interrupted. She held out a hand. "If you insist on violating the Ordnung, you can't be here either. Give me that thing. I have to take it to the deacon."

"No!" Emma set the glass of water on the windowsill. "If you do, Deacon Pierce could ask him to leave."

"Josiah knew the consequences when he brought the phone in here. Now that we know what he's done, we're at risk if we *don't* take it to the deacon." Leah gave Emma a stern look. "You know that. You know we must do the right thing. He's brought a phone into our house. That is forbidden."

Her heart pounding, Emma tried to think. Josiah did know. She'd warned him already. She let him get away with it after the funeral because she knew how anguished he was about Mudder and Daed. "Give him another chance. Please, Leah. He's been through so much."

"We've all been through a lot, and we're not using telephones to talk to New Order Mennonite girls or listening to music on iPods." Frowning, she shook her head. "Yes, I know all about it. I'm not a fool, and neither is your brother. Think about Mark. Do you want him influenced by these outside forces? What about Lillie and Mary? Do you want them to lose their innocence? And my boys. I have to protect my boys." Her hands went to her stomach in a protective gesture. "And my baby. Give me the phone."

Angry tears bright in his eyes, Josiah shook his head. "I can't." He looked at Emma, his face beseeching. "It's the only way I can talk to Sarah. Her father won't let me see her anymore, thanks to Luke."

"You give me no choice." Leah took a long breath. "I'll ask Luke to talk to the deacon. He'll come to you to investigate your infractions. That will be worse."

"Whatever."

Josiah's defiant tone told Emma all was lost. "Please, please don't do this, Josiah."

"I love her."

Emma laid a hand on his shoulder. His tight, knotted muscles tensed under his cotton shirt. "What about Miriam? You two seemed to get along so well when you started going to the singings last year. She likes you a lot. She's waiting for you to shine a flashlight in her window again."

"Miriam...Miriam's nice. I like her. She's a good person." He jerked away. "But I love Sarah."

He fled, leaving Emma in the hallway with Leah. Emma gathered her courage. "Please don't go to the deacon. Let's talk about this as a family. Tonight, when Luke gets home."

Leah rubbed her temple, her face pale against the flowing fabric of her dark green dress. "I wouldn't do anything without speaking to my husband first. Surely you know that."

"Of course."

Leah lumbered away, one hand on her lower back. Emma waited until she disappeared into her bedroom and the *thump, thump* sound signified she sat at the treadle sewing machine, pumping the foot peddle. Then Emma scurried the other direction toward the room Josiah shared with Mark, and now Joseph and William. She peeked around the corner. Josiah bent over something on his narrow bunk bed. She hesitated. He turned and grabbed a shirt from a hook on the wall, then another. They disappeared into…a trunk. He had a trunk open on his bed. His movements were quick, almost frantic. He didn't look up and he didn't hesitate.

Her heart banged against her ribcage. He couldn't leave. She couldn't let him. A wave of memories washed over her, making it hard to breathe. Carl standing on the porch. Carl tearfully apologizing. Carl walking away.

Not again.

The definitive snap of the trunk lid made Emma jump. She rushed to squeeze between Josiah and the quilt-covered bed where the trunk sat. "No. Don't go. Let's talk about this."

Josiah's sad smile didn't reach his walnut-colored eyes. "We've talked and talked. There's no more talking to do."

Emma couldn't let him go. Somehow their future as a family depended on her being able to convince him to stay.

She snatched at the handle, but Josiah brushed her hand away. His long, knobby fingers touched hers with a surprising gentleness that brought tears to her eyes. He hadn't changed from his black pants and suspenders, but the lack of a straw hat to cover his unruly thatch of hair told her a decision had been made. The talks with Carl hadn't helped. Her admonishments hadn't helped. And Leah's intervention certainly hadn't helped.

He straightened. "It's done. I'm going."

"No, no, it's not. Please."

He grabbed the trunk, looked around the crowded but neat bedroom as if memorizing it, and then moved away from her. "It's for the best. I'm only causing more problems. It's too crowded here with all of us and all the memories of Mudder and…" His voice broke. "You know…"

"Where will you go? You can't go to Sarah's!"

"I'll talk to her father. Explain the situation. Maybe when he knows I'm leaving the community for good, he'll change his mind. If not, I know an Englisch family I can stay with until—"

"Until what? What will you do?"

"Get a job. Go to school or get a GED. I'll learn things. Things you'll never get to learn."

After throwing that piece of certain truth in Emma's face, he marched out the door, his skinny teenager legs carrying him away from everything he'd ever known.

Emma closed her eyes for a second. His words hurt, even though they rang with a truth that the teacher in her recognized. Still, knowledge wasn't as important as faith. The jumbled words of prayer milled around in her head, incoherent. Josiah couldn't go. If he did, she might never see him again. She'd lost her mother and father. She couldn't bear to lose a brother, too.

Father, please help me find a way to save him. Not for me. But for him. Go after him.

The voice in her head whispered the words with a sharp clarity that startled her into action. She rushed down the hallway toward the closing door. Josiah's hand clutched the outside knob. The door shut. Emma grabbed it and pulled.

Josiah leaped over the last porch step and started across the heat-scarred grass.

She scurried after him, her long skirt hampering her headlong struggle to reach him. "Josiah, wait. Just stay one more day. Talk to Carl again." She couldn't believe those words came from her mouth. Carl who had abandoned her. "He understands what you're going through."

"The difference is that he had a chance to find out for himself what he wanted. He got to see what's out there." Josiah stopped and turned. "I need to see the world out there. I have Sarah. Her family will accept me as I am. I won't be alone."

He didn't need Sarah and her family. He had his own family. Aunts and uncles and cousins—an entire close-knit community of people who loved him. "You have me and Annie and Catherine and Luke and Mark and the twins." She struggled to keep her voice from breaking. "Miriam wants to make a life with you. She's waiting for you to see that. You belong here."

"Miriam knows I care for someone else. She'll find someone new. I've already arranged for a ride. I asked George Johnson if his dad could pick me up at the road." Josiah's voice cracked over the name of the Englisch boy who had helped him go to Wichita before. "I'll walk to the crossroads to meet his car."

He was trying to spare her from having to watch him drive away. "Don't go."

He kept walking. She stood there, watching, until he disappeared from sight, and then long after.

Chapter 17

Emma folded the tablecloth she was embroidering, laid it in her sewing basket, and plunged her needle into the pin cushion. She wanted to finish this piece. It was intricate enough, pretty enough, that it should sell quickly at the produce stand. The Englisch people liked these things almost as much as the quilts. But her eyes were too weary for the intricate cross stitches, and her tired fingers couldn't maneuver the fine daisy and French knot stitches anymore. The dusky evening quiet soothed her tangled thoughts of Josiah and where he would lay his weary head tonight.

She sighed. Her mind wouldn't stop going round and round, trying to find another ending to the story. None came. The children had been asleep for at least an hour. Luke and Leah were in their room. Emma extinguished the kerosene lamp. She should join Annie and Catherine, who were surely asleep by now. Yet the restlessness consumed her. She glanced out one of three large open windows that lined the far wall, allowing a soft, cooling breeze to chase away the heat of the day. The sun burrowed on the horizon, almost gone from sight. Time to go to bed.

Emma cranked her head from side to side to loosen the tense muscles in her neck and shoulders. It didn't help. The stairs beckoned. She hesitated. Instead, she went to the kitchen where she turned on the gas stove and set the kettle on the burner. Maybe a cup of chamomile tea would assuage the empty feeling inside her.

Supper had been a quiet affair, with no one bringing up the fact that a family member was missing from the table. Apparently all the words about Josiah's infraction and departure had been said earlier when Emma had listened to the rise and fall of Luke and Leah's voices behind the closed door of their bedroom.

Luke's only words at the supper table were the "Amen" after his silent prayer before the meal and to ask for more fried potatoes.

The image of Josiah trudging down the road, his trunk banging against his leg, miniature puffs of dust rising up with every step, assailed her. Where was he now? Had Sarah's father welcomed him into the Kauffman home? Surely he had taken pity on a young man whose heart hung so precariously on his sleeve that he was willing to give up his home and family for the man's daughter.

She wiped the counters even though Catherine and Annie had left them spotless. Annie's ingredients for the pies she would make in the morning sat in a neat row on her preparation table. The biscuits for breakfast were wrapped in a towel and nestled in a huge basket. Emma sniffed. *Go to bed.*

Resolute, she turned off the burner and marched down the hallway to the stairs that led to the bedroom she shared with her sisters. Something moved outside the open living room windows. She stopped at the bottom of the stairs. What was that noise? The rustling sound grew louder. She stood very still. Someone lurked in the grass outside the windows.

Her hand went to her throat. Who would visit this late? Her heart lurched. Thomas had said he would figure out a way. Maybe Deborah Brennaman enjoyed having her grandchildren spend the night now and then to give her son a break from double parenting duty. Emma had no way of letting him know that things had changed since their conversation. Doubts pummeled her. Thomas made no promises, but his track record showed him to be an honorable man of his word. He would never leave Bliss Creek. He might also never find the time to court. She had a history with Carl. Once she gave her heart away, could she really get it back?

Emma slipped over to the windows and peeked out.

A beam of light flickered over her head. She craned her neck and looked up. The light waved back and forth, touching an upstairs window. The window to her bedroom. Thomas had said he was too old for flashlights and covert courting, but as a Plain person, Thomas also stood on tradition.

She peered through the dusk, trying to see beyond the light. The shadowy figure had no features against the dark expanse of sky. She opened the door. "Thomas?"

"Thomas? It's me, Carl."

Thomas shook the reins and clucked. The new mare—Eli and Rebecca were still debating its name—picked up its pace. The full moon hung heavy in the sky. A good night for courting. He tugged at his hat, his palms damp. It had been a very long time since he had picked up a young lady and taken her for a ride in a buggy.

His courtship with Joanna had been a long one. For a Plain girl, she was a quietly stubborn young lady with a surprisingly sharp mind of her own. No one hurried her into making a decision. She wanted to be sure she was doing the right thing—for both of them. She'd kept him waiting. Something she regretted when she came to realize their time together would be so short.

He brushed away the memories. Not tonight. Tonight, he planned a new beginning. The children were safely tucked away with their groossmammi and groossdaadi. Thomas had all the time he needed to convince Emma to take a buggy ride with him.

He turned on to the road that led to the Shirack house. To his surprise, lights shone in his face. He heard the clip-clop of horses hooves before his eyes adjusted. A horse pulling a buggy trotted briskly along the other side of the road. Thomas ducked his head, knowing that his own battery-operated lights would allow some other courting couple to see him. Given the fact that Annie and Catherine were of age for seeking a husband, he should've been prepared for that.

As the buggy passed, he couldn't help but glance toward it. He almost dropped the reins. Carl Freiling. Thomas sucked in air. With Emma? Surely not. He dared a quick second glance. Emma. Stunned, Thomas snapped the reins and the horse picked up his pace again.

It took a few seconds to understand. Carl had convinced Emma to give him another chance. Thomas's fingers tightened on the reins. Anger flashed through him. He tapped it down. It was selfish of him. If Emma could finally find happiness with Carl then Thomas should be happy for her.

He leaned back in the seat and tried to relax. Emma would surely be hurt again. Carl had no claim to the title of gentleman. That much everyone knew. He hadn't treated Emma well, although her faith dictated that she forgive him for those past transgressions. And she had done so. Thomas would have to live with this scenario. It was his own fault for waiting so long to approach her and then being so wishy-washy about finding a way to court her.

He tugged on the reins and brought the buggy to a halt in front of the Shirack house. He covered his face with his hands and sat, not moving. The emotions that battered his already scarred heart paralyzed him in an agony of regret. Emma, with her brilliant blue eyes and fair skin. Emma, with her careful, crisp way of speaking her mind, and her honed sense of right and wrong. The crinkle at the corners of her lips when she smiled. Her image wavered and then dissolved beyond the horizon, beyond his grasp. He'd never felt more alone.

A darkness-cooled breeze washed over him, taking with it his sense of uncertainty and despair. Thomas raised his head and stared at the beautiful starry sky. The soft white glow of the Milky Way drifted above him. The enormity of God's creation dwarfed him. He felt oddly comforted by that fact.

Don't give up.

The words rang clearly in the night sky. *Don't give up.*

You're not alone.

Emma stared into the darkness, glad that clouds found their way across the moon, blocking out the light for a few seconds so Carl couldn't see the red that burned her face. Thomas had come for her. Four years she'd gone without courting and tonight, two men had come for her. What would she have done if Thomas had been a few minutes earlier? She gripped her hands in her lap to keep them from shaking.

Carl continued to talk, recounting his day at a horse sale and the long hours in the field with his father and brother. He managed to make everything sound like a funny story. Carl loved to talk, which worked out well at the moment. She couldn't have spoken if she tried.

"I know it's been a long time, but surely you aren't nervous around me." Carl clucked and snapped the reins. The horse picked up speed. "Cat got your tongue, or have I put you to sleep with my boring stories?"

A high-pitched half-giggle escaped her mouth. She sounded like a teenage girl. "No, I'm not nervous."

"Good, because I promised myself I would entertain you. I've been saving up my stories all week. Shall I finish with a joke I heard at the feed store yesterday?"

Emma tried to smile. Her lips wouldn't work. "I'm wondering if this is a terrible mistake."

Carl shook his head. "Don't do that. Remember, we're starting fresh. We've just met. This is our first time out. I said how do you do, you said fine and dandy. We might even go to a singing, how about that? Would you like that?"

As if she wanted to pass the evening with girls and boys not too far removed from her schoolroom. Her face heated up again at the thought. She leaned back and stared at the clouds that floated across the sky. A light breeze lifted the strings of her kapp. "If only it were that easy to go back. You know it's not."

"Yes, it is." Carl tugged at the reins and the buggy veered left onto a dirt road that led to his parents' farm. "It's that easy. That simple."

"Only because you were the one who left and had all the adventures while I stayed here and watched my friends marry, one by one. They all said the same thing. Someone is waiting just for you. You'll teach for now, but one day, the right man will come along. But he never did."

"Because I'm that man."

Emma snorted. It wasn't a ladylike sound, but she couldn't help herself. "You had a funny way of showing it."

"Did you ever wonder if it is really possible for people to find their heart and soul mate at age eighteen or nineteen? We're barely grown, barely out of a schoolroom where we learned two plus two and how to speak some English and we're supposed to be sure about something that we commit to until we die."

Leave it to Carl to question something that was time-tested, something that had worked for generations of Plain people. Had he shared these thoughts with Josiah? "My parents did it this way, as did their parents before them and my great-grandparents. Just as yours have done." Emma struggled to keep her voice down. No man liked to have a woman argue with him. "It's our way. We know from the time we are old enough to understand that we will have book learning for a short time, but it's the learning with your mudder and daed that is important. Every Plain child knows it."

"Because they know nothing else."

Emma pushed back a tendril of hair escaping from her kapp. "But we're not eighteen anymore. I'm twenty-three. You're twenty-four. We've grown up. You especially know something different. You saw something different out there, and now you can't forget it. You can't erase it. You've become worldly."

"No. No, that's not true." Carl yanked on the reins. The horse snorted and reared its head, and the buggy came to an abrupt halt in the middle of the road. "Easy, girl, easy. Sorry."

Emma couldn't be sure if he were talking to the horse or to her. "You're changed, Carl. You've been changed by what you saw and what you did. There's no denying that."

"So I've changed. It's made me value what I have here. I value you."

His voice choked, and he stopped. The only sounds for several seconds were his harsh breathing and the rustle of the wind in the trees that lined the road.

Emma opened her mouth and closed it. She had no words to describe the tumult inside her.

"Giddy-up." Carl clucked and tugged the reins. The buggy circled round. "I'll take you home."

That's what she wanted, wasn't it? To go home. She bit her lip until it hurt. "Wait. Not yet. Let's just ride a little bit more."

He tilted his head toward her, his face dark under his hat. "Are you sure?"

"Yes. It's a beautiful night." She held on tight to the side of the buggy with one hand. "Let's just see where it takes us."

The buggy lurched forward. "And Carl, could we just not talk for a while?"

She couldn't see his face, but she felt the tension that jolted through him. "If that's what you want."

"That's what I want."

Chapter 18

Finally. Emma inhaled the crisp early morning air. The first day of school. How she loved the first day. All those smiling faces, scrubbed, brown from the sun, lined up in her classroom. She forced herself to slow her pace. The twins' short legs couldn't keep up with the bigger children.

Normally, Emma went early to prepare her lessons and herself for the task of coordinating the education of more than twenty-five children who ranged in age from five to thirteen, no easy feat. Children who still needed to learn the alphabet and English. Children who were readers. Older children who would soon leave formal education behind. But today, she served as chaperone for the four children coming from the Shirack house. Mary and Lillie chortled over some silly thing. If they had any qualms about starting school, it didn't show. Her lunchbox containing sausage on a bun in one hand, Mary stuck her other sticky hand in Emma's. "See the pretty butterfly, schweschder? Mudder liked the pretty butterflies that came into the garden."

Emma squeezed her sister's small hand. In their own sweet way, the twins did know the significance of this milestone. And celebrated it without their parents. A bittersweet ache filled Emma's throat. Mudder always stood on the porch and wished her a good day on that first day.

Not today.

The schoolhouse came into view, bright with its new coat of white paint. The men had painted the trim a dark green. The windows shone in contrast. She smiled. Life went on. Even though she had no idea what to do about Carl. Or Thomas. Carl hadn't been back to the house since he dropped her off that night two weeks earlier.

Thomas had not returned to the house, either, and she certainly didn't expect that he would anytime soon. The man probably felt humiliated. Shame ebbed and flowed through her, as it did every time she thought about it. She swept the thought away. Today she would focus on her students, not on herself. Today she would do good for others all day. And every day for the rest of the school year.

Laughing and chattering, children clustered near the porch. Some boys chased each other through a stand of nearby oaks. A volleyball bounced past her and rolled into the high grass on the other side of the road. "Teacher!" Helen Crouch's daughter Ginny called out. "Teacher's here! Play volleyball with us!"

"Welcome back. Welcome back, everyone." Emma smiled and waved. No time for play this morning. She had her devotions picked out and the children would select the first songs of the school year, but she wanted to write her assignments on the board. "No volleyball this morning. It's almost time to go in."

The *clip-clop* of horse hooves made her glance to make sure the children weren't in the road. Thomas pulled his buggy into the yard. Suddenly Emma felt warm, despite the balmy early morning breeze. It must have been so hurtful to see her with Carl. Guilt mixed with regret ate at her like a canker sore. Carl said words lightly, while Thomas did not. Thomas didn't deserve to be hurt. He deserved someone with whom to go forward in his life, to be happy after all he'd lost. She didn't deserve his attention, not after standing him up for Carl.

His hat pulled down on his forehead, he sprang from the seat with ease, turned and helped Rebecca down without making eye contact. "Good morning."

He appeared to be talking to her shoes. "Good morning."

He turned his back to her and spoke to Eli. "Behave yourself, son. Emma has a full classroom this year. She doesn't have time for silliness."

"Eli is silly all the time." Rebecca grinned. She'd lost a front tooth sometime during the summer. "That's what Daed says."

"Your father is wise." Sometimes. About some things. Emma clapped her hands together twice. "It's time to begin our first day. Everyone inside. Quickly, now."

Mark opened the door and the children poured in. As they passed through, she began to count how many she would have of each age group. She didn't see any unfamiliar faces. *Gut.*

"Emma." Thomas's hoarse voice spoke volumes even as he whispered her name. He stood only about a yard from her. "I thought you were—"

She glanced at the children. They took their seats in a semi-orderly manner. Giggles and whispers ensued. She only had a few seconds before restlessness set in. She turned to him. "Thomas, I—"

"I came to your house."

"I know. I saw you."

"I thought you...you said we could...I don't understand."

"I didn't anticipate Carl's visit. I'm sorry. He took me by surprise, and I felt obligated to hear him out."

"Obligated? After what he did to you?" Thomas snorted. He lifted his hat and slapped it down on his head. "I'm too old for this."

Always with the same excuse. If he kept saying it, they might both start to believe it. She folded her arms. "Then I guess it doesn't matter whether I see Carl. If you really believe you're too old to court, why did you approach me to start with?"

He held up a huge hand. "Because!" His voice had risen. A couple of children looked back. He stepped closer to Emma. His face darkened with emotion. "I like you. And I'm...I'm lonely."

Emma's hand went to her heart. She knew the stark gray of that feeling. She had plumbed its depths. "I'm sorry, Thomas." She gestured toward the classroom. "It's time for devotions. And I have to teach."

His gaze drilled hers. He nodded, backed away, almost missed the step, then righted himself. "I hope Carl treats you well."

The gruffness of his voice spoke of emotions tethered. Tears pricked Emma's eyes. "Carl hasn't been back since that night. It didn't...it didn't go well. I'm not sure what I want to happen with him."

Thomas shrugged. "I hope you figure it out. Have a good first day of school, teacher."

Those were the words Mudder always said on the first day of school. How did he know these things? He couldn't. She breathed a sigh. "Danki."

Without another word, he pounded down the steps.

Tempted though she was, Emma didn't have time to watch him drive away. She had children to teach. The thought steadied her. At least that was something she knew how to do.

Chapter 19

Emma chunked another piece of wood in the fireplace, careful not to singe her fingertips. "*Brrr*, it's cool this morning." She wrapped a wool shawl around her shoulders and picked up her cup of hot tea. "Fall is turning into winter already. Before we know it, it'll be Thanksgiving—and then Christmas."

Cousin Ruth nodded, but the way she studied her oatmeal-raisin cookie as if she'd never seen one before told Emma her cousin hadn't really heard the words. Their conversation had gone on like this ever since Ruth arrived in an impromptu visit. Emma enjoyed her company, but usually they exchanged news and laughter among all the women folk. Today, Catherine had gone to clean houses and Annie had to take a special order of a dozen pies to some Englisch folks in town. Leah's boys were down with colds, so she had her hands full.

That left Emma with Ruth, who had been practically mute since her arrival. If they weren't going to visit, Emma had things to do on this fine Saturday morning. Teaching all week put her behind on her chores at home. Catherine and Annie took up the slack, helping Leah, but still, Emma intended to do her fair share, especially with the baby coming in December. "Ruth? Ruth! Are you listening to me at all?"

Ruth's face creased in a dreamy sort of smile. "Yes, yes, I'm listening. It's just…just…"

"Just what?" Emma sipped her chamomile tea. She added a smidgen more honey. She liked it sweet. "You're downright silly today. Why so preoccupied?"

Ruth smoothed her kapp. She smiled, then sighed. "David Fisher and I plan to marry. The bishop will publish the announcement at the prayer service tomorrow."

Emma's heart contracted and then became stuck, as if it might not beat again. She rubbed a pain in her collarbone with two cold fingers, willing herself not to cry. "Wonderful. What wonderful news, Ruthie." She rushed around the table and threw her arms around her. "Congratulations."

"I came to tell you first because I wanted to ask you something. I know it's been a hard year for you, what with your parents passing and all." She sniffed and wiped at her nose with a hankie embroidered with roses. "Carl came back. Josiah left. It's hard, I know, but I hope you'll do me the honor of being one of my attendants."

Her little cousin Ruth, nineteen years old, would marry first. Emma swallowed hard, took a breath, and smiled. "Of course I will. I'm honored you asked me."

"Molly Kruger will be the other one. Jonathan Yoder and Michael Kelp will be David's attendants." Ruth hugged Emma. "Oh, there's so much planning to do, so many preparations to make. The wedding is to be a week from Thursday. Mudder bought the most beautiful blue material. I'll start sewing the dress tonight."

Jonathan Yoder. He was Annie's age, baptized the same week. Emma nodded, her fingers twisted in a painful grip in her lap.

Ruth popped up from the table. "I have to go. There's so much to do. We'll talk more after the service tomorrow, all right?"

Emma followed her to the door. "Of course."

All smiles, Ruth hugged her yet again. "I can't believe David asked me to marry him. I so wanted it. I thought he would, but I wasn't sure. We'll be so happy. And there'll be babies." Her hands fluttered to her pink cheeks. "I can't help it. I'm floating, I'm so blessed by everything."

Emma smiled. The happiness saturated the air, making the day bright with anticipation. Who could be sad at a time like this? "As you should be. It's a wonderful day. It truly is a blessing."

She stared down the road long after the buggy disappeared.

"You're letting a cold draft in."

She turned to find Leah in the doorway. "Sorry." She whipped the door shut. "How are the boys?"

"Feeling well enough to be ornery. They think they should be able to play catch with the baseball in the house, since I won't let them go outside." Leah grimaced and clutched at her apron. "I would like for them to go outside, if only their fevers would go away."

Emma took a step forward, stopped. "What's the matter? Are you in labor?"

Leah rubbed her belly and rested her other hand on the wall. "False labor. It's too soon for this *bobbeli*, as much as I would like for it to be time."

"Are you sure?"

Leah's fleeting smile transformed her plain face for a second. "I've done this before."

"Of course." Emma tried to ignore the bitter taste in her throat. No need to rub it in. "Let me make you some hot tea. It's cold in here today, and I've made it worse with the door—"

"Wait. I want to say something" Leah tensed and rubbed harder. "I'm sorry about Josiah."

Emma studied Leah's face. No trace of judgment resided there. Only a soft sadness. "It's not your fault."

"If I hadn't threatened to go to the deacon, he might still be here." She sank onto the bench at the table. "I know that's what Luke thinks."

"Luke thinks you were right, that the Ordnung must be followed."

"What do you think?"

"It doesn't matter."

"It does." Leah smoothed the table's wood with both hands in an absent motion. "We live in the same house, and your resentment is obvious."

"No. I don't resent..." Emma stopped. "I'm sorry. It's not about

Josiah. It's true I miss him and it's hard when it's your own brother, but you were right."

"Then why are you so distant with me? We've been sisters-in-law forever, and yet I still feel as if we're barely acquaintances. I remind myself over and over that you've suffered a terrible loss, but it's not easy for me either."

Emma sank onto the bench across from her sister-in-law. "You know what it's like to have your own home. People have routines and ways of doing things. Ways of disciplining children. Traditions. It's hard to change that."

"The truth is I feel like I'm a visitor here. A permanent visitor. An unwanted visitor."

Emma walked a long mile in her sister-in-law's worn shoes. "I'm sorry to have made you feel that way."

"Am I so unlikeable?"

"No." Regret and shame melded in a sharp needle that poked Emma full of holes. "Of course not. You're hardworking and just as God made you. Why don't I make that tea?"

"Hardworking? High praise, but it saddens me that it is the only attribute you find in me to like. You know, Emma, we were brought up differently." Leah plucked a loose stitch on her apron. "My family is conservative."

"As is mine."

"Not nearly as much. My father barely acknowledged the rumspringa. He didn't allow us to associate with those of other faiths, not even the Mennonites." Leah glanced up. "My father...he frowns upon silliness. Upon frivolity. He says one thing leads to another."

"Like it did with Josiah."

"Exactly."

"Josiah will come back. He'll be back."

Emma rose and headed to the kitchen. Her parents were gone. It was wrong to criticize them now. They allowed Catherine to continue to work in the Englischers' homes even after her baptism. But the bishop had blessed that decision. In these hard economic times some slight changes in the rules were necessary. It would stop when she married. Maybe they should've drawn the line at letting Josiah go to Wichita. Emma slapped the kettle on the stove and turned up the flame. Hindsight.

"No matter what I do, I make you angry." Leah stood in the doorway, her face white against her dark dress. "I am truly sorry they're gone. I mean no disrespect. I simply believe that we must be vigilant against those things that would lure us into worldliness. Into temptation."

"As do I. You think if my parents hadn't been so lax, you'd be in your own home, and Luke would be at his shop, and everything would be the way it was before." The words caught in Emma's throat. She turned. "Shall we have biscuits and honey with the tea?"

"What about Josiah's eternal salvation?"

Emma closed her eyes. "It's in God's hands. To worry is to show a lack of faith." If only she could stop herself from worrying. Her lack of faith and forgiveness filled the room. "None of us know if we will go to heaven."

"That's true." Leah shuffled forward. "We didn't laugh in the house I grew up in. Here, you laugh. I like that. It's obvious you like each other's company. My family isn't like that. We don't show our feelings. It's not considered appropriate."

Leah liked *es gelechter*. Emma certainly couldn't tell that. She'd never even heard Leah laugh outright. An occasional small chuckle behind her lifted hand, but that was about it. Emma kept her gaze on the teapot. She dropped the tea ball into it and poured the steaming water in. "You should sit. You look tired."

Leah sighed. "My back aches so much that I can't sleep at night."

It seemed no one was sleeping well. Even Annie whimpered in her sleep, waking Emma from her own troubled dreams. "It won't be long." She brought the teapot to the table along with two thick china mugs. "I'm sorry to have made this harder for you. I'll try to do better."

"I'm sorry I'm not as lighthearted as you are."

"You must think we are awful, laughing so soon after—"

"No, no, I envy…I know envy is wrong, but there is no other word. I envy it and I worry that Luke is—"

Alarm rocked Emma. "What about Luke?"

"He doesn't smile anymore. He used to be more…patient with the boys. More patient with me. He tried to make me laugh because he knew it didn't come easily. He wanted the boys to take joy in small things. Simple things. Now he works, he eats, and he sleeps. He barely speaks, let alone jokes."

Emma poured the tea, then took a sip from her cup. It burned her tongue. She welcomed the small pain as a distraction from Leah's words. "I'm sure he still does want that for them and for you. He's just working very hard to take care of all of us. To keep the farm going. He's tired."

Leah's face crumpled. "He's lost his joy. He doesn't see me anymore. He looks through me to a distant place where he might someday be able to rest." Tears wet her cheeks. "He's sad. I don't think he's even thankful for this baby."

"No, that's not true. Luke loves his children and a baby…a baby gives us hope for new life, a new beginning." Emma let her hand creep forward until it covered Leah's. "Luke won't always be sad. Aenti Louise says these things take time. But they shall pass. It will get better with time. She promised me." She patted Leah's hand and withdrew hers. "Let's talk about happy things. Cousin Ruth is getting married to David. I'm to be her attendant."

Leah dabbed at her face with a napkin. "What wonderful news. I suspected as much."

"You did? I had no idea." Emma forced a smile. "She's so happy."

Please God. Don't let us always be sad.

Chapter 20

Despite the hard surface of the Sunday benches that had been carted into the Dodd barn for the wedding, Emma couldn't contain a blissful sigh. Ruth glowed in her blue dress. She'd emerged from the *abroth* looking like she might float away. Emma doubted that her cousin had anything to admit to the bishop or for which to be admonished. Her rumspringa had been very mild compared to many. She confided in Emma that she found the Englisch ways very disconcerting. The boys too forward. Her eyes were only for David. Her rumspringa had been brief; her baptism right behind it.

The couple had completed the questions that served as their vows and returned to their seats more than an hour ago. The service was almost over. Everything was ready for the noon meal. Immediately after they would begin cooking the wedding supper. The cakes and ice cream were made. With more than one-hundred-fifty guests coming from as far away as Ohio, the food preparations had been massive. Thankfully, Ruth had four sisters and a bevy of cousins to help.

The bishop said the words that ended the service. Emma immediately stood and rushed to Ruth's side. "Congratulations." She hugged Ruth. "Are you ready to change your kapp?"

Ruth's cheeks turned pink. "Let's go to my room."

Together they scurried across the yard to Ruth's home. In her room, the bride carefully removed the pins that held her black kapp in place, laid it aside, and placed the white one over her dark brown hair. A tear slid down her cheek. "I can't believe it."

Emma patted her arm. "Believe it, Mrs. David Fisher."

Ruth touched the kapp with a shaky finger. "I'm nervous…about being…a wife."

Emma's cheeks heated up. She ducked her head, searching for the right words. "David's a good man. He'll be patient. And I'm sure he's as nervous as you are."

"Really?" Ruth looked relieved. "I didn't think of that."

"I'm sure of it." Men liked to act like they knew what they were doing, but Emma was sure they were just as uncertain about these things. "Right now, it's time to eat the noon meal. There'll be gifts to open and singing this afternoon. And the wedding feast this evening. All those young, single boys and girls out there are chomping at the bit to be paired off. You need to eat well; it'll be a long, wonderful day."

Ruth shook her head. "Right now, I don't think I could swallow a bite. I'll meet you in the barn. I just want to have a word with Mudder before I go find David."

"He's probably already wearing his new hat and being congratulated by every man in the district. He'll wait for you." Emma didn't blame Ruth for wanting to get those words of motherly advice. She no longer tried to imagine her wedding day. It was too painful to think it might never come, and if it did, Mudder and Daed would not be there to see it. "I'll be in the kitchen. There's plenty of food to carry out."

She marched through the Dodd house, almost an exact replica of her own, to the kitchen, where a contingent of women swarmed, scurrying to and fro with bowls and platters and trays. Catherine handed her hot pads and a deep, heavy dish of dumplings. "Take these." She wiped at her forehead with the back of her hand. "I'll bring the roast."

Together they trotted across the yard to the barn where the men had rearranged the benches with tables between them. Emma watched the uneven ground to make sure she didn't stumble over something and drop her dish.

"Emma."

Thomas. She slowed, then sped up. "Good morning."

"Can I have a moment?"

He stepped in her path. Catherine looked back, but kept going with her heavy dish. Emma wavered. "This is hot and I must get it inside. The festivities are beginning."

He tugged the brim of his Sunday hat so it shaded his eyes. "Weddings always make me think of Joanna."

His words sliced her heart like a sharpened butcher knife. Weddings made her think of the future. They made Thomas think of the past. It was ungracious of her, but Emma couldn't help but feel that it was a sign they had no future together. She shook free of the thought and tried to focus on his feelings. "I'm sorry for your loss. I know it still grieves you."

"No, it's not a sad thought." He smiled. He did have such a nice smile. "I've learned to be content with the time we had. And the children are a blessing."

Emma shifted. True on both counts. Maybe someday she would be able to feel that way about the loss of Mudder and Daed. But not today. Not yet. The heat of the dish seeped through the hot pads. People filtered around them. A curious glance or two came her way. "I'm glad you're not sad anymore, Thomas, but I really have to go."

He glanced at the guests passing by. "I know this is not the right time. But I'd like to talk to you. I'm sorry I didn't say things better at the school. I didn't mean to burden you. I try hard to be content, but when I see you...today is too busy with the wedding festivities, but tomorrow evening...later."

She studied his face. "I don't know, Thomas. Things are so confusing right now."

He took a half step closer, but the distance between them remained more than proper. He smelled like wood chips. "You said you weren't sure about Carl. I must take my chances before you make up your mind about him. I would like to make things less confusing. For both of us."

Weddings promised new beginnings. Carl promised a new beginning, but seemed to deliver the same old heartache. Despite his little jokes and funny stories, they still spent most of their evening together rehashing old memories and hurts. She was trying to make room for the possibility Carl might have changed in the past four years. In some ways, he had clearly changed. He knew more words, big words, lots of words no Plain farmer would have cause to use. He walked with the assurance of someone who knew where he was going and why.

Carl wanted her to walk with him. So did Thomas. She feared being hurt again, yet she longed to trust. The truth knotted in her throat. Could she risk being hurt by Carl or any man? Even someone as sturdy and kind and faithful as Thomas? She was afraid to hope. Afraid to trust.

Thomas stared at her, waiting for some kind of response. His expression said he was as confused as she was. Emma swallowed the painful lump, hoping her feelings weren't etched across her face. "Less confusing would be good."

He tipped his hat and moved away just as another gaggle of women rushed past her, carrying more food.

The rest of the afternoon passed in a blur of eating and laughing and singing. By evening some of the older folks had moved into the house where they napped or played board games with the younger children. Too busy to be tired, Emma was nevertheless relieved when they finally grouped around the supper tables. The girls and boys who were courting age anxiously milled about on the edges until Emma and Jonathan began to pair them off for the seating, couples already courting on one side, those who were interested in each other on the other.

To Emma's surprise, Annie actually giggled when Jonathan left a place at the table—next to him. On the other hand, Catherine was nowhere in sight. Emma hated to see the disappointed look on Michael Glick's face. Nor was it fair to the girl who was seated beside him.

Emma didn't have time to linger over the thought. She touched Miriam's arm. The girl smiled, but her brown eyes were sad. "I was so hoping."

"I know. Me too." Emma had sent a letter to the Kauffmans' address.

Even though Mr. Kauffman surely didn't allow Josiah to court Sarah, Emma believed they would watch over him, make sure he was faring all right in a fancy world. They were good people. "I still believe he will come home. He's sowing wild oats, but he is a Plain person at heart."

Miriam shrugged. "It's been almost three months. I keep thinking Josiah will miss me—miss all of this. I can't imagine what it must be like to not see your family or friends, the people you grew up with."

Emma drew her toward one of the tables, leaned forward, and patted the bench. "We can't imagine, because this is all we've ever wanted. We have to accept Josiah's journey as God's will for us. We don't know how it will end, but God does." She commanded herself to believe the words she spoke. "And so we go forward."

Miriam's gaze flitted to William Zook as he dropped onto the bench next to the empty spot Emma had assigned to Miriam. She looked up at Emma, her eyebrows raised. "Emma—"

Emma offered her an encouraging smile. Time for both of them to move on. "I've got so much to do. We'll talk later. Enjoy the meal."

She rushed away. She wasn't giving up on Josiah coming home, but she couldn't let Miriam languish the way she had, waiting and waiting for the man she thought she loved to come home. Even if he returned, he wouldn't be the same. He would be the sum of his experiences and the things he'd learned. Carl wasn't the only one who had changed in four years. For better or for worse, so had Emma. Just as Miriam would, the longer Josiah stayed away.

Absence didn't always make the heart grow fonder. Sometimes, it gave the heart time to grow up.

Chapter 21

The evening after the wedding, Emma puttered around the house long after the others had gone to bed. The excitement of the festivities, the visiting with old friends and family, the enormous mountains of food had left her with a pent-up tension that she couldn't relieve. Restless, she folded the last of the clean laundry. Mended a stack of the boys' socks. Wrote a letter to her cousin in Ohio. Read an old edition of *The Budget* newspaper a third time.

Finally, knowing how early the sun would rise on the next day's chores and school, she extinguished the kerosene lamp. A light flickered through the darkened windows. She forced herself to walk calmly to the glass and peek out. Thomas waved a flashlight. He'd come. The fact that'd he'd chosen the traditional signal touched her. He honored their traditions. He wanted her to know he'd overcome obstacles to court her. She heaved a sigh. His overture took courage in light of what he believed her relationship to be with Carl. Her palms damp, she slipped on her heavy wool coat, carefully closed the door, and ran down the steps.

Without a word, Thomas offered a hand to help her into the buggy, then rushed around to his side. He tucked a thick robe over their laps and picked up the reins. He clucked softly and the buggy jolted forward. Emma inhaled the cold, damp air and waited for him to give her a hint of what he was thinking.

He cleared his throat. "I'm glad you came out."

"Me, too. I mean, I'm glad you came to get me."

More silence. Carl never stopped talking. Emma found Thomas's quiet refreshing. Thomas was comfortable with himself. He didn't seem to mind a companionable silence. It gave her time to collect her thoughts. The clip-clop of the horse's hooves lulled her. She relaxed for what seemed like the first time in forever. Because of Thomas. But it was cold and the ride would be short. She wanted it to be fruitful for both of them. Thomas had paid her a great compliment by waiting patiently for this moment, and pursuing it despite what had happened on his first attempt to court her. "I—"

"I—"

They both laughed, Thomas's gruff sound mingling with her higher peals in the night air. He held up a gloved finger. "You first."

Emma chose a topic she knew would warm a father's heart. "Eli's reading has improved so much this year. He's quite the scholar. He's helping Rebecca learn to read. And he's helping her with her English, too."

Thomas's face dissolved into a big smile in the moonlight. The sight of his full lips stretched across a sculpted face under dark, warm eyes diffused the cold air around her, making the evening seem suddenly warm as a May night. "He has a good teacher." Thomas snapped the reins and the horse picked up his pace. "He and Rebecca natter on about school all through supper. A sure sign they enjoy the time they spend with you."

The high praise made Emma happy, yet a little uncomfortable. She didn't need praise for a job well done, but still, it was lovely to receive. "I'm glad."

"So am I." He glanced at her and away. "I enjoy the time I spend with you, too."

"Can I ask why?" She didn't want him to think she would fish for compliments, but she truly did want to know why. What did Thomas see in her that caused him to seek her company?

He didn't answer right away. Knowing Thomas, he would take the question very seriously and give her a carefully thought-out answer. "I'm not much of a talker."

"No, you're not."

"You don't make me feel bad about it." He ducked his head. "The words are sweet, but so is the silence."

She nodded, even though he wasn't looking at her. She could see how courting would be difficult with women who expected a man to hold up his end of a conversation. It was just easier on those first buggy rides. "You feel comfortable?"

"Yes."

"I'm glad."

"It also helps that you're pretty."

The warm rush of a deep blush coursed through her. "Thomas!"

"The truth is the truth."

"For a man of few words, you know which ones to pick."

Again, with that smile. Emma tried to breathe, but the air caught her in throat. She felt a little faint. She couldn't have spoken if she'd tried.

Thomas guided the buggy onto a dirt road that cut through her family's fields and ran alongside a pond where the kids loved to fish on hot summer evenings. After a while he tugged on the reins. The horse stopped along the banks of the pond. The reflection of the moon wrinkled in waves stirred up by a damp breeze out of the north. The scent of grass and wet earth made a lovely autumn perfume. Thomas hopped from the buggy and offered her a hand. "Shall we walk?"

She nodded and let him help her down. His big hand was warm and steady on hers. His smile hung crooked on his face. He let her hand drop and grabbed another blanket from the back seat. They walked in silence along the edge of the pond, its water polished silver.

Walking made conversation easier for Thomas. He spoke more words than she'd ever heard him string together in a single visit. He asked questions about school and her scholars. Emma told him stories of their antics that made him laugh.

"Mary and Lillie played Hide and Seek the other day," she told him.

"Not unusual for little ones their age."

"Except when I rang the bell to signal the end of recess, they stayed hidden."

"For how long?"

"Until I found them hiding in that grove of elms south of the building ten minutes later."

Thomas chuckled. "What did they have to say for themselves?"

"They said Eli told them to stay hidden until someone found them. He said that's how you play the game."

"My Eli?"

"Your Eli."

Thomas shucked off his gloves and stuck them in his pocket. Then he lifted his hat and scratched his head. "That's my boy. Always wanting to be in charge. I'll talk to him."

"No, no, don't do that!" Without thinking, Emma grabbed his arm at the elbow and hung on with one hand. "He didn't know they would take him so literally. Besides, it's just Hide and Seek."

His big hand fell on top of hers and tightened. He halted, forcing her to do the same. She looked up at him, aware of her heart pounding in her chest as if she'd run a mile. "Thomas?"

He shook his head. "You're not so far removed from schoolyard games yourself."

"Far enough."

"Are you sure?"

She nodded. His hand slid away from hers. She let go of his arm, and they started forward again.

Neither spoke. Their shoes crunching in the dead leaves along the banks of the pond made the only sound for a few minutes. She waited, not trying to fathom what might be going on in his head at this moment. She'd come to realize Thomas thought about things more than anyone she'd ever known.

"That night, when I came to see you…" Thomas spoke softly, as if not to wake the creatures that lived in the nearby stand of trees that buffered the pond from now-empty fields. "When I realized you were leaving with Carl, I felt so…foolish. I thought we had an understanding."

Emma ran her hands up and down her coat sleeves, suddenly chilled. She'd known this moment would come sooner or later. "His visit represents no commitment and he knows that, yet he is persistent."

Thomas walked more quickly, forcing Emma to skip to keep up. "I have much to consider, because of the children."

A true statement, but Emma couldn't change the situation. "They don't know where you are tonight?"

"No. They don't. I don't want to create an…an expectation that could later become awkward. You're their teacher. They love you."

They were both quiet for a few minutes. Bullfrogs sang in the distance. Emma sighed. "I love them, too."

Thomas picked up a rock and chucked it in the pond. Then another. "You love all your children."

She picked up her own rock and chucked it. It skipped over the water, making rings that rippled outward. Luke had taught her to do that a long time ago. She missed their time of big-brother, little-sister. "That's true, but I want to be a mother as well as a teacher." And more. She should be brave enough to say it. "I want to be a wife."

Thomas handed her another rock. Their fingers brushed for a fraction of a second. Their gazes held. "You'll be a good one."

"You think so?"

"You do everything well. Even skip rocks."

Her breath gone, Emma focused on the rock he'd given her. It felt smooth and cold in her hand. She forced herself to inhale.

Thomas's face hovered over hers, his eyes muddy water in which she could fathom nothing. "Do you still love Carl?"

"No." *I don't know.*

"Your face says differently when you're talking to him."

"You're mistaken." *Surely, you're mistaken.*

He spun away from her and stalked ahead for several yards, then stopped. There, he spread the blanket on the grass. "Please sit with me." He bowed slightly at the waist. "I know it's chilly. Just for a few minutes."

Hoping her face didn't give away how much he disconcerted her, she sank onto the blanket and looked out at the pond. She concentrated on the ripples in the water caused by a sudden, cold breeze. Better to do that than look at his face. He would know. Know that she wasn't sure of anything, least of all how she felt about him. Thomas stirred feelings in her that she had never felt for Carl. Feelings so strong they made her legs weak and her hands tremble. Did love feel like the flu? She wished Mudder were around to answer that question. With Carl, the flame had been steady. With Thomas, it leaped and swirled, threatening to devour everything in its path. The thought made the hair stand up on her arms.

He wiggled next to her like a child, his long arms and legs sticking out in all directions. He was too tall to sit comfortably on a blanket. Emma peered at him out of the corner of one eye. His face was half-hidden in the shadows. He spoke so little, but when he did, the words resonated with her. He saw things, knew things about her that others failed to see and understand. Although her feelings for him were rooted in Thomas's steady calm, kind eyes, and thoughtfulness, the feelings were far from steady or calm. He was a man when Carl seemed to still be a boy. She worked to clear her thoughts. "What about you, Thomas?"

"What do you mean?"

"You and Joanna."

He ducked his head so his hat hid his face. "It's been four years."

"It doesn't matter if it's been ten years. Are you ready to move on?"

His face still hidden, he plucked a blade of grass. "I have to. For the sake of the children, I must."

"That's not what I asked you."

"I know, and you deserve an answer." He tossed away the grass and leaned back on his elbows. She could see his face, but his expression remained inscrutable. "All I know is that I think about you more than I should. I'm acting like a boy. It's been a long time, but I'm fairly certain that means something."

"That you're a man?"

He laughed, a low sound that warmed her. "Perhaps that's what it is. I want to believe it is more. Do you?"

Afraid to trust her voice, she nodded. But what about Carl?

As if he read her mind, Thomas sat up. "There can be nothing between us as long as your feelings for Carl are ambivalent." He leaned so their faces were close. "I know what I feel. I will wait for you. For however long it takes."

No hurry. Emma twisted her fingers together tightly in her lap. "It may be selfish of me, but I long to have my own children, to have my own home, and to share it all with my husband. Not later. Now."

"You deserve that." His voice sounded ragged. "Your life, your future, are in your hands."

It didn't seem that way to her. It seemed that so much depended on others. She was needed at home and at school. Catherine needed her. Josiah needed her. Her scholars needed her. Even Carl said he needed her. "Many people are depending on me. Maybe God's plan was for me to be a teacher and helper, not a mother."

"I think you're afraid of being hurt again." Thomas didn't move away from her. His face was so close she could've touched it. The thought made her scoot back. He didn't follow. "Aren't you?"

When she didn't respond, he sighed, a melancholy sound that mingled with the bullfrog's concert. "For Eli and Rebecca's sake, I must make very sure this is right, but in my heart, I already know. I know it's you. The question is—do you know?"

Emma pressed her chilled hands to her warm cheeks. "I don't want to do anything to hurt your children."

"So you think it's better not to try? That they remain motherless?"

Others would jump at the chance to be with Thomas and his children. "What about Helen? She's a good mother to her own children. She's shown by her actions that she cares for you." Emma scooted to the farthest corner of the blanket. "Could you not give your heart to her?"

Thomas stood. "You're matchmaking at a time like this?"

It was the closest Emma had ever heard him come to sounding angry. She popped up to face him. "No—"

"That's your answer, then." He settled his hat and snatched up the blanket. "After all he's done to you, you would choose Carl."

"I never said that. I—"

He slapped the blanket together in a haphazard wad. "We should go back. It's late and tomorrow I have much work to do."

Her cheeks burning, the muscles in her shoulders and neck knotted, Emma walked behind him, not bothering to try to keep up with his long strides. He glanced back. "Don't dawdle. Be careful of the holes. Don't step in one and twist your ankle."

"I'm not one of your children." Even though she sounded ten. She picked up her pace. "Don't treat me like one."

"Then don't act like one."

"I'm not! You're just mad because…because…" Because he cared about her and she had hurt him somehow. "I didn't mean to hurt you."

Without a word, he tossed the blanket on the floor of the buggy and held out his hand. She took it and he helped her in.

They rode in silence until the house came into view. Silent rides were becoming a habit. Thomas tugged on the reins and brought the buggy to a halt. "Decide what you want. I meant it when I said I would wait, but you have to decide."

"Thomas."

He shook his head. "We're done talking. It's time to think and then to do."

She stood on the porch, watching him drive away until darkness cloaked the buggy. It was all she could do to keep from slamming the screen door. Twice she'd gone out in a buggy, twice she'd come home in a huff. Somehow she remembered courting as being much nicer than this.

Chapter 22

E mma strolled down the aisle between the desks watching the younger children cut pumpkins from construction paper. Her hands on her hips, she surveyed the real pumpkins and dried leaves the children had used to decorate the schoolroom. A shiny, sleek one sat on her desk, leaves strewn around it. The festive decorations lifted her spirits. Thanksgiving had always been her favorite holiday, and she was determined to count blessings as always. It would be the first big holiday without Mudder and Daed, but all the more reason to find joy in it. Lillie, Mary, and Mark needed the older brothers and sisters to lead them in the way of always finding something for which to be thankful.

She stopped to look over Mary's shoulder at the pumpkin her sister was cutting from construction paper. "What a nice job you did cutting out your pumpkin."

"It's orange!"

She smiled at the little girl's enthusiasm. November and Thanksgiving were such a lovely time of year, even if the events of the past year had been difficult. There was still much to be thankful about. "Yes, it is, very orange. What are you going to draw on it? What are you thankful for?"

Lillie wrinkled her nose. She tilted her head. "Hmm...I'm thankful my sister is my teacher."

"That's very sweet. Thank you, Lillie."

One of the older boys snickered. "Teacher's pet."

Emma fixed him with a stern stare. "Do you need to spend some time writing an essay on how to behave oneself in school, Robert?"

The boy ducked his head. "No."

"Then mind your manners and finish grading Rachel's spelling test."

"Teacher, look at my pumpkin."

Emma turned her attention to Rebecca, who held up a neatly cut circle with a protrusion at the top. She'd used a crayon to color the stem brown.

"It's lovely, Rebecca." Thomas's daughter had proven to be a bright, willing student who moved easily from Pennsylvania Dutch to English and learned numbers just as quickly. "What are you thankful for?"

The girl bent over her creation, the tip of her tongue peeking through her lips as she labored over her drawing. "Daed, Groossmammi, Groossdaadi, and Mudder in heaven." She sniffed, her tone years older than her age. "I'm happy Mudder's in heaven."

Rebecca dropped the brown crayon and picked up the black. She peeked at Emma without raising her head. "Can I tell you a secret?"

Emma debated. Did secrets between a teacher and her scholars present any problems when the child was Thomas's daughter? She was only six, after all. "Of course you may."

She leaned down, and the girl's warm breath touched her ear. "I'm happy Mudder's in heaven, but I really wish she were here so we could make a quilt together. And bake bread. And she could teach me to sew dresses. Is that bad, that I wish she were here?"

Emma straightened and patted the girl's shoulder. "I understand why you feel that way, but you know that your mother is in a special place with our Heavenly Father. That is a good place to be."

"I think Daed wants her to be here, too."

Emma stiffened. Therein lay the problem with confidences from a little girl who was the daughter of the man she might be courting. Thomas had visited her only once since that first night and then had stayed only a short while, pleading concern over Eli being sick. He had made no mention of their earlier walk along the pond. He was waiting for her to make a decision. To do that, she had to figure out what to do about Carl. Forgive him and move on. That's what she needed to do, somehow. Then she'd be able to cast away the fear the thought of making herself vulnerable to Thomas brought every time she entertained it.

She must not take advantage of Rebecca's confidences. Yet children could be so observant, much more than adults realized. Curiosity reared its ugly head. Emma fought it back into its corner. "Your father is a strong, faithful man. He's fine, Rebecca."

The little girl sighed. "Then why does he look so sad? Today I showed him the rip in my hem, and he was very sad. I think it's because he doesn't have Mudder to sew it."

Or do all the other things wives do for their husbands and children. "You know how you can help him?"

"By being good and working hard and making breakfast?"

Emma nodded. "And by learning to mend those rips yourself."

The girl frowned, making tiny little lines between her eyes. She looked so much like Thomas. "Aunt Molly is teaching me, but I'd rather bake pies."

Emma forced a smile. "Me, too, but we must all do things we don't necessarily like. And think how helpful it will be when you can sew clothes for your father and your brother. Now finish coloring your pumpkin."

"Yes, schweschder, finish coloring your pumpkin," Eli piped up. "I want you to learn to sew, too. I need some new pants." He pointed to his pants, which were very obviously too short. The boy grew like a weed, just as Mark, Lillie, Mary, and Leah's boys did. "Think you can do that?"

Rebecca made a face, then grinned. "I can. I know I can. I'll ask Aunt Molly to help me learn faster."

"Good, because I look like I'm going wading in the pond."

The children laughed. Emma shushed them. "Finish your pumpkins."

They were sweet children. Surely Thomas's sisters and his mother were keeping up with the needs that he could not handle. Even though they had their own families, they would make every effort to fill in the gaps for Thomas. Sadness a mantle around her shoulders, she moved on to the older children, who were working on arithmetic problems. She glanced at the battery-operated clock that sat on her desk. "It's time, boys and girls. You may get your lunch boxes and coats and return to your seats."

Their faces bright at the thought of the two free days ahead, the children chattered loudly as they gathered their books and donned coats before returning to their seats. The girls covered their kapps with bonnets to keep their heads warm. "You are dismissed."

They maintained the expected decorum, leaving their seats row by row until they reached the door, where it was a mad dash down the steps and away. They all had chores to do when they arrived at home, just as they had before coming to school, but still there would be games to play and fun to be had. They needed to spend time running around in the snow, chopping wood, ice skating, hunting—anything but sitting and reading in tortured English or doing multiplication tables until they could do the nines without faltering.

Emma straightened her desk and made sure the fire was out in the stove. She took her time, sweeping the floor and cleaning the blackboard. She enjoyed this part of the day, the quiet, the letting go of that sense of needing to be in control. Whatever formal education these children received came from her. She served as their only teacher. She took that honor and privilege very seriously.

Her feet tired from standing all day, Emma closed the door behind her and started down the steps. A blessed silence enveloped her. She needed to work, the kind of physical work that made her muscles burn. She increased her pace, intent on a lovely walk home through the snow, brisk, clean air that smelled of evergreen trees filling her lungs. A movement caught the corner of her eye. She wasn't alone after all. A child who didn't want to walk home alone? "Who is that? Mark, is that you?"

"It's me." Carl sauntered across the yard, his boots making a squelching sound in the slushy snow. He had a stack of firewood in arms so big, he staggered under its weight. "Were you expecting someone else?"

"I expected no one." She tightened the strings of the wool bonnet she'd placed over her kapp. "If you're looking for your nieces, you're late. They've already gone."

Carl dropped the wood in the wood box next to the front door. "My sister said it was our turn to bring wood. She also said to tell you they would be happy to host the next school singing at their house."

Not wanting to appear ungrateful, Emma waited until he clomped back down the stairs. "Tell your sister I said danki. The children are almost ready with the songs in Deitsch, but the English ones still need work."

"Whenever they're ready."

His gaze made her want to squirm. She forced herself to move toward the road. "I best be getting back to the house. I have papers to grade."

"I thought I'd give you a ride home." He flung an arm toward his buggy. "You must be tired."

Time alone with Carl was the last thing she wanted right now. She had too much on her mind, and she couldn't think straight with him so near. Uncertainty scampered up her spine and wrapped itself in a knot around her throat. "The walk will do me good." She straightened her shoulders and quickened her stride once again. "I've been cooped up inside all day. My mind is full of cobwebs."

"Then let me walk with you."

"And leave the buggy here? It'll be a long walk back. I reckon you have work to do."

"I chopped wood first thing this morning. I spent several hours mending the fence to keep the cattle from breaking out again." Carl scratched his nose with a gloved finger. "I also repaired the chicken coop door and cleaned the stalls in the barn. Until it's time to feed the animals again, I'm done."

Despite her thick shawl, the cold seeped into Emma's bones. She pulled it tighter around her shoulders. "Why are you here?"

He shook his head, his expression bleak. "I came to pick you up the other night. I shone the flashlight. You never came out."

Heat seared her face. She breathed in and out. "I didn't know. I didn't see you."

"I'm surprised Annie or Catherine didn't tell you."

"They're heavy sleepers." Or they didn't want her to resume courting Carl. "Besides, they couldn't come down in their...at night to talk to a man outside the door."

"Even if it's to ease his troubled heart?" His hand caught hers. "Even if it's to save him a night of regretting all he's done to push the woman he loves away?"

She tugged at her hand. "Don't! You don't touch a Plain woman who is not your wife. You're a Plain man."

He stopped walking. She halted beyond his reach. His breath came in hard spurts. His eyes shone with unshed tears. "Don't you think I've tried? I came back here to be with you, and you're seeing another man. I might as well leave again."

Emma closed her eyes against the memories of turmoil and anguish Carl had caused her. If she didn't start over with him, he might lose his faith. She would be responsible for that. "Don't do that, Carl. Don't leave. Don't make that decision based on what I do. Make the decision based on your faith."

"If you truly forgive me, you'll give me another chance."

That wasn't fair. "I want to forgive you. I *should* forgive you. I know that. I want to make amends." She fought a sudden wave of nausea. "But that doesn't mean we can start over. I grew up while you were gone. I value different things now. I want different things in the man I marry. Stay in Bliss Creek and find a fresh start with a girl who will love who you are now."

"I don't want a girl—"

A shout in the distance cut short his response. Emma shielded her eyes against the glare of the sun on the drifts of snow the boys had shoveled from the road. Luke hurtled toward them in the buggy, the horse at a full gallop. Too fast for Emma's taste. She lived in fear of another buggy accident. He needed to slow down. Nothing could be that important. Another sickening thought hit her. What would he think about her being out here alone with her former beau?

"Emma!" He halted the buggy a few feet from where they stood. His face a dark, wind-whipped red, he gasped for breath as if he'd been running. "It's Josiah. Something has happened to Josiah."

Chapter 23

Emma grabbed the handle and hoisted herself into the Carmichaels' van. It still had an odor of leather and plastic that she only smelled in cars. She'd ridden in one like it before, when her parents had taken them on a family outing to the Wichita zoo. This time no feelings of anticipation crowded her, only fear. "What did Sarah's father say? Did he tell the bishop's wife if Josiah was badly hurt?"

Without answering, Luke pulled the door shut and sank onto the seat across from her. The van easily held the five of them. Josiah needed his family around him. Only the twins stayed back with Leah. The aunts would help with the work. The uncles would take care of the chores for as long as necessary. Luke had been terse about the call that came to the phone in Bishop Kelp's barn—the phone used only for district emergencies. Emma tried again. "Luke, what did he say?"

"I didn't talk to him myself. The bishop's wife said Roy Kauffman wanted us to come right away."

She followed his gaze to Mark, Annie, and Catherine. They sat stiffly in their seats, gazes directed toward the broad windows, watching the scenery flash by. They were listening, though, and he wanted to spare them. It was that bad.

"How did it happen?" Emma leaned forward and dropped her voice to a whisper. "Was he in a car accident?"

"She said something about a fall."

A fall.

Ach, Josiah.

Luke leaned toward her. His whisper did nothing to alleviate her fear. "He'd been drinking…alcohol. Sarah Kauffman was with him. They were arguing."

And now the bishop knew about Josiah's behavior. A shudder ran through Emma. The bishop might be the least of Josiah's problems right now. "Was the fall an accident?"

Luke shook his head. "I don't know."

Emma stared out the window. The wings of exhaustion fluttered all around her. She closed her eyes, but the motion of the van sent a wave of nausea through her. She opened them again. Better not to focus on the rushing pavement under them or the air whooshing around them. It reminded her of the night she and Luke told Josiah about Mudder and Daed. So much had happened since then, yet nothing seemed changed. They still struggled day after day against a poor economy, against the fear that Josiah might never come home, and for her, against the odds of marrying and having children.

Now Carl Freiling claimed he still loved her. Thomas wanted her to choose him. She had to make a choice. Determined not to think about it, Emma closed her eyes and let herself drift. Went with the motion instead of fighting it. That's what Thomas would do.

Thomas, with his earnest, simple ways. With his kind eyes and gentle heart. It was time she opened her heart to the possibility. He would always love Joanna and cherish the memories he had of their life together, but he had shown Emma that he was ready for a new season in his life. He was ready to make new memories. It was time for Emma to leave behind the past and to make new memories, too—memories that didn't involve Carl or the past.

"This is what happens when a Plain person ventures into the world." A tiny note of vindication flitted about in Luke's sudden words. "Josiah will come home now."

Emma forced her eyes open. Josiah reminded Emma of herself.

Stubborn. Besides, he thought he was in love with Sarah. If he hadn't met her, Josiah wouldn't have gone to Wichita, and he wouldn't be in a hospital now. Sarah shouldered much of the blame. "Maybe. As long as Sarah is in the picture, I don't think he'll leave her. She holds too much sway over him. This is her fault."

"It isn't about blame. She's only a girl." Luke's hands balled in fists. When he saw Emma's gaze, he shook them out. "Besides, we don't know what happened. He was drinking, maybe drunk. That's not her fault."

"If she hadn't lured him to Wichita, none of this would be happening."

"She isn't to blame, and even if she is, we'll forgive her."

Emma turned to the window. She no longer wanted to talk to Luke. He demanded too much of her. God demanded too much. She leaned her forehead against the cool glass and waited. Waited to see if her brother would live or die. Would come home or stay. Would grow up or fade away. The minutes seemed to pass in slow motion. The van went faster than she'd ever traveled in her life, yet it seemed to crawl toward Wichita and her injured little brother. Time was not her friend.

"We're here."

Mr. Carmichael's soft words made Emma want to whimper. Finally. Finally, they would know how badly Josiah was hurt and then they could do what needed to be done. The *whoop-whoop* of sirens screaming confirmed the driver's words. The noise beat on Emma's already throbbing head. They spilled out of the van and followed Luke's lead into the emergency room. The startling clean smell of antiseptic mixed with the odor of people, lots of people, some of whom hadn't bathed in a while. Bright lights. Official looking people scurried about. She tried to take it all in and nearly collided with a woman in green pants and a green shirt.

"Watch it!" The woman kept going. "Orderly, over here!"

"Sorry. So sorry." Emma stumbled back a few steps. She grabbed Mark's hand and rushed after Luke. "Catherine, Annie, keep up. Stay together."

Mark dug in his heels, forcing Emma to slam to a halt. "What?"

He pointed to an enormous television screen mounted on the wall above the rows and rows of padded green chairs in the waiting room. The people in the chairs watched girls in skimpy bathing suits playing volleyball on a beach, the ocean glistening in the sun behind them as they squealed with laughter.

"Never you mind." Emma pulled him forward. "We're here for Josiah."

Luke paused at a long, narrow counter. It took three attempts to get her attention, but the lady finally looked up. Josiah had been admitted. Paperwork needed to be done.

"We don't have insurance."

The lady's knowing glance took in their clothes and frightened faces. She slid some papers toward Luke. "We still need these filled out. Your brother will be treated, regardless. Payment plans are available. The hospital knows your kind are good for it."

Your kind. Good for it. Emma tried to take no offense. The woman was right. The community would help them with more than chores and food. They'd help pay the bills.

"Where is he?" Luke's voice choked. His fingers gripped the counter. His knuckles whitened. "We want to see him."

Her face a little kinder, the lady picked up the telephone. "Fill out the paperwork while I contact the doctor."

Luke snatched up the papers and pen. He surveyed the waiting room, his expression desperate. The commotion and noise, the people, they were all too much for him, too. Emma touched his arm. "Let me do it."

She turned to Annie. "Take Mark and Catherine and find a seat."

She tugged the papers from Luke's hand and began to answer the questions as best she could. Amazing the things they needed to know, but anything was better than simply waiting, each second ticking away as she wondered.

Finally, a nurse appeared and shepherded them down a long hallway to an elevator. Mark's mouth remained open the entire ride. The new waiting room held half a dozen people, including one Emma recognized. Sarah Kauffman. Her face wet and puffy, the girl flew from her chair. "Did they tell you anything?"

"Sarah, sit." A tall, angular man in a straw hat stood and held out a hand. He introduced himself as Roy. Sarah's mother's name was Grace. "We're sorry to meet you under these circumstances."

Luke shook his hand. He made no introductions. "Where's the doctor? What does he say?"

"They just keep saying the doctor will come out to talk to us when he can." Roy waved a hand toward a chair, but Luke remained standing. Emma stood next to him in silent support. Roy acknowledged her presence with a slight nod. "Josiah arrived unconscious. He has a possible head injury and broken bones. He fell from a second story balcony."

Someone cried out. Emma couldn't be sure if it was Catherine or Annie. Or maybe it was her own voice. Her stomach rocked. A buzzing sound filled her ears. She teetered a few steps and sank into the closest chair.

Sarah began to sob into a hankie. Roy's gaze sought his wife. She went to her daughter and put an arm around her. "Come. You need to wash your face and get a hold of yourself. All this crying doesn't help anyone."

She shooed her daughter from the room with a soft, kind whisper that touched Emma's aching heart. She wanted her mother to be here, to put an arm around her and say those words. To take the load she'd been carrying for the past few months. "How did this happen?" She didn't recognize her own voice, it sounded so light and breathless. "What second story balcony? Was he pushed?"

Roy smoothed his beard, his expression pained. "Sarah is forbidden to see Josiah. He's been staying with another family, but the temptation apparently became too great. After school Sarah slipped out of the house and met your brother at an Englisch friend's apartment where they were going to play video games." The anger in his face matched the anger in Emma's heart. "No adults were there. These boys sampled the parents' liquor cabinet. Josiah became drunk and then, according to Sarah, he asked her to marry him. Showing the first bit of good sense in a long time, she said no. Your brother became angry."

"That doesn't explain how he ended up going over a second floor railing." Luke paced the carpeted floor. "What does Sarah say about that?"

"He stood on the railing and threatened to jump if she didn't change her mind." Roy hesitated for the first time in telling the story. "I'm not sure what happened next. Sarah says it happened too suddenly for her to know exactly what he did or didn't do."

Roy didn't voice the words, but the question floated in the air, heavy with ominous uncertainty.

Had Josiah tried to take his own life?

Chapter 24

"*Ach*, Josiah." Emma couldn't keep the words from bursting out. Nor the tears that followed. Worldly ways had brought him to the hospital and to this awful, perilous possibility. A Plain boy would not do what Roy Kauffman insinuated. Not Josiah. Not the brother she knew. She turned to Luke. "He's mixed up, bruder, but not that mixed up. He values his life as much as you do, as much I do. He knows how much we've lost already—"

Mark tugged at her sleeve. "Why would Josiah drink alcohol? Deacon Altman says it's bad. Mudder said we should never have alcohol."

Emma swallowed the torrent of words that threatened to overcome her. She hugged her little brother. "Sometimes people make bad choices. You're good to remember what Mudder said. Never forget it."

She was thankful Mark wouldn't be faced with these choices any time soon. Not for another six years, when his own rumspringa began. The thought sent an arrow plunging into her heart. Luke was right. New rules. Rumspringa or no, Mark would not be exposed to this world.

Before she could voice the thought, a short, brown man entered the room. With his white coat and stethoscope around his neck, he had to be the doctor, although he looked very young. He glanced around.

"Are you Josiah's father?" He directed the question to Roy, who shook his head.

"His parents passed away." Luke's words held no emotion. "I'm his brother. We're his family."

"Could you excuse us for a few moments?" Again the doctor spoke to Roy. "For a family conference."

Sarah and her mother stood at the door, but Roy herded them off. They gathered their things and straggled from the room. Sarah trailed after them. She kept looking back, her face full of sorrow and longing. Emma almost took pity on her, but the thought of Josiah on that railing kept her from opening her mouth. Again, forgiveness eluded her.

After introducing himself, Doctor Chavez asked Luke to sit, but he remained standing as if he wanted to run from the room. Maybe he wanted to rescue Josiah and take him home. "How is he? How's Josiah?"

Doctor Chavez sat down across from Emma and steepled his stubby fingers. "Your brother is a very lucky young man."

Luck was a foreign concept. One did not have luck. Things happened according to God's will. Emma tried to concentrate. "But he's hurt."

"He fell from a second story balcony. Fortunately, his fall was broken by bushes outside the building. As a result, he suffered a concussion, a broken collar bone, broken ribs, two broken fingers, contusions and abrasions—bruises and cuts—but he's in remarkably good shape considering how bad it could've been."

Catherine began to sob, Annie with her. The two clung to each other. Emma gritted her teeth and tried to stop the flow of her own tears. "But he'll heal?"

"Yes, in time."

"How much time?"

"It's hard to say. We'll know more when he's awake." Doctor Chavez tilted his head, his lips pursed. "But to be honest, I'm more concerned about your brother's mental state."

"Mental state?" Luke's gaze turned steely. "What do you mean?"

"The officers at the scene reported that there's a possibility that your brother jumped. Witnesses said he was intoxicated and behaving erratically prior to the accident."

"You've hit the nail on the head, Doctor." Luke crossed his arms, his posture tense. "He was drunk. It was an accident."

"All the same, I'd like to have him evaluated by a mental health professional before he's released."

"He'll be fine as soon as we get him home." Emma wanted her brother to sleep in his own bed. She wanted to care for him herself. Surrounded by love, he would get better much more quickly. "He needs his family."

"I'm sorry. In this particular case, it's not up to you." Doctor Chavez's tone was apologetic, but firm. "We have protocol to follow in incidents such as this."

"What do you mean?"

"When someone is brought into this hospital who is a possible threat to himself or others, we have an obligation to treat those problems as well as any physical problems."

A threat to himself or others. Josiah felt things more deeply than most, but he would never hurt anyone. "We want to see him." Emma rose. "We want to see him now."

"Your brother is sedated." Doctor Chavez's kind tone never wavered. "We're monitoring him closely for brain swelling. He'll remain sedated at least until tomorrow. You should all get some sleep yourself."

The doctor rose and walked to the door where he paused, one hand on the frame. "I know this is overwhelming for you. It's certainly not what you want to hear, but I promise you we'll do everything we can to help your brother. He will get better. You've had a long, stressful day. You probably haven't thought to eat. I suggest you visit the cafeteria." His gaze traveled to Mark and the girls. "There are several good hotels in the vicinity. I'll ask the office staff to advise you regarding their locations."

Luke moved so he stood next to Emma. "We're not leaving until we see him."

The doctor nodded. "He'll be transferred to the ICU shortly. You may look through the window at him then, but that's as close as you can get for now. I'll let you know when the transfer is made."

"I appreciate that." After the doctor disappeared down the hallway, Luke turned to Emma. "Take them to the cafeteria. I'll stay here until he comes back."

"But what about the hotel—"

"One thing at a time, Emma."

The calm determination in her brother's face comforted her. Luke would handle this. He would know what to do. "Should I bring you something?"

"No." The bob of Luke's Adam's apple told Emma he felt the same nausea she did. He gripped his suspenders with both hands, his knuckles white. "I'm not hungry."

Emma hated to leave him, but the determined set of his shoulders told her he wouldn't budge. After a few trial and error turns, she managed to guide the others to the cafeteria. The aroma of fried meat and baked breads mingled together led them through the double doors. The array of food behind the long counter boggled the mind. So did the prices.

"Cheeseburger and French fries." Mark sounded faintly hopeful. He picked up a tray and grabbed silverware wrapped in a paper napkin. "Could I have that?"

Emma exchanged glances with Catherine. Her sister nodded. "Annie and I can share a plate. I'm sure it'll be too much food for one person. What about you, Emma?"

Her imagination robbed her of her appetite. Poor Josiah's bruised and battered head taunted her. "I'm fine. Maybe later." She mentally counted the dollar bills and coins in her bag. She could cover the meals. But it was too expensive for all of them to stay for very long. And a hotel? How much would a room cost? Could they all stay in one room? She had no idea.

After they were settled at a table, meals in front of them, she stood. "When you finish, come back to the waiting room. Remember, the third floor."

"Why are you leaving us?" Mark dropped his hamburger on his plate. Catsup splattered on his sleeve. It looked like blood. "Where are you going?"

"I'll be in the waiting room with Luke." Swallowing against the bile in the back of her throat, she worked to hide her own panic. "I don't want to leave it all on his shoulders. I'll take him a cheeseburger."

She wanted Luke to eat, whether he liked it or not. A hamburger would be a treat, of sorts. She found him sitting with the Kauffmans. Apparently he'd shared the doctor's news. Sarah sobbed quietly in the corner, a younger girl at her side.

"I brought you this." She held out the paper bag. Grease made a widening circle on it. "You should eat."

He took the sack. "Did you?"

She shook her head. Luke offered the food to Roy. "Maybe one of your children?"

Roy inclined his head in thanks and took the bag to his wife.

Luke pointed to the chair next to him. Emma sat down, and he leaned back until his hat touched the wall behind him. "I have a plan."

He had a plan. *Thank You, God.* "I have to go back. There's work to be done, and I can't leave Leah with the baby coming soon. I'll take Mark and Catherine with me." He leaned forward and put both hands on his knees. "You and Annie will stay here to be with Josiah for the first shift. We'll take turns."

"What about school? What about Annie's pie orders?"

"Catherine will do her house cleanings until she can find someone to substitute for her. Leah and the rest of the women can handle Annie's pie and dessert orders for a while—unless the baby comes early." Luke's voice got stronger as he went on. Having a plan had taken some of the fear out of him. He had control. "I spoke to the bishop. The deacons will meet this afternoon with the parents, and they'll choose a teacher to substitute for you for one week. Then you're to return to finish out the semester and the Christmas pageant."

The words sank in, but the topsy turvy place that was now her world couldn't seem to process anything. "You used the phone?"

"Jah, this is an emergency."

"I know that—"

"The bishop has agreed to our plan. He'll talk about the financial needs with the deacons—"

"They just helped us with the barn." Emma bit back a groan. The community did so much for them. She hated to rely on them once again. "They've done so much for us already."

"They don't begrudge us. We'll help others when the need arises." Luke frowned and rubbed a spot on his temple. "I'll get a hotel room close to the hospital so whoever is staying can walk to and from. You have to be careful here. It's different. Don't walk alone after dark. You and Annie stay together when you're outside the hospital. And it doesn't matter where you are, the Ordnung still applies. Do you understand me?"

Her heart beating a staccato in her throat, she nodded. She'd never been on her own away from Bliss Creek. "I know that." She had no desire to sample the life Josiah had been living. Look where it had led him. "We brought nothing with us."

"Someone will bring your things. We'll take turns. It'll be fine." Luke talked fast, as if he couldn't wait to leave this place behind. "As soon as the doctors will let us, we'll take him home. It'll be best for everyone. He'll heal faster among family and friends."

Emma thought the same. She hoped they were right, that they weren't underestimating the severity of Josiah's injuries. What if he needed surgery on his brain? She knew little about these things, but the doctor had been very serious. Words like *swelling of the brain* made the hair on her arm prickle with fear and her stomach wrench into knots. "What if—"

"It's wrong to question God's will." Luke's tone brooked no argument. "Don't worry. Put your faith in God."

The sharp tone stung. Luke had changed so much since their parents' death. Lost his joy. That's what Leah thought. The burden on his shoulders weighed him down. He needed her help. She straightened. To help him, she must meet the problems head-on. "What about

Sarah? He's not going to let her go that easily. He asked her to marry him."

"He'd been drinking. That's over. Roy will keep a much closer eye on his daughter now. And Josiah will see this life isn't for him."

Maybe. "She'll want to be here for his recovery. I'll talk to her about what's best for Josiah."

"And I'll talk to her father," said Luke. "I'll let him know we're taking Josiah home where he belongs. There'll be no further contact."

Please God, let Josiah see the error of his ways. Luke didn't know much about these things. He'd courted no one but Leah. They'd been baptized on the same Sunday and married not long after. He never seemed to have any reservations or regrets. Josiah might always have both.

She settled back in her chair, uncomfortable with its straight back and rough fabric. Nothing to do now but wait. And pray. His elbows propped on his chair, long legs stretched out, hands clasped tightly across his flat stomach, Luke leaned his head on the wall and closed his eyes. Emma couldn't tell if he prayed or slept.

She tried to relax and let her mind drift. Living in a hotel room with her sister. The strangeness of it all pressed on her. The stares of strangers would follow them. The room would have electricity and a phone and a television. Those things didn't matter. Only Josiah getting better mattered.

"What was Carl Freiling doing at the school?"

Luke's hoarse question brought her upright in the chair. "Nothing." She nibbled her lower lip. Not true. She couldn't lie. "He wanted to talk to me."

"About what?"

"Private matters."

Luke opened his eyes. "There are no private matters between you and Carl."

His stern tone riled her. Emma breathed. Luke had her best interests at heart, and he was the head of her household. "We've seen each other a few times…lately."

"It's not for me to know then." Luke's jaw worked. Disappointment showed in the way he stared across the room. "I had hoped you would choose another."

"I haven't made up my mind about anything." Emma struggled with how much to say. "He's persistent, but I have thoughts of…another."

"Thomas, you mean?"

Of course, her brother knew. He and Thomas were friends. Had they talked about her? Discussed her? Her face burned. "Did he say something to you?"

"Of course not." Luke shifted in the chair, a look of pain on his face. For a place of waiting, this room had awful chairs. "Do they know about each other?"

"Yes."

"And they don't mind?" His eyebrows tented. Incredulity filled his voice. "I can't believe Thomas doesn't mind."

"Of course he minds. I mind. I didn't choose this."

"But now you do need to make a choice. And do it quickly, before the deacons find out you're courting two men."

Chapter 25

Much to Emma's relief, the entrance of Doctor Chavez ended the uncomfortable exchange with Luke. Her brother was right. She needed to finish her conversation with Carl when she returned to Bliss Creek. Then she could reach out to Thomas with a clear conscience, the past behind her. Resolute, she stood, her attention focused on the doctor and news about Josiah. "How is he?"

"He's in the ICU. You may take a peek now."

The walk back through the hallway seemed to take forever. Emma stood next to Luke at the window. Josiah looked very far away, but not so far that she couldn't see his bruised face, swollen eyes, and purple lips. Machines made beeping noises in a monotonous tone that still seemed to shriek in the quiet of the ICU. A clear bag of some sort of liquid hung from a bar over his head, its tube running down to his arm. His shaggy brown locks of hair were damp and matted to his head.

"He'll want his hat...now that he's coming home." It was a silly thing to say. As if Josiah would open his eyes and worry about his bare head. She couldn't keep the tears in check. "We'll have to fetch his hat."

"Don't cry." Luke's hoarse voice said the admonition was meant as much for him as for her. "Tears won't help him."

She swallowed hard and sniffed. "I'm not crying."

Luke adjusted his own hat. "I'll go then. The Carmichaels are waiting to take me to a hotel they recommend."

Panic enveloped her. She pressed her hands against the glass, willing herself to be strong. "In the middle of the night?"

"Emma, it's morning now. Day has dawned."

Surprised, she looked around. With no outside windows, she'd lost all sense of time. Only the weariness in her bones told her it had been a long time since she'd slept. "So you'll go. And I'll wait here with Josiah."

"We'll drop Annie off here before we leave to go home. She'll have the room key and all the information. The two of you can go back to the room so you may sleep and wash up."

She couldn't leave Josiah. What if he woke up? She simply nodded. Luke would be gone. What happened after that would be up to her.

Chapter 26

The morning passed in a series of fits and starts. As hard as she tried, Emma couldn't keep from drifting off. She awoke with a crick in her neck, embarrassed that the nurses might have watched her sleep. She shifted in her chair a few feet from the ICU and willed herself to keep her eyes open. Maybe if she moved around...

She stood, pushed through the double doors, and strode down a long hallway. In the bathroom, she splashed cold water on her face for a good two or three minutes. Then she washed her hands with the foamy, green liquid soap that came from an enormous upside-down dispenser. She inhaled its odd, harsh smell of apple. Her stomach heaved. Quickly, she fled the bathroom and began marching back and forth in the hallway.

"Hello, Emma."

The timid voice pulled her from a painful reverie. With great reluctance, Emma looked up. A huge pink purse on one shoulder and a cell phone in her hand, Sarah stood at the double doors. "How he is?"

Emma returned to her pacing. "The same."

A tiny sob burbled from the girl's lips. She brushed away tears that made her eyes so puffy Emma couldn't tell what color they were. "I know you blame me. My mother says I should leave you alone, but I came to say I'm sorry. This is all my fault. He wouldn't have been out on that balcony if I hadn't asked him to come to Wichita."

Now that the time had come to confront Josiah's friend, Emma found she couldn't form the sentences. Exhaustion made it hard to remember what she needed to express to the girl. Emma rooted around in her small carry-all bag until she found a handkerchief.

She held it out. "Here. You need to stop crying. It only gives you a headache. I've been wanting to talk to you, anyway. Let's sit down."

Sarah's cell phone buzzed. She looked at it, typed something using both thumbs, then turned back to Emma as if there'd been no interruption. "I didn't think you would ever talk to me again."

Despite all the worldly influences she was such a child, this object of Josiah's affection. At seventeen, Sarah still had that innocent, naïve way about her. A maternal instinct flowed over Emma, leaving a bittersweet ache where her heart should've been. Whatever lay in the future, Emma wanted only to be kind. Firm, but kind. "Not speaking won't help Josiah. Being angry with you won't help him."

She waved Sarah into a chair and sat across from her. Her hands tightly entwined in her lap, Emma searched for a way to begin. "What has Josiah's life been like these last few months?"

Sarah relaxed against the chair's rough fabric. Her eyebrows lifted and she cocked her head. "Well, pretty regular. I mean, he's been fine. Except that my parents wouldn't let me date him. We had to..." Her fair cheeks stained red. "We sort of snuck around so we could see each other. But he passed the test to get his GED. You must be a good teacher, Emma. He did great, with hardly any studying. He's looking—was looking into taking classes at the community college."

Just for a fleeting second, Emma allowed herself to feel a smidgen of satisfaction. Then the familiarity of the situation sank in. Carl too had gotten his GED. Carl had gone to community college. History repeating itself. She couldn't let that happen. She forced herself to focus on the young girl sitting across from her. "It's Josiah who is a good scholar."

"Even so." Sarah shrugged. "He wants to study agriculture. He says there are better, more efficient ways of farming that will produce more food. In this world where there are so many starving people, that's important."

Josiah thought about starving people. How little she knew about him. Emma took a deep breath. "You know he has to come home. It's best for him. The influence of the Englischers is destructive for people like us. It'll destroy Josiah. You can see that, can't you?"

Sarah's face crumpled. She wadded up the hankie. "I know." Her voice sank to a whisper. "I've always known he would go home. He missed you all something awful, even though he didn't let on."

"You have to tell him it's all right for him to leave you. That you understand. That you want him to go."

Sarah sniffed and wiped at her face again. "I know."

"Will you promise me that you'll do that? For his sake, don't ask him to stay."

Sarah raised her face. Her chin trembled, but she nodded. "For his sake, I will."

"Thank you." Emma wiped her own face, surprised to find it wet with tears. "Thank you."

The double doors popped open and Luke entered, followed by Annie, Catherine, and Mark. Emma stood. After a second, Sarah joined her. The uncertain look on her face said she wasn't sure what to expect from Josiah's older brother. Luke nodded at her, but turned immediately to Emma. "The Carmichaels are waiting outside. Annie has the key card to the room, and she knows how to get to the hotel." He handed Emma an envelope. "The room is paid for. This will cover your meals. Spend it carefully."

"When are you coming back?"

"I'm not sure, but I'll send someone with your things tomorrow or the next day at the latest."

She glanced at her wilted dress. She could get by. "We'll be fine."

Luke's expression didn't change. "Remember what I told you."

She nodded. Catherine gave her a quick hug, followed by Mark. Then they were gone.

"He didn't speak to me. He's mad at me." Sarah's gaze traveled to Annie. "You're all so mad at me. For good reason, I know, but I never meant for any of this to happen."

The arrogance of youth to think it was all about her. Emma shook her head. "Luke has a lot on his mind. An injured brother, a wife expecting, a farm to run, children to worry about. He doesn't have time to think about you or worry about your feelings." No, he'd left that one detail to Emma. "You should go, Sarah."

The girl clutched her pink bag to her chest. "Please, I just want to talk to him one last time. I want to say good-bye to him."

"Not today." It seemed unlikely that any of them would be able to talk to him today. "The doctor says he's sleeping. Come back in a few days."

It was Sarah's turn to root around in her bag. She came up with a pen and a scrap of paper. "I know you don't want to use the phone, but if anything happens, good or bad, could you call me?" She scribbled a number on the paper. "Or ask the nurse to do it, if you don't want to."

Emma took the paper, but she made no promises. "He'll be fine." She said those words with more confidence than she felt. Would Josiah be fine?

Only God knew. She would have to trust Him.

Chapter 27

E mma sighed and shifted in the chair. Her neck ached, and a muscle in her shoulder twitched. She had no one to blame but herself, but she couldn't face sleeping in the strange, cold hotel room. What if Josiah woke while she was gone? The odor wafting from her dress made her wrinkle her nose. She glanced at the clock on the wall across from Josiah's bed. One-thirty. The light filtering from the blinds on the two windows beyond the bed told her it was afternoon. Otherwise, she'd have no clue if it were day or night. Josiah had been asleep for forty-eight hours now. The doctor had allowed her and Annie to take turns sitting with him for the last twenty-four. She rubbed the sleep from her gritty eyes and went to his bedside.

"How are you, bruder?" She brushed a hand across his forehead. His skin felt cool. "It's time for you to wake up now."

The doctor had weaned him from the medications, but still he slept. Doctor Chavez said it gave his body time to heal. For Emma, the waiting was excruciating. She wanted him to be better. She wanted to go home. She missed the school and her students. She even missed Leah. She took Josiah's hand and held it tight in hers. "Please wake up. I want to talk to you. Thanksgiving is in a few days, and we want to take you home so we can all celebrate together."

His still face, with bruises the color of plums and Granny Smith apples, gave no indication he heard. She picked up the pitcher of water on the nightstand. The dry air in the hospital made her thirsty all the time. Josiah's fingers curled around her other arm and tightened. "Josiah?" She leaned in closer. His eyes opened. She set the pitcher down. "Josiah, you're awake!"

He licked dry, chapped lips. His eyelids fluttered. He winced and his free hand went to his face. His fingers touched his bruised cheek. "Where am I?"

"The hospital. I'm so glad you're awake. I'll get the nurse."

The hand on her arm tightened. "Wait. Wait."

She stayed by his side. "What is it? Everything's fine. You're fine. As soon as the doctors will let us, we're taking you home."

"Luke?" His voice sounded scratchy. "Here?"

"He had to go back to the farm for a few days, but he'll come to get you and take you home as soon as you are able to go."

Tears leaked from the corners of Josiah's eyes and ran into his shaggy hair. "He wants me back?"

"Of course, he does. We all do." Emma squeezed his hand. "Everyone wants you to come home."

A suppressed sob made his skinny chest heave under the thin sheet. "I don't want to hurt Sarah."

"Sarah will understand, I promise."

"I can't stay in the city anymore." Emotions crowded his bruised face. "It does bad things to me."

"She understands that." Emma breathed a silent prayer of thanks that Josiah understood it, too. "I've talked to her."

"You talked to her?" Josiah tried to sit up, winced, and sank back on the pillow. "What did you say? You didn't make her feel bad, did you? I need to talk to her."

"I didn't blame her for anything." Not aloud. "It's better if you don't see each other anymore—for both of you. Saying good-bye will be so hard."

"I have to apologize for the way I acted when…when this happened. I have to say good-bye." The accident hadn't changed her brother's stubborn nature. "I'm not leaving Wichita without talking to her."

Emma swallowed her fear. Sarah would live up to her promise to let him go. To send him away if necessary. "You'll see her before we go home, all right? I'll talk to her father. Don't worry. Just get better."

"I am better." He struggled to sit up again and then tugged at the tube taped to his arm. "I want out of here."

"Settle down. You can't go anywhere until the doctor says you can." She tried out her teacher voice on him. Josiah had never given her trouble as a student, only as a brother. "You have a concussion and broken ribs and fingers."

"No wonder my head hurts." He rubbed his forehead with the splinted fingers, then turned his hand back and forth, looking at the splints. "I have the worst headache. It's a hospital—you'd think they could do something about that."

Emma managed a smile at his attempt at a joke. She pulled the chair close to the bed. She didn't know where to start, but they had to talk about it. They couldn't sweep this out with the crumbs on the floor. "Do you remember what happened? How you ended up here?"

He wiggled so he laid on his side facing her. "It's a little blurry." He grimaced and rolled to his back again. "Can I have a drink of water?"

She poured it for him and helped him sit up long enough to drink. "What's the last thing you remember?"

"Sarah and I went to some friends' apartment to play video games after she got out of school. We weren't supposed to be together, but we didn't care." His face reddened. "I remember being offered a drink. I took it."

Emma gripped his hand. "And then what?"

His eyes closed. He didn't answer.

"Josiah, then what happened?"

"You already know, don't you? Sarah told you."

"Sarah told me her story. I'm asking you to tell me yours."

"Why?"

"Because Doctor Chavez thinks you need help. I want to know what happened so I know whether I need to convince Luke to get you that help."

"I didn't jump. I slipped."

Emma took a deep breath. He didn't jump. He didn't mean to do it. "You were upset at Sarah because she said she wouldn't marry you?"

"No. My head was all messed up because of the liquor. I would never have asked her if it wasn't. I got up on that railing to scare her. That's all." His voice cracked. "I don't want to die. I want to go home."

"Good." Tears rolled down Emma's face. She didn't bother to brush them away. "That's good, bruder. We want you to come home."

He closed his eyes. Tears trailed down the sides of his face. "I was messed up before the liquor." The words came in jerky fits and starts. "I'm messed up about Mudder and Daed dying. I wasn't there when it happened. I never got to see them again. I never got to say I'm sorry."

"Sorry?"

"That I was so rebellious. I made them worry. Worrying is a sin."

Emma squeezed his good hand through the bed railing. "They loved you. Hang on to that."

His fingers curled around hers and tightened.

She bent her head and breathed a prayer of thanksgiving. Josiah wanted to come home.

The door opened and Doctor Chavez strode in. "You're awake! Outstanding! How are you feeling, Mr. Shirack?"

Josiah let go of her hand. "Like I want to go home."

The doctor's energy filled the room. He took a pen from his coat pocket and flipped open a chart. "Well, let's just see about that. Hmm." He tapped the pen against the chart. "Physically, you're coming along surprisingly well. I would still like to have a colleague of mine do an evaluation."

"To see if I'm psycho kid?" The sharp edge of Josiah's words cut the air. "I'm not."

"Humor me, then." Doctor Chavez dropped the chart at the foot of the bed and began examining Josiah's eyes with a small flashlight. "Good. Good. You must have a very hard head, young man, because you came through this relatively unscathed. Still, you need to stay here a few days under observation. The evaluation won't take much of your time. It'll give you something to do."

"How long will you keep me here?"

"Until I'm sure this won't happen again."

"It won't."

"Unfortunately, I can't take your word for it, Mr. Shirack."

"He says it was an accident." Emma couldn't believe she had the courage to argue with a doctor. An educated, fancy person. But this was Josiah, and he needed to go home. "He fell. That's all. He'll get better at home among his family and his friends. If he agrees to your evaluation, can he go home right away when it's over?"

"To be honest, he doesn't have to agree. He can't leave without it. I was humoring him." Doctor Chavez's smile didn't take the sting out of the words. His gaze shifted to Josiah. "You can go home when I'm satisfied that the concussion isn't going to cause you problems. In the meantime, I'll have the nurses give you something for the pain."

He picked up the chart and headed for the door. "You can have visitors now. I'll ask Doctor Morris to come by as soon as he can work a consult into his schedule."

After the doctor left, Josiah stared at the ceiling, his face morose. "I didn't do it on purpose."

Relief surged through Emma. Josiah had made a bad choice, but he wasn't suicidal. The doctors would see that and then they would be able to go home. Soon, she'd sleep in her own bed, cook and clean and wash clothes in her own house. Teach her students. "I know you didn't. That's good. You'll go home soon, that's the important thing."

"I want to see Sarah."

"I'll see what I can do, all right?" Emma debated. She needed to get word to Luke. And she needed to talk to Sarah's father Roy. Which meant using the phone. "Why don't you rest a while? Annie is in the cafeteria. I'll get her. She'll be so happy you're awake."

Josiah didn't need much prompting. His eyes were already closed. Ten minutes later she had Annie planted in the chair by her brother's bed. The slip of paper in her shaking hand, she went to the waiting room and sat down next to one of two telephones. She smoothed the piece of paper. The numbers wavered in front of her. The calls needed to made. No one would consider it a frivolous thing. She picked up the receiver.

"There you are."

She jumped. The receiver dropped from her hand and landed on the carpet. "Thomas! What are you doing here?"

"You were calling someone?" The note of surprise in his voice dismayed her. Thomas moved into the room, his expression uncertain. "Did something happen?"

"I can't believe you're here." She smoothed her dress, conscious of the fact that her clothes were rumpled and her hair straggled around the edges of her kapp. What must he think of her looking like this? "I need to call the bishop and ask him to tell Luke that Josiah is awake. Luke should come. I want to take Josiah home as soon as possible."

"It's good news that he's awake." Thomas dropped Mudder's ancient suitcase at her feet and sat down in the chair closest to her. "I brought clean clothes for you and Annie. Leah picked them out. She said it should be everything you need."

Emma inhaled his earthy scent of sweet hay and light sweat. A knot formed in her throat. She missed home so much. "I'm so glad you're here."

"You are?" Surprise caused his bushy eyebrows to rise and fall. He ducked his head and studied his long, narrow shoes. "I thought you might prefer Luke at a time like this."

"Thomas, when will you stop doubting?" Frustration at this awkward one-step-forward, one-step-back relationship bubbled up in her. "You live up to your namesake in the Bible."

"When you make your choice." He pushed his hat back, raised his head, and met her gaze straight-on. "The last time we talked, you said I should be courting another woman. That doesn't give me much reason to think you see any future for us. Who is the doubter, really?"

Anger clipped his words. Emma bit her lip, pushing back her own anger. She didn't want to argue with him. "I'm sorry. I didn't mean to offend you that night. I was trying to think about what is best for you and for Helen and for your children—yours and hers."

The anger in his face gave way to sadness. "We seem to need to say we're sorry a lot. I'm not a wishy-washy person. I know what I want. I've given this much thought. I can't see what a woman like you would see in a man like me. Older, yoked with children, just this side of ugly. Carl is younger and good at talking. Perhaps he is best for you, just as Helen would be a better choice for me."

Yes, Carl loved to talk and he knew just what to say. But he wasn't so good with the follow-through. He never had been. Thomas would be there for the woman he chose. Helen deserved such a man. Emma sighed and threw up her hands. Too many conflicting feelings battered her. "All I know is right now, you are a sight for sore eyes, Thomas."

His hand touched hers for the briefest of seconds. The sudden, insistent beep of the phone made her jump back. "Did we break it?"

"No and likewise, I'm glad to see you. Let's leave it at that for now." Thomas picked up the receiver, and returned it to its base. He smiled at her. "We should focus on others now, not ourselves. Luke wanted someone to check on you. He's beside himself not being able to be here. I asked my sister to keep the children so I could volunteer. That way Luke can stay close to Leah and the boys."

So he did it for Luke, not for her. Emma accepted that. His intentions were good, even if they weren't directed at her. "How is everyone?"

Thomas shared his news from home and then Emma filled him in on everything the doctor had said about Josiah's injuries, the psychological evaluation, even the situation with Sarah.

"Do you want me to make the call to Sarah's father?" The kindness that radiated from Thomas's eyes warmed Emma. He was sorely mistaken to think he was "just this side of ugly." "I don't mind."

Relieved, Emma handed him the piece of paper where she'd written the important telephone numbers.

Thomas handled the phone like he'd been making calls all his life. Surely there had been times during Joanna's extended illness when he had found it necessary to use it.

He spoke quietly, quickly, then hung up. "Roy will bring Sarah here when she gets out of school. He's reluctant, but he understands what's at stake. The bishop's wife will get the message to Luke. I imagine he'll want to come to the city himself."

"It's kind of you to be so helpful." She stood. "I should get back to Josiah."

He picked up the suitcase. "May I look in on your brother before I leave?"

He had such good manners, too. "Jah, Josiah would like that."

Together, they walked to Josiah's room. Emma sneaked a peek at Thomas's face. He seemed lost in thought. She wanted to peek into his mind for a second. "Does being here bring back memories?"

"Jah."

When he didn't elaborate, Emma wished she'd left the question unasked. "It's a strange place, a healing place, but yet so cold and impersonal. It seems to me people would get better faster at home, among friends and family."

"Sometimes the need for powerful medicine is greater. Sometimes monstrous battles are fought inside these walls." Thomas's pace slowed. "My thoughts get jumbled up here. It's painful to remember those last days with Joanna, yet more painful to try to forget them. I saw her alive for the last time in a room in this hospital. She was a cheerful soul to the last breath she drew. I don't want to lose a single memory of her, even if that memory is here."

It was the most words Emma had ever heard him speak about his wife. As painful as it was, he'd been willing to come here to help out a friend in need. "You're a good friend to come here."

"You think of me as a friend still?" His smile didn't reach his eyes. "I continue to hope for more."

"Sometimes the strongest feelings are rooted in friendship."

He nodded, his expression grave. "That's a wise thought. We'll leave it at friendship then."

After that they didn't speak. Finally, they reached the stretch of hallway that led to Josiah's room. To her surprise, Annie paced outside his door.

"What's going on?" Emma hastened toward her sister. "Why are you out here?"

Frowning, Annie stopped pacing. "Thomas, I didn't know you were here—"

"Why aren't you inside with Josiah?"

Annie threw up her hands. "Because the psychologist wanted to interview him in private. He's in there now asking Josiah who knows what."

Emma started toward the door.

Thomas stepped in front of her. "Let it be."

"Josiah's a minor."

"This needs to be done. Your brother went through something that's hard for us to understand. He needs help."

Emma struggled against the desire to push her way past Thomas and into that room.

Thomas towered over her. "Think about what's best for him."

What would be best would be for him to come home.

Chapter 28

After fifteen minutes of pacing in the hospital's long hall, Emma plopped down in a chair covered with cloth that felt like a rug under her fingers. "How long does this take?"

Thomas leaned against the hallway, his head down, his hat covering his face. He looked like he'd slept standing up. He stirred. "It'll take however long it takes."

"Such a sage man," Annie murmured. She wiggled in the chair next to Emma. "I can see why you like him."

"Hush! At least he—"

"Emma. Annie. Is he really awake? Is he all right?" Sarah barreled down the hall, her shiny boots smacking on the tile. "What does he—"

"Sarah, quiet, please." Roy approached them at a more sedate pace. "It's not necessary to shout out questions in a hospital. People are resting, trying to get better here."

Her face stricken, Sarah slowed. "I'm sorry. I'm just so excited he's awake. Have you talked to him?"

"Yes, and he's fine. He remembers everything." Emma stopped at the implication of those words. Sarah had to know Josiah remembered the question he posed and her answer. "He's not upset. He's fine."

"Why are you sitting out here then?"

Emma explained.

"They think he's suicidal?" Her expression befuddled, Sarah turned to his father. "That is not true. It was the alcohol."

Mr. Kauffman didn't look convinced. "That's best left to the professionals."

"We believe Josiah is fine." Emma patted the chair on the other side of hers. "You might as well have a seat. We can't go in until the psychologist comes out."

As if he heard the words, a man in a gray suit exited Josiah's room. His expression solemn, his gaze skipped from person to person. "Well, I see Josiah has quite the cheering section. That's excellent." He held out his hand to Mr. Kauffman. "I'm Doctor Morris."

Again, the need for that painful explanation. Josiah's father wasn't here to go through this with his son. Emma was glad Mr. Kauffman did the necessary explaining. Doctor Morris turned to her. "Very well, then, are you the legal guardian?"

She shook her head. "My brother Luke."

"Ah, and where is he?"

"He had to return to our farm, but he'll be back."

"I see. When he does return, please ask him to make contact with the staff to set up an appointment to discuss Josiah's treatment with me."

"His treatment? He's fine. We're ready to take him home."

Doctor Morris pursed his lips. "Your brother will be fine." There was an emphasis on the word *will* that bothered Emma. "I still want to speak with your brother before Josiah's released."

"Doctor, Thanksgiving is in two days. We want to have him home for the holiday. It'll do so much to improve his spirits."

"How quickly can your brother get here?"

Thomas eased away from the wall. "I'll have him back here by tomorrow morning."

"Tomorrow morning it is." The doctor walked away.

Emma swallowed hard against that knot in her throat. "You are a good friend, Thomas."

"Friends help friends." He tipped his hat and strode away, his long strides eating up the hallway. Emma stared after him, trying to decipher his tone. Resigned? Or determined?

"Can I see him now?"

Emma had momentarily forgotten about Sarah. Next hurdle. "Let's go in together."

Josiah's eyes were closed when they entered, but they flew open at Sarah's whispered words of greeting. Her hand closed around his. Emma had to look away. Should she leave them alone? She didn't want to do that. Instead, she hung back, allowing them one small moment.

Sarah wiped at her face with her free hand. "Josiah, I'm so sorry." She glanced back at Emma. Emma nodded in encouragement. "I came to tell you I'm sorry."

"Is that it? You're sorry?"

Sarah flinched. She glanced back at Emma again.

Emma couldn't take it. She bustled over to the bed. "How are you feeling? Do you need some water? Sarah wants to talk a bit. Are you up to it?"

"Not really." He studied the ceiling with exaggerated nonchalance. "I'm tired."

His change of attitude baffled Emma. "You told me you wanted to see her."

"I changed my mind."

"No you didn't," said Emma. The way Josiah kept sneaking glances at Sarah belied the bravado in his words. "You're just afraid."

His good hand fisted. "Afraid of what? I'm not afraid of anything."

"You're afraid of saying good-bye."

"You're afraid? So am I." Sarah raised both hands to her face and wiped tears from her cheeks with trembling fingers. "I'm afraid of never seeing you again."

No, no. They weren't going down that road. "Josiah is tired, Sarah. Maybe you should go."

Sarah hung her head.

Emma felt like an overprotective parent, but it had to be done.

Sarah squeezed Josiah's good hand. "Good-bye, Joe."

"Wait." Josiah grasped at her hand on the railing. She withdrew it. His eyes glazed with understanding. "Will I see you again?"

She backed away, her arms wrapped around her chest. "I don't think so," she whispered. "It's best if we don't."

Then she was gone.

Josiah's chin trembled. A pulse beat in his jaw. After a long second, his gaze sought Emma's. "I want to go home. Please."

"Soon, bruder."

He rolled over and faced the wall.

Chapter 29

Thomas raised a finger to his lips and shook his head. Eli closed his mouth. His son didn't quite have the hang of the concept of being quiet when hunting. Together, they slipped through the narrow stand of oak trees and followed the stream toward the knoll where wild turkeys sometimes roosted. Thomas led the way, his rifle balanced in the crook of his arm. He tried to shake off the irritability that had plagued him since he returned from the hospital the previous day. He should be enjoying the crisp air, the late afternoon sunshine that took some of the chill from the air, and teaching his young son how to hunt.

The temperatures had risen enough on this fine late fall day that the snow had started to melt a little. He tread lightly through the slush, his gaze searching the nooks and crannies of the woodland's edge for turkeys. His mother would be so pleased if they could bring home a fresh one in time for Thanksgiving tomorrow. Unfortunately, so far they hadn't seen even one of the fowl. It was as if the turkeys knew tomorrow was the big day. They were hiding out. The nonsensical thought raised his spirits.

Successful or not, hunting gave Thomas an excuse to turn down Luke's offer to ride along with him to Wichita. Until Emma moved beyond her past with Carl Freiling, it served no purpose to continue to try to court her. Thomas would have to be happy with the friendship they kept talking about. The thought sent his mood plummeting again.

Luke's offer had surprised Thomas. Why would Luke want him to go back to the hospital? It served no purpose. The plan was to discharge Josiah from the hospital as soon as Luke met with Doctor Morris. They would be home later this evening. Thomas's help wouldn't be needed.

Maybe it wasn't about Josiah. He tightened his grip on the rifle. Maybe Luke knew about Carl. Even an old man with two children would be preferable to Carl as a suitor for Emma. It didn't matter. Only Emma's feelings—or lack thereof—mattered.

"Daed!" Eli's whisper could be heard for several hundred feet. "Daed, look!"

"No talking." Thomas shot Eli his most severe stare. They would never find a turkey at this rate. He shook his head. "Hush."

Looking as if he'd burst from the effort to keep his mouth shut, Eli raised an arm and pointed toward the stream. Thomas followed his gaze. He stopped. Barely breathing, he tugged Eli's arm down. "Get behind me," he whispered. "Slowly."

A grizzled coyote dipped its snout into the flowing stream. It was big and rangy with a sharply defined muzzle and fur that mixed gray and yellow with darker patches along its back. Its powerful jaws were perfect for tearing his prey—like Thomas's chickens and calves—into ragged pieces. A half dozen of his livestock had been lost to this predator or one like it in the last few weeks.

He raised his rifle. The coyote's head came up. For a second, it seemed to stare at Thomas, a challenge in its bright, glowing eyes. A low growl emanated from deep in its throat. Thomas peered through the sight. A clean kill shot would be best. He had no desire for the animal to suffer.

"Let me shoot 'em, Daed!" Eli whipped around Thomas and raised the rifle he'd received for his last birthday. "I can get 'em!"

At the sound of Eli's high, excited voice, the coyote growled again. He bared his yellow fangs, crouched, then darted into the trees, his powerful haunches leaping over a nearby boulder. Thomas didn't dare take the shot, not with Eli in front of him. The coyote disappeared from sight without a backward glance.

"When I tell you to get behind me, that means *stay* behind me." Thomas shoved down the barrel of Eli's rifle so it pointed at the ground. "Did I not tell you to keep quiet?"

The boy slapped a hand over his mouth, his features woebegone. "I'm sorry. I got so excited I forgot!"

"Forgot?" Thomas sucked in air and blew it out. "In two seconds' time, you forgot?"

"We could go after it." Eli's lower lip trembled. "You could still get it."

"You disobeyed me, son. You put yourself in danger. That tells me you aren't as old as I thought you were. You'll hang the rifle up in my bedroom until I decide you are ready to hunt." In any event, Thomas had no desire to hunt an animal as dangerous as a coyote with his eight-year-old son in tow. He bottled up his anger—brought on by fear for Eli's recklessness—and lowered his voice. "We need to get back. It'll be dark soon, and there are chores to be done."

"But we didn't get the turkey." His face crestfallen, Eli ducked his head and kicked at the snow with his boot. "Groossmammi will be disappointed in us."

Eli was the one disappointed, but he had to learn.

"You scared away every turkey within five miles." Thomas started walking. "Lesson learned, I hope."

Together, they trudged through the trees toward the open field. The dirt road that led to his house was just behind it.

Now that there was no need to be quiet, Eli didn't say a word. Thomas understood his disappointment, but right now, he was more concerned with teaching Eli to behave himself properly on a hunt. Otherwise, he could hurt someone—or himself. Thomas wanted that coyote dead, but he would get it another time. The right time.

The *clomp-clomp* of horse hooves made him look up. James Daugherty and his wife Susannah drove toward him. Thomas could see where Helen Crouch got her roly-poly build. She looked just like her mother. He tipped his hat to them. "How goes it?"

James doffed his hat. "We had to pick up a few last-minute things in Bliss Creek. We have a houseful of visiting relatives here for Thanksgiving."

"Good for you." Thomas expected them to keep moving, with all the preparations they surely had to make for tomorrow. To his surprise, James tugged the reins and brought the buggy to a halt. His wife craned her head at him, an earnest look on her face. "Why don't you come by tomorrow for a piece of pie? Helen is baking. She makes the best pumpkin pie in this part of the state." Susannah looked so pleased with herself. "I'm sure your mother won't mind if you stop by after her feast. Bring the kids. Rebecca loves to play with Betsy."

Another thing Helen must've inherited from her mother—the gift of gab. Thomas plunged in when she stopped for air. "Thank you, but—"

"No buts. The more the merrier!"

"Fine. I'll…we'll be there." Flustered, Thomas backed away. "I better get moving. Chores to do."

"Wonderful. We'll see you tomorrow."

Still looking pleased with herself, Susannah kept waving even as they moved off down the road.

Thomas shook his head.

"What, Daed?" Eli looked puzzled. "Don't you like pumpkin pie?"

Thomas stared at the disappearing buggy. He liked pumpkin pie just fine. It was the matchmaking that bothered him.

Chapter 30

Every muscle in Emma's body sagged with relief. She sank onto her bed and sat still for a few minutes. The sheer joy of being in her own house and in her own bedroom buoyed her. Annie's tiny, ladylike snores told Emma her sister had succumbed to sleep not long after her head hit the pillow. After wondering aloud where Catherine was, Annie had been too tired to wait up for her. Courting maybe? Emma hoped so. Catherine might be moving on, leaving the horrors of last summer behind.

She brushed her hand over the rough patches of the quilt. Perfectly stitched with love and laughter. Nothing like that in the hotel room. The lovely quiet of her home deserved its own prayer of thanks after the relentless noise of the city. Even in the middle of the night, noise beat at the windows—people argued, horns blared, sirens screamed. The trash trucks clanged every morning with their huge pincer-like lifts that whined and shrieked under the weight of the enormous trash bins in the hotel parking lot.

Emma slid under the cold blankets and breathed in the nippy air. No dry heat like the hospital. She embraced the cool freshness as she stuck her hands under her pillow and snuggled closer. Her fingers encountered something hard and square. Surprised, she pulled the package out and squinted at it in the murky darkness. It felt like envelopes.

She threw back the covers, snatched her robe from the hook, and tugged it on. Shivering, she padded downstairs and lit the kerosene lamp. She held seven envelopes tied together with a white ribbon. Catherine's neat script covered a note slipped under the ribbon. *Carl left these for you the day after you went to Wichita. He made me promise not to tell anyone and not to read them. I kept my promise.*

Emma ran her fingertips over the top envelope. It was addressed to her in Carl's outlandish, swirling cursive. It looked yellow with age. Nibbling at her lower lip, she plopped into the rocking chair. Her legs felt too weak to hold her. What did Carl hope to accomplish by giving her these letters? He had been right not to correspond with her during his long absence. But now, now she could know what he had been thinking and doing during those difficult days after he walked away. While she cooked and sewed and cleaned and tried to forget. Her mind said to let it go. Not to rip open old wounds. But her heart, despite its still tender scars, wanted to know.

Taking a deep breath, she carefully pulled out the flap on the first envelope and removed the folded paper with trembling fingers.

Dear Emma,

Greetings. I hope you are well. I know you're angry with me, but I also know you will want to forgive me. It's your nature and that of your faith. In this, I find comfort. I don't deserve to be forgiven, but yet you will forgive me. For that, I'm thankful.

I don't know if you'll ever read this letter. Even if I send it, you probably will choose not to open it. That would be the proper choice. Even so, I can't help myself. I have to write to you. I'm bursting with things I want to tell you. I left you and yet, every time something happens, you are the first person I want to tell. I want to share all my thoughts with the woman I love.

You can't imagine how much I wanted to share this adventure with you. I knew it would be wrong to ask that of you. I didn't want you to sacrifice your faith and your family. Eventually you would come to resent me for taking you away from everything and everyone you love.

So here I sit in my little, one-room apartment in Hutchin-
son. It has a sofa bed, a table with two chairs, and a tiny
kitchen with two pots and one skillet—more than plenty for
me. The walls are a funny tan color like wet sand. I took my
GED test today. I also enrolled in driver's education. Yes, me,
behind the wheel of a car. Well, not yet, but soon. I applied
for three jobs, at a hardware store, a nursery, and a restaurant.
Now I wait for interviews. As soon as I receive my GED cer-
tificate and earn some money, I'll start classes at the junior col-
lege. I think I'll take accounting courses. You remember how I
loved numbers in school? Maybe not exciting for the rest of the
world, but everywhere I turn there is something new to experi-
ence and touch and learn. As a teacher, surely you understand
the joy in that. Did you know you can heat soup from a can in
a microwave in about two minutes? Two minutes to prepare a
meal. Imagine all the free time you could have for reading and
learning if you didn't spend so much time cooking.

Yes, there are times at night when I sit here alone that I
ask myself, what have I done? I miss the smell of earth. I miss
your smile and your laugh. I miss my sisters and brothers. I
miss the quiet. But I've made my choice. I hope you can learn
to accept that.

It would be perfect, if only you were here.

With all my heart,
Carl

Emma folded the letter and slipped it back in its envelope. She
blinked back burning tears. Carl counted on her forgiveness. He
thought of her as being better than she really was. In her mind's eye,
she could see him pouring over his books, studying, doing algebra
problems just as he had in school. Always quick with numbers, he
delighted in trying to stump her. Their friendship began in the
schoolhouse. Those had been lighthearted, carefree days.

She held the stack of letters to her chest and willed the tears not to fall. Despite her best efforts, a few refused to obey. They slipped down her cheek, traitors every one of them. She wiped at them with the back of her nightgown sleeve. It came away wet. If Mudder were here, she'd shake a finger at Emma and remind her of the importance of a handkerchief. Mudder. Emma longed to hear her soft voice, so full of love and wisdom. She'd know what to do. Mudder would tell her to get a backbone. Chin lifted, Emma swiped at her nose. She was a mess. She straightened her sagging shoulders and sniffed hard. A creaking noise made her jump. The front door. Someone was coming in. She stuffed the letters under her robe.

"Emma? Are you all right?"

With another quick wipe of her face, Emma turned to face Catherine.

Her coat tucked over one arm, Catherine gave her a tentative smile. "What are you doing up so late? I thought everyone would be asleep."

"I guess I'm off track because of the time at the hospital." Emma swiped at her face with the back of her hand.

Her expression suspicious, Catherine cocked her head. "Have you been crying?" She stuck her hand in her apron pocket, pulled out a handkerchief, and held it out. "Your eyes are red and your nose is running."

"I could be getting a cold." *God, forgive me a small lie.* Emma snatched at the handkerchief. She needed to move the conversation away from the telltale signs on her face. "*Danki.* What about you? It looks like you had a good evening."

"I'm...I was...just you never mind!" Her smile grew brighter. "It's late. I'd better get to bed. Tomorrow will be a wonderful day of thanksgiving."

She started to turn, then stopped, her smile gone. "Did you find the letters?" She frowned. "I almost didn't accept them, but then I thought that it wasn't for me to decide. You could return them, if you wished."

"It's fine. Don't worry about it. We should get to bed." Gripping the letters, Emma stood. "Tomorrow will be a great day."

Her face puzzled, Catherine nodded. "I'll be up as soon as I get a drink of water. Pleasant sleep."

Upstairs, Emma slid the letters back under her pillow, the best place for safekeeping. She rolled over and stared at the ceiling, contemplating whether she would read more. Her head and heart continued to argue. Carl had given her the letters to reestablish a connection severed by time and distance. Instead of going forward, they were going backward.

Emma knew that. She also knew she would read the rest of the letters. It would be like picking at a hangnail. She couldn't help herself.

And Carl knew that.

Chapter 31

H er shawl wrapped tightly around her shoulders, Emma shuffled down the stairs and padded through the living room. A cup of hot coffee would help keep the pre-dawn chill at bay and chase away the cobwebs left from spending time reading a letter instead of sleeping. Resolutely, she pushed away the thought of those letters, safely tucked under her pillow. Thanksgiving ranked as one of her favorite days of the year. She wouldn't allow it to be spoiled by ancient history. She glanced at the windows. A tiny bit of pink streaked the dark above what must be the very edge of the world, heralding a dawn yet to come. *Thank You for another day.*

The first thank you of a day dedicated to giving thanks. She smiled. Their first Thanksgiving without Daed and Mudder. The painful prick subsided after a few seconds. Daed and Mudder would be present in each one of her brothers and sisters and each one of her aunts and uncles and cousins. She would be thankful for the wonderful memories of two loving, caring parents. She would be thankful for all they had taught her, how they'd brought her up in the Plain ways and helped her build a fortress of faith. For that she was determined to be thankful.

Besides, they had much to do to prepare the food they would take to Uncle Noah's for the feast. But first chores had to be done and then they would gather for devotions, as they always did on Thanksgiving morning. She headed toward the kitchen. Soft voices mingled, rising and falling beyond the doorway. She slowed. Someone had risen earlier than she. That didn't happen much.

She cocked her head, listening. Maybe Annie had decided to make one more pecan pie or another pumpkin pie. That would be so like her. She sometimes sang church songs as she worked. No, it was Luke's deep voice mingled with Leah's softer, higher voice. Emma approached the door, intent on saying good morning and praising the day. Something in the murmured tones made her bide her time. She peeked around the corner.

Luke stood in the middle of the kitchen, his hand on Leah's enormous belly. Emma started to back away. Neither her brother or sister-in-law seemed aware of her presence. Luke had tears on his cheeks. "I am thankful for this, Leah, believe me."

"You've been so far away for so long, I'd begun to think you no longer cared for me," Leah whispered. "Or for this baby."

Luke's face contracted. "It's hard for me. You know that. It's hard for me to say the words. You want me to be someone I'm not. You think that's easy for me?"

"As hard as it is for you, you know I need to hear those words. Not every day, but often enough to know." Leah's voice faltered. "Every day I'm thankful for you. I'm thankful for my boys, but living here is hard."

Emma winced. She had to do more to make Leah feel that she lived in her own home now. They all did.

Luke's arms went around Leah in a hard embrace. "Forgive me?"

"What's going on?"

Emma turned at Josiah's voice. She lifted a finger to her lips. He slipped closer and peeked around the corner. To her surprise, he smiled and jerked his head toward the living room. Alarm raced through her. He wore his coat. The sling that cradled his arm close to his shoulder was gone. "You're not leaving, are you? Where are you going?"

"The chores won't do themselves." He pulled on a woolen glove. "I'm doing what we do every morning. The livestock need to be fed."

"Luke doesn't expect you out there your first day back. The doctor said you could come home if you took the time to heal from your injuries."

"I can feed the animals, at the very least." Josiah tugged at the cast on his arm. "This thing itches. It's time that I start pulling my weight around here."

His words sent relief and hope rushing through her. Something else for which to be thankful. "You have plenty of time for that when you're better."

"I have to make up for lost time."

They smiled at each other. "Happy Thanksgiving."

Mary and Lillie flew down the stairs, their little shoes making clickety-clackety sounds on the wood. "Happy Thanksgiving!" Mary tore by them. "We'll feed the chickens real quick."

"Don't forget the mama kitten!" Mark's boots made a heavy thudding sound on the steps. "Luke says she has to keep her strength up so she can feed her babies. I'll take care of the horses and the pigs."

With one long stride, Josiah made it to the door in time to open it for his little sisters and his brother. He grinned at Emma. "It's good to be home."

He clomped out. Still smiling, Emma went into the kitchen. Leah hummed at the stove, and Luke was nowhere in sight. He must've gone out through the back door.

"The bacon's on. I'm making pancakes." Leah actually smiled. "Will you fry the eggs?"

"It would be my pleasure." Emma smiled back. Thanksgiving brought out the best in everyone. "I think we should have some apple muffins, too. I'll put out the honey and the peach preserves."

Breakfast passed in a medley of laughter and conversation. Emma savored every moment.

Both the animals and the humans fed, it was time for devotions. Even the little ones joined in. After prayers, Luke looked around. His face as relaxed as Emma had seen it in months, he pointed to Lillie. "You start, little schweschder."

Lillie giggled, obviously pleased at the honor. "I'm thankful for the dollies Leah made Mary and me for our birthdays. Oh, and for the turkey we'll have at Uncle Noah's house."

It was Leah's turn to look pleased. "I'm glad you like the doll. What about you, Mary?"

Mary squinted her eyes, as if thinking hard. "I'm thankful for my coat when it's cold and the stove that makes the water hot when I have to take a bath."

Emma laughed, in spite of herself. Everyone knew Mary didn't care for taking a bath. On around the circle they went, each selecting small, simple blessings.

Catherine's turn came last. Her face, usually so shuttered, reflected a mix of happiness and trepidation. Her gaze skipped around the room, lighting everywhere except on her family. "I'm not sure how to say this. With Mudder and Daed gone everything's changed, and I don't know how you're supposed to do this…" Her voice sounded higher than usual. "So I'm just going to say it. My blessing is…well, Melvin Dodd asked me to marry him and I said yes. Luke, we'd like to ask you to make the invitation after the prayer service on Sunday."

Stunned silence prevailed for a long second. Then Leah hopped to her feet, more nimble than seemingly possible with her girth. "Congratulations! What wonderful news!"

Then everyone talked at once. The twins clamoring to get into Catherine's lap. Annie and Josiah took turns patting her shoulder. The boys ran around the room, cheering. Emma couldn't bring herself to move. Her gaze connected with Luke's. He shrugged. After a few minutes, Catherine untangled herself and peered around Leah. "You're not saying anything, Emma."

Emma sat up straighter and pushed back all the words that threatened to tumble out. Catherine would marry first, before Emma, before Annie. It didn't seem fair. *This isn't about fair.* Emma should be happy for her sister, thrilled, in fact, that she had overcome the horrors of the accident to find happiness. Still, she couldn't ignore the ugly envy that threatened to take root in her heart. "You two were very quiet, indeed. I had no idea you were even courting until last night. Has it been long?"

"Long enough." Catherine plucked at her apron. "We've been visiting for a while. At Ruth's wedding, we realized we had something special. Everything fell into place."

"But you didn't even come to the noon meal," Emma objected. "I was going to seat you next to Michael Glick."

"Didn't you notice Melvin wasn't at the table either?"

"Congratulations." Emma went to her. "I'm so happy for you. What a blessing. I know you and Melvin will have a good life together."

"Thank you," Catherine whispered. She clasped Emma's hands in hers. "Your turn will come, I know it will."

Emma forced a smile. "I know you're right."

If only saying it would make it so.

Chapter 32

E mma tugged boots over her thick woolen socks. Then she shrugged on her heaviest coat. They needed two buggies to carry the entire family to Uncle Noah's house. Since the new one didn't have a kerosene heater, Luke took Leah and the smaller children in the old buggy while Emma and the older siblings dressed for the weather. She added a woolen bonnet and tucked a scarf around her neck. "I'll drive," Josiah said as he stalked past her and opened the front door.

"No, you won't." She scurried after him. "You'll put a strain on your shoulder and your ribs. What if the horse spooks and jerks the reins? I'll drive."

Josiah clomped down the steps. "I'm not being driven to Uncle Noah's by—"

"By a girl?" Emma laughed, her breath making white puffs in the icy air. "Pride goeth before the fall, little bruder. Doctor Chavez said no driving."

"He meant cars."

"Buggies are worse." Emma pulled on her gloves. Doctor Chavez also intended for Josiah to go back for a series of follow-up visits to him and to Doctor Morris. Josiah had made it clear he intended to do neither. "Forget it. You're not driving."

Mark hurled himself past them and rushed toward the buggy. "I can drive. Let me!"

"Where are your gloves?" Emma called after him. "Back in the house, right now."

Josiah rolled his eyes and groaned. "Which is worse? My sister or my little brother—"

He stopped. Emma followed his gaze. Annie sat in the driver's seat, the reins in her hands. "How about your other sister?" She grinned. "All aboard, we're losing time. I told Aunt Sophie I would make my green bean casserole when I get there—that way it will be fresh and hot."

Chattering and laughing, they huddled together under thick, soft buggy robes. Annie clucked and shook the reins. They were off to Uncle Noah's. Emma glanced back. Catherine raised her face to the late morning sun as if soaking up its warmth. Emma turned and did the same. How could one be burdened by sorrow and discontent on such a beautiful day? Catherine deserved all the happiness she could find. Melvin Dodd was a fine young man who worked hard on his father's farm. He would make a good husband. They'd done a good job of keeping their courting private.

Unlike Emma. Everyone seemed to know about Carl and Thomas. Seeing Catherine so happy brought Emma's dilemma front and center in the bright morning light. Carl with his letters. She tried not to think about the letters. She'd been tempted to read another this morning, but there hadn't been time. Reading the letters didn't mean she believed they could overcome the past. It only meant she was allowing herself to revisit those days. It might be the only way to heal from what Carl had done.

Then there was Thomas. Their talk at the hospital had made her believe they might have a chance. What would he say about the letters? Let the past lie? Let Carl go. Or would Thomas bow out? The thought stabbed her. She didn't want that. She should return the letters to Carl without reading more. She sighed and closed her eyes. She had to make a decision. Soon. After the holiday, Thomas might see fit to visit her again. Today he would be celebrating with his family and so was she. She should be happy in the moment.

She opened her eyes. They were turning off the dirt road onto the highway. The produce stand sat empty today. Flashes of the scene battered Emma. Bits and pieces. The sounds more than the sights haunted her. The horse's screams. The wailing of the sirens. Catherine's sobs and Luke's ragged breathing. The sounds echoed loudly in the silence that descended on the buggy.

"Maybe we should pray." Annie offered, her voice small and tentative.

"Yes, yes, we should." Emma bowed her head and whispered a prayer for Mudder and Daed and for all the families who celebrated a day of thanksgiving with empty spots on the benches.

"Look, there's Thomas." Mark's voice broke the silence. "And Eli. Hi, Eli! Hi, Rebecca. Happy Thanksgiving!"

Annie pulled even with Thomas's buggy. He waved and wished them a happy holiday in return.

"We're going to Groossmammi's," Rebecca called. "And then we get to go to Helen's house for pie. I'll get to play with Betsy today. That's what I'm thankful for."

Thomas's gaze met Emma's. He didn't blink. She stared back. The connection she'd felt at the hospital somehow had been broken. Surely, she could blame no one but herself. She offered friendship. He had taken it. She told him to consider Helen Crouch. Apparently, he'd decided to take her advice.

"It was neighborly of Helen's parents to invite us for dessert," Thomas said, his bleak expression belying his words. "I've heard Helen makes some of the best pumpkin pie in this part of the state."

Emma lifted her chin. "I'm sure it's wonderful. Your family doesn't mind?"

"With the brood that my mother will have at the house, they'll hardly miss the three of us after we've eaten turkey. It'll be naptime for her. Besides, she's always…" He stopped. His face suffused a red that had nothing to do with the brisk northerly wind that buffeted them.

"Anyway, we better get going. Mudder doesn't like for the turkey to sit too long after it comes out of the oven."

"Us, too." Annie said when Emma didn't respond. "May your day be truly blessed."

Thomas's nod seemed to take in everyone except Emma. She didn't speak again until his buggy turned off on the road that led to his parents' farm. Then she couldn't hold it in any longer. "Not to be ugly or anything, but I think Annie's pumpkin pie is the best in this part of the state."

Annie burst out laughing. After a second, Josiah, Catherine, and Mark joined in. "What? What are you laughing at?"

"You, schweschder." Annie shifted the reins to one hand for a second and squeezed Emma's arm with the other. "You're so good most of the time, you try so hard, and then sometimes you're so human. It's nice to know you're only human. Things get to you just like they get to me or Josiah—"

"Or me." Catherine chimed in.

"Of course, they get to me." They could never know how much. Emma couldn't believe they didn't realize how flawed she truly was. "But it's not nice and you shouldn't laugh. It's not a competition. We should be happy that Helen makes great pies. We should wish her the very best with her pies. And with Thomas." She almost choked on the last three words. "That would be the nice thing to do."

Annie whooped so loud Emma jumped. "See, there's that nice Emma again." She giggled. "You're right. But you don't mean it. You like Thomas. And if you want to be with him, you need to start working at it a little harder."

"Hush. That's a private matter between Thomas and me."

Annie shrugged. Emma glanced back at her brothers and sister. "All of you, hush."

No one said another word, but Emma could feel their smiles warming her back all the way to Uncle Noah's house.

Thomas eased onto a bench. He needed to get out of Helen's way. She'd been fluttering around the crowded room ever since he arrived. Clucking like a hen over Eli and Rebecca as well as her four children. They were like stepping stones, one right after another, clean, neat, soft-spoken. Their respectful demeanor spoke well of Helen and her parents. He turned down her third offer of more pie. "I really couldn't eat another bite."

"Some coffee then, to take the nip out of the air."

Between the fireplace and the overflowing crowd of relatives, the room was plenty warm already. Thomas gently refused the offer yet again. He had to raise his voice to be heard over the gaggle of children playing Dutch Blitz on the piece-rag rug on the wood floor. Helen navigated around Eli and Rebecca, but nearly tripped over her son Edmond's long, gangly legs. "Whoa!" She teetered, did a strange little two step, caught herself, and managed to save the pie tin.

Eli giggled. Thomas stared. His son quickly shut his mouth and went back to the game. Thomas stood. "I think it's time for outdoor games. Eli, Rebecca, run along. Work off all that food with a good run about the farm. Go on!"

"Good idea!" Helen looked relieved. "Edmond, Betsy, out you go. You too, Ginny and Naomi. You can keep an eye on the younger ones."

They didn't need another invitation. In seconds the games were put away. Coats in hand, they were out the door, giggling and skipping. Their absence brought a little more space to the room. Thomas stretched his legs at the table and relaxed.

Helen's mother gave him a sympathetic smile. She turned to her daughter. "Helen, why don't you sit down for a minute." She had to raise her voice to be heard over the good-natured chatter of half a dozen teenagers playing Parcheesi at the other table. "I'm sure Thomas would rather talk with you than watch you fly around like a frightened bird."

"Yes, Mudder, you're right." Still, she took time to add more wood to an already blazing fire. Then she plopped down across from him. Wisps of brown hair escaped her kapp and hung in her eyes. She held up the pie tin. "Are you sure you won't have another piece?"

He dabbed at his face with his napkin. The blazing fire coupled with the crowd of relatives made for a stuffy, warm room. "I couldn't eat another bite."

Helen fanned herself with a napkin. "It's rather warm for late November, isn't it?"

Thomas hid a smile. She compounded the warmth of the fire with her propensity to dash about, always in a hurry. Despite her small stature and rather round figure, she did everything in a rush. His measured approach left him eating her dust. So to speak.

James slapped his mug on the table and leaned back, thumbs hooked on his suspenders. "How is that sow you were having problems with?"

"I had to put her down. The vet said she couldn't be saved."

That was all the prompting James needed. They spent the next hour discussing livestock, the price of cattle, and whether it made sense to plant winter wheat, given the downturn in the economy. Time passed much more quickly. At some point Thomas noticed Helen wasn't in the room anymore. He had no idea when she left.

"I should be going," he said. "The animals won't get fed on their own. I truly appreciate your kindness in inviting us to share the holiday with you."

"I better get on with chores, too. After all this excitement, it will be good to turn in early tonight." James yawned and stood. "Know you're always welcome here, Thomas. We have plenty, and we are pleased to share with you."

His throat tight for some unknown reason, Thomas swallowed and nodded. "I appreciate that."

Tugging at his gloves, he clomped down the front steps and inhaled the brisk air. When he exhaled, some of the thick, heavy feeling brought on by the warmth of the Daugherty house and all the food he'd eaten went with the air. He liked the cold. It made him feel wide awake.

Something icy and wet smacked his hand. "What?" Startled he held up his fingers, coated with snow. "Who did that?"

Another snowball collided with his shoulder. He whirled in time to see Helen duck behind the porch's corner. "Helen Crouch! What do you think you're doing?"

She trotted away from the house, her face creased with a big smile. "That's your punishment for trying to leave without saying good-bye."

Thomas glanced around. They were alone. He swooped down and scooped up a handful of snow, packed it together with both hands, and took aim. Helen ducked. The snowball sailed over her head. Her laugh sounded like the chortle of a young girl. "Missed, missed!"

He tried again, this time making sure he didn't get anywhere near her. She laughed even harder. He couldn't help but laugh with her.

She stopped a few feet from him, still smiling. "Could we be any sillier if we were teenagers?"

"It's the season." Thomas couldn't be sure when the holidays had ceased being a time of bittersweet reminiscence and become once again a time of joy. It had taken years, but now he could look forward with anticipation to the holidays. With a sudden reluctance that surprised him, he turned to hitch the horse to the buggy. "But now, I do need to get home and do the chores. The animals don't know it's Thanksgiving. I would've said good-bye, but I figured you were busy."

"I'm used to getting things done. No sense in slacking off. Just makes more work later. But I was lax in my duties as your hostess. I apologize."

Remorse touched Thomas. She needn't apologize. He had chosen conversation with her father, and she had done the correct thing. Taken care of matters in the kitchen. She had practice being a good daughter, good wife, and good mother. "We enjoyed our visit, Helen."

Helen slapped her gloved hands together, making a tiny shower of snowflakes fall from them. She smiled up at him. "I think we dirtied every pan in the house making that feast. Can you believe six pies are gone?"

"It was really good pie." Thomas patted his stomach. Helen cooked well, too. In her, he could see everything he sought in a woman. So why didn't it feel quite right? Maybe he needed to recognize that practical matters were more important. He couldn't expect to have the sort of joyous union he'd had with Joanna a second time. "Now I need to go work some of it off. By the time we get home, it'll be time to start the evening chores. It gets dark early this time of year."

"I'm looking forward to the new year myself." Her breath came in cloudy puffs. "Spring is always a fresh, new start, isn't it?"

The wistful look on her face touched a sore spot in Thomas's heart. He understood her loneliness far better than most. He smoothed a hand across the horse's rump. "I've always believed we can make our own fresh, new starts any time of the year. Christmas will be here soon when we celebrate a special new beginning."

"You're a wise man." Helen's face brightened. "We'll see you at the children's Christmas pageant."

"That you will." He tightened the harness, aware of her hopeful glance. "Eli and Rebecca both have parts in a skit. They've already started practicing."

"You'll be helping to build the set, then?"

"I wouldn't miss it."

She took a few steps closer. "I'm sewing costumes for—"

A wail cut the air. A child in distress. "Help! Help us! Mudder! Groossdaddi!"

Before Thomas could react, Helen shot across the hard-packed snow. Despite her flowing skirts and shorter legs, she was the hare to his turtle. Thomas picked up his pace until his long legs ate up the distance between them. It could be Eli or Rebecca hurt or worse. "We're coming!"

"What is it?" Helen called. "Where are you, Ginny?"

"Here!" Helen's middle daughter raced up the path that led to a small pond. "It's Edmond." She stopped and put both hands on her knees, her breath ragged and panting. "He was skating on the ice and it cracked. He fell in."

"It's too early in the winter to be ice skating!" Helen darted past her daughter. "That child has the common sense of a goose."

She stumbled, fell. Thomas grabbed her arm and tugged her upright. They slipped and slid down the icy path. The trees parted on the clearing that led to the pond. Helen's nephew, Michael, sprawled on the ground, his hand outstretched toward Edmond's. The boy's lips were already purple. His teeth chattered.

Michael stretched out farther. "It's too far! The ice is cracking." He rolled up on his knees. "I can't reach him from here."

"We need something—a pole or a branch." Thomas glanced around, searching. His gaze fell on Eli and Rebecca. They huddled on the shore, their eyes big in white faces. "Look for a big branch, but stay away from the edge of the pond!"

They scattered.

"Here." Helen rushed at him, dragging a branch almost as tall as she was. "Use this."

Thomas flattened himself against the ground. He ignored the icy burn of the snow against his neck and cheek and shoved the branch out as far as he could. Edmond's frightened face stared back at him from the black hole. He clutched at the jagged ice. Thomas pushed the branch as far as he dared. "Take it, Edmond, grab hold!"

"If I let go, I might…" Edmond gasped. "I'll go under."

"You have to let go long enough to grab the branch. Come on, you can do it!" Thomas put all his authority into the words. The boy had to believe. His life depended on it. "I'll get you onto dry land, I promise."

The boy sobbed once. "I can't."

"Yes, you can."

"Edmond Crouch, do as Thomas says." Helen's voice rang with authority. "This second."

Thomas didn't dare break the hold of his gaze on Edmond, but the look on the boy's face told him Edmond always did what his mother told him to do—especially when she employed that tone.

A second later Edmond's fingers wrapped around the branch.

"Good boy!" Thomas tugged hard with both hands. The sound of Helen's tortured breathing filled his ears. She couldn't suffer another loss. *God, please!* In what seemed like an eternity, he tugged the boy forward, slowly, praying the ice wouldn't break again.

Finally, he dragged him to the shore. Helen squatted and grabbed her son by both arms. Together, they tugged him onto the packed snow, well beyond the ice. "My son, my son," Helen muttered. "*Ach*, my son."

Thomas doubted she even knew she spoke. His lungs about to burst, he remembered to breathe. His heart pounded against his breastbone. "Are you all right? Are you hurt?"

Edmond curled up in a shivering, wet ball. "I'm so cold."

Helen ripped off her coat and wrapped it around him. "You're fine. You'll be fine." Her voice wobbled, but she tugged her son to his feet. "We'll get you inside and get you warmed up."

Edmond leaned into his mother. His whole body shook as he looked up at Thomas. "Danki."

"Here, take my coat, too." Thomas shrugged it off. "We need to get you warm."

Helen waved it away. "It's a short distance. Don't get it any wetter than it already is. You'll need it for the drive home."

Thomas hugged the coat to his chest. Eli and Rebecca descended on him. He put a hand on each child's shoulder and squeezed. They were safe and dry, unlike Edmond, whose boots squeaked when he walked. "Are you sure—"

"Let's get him inside." Helen didn't appear to feel the cold or notice her sodden, muddied dress. Her entire being focused on her child. "Everyone inside. I'll make coffee and cocoa. We need to get you warmed up."

She glanced back at Thomas. "You're welcome to stay." She started up the path before he could respond, her arm around Edmond, who staggered a bit. Ginny, Betsy, and Naomi crowded their mother and brother, holding each other up. Michael followed, the look of relief on his face so intense, Thomas feared the young man would collapse under it.

Thomas squeezed his two children to him for a moment longer, letting the horror of what might have happened fade away. Helen's quick action had helped to save her son. She masqueraded as a roly-poly hen, but she could be a fierce eagle when it came to protecting her children. She had to be. He admired her stamina. Admiration—could it become more? "Come on, children. We need to get home."

Rebecca looked disappointed. "No cocoa for us?"

"We'll have it at home." He brushed snow and dirt from the coat and slid it back on as he walked. It did little to stop the cold that seeped into every bone in his body. The frigid wind picked up. He glanced at the sky. Where it had been cloudless earlier, dark clouds now rolled across the expanse, hiding the sun. He trudged faster. "Helen, we have to go. It looks as if we might get some more snow."

She barely acknowledged his words, so obviously intent on getting Edmond inside. Cold and bedraggled, they marched up the path to the house. When they arrived at the buggy, Helen stopped barely long enough to say a proper good-bye. "Your help was much appreciated."

"I'm thankful we were able to get him out."

"We have much to be thankful for." Something in her expression told him she was thinking of the loss she'd already suffered. "I better get him warmed before he catches pneumonia. Happy Thanksgiving."

"Happy Thanksgiving."

He watched until she closed the door behind her.

A package should never be judged by its wrapping.

Chapter 33

Emma swished the platter in the dishwater and scrubbed it a second time. She handed it to Annie, who dried it and set it next
to a large stack of clean plates. "One down, fifty to go," her sister said,
smiling. "I'll put the kettle on to heat some more water. One thing
about so much good food and fellowship, it means so many dirty
dishes. Are you sure you don't want to dry?"

Emma used the back of one wet hand to rub an itchy spot on her
nose. The mouth-watering aroma of turkey that had been so alluring
earlier still hung in the air, but now it made her feel a little sick. She'd
eaten too much. "I like washing. I don't mind drying, but I like washing
better."

"That's because you like a challenge. The bigger the better."

The voice behind her caused Emma to crane her neck around to see
Aenti Louise trot into the kitchen lugging another stack of dishes. "I
think we dirtied every dish, every pot, every pan, in your Aunt Sophie's
kitchen," she chortled. "They'll be eating leftovers for a week."

"I'm sending the leftovers home with all of you." Sophie bustled
into the kitchen with another pile of dishes. She grabbed a washrag
from the counter and headed for the door. "I'll wipe down the tables."

Annie took the serving dishes from Aenti Louise and handed them
to Emma. "I do like leftover turkey and mashed potatoes and gravy."

"And pumpkin pie." Aenti Louise swiped a saucer with an already cut piece of pie on it from the cabinet and sat down in a chair at the prep table. It was her third piece of pie. Where did she put it all? "With ice cream."

"Ice cream?" Emma laughed. "Next you'll want pretzels or popcorn. Enough, Aenti. Tell us stories while we work."

"Salt and sweet, my dear, salt and sweet. But I'd rather hear what you think about your sister's wedding plans."

Emma almost lost her grip on a wet, slippery bowl. "She told you?"

Aenti Louise put down her fork and folded her hands in her lap, looking all prim and proper. "Of course not. She has to wait until the deacon makes the announcement on Sunday."

"Then how…"

"My eyesight may be going, but my hearing is as good as ever." Aenti Louise adjusted her glasses for good measure. "I overheard Luke and Leah discussing it. They felt Melvin should've come to them for permission, but still they sounded pleased."

Emma dumped two pots into the water. It splashed on her apron and ran down the side of the tub. "Whoops!"

They all laughed. "Are you taking a bath or washing dishes?" Aenti Louise picked up her fork again. "I think they're pleased that one sister is taken care of. You also seem at ease with her announcement."

Emma kept her gaze on a gravy-encrusted pot. "Why wouldn't I be?"

Aenti Louise smacked her lips and tossed her fork on the table "Emma Shirack. This is your Aunt Louise speaking. Have respect."

"Yes, Aenti." Emma dropped the pot into the rinse water and turned to face her. "It seems a little sudden."

"To someone who's been waiting for years, it would."

"That's not it. Catherine suffered a terrible trauma when Mudder and Daed…when they…when…"

"So did you. So much so that even after six months, you still can't say the words."

"When they died." Emma dried her hands on a towel and laid it on the table. She sank onto a chair across from her aunt. "She suffered so terribly she couldn't eat or sleep. Now she's marrying a man whom she's barely begun to court."

"That's because I know how short life is and how suddenly it can end." Catherine strode through the doorway, an almost empty basket of rolls in her hands. "I saw what happened to my parents. I was there when they took their last breaths. Did you know Mudder called for Daed—before you ran up—she called his name? They so loved each other. I want to have that before it's too late."

"Catherine, I'm sorry." Emma rushed across the room to her. "I am happy for you, very happy."

"I know you don't believe that I'm better, but I am." Catherine thrust the basket at her. "You're the one who can't seem to look ahead instead of behind. You know who else knows how short life is?"

Emma set the basket on the table. "What do you mean?"

"Thomas. Thomas knows."

Catherine whirled and left the room. Emma stared at the empty doorway, pondering.

"She's right, you know."

Emma closed her eyes for a second, then turned to face Annie. "I do know, but it's a hard decision. A hard choice."

"No, it's not. Carl left you. Thomas never would." Annie polished the plate in her hand with such vigorous strokes, it was a wonder it didn't break. "I wish…I wish I had choices. I wish someone shone a flashlight in the window for me."

She sounded so sad. Emma covered the space between them in three quick steps. She patted Annie's shoulder. Her sister's eyes were bright with tears. Emma felt her own tears well. "I'm sorry. There will be someone for you."

"Maybe not. I need to face that fact."

"Not yet. It's too soon to think that way."

Annie sniffed. "I'll get along fine, just like you have."

"What do you mean?" Surviving. Surely God intended that life be more than a bare minimum. "I'm not doing much of anything."

"You can't call teaching children not much of anything. The community trusts you with their children." Annie went back to drying dishes. "I can't teach—that's your calling. But I can cook. I mean to ask Luke to let me try to get a job at the restaurant in town. Soon. I keep saying that, but this time, I'm going to do it. What's the worst that could happen? He says no?"

The thought of working all day surrounded by fancy folks sent a tiny shiver through Emma. She'd grown used to their stares. Even the photo taking. But a steady diet of it would be trying. "Are you sure?"

"I can be much more help with the finances that way."

Luke hadn't said much about their finances since the discussion that occurred right after their parents' deaths, but Emma had watched his face darken and the sun lines around his eyes deepen as he stared at paperwork spread over the table in the evenings after long days of hard work. "Would you be happy working in town?"

Annie's face brightened. "I love to cook. When people enjoy the food I prepare, it gives me a sense of accomplishment. Is that wrong?"

"No, my child, it's not wrong." Aenti Louise put a gnarled hand covered with ropey veins to her mouth to hide a gentle burp. "I like your food very much. Preparing the food that people break together is an honor and a privilege. Ask your brother. See what he says."

Annie hugged a clean pot to her chest. "I will."

"Give me that pot. I'll put it away." Aenti Louise slid from her chair and held out a hand. "Time to make myself useful."

They worked in silence for several minutes. Emma sank her hands into the soapy water. She fought drowsiness. Too much turkey and not enough sleep. There would be time for a nap later. Right now, the stacks of dishes didn't seem to be shrinking fast enough.

"You don't realize how blessed you are, Emma."

Emma almost dropped a serving dish that still had chunks of mashed potatoes clinging to the sides. Aenti Louise's words pierced her. Emma claimed to be blessed. She spoke the words. She even thought them. But did she believe it? She met her aunt's gaze. "Carl Freiling is trying to convince me he's changed by giving me letters he wrote to me while he was away, but never sent. Thomas Brennaman claims to have feelings for me, and he's having dessert at Helen Crouch's house. I don't feel blessed. I feel…I feel confused and afraid I'll make the wrong decision."

Aenti Louise sighed. *"Pffft."*

"Pffft? What does that mean?"

"It means you have yet to seek the will of God in this. If you had, you'd know what path you must take."

Emma went back to washing dishes. She didn't respond to her aunt's claim. She had no answer. If God was telling her something, she had no idea what it was.

"Do you know the story of Jacob?"

As a child, Emma had loved her aunt's stories told by the fireplace in the evenings before bedtime. After she delivered babies, she often stayed and took care of the smaller children, giving mothers a day or two to recover and take care of the new baby. Her services were in great demand in those days. "I remember you telling us the stories. He stole his brother Esau's birthright."

"I was thinking of later, when he was a grown man. When he wrestled with the angel of God. Remember that story?" Aenti Louise stooped to put away a large pot. She put a hand on her hip when she straightened, wincing in pain. "Why do you think God sent an angel to wrestle with this man?"

Emma glanced at Annie. Her sister gave her a sympathetic smile. There was no stopping Aenti Louise when she started with a lesson. "Because He wanted Jacob to realize who was in control."

"And who was that?"

"God," Emma whispered.

"Yes. The angel fought with Jacob all night. He could have overpowered him at any time. Instead he kept fighting and fighting until Jacob was too tired to fight anymore. Then the angel touched Jacob's hip socket and with one touch defeated him. That's when Jacob knew God was in charge. Who's in charge of your life, Emma? Who are you wrestling with?"

Emma bowed her head and tried to hide her tears. "Plain people don't wrestle. We don't fight."

"Don't get sassy with me, little girl. We don't fight physically. But we struggle with God's will all the time. What are you wrestling with God about?"

"Why did He let them die?" She swallowed hard against the lump in her throat. "Why?"

"I don't know." She touched Emma's face with a wrinkled hand. "But in the darkest hours the only place to turn is to Him."

Emma turned and accepted her aunt's hug. "I'm trying."

"I know. Stop trying so hard and let it be. Stop and listen. Be still and hear. Just be."

Just be. It sounded so restful. And so impossible.

Chapter 34

Dear Emma,

Today I drove a car. It's an amazing feeling, but strange. Not at all like driving a buggy, really. The instructor said I did well. I wonder if he tells everyone that. You turn the wheel and push on a gas pedal and a machine that weighs thousands of pounds does what you want it to do. I find that to be a good feeling. But it has responsibility. If I push the gas pedal too hard and the car goes too fast, I might lose control. I might not stop at a stoplight. I might hurt someone. Life is like that, isn't it? If we go too fast or make a wrong decision, we hurt people. I know I hurt you. Have you forgiven me? I hope so. Tomorrow, I'll take another lesson. Eventually I won't worry so much about losing control. Or making a wrong decision while I'm driving. If only life were as easy to learn.

With all my heart,
Carl

Emma folded the letter and slipped it back into the envelope. If only life were as easy to learn. Aenti Louise's words that afternoon sang inside her head. Be still. Listen. Let God be in charge. She closed her eyes and sat very still. *God?* The image of Carl sitting behind the

wheel of a car floated through her mind. Did he play the radio while
he drove? Did he open the windows and sit with one arm dangling
outside like she had seen the Englisch men do? Did he stick his head
out and let the wind blow his hair? He wouldn't have worn a hat, surely.
How fast had he driven? She thought of the speed limit signs on the
highway. Seventy miles an hour. Who could compete with that kind of
adventure? She smoothed the envelope with a shaking finger. Carl may
have walked away from that sort of worldliness, but the fact remained
that he still wanted control. Control of her.

Who is in control? Who's in charge? Aenti Louise loved those kinds of
questions. Emma hated them.

She tried to listen to the silence again. After a long, fun-filled day
with a house full of aunts and uncles and cousins, nieces and nephews,
the quiet was lovely. But empty. No words of wisdom came. Everyone
had turned in early except her. She couldn't seem to find the peace
necessary to sleep.

Still, it had been a good day. Despite the encounter with Thomas.
Despite the empty spaces where Mudder and Daed should've been
seated. Despite the discussion with Aenti Louise, Annie, and Catherine.
Despite the uncertainty in her life. God did have control. *I'm trying, God.*

Instead of going to sleep, she read two more letters. They contained
lengthy descriptions of Carl's life in a fancy world. He went to the
movies, saw a play, watched cartoons on TV like a small child. He
said he missed her, but every letter brimmed with excitement over
some new adventure. Even learning to use a dishwasher and going to
a Laundromat filled him with awe and wonder. He described meals in
fast food restaurants and conversations with strangers on the bus. He
painted a world where everything was something to write home about.

She slapped the fourth letter back in its place. Why? Why did he
want her to read all this? Four years later. What difference could it
possibly make in her feelings for him now? So he had his adventure and
he wanted her to say it was all right that he left for four years to do it. So
far, she couldn't find it in herself to say that. Or feel it. Or forgive him.

She extinguished the lamp and waited for her eyes to adjust to the inky darkness. A knock on the door made her jump. She gasped and put a trembling hand to her chest. After a few seconds, another knock, this one a little louder. She rushed to the door. "Who is it?" she whispered, her hand on the knob. "It's late."

"It's Carl." His hoarse whisper sent another tremor through her. "Open the door."

She nibbled at her lower lip. After a few seconds she did as he asked. "It's late and it's too cold for buggy rides."

"I'll only stay for a few minutes."

He held her gaze. She sighed. "Come in."

Pulling gloves from his hands, he brushed past her. He smelled like the smoke of wood burning in a smoldering fireplace.

Emma relit the lamp and waited until he chose a chair. She lowered herself into a hickory rocking chair a discreet distance away. She folded her hands in her lap. "Happy Thanksgiving."

"Same to you." He fumbled with the eye-and-hook on his black woolen coat. "Did you have a nice day with your family?"

"I did. And you?" She studied her hands. She was too tired for awkward conversation. "Carl, don't take your coat off. I'm really too tired for you to stay—"

"Did you read the letters?"

She raised her head to meet his gaze. His hand was still on the last hook, as if he'd forgotten what he was doing. His eyes blazed with emotion. She looked away. "Four. I've read four."

"Will you read the others?"

"I'm not sure."

"Promise me you'll read them." He slapped both hands on his knees and leaned forward. "I need for you to read them. So we can talk... about everything. Once you've read them, if you can't get past what I've done, then I'll stop bothering you."

What he had done? Abandoned her. Adopted a way of living that flew in the face of everything they believed in. Only Carl could believe someone like her could get past all that. "Carl—"

"I know you want me to give up so you won't have to make a decision, but that's not going to happen." His gaze seemed to pierce her skin and peer at her heart. "You're the only one here who will understand and forgive."

"You've already been forgiven by your parents and your family. What are you talking about, Carl?" And what did he know about what she wanted? She didn't know herself. "I haven't made a decision because there isn't one to make. There's nothing between us anymore."

"That's not true and you know it. We bonded for life. I'll not give up. I won't make it easy for you. Thomas might, but I won't. I came back here for you."

He rose. Her heart sliced to ribbons by his words, she followed suit. "I don't know what to say."

"Say goodnight."

He came back for her. "Goodnight, Carl."

"Now that I've spent a few minutes in your company it is a good night." He touched the brim of his hat and moved to the door. "Until another day."

He slipped through the door and closed it behind him, leaving her standing in the middle of an empty room. After a few seconds, she returned to her spot by the lamp. His strange, emotional insistence propelled her to pick up the stack of letters once again.

The next one was short. It had been written about a month after the letter describing how he watched cartoons on the television while the dishwasher took care of his lonely plate, fork, and spoon.

Dear Emma,

I went to a church service today. It's the first time I've been to a service since I left home. It was a nondenominational church about a block from my apartment complex. In some ways it was very different. There were musical instruments and lively singing, candles, and flowers. But in other ways, it was exactly the same. Nondenominational means they have no ties to a larger community of like believers. They stand alone. You know what's so amazing about that? They believe Jesus was the

Son of God, that He was crucified, died, and buried, and on
the third day He arose and ascended into heaven to sit at the
right hand of God. Sound familiar? Why are Plain folks so sure
everyone else is so different? We believe in the same Jesus and the
same God. I was far, far from you on Sunday, yet I worshipped
the same God as you. Is it not a little prideful to think of our-
selves as being different? I'm not trying to shake you from your
faith. I only want you to think about it. To test your beliefs to
make sure you are strong in them.

With all my heart,
Carl

Emma let the letter flutter to her lap. Was he asking her those
questions or himself? Plain folk didn't think of themselves as better for
being different. Not different, but set apart. Humbly accepting God's
providence. Not expecting it or earning it.

She slapped the letter into the envelope. Two remained. She studied
the envelopes, tempted to continue reading. Carl had been so adamant
about it. The light-hearted joker had disappeared into a man buffeted
by his own emotions. Why? What had he written that he couldn't say
to her? He'd written the dates in the upper left-hand corner, where
normally one found the return address. He probably never intended to
send them and having the dates allowed her to read them in the proper
order. Puzzled, she examined the last two side by side. The gap stared
back at her. After the next letter, Carl hadn't written another one for over
three years. He'd written six letters in a few months' time, then stopped.

She tapped her finger on the next envelope. She started to open
it, then stopped. If she didn't go to bed now, she'd be a wooly-headed
teacher tomorrow. Her responsibilities called to her. She'd spent enough
time mooning over Carl this evening. Time to go to bed. Resolute, she
tied up the envelopes in the ribbon and climbed the stairs.

Carl had waited four years to come back to Bliss Creek. A stack of
letters couldn't change that, no matter what secrets lay on those pages.
She would tell him so—after she finished reading the letters.

Chapter 35

"A men." Luke cleared his throat and looked up. "If this ham tastes as good as it smells, we are having a real feast tonight."

Pleased at her brother's obvious good mood, Emma slapped a thick slice of the baked ham on Luke's plate and another on Josiah's. Annie followed behind her with a bowl of fried potatoes, while Leah served the children, who were chattering among themselves about a coyote they claimed to have seen on the walk home from school. Emma hoped they'd mistaken a stray dog for the wild creature. Coyotes had been destroying their livestock. She hated to think of the children running into one of them out in the middle of nowhere. "Did you get the pigs back behind the fence?"

"Jah, but the coyotes killed two of them." Luke dug a fork into the ham and began to cut it with his knife. "We closed the hole up completely. We can't afford to lose any more livestock."

"It seems like the coyotes are getting closer this year," Josiah mused. "Mark told me the carcasses you found were up on the knoll that overlooks the pond. That's right in our backyard, practically."

"The snow's come earlier this year. It forces them to hunt closer to us. They have to look harder for food." Luke shook his head. "It is so cold out there, I think my breath froze. What about you, Josiah? How were things at the blacksmith shop?"

Emma couldn't decide if Luke sounded a little wistful. If he missed working in his shop, he never mentioned it. Josiah had gone back to work the day after Thanksgiving, despite his cast. The bruises on his face had turned an odd shade of yellow and green.

"Very quiet." Josiah spoke with a mouth full of ham. Emma had to stop herself from chiding him. Josiah was a grown man now. "I cleaned the stables and restocked all day."

Luke looked pleased. "Good, honest work."

"I'm not complaining." Josiah loaded his fork with potatoes. "It was cold, but I like that better than the heat in the summer. When you get the forge going, it's like being inside a fireplace all day."

"Walking home from the Jensons' house this afternoon, I nearly froze my toes off." Catherine passed a basket of hot-from-the-oven bread to Annie. "Tomorrow I'm doubling up on my socks if I can still get my feet into my boots."

Annie laughed. "You could wear mine. My feet are bigger than yours."

"I'm glad tomorrow is my last day cleaning. I need to get my dress done and the house cleaned."

"We have everything we need for the meal," Annie said. "I'm so glad the bishop decided to allow gas-powered refrigerators. It makes it so much easier to make food in advance and store it."

"No more going to the common freezer at the bishop's house," Catherine agreed. "And everything keeps so much longer."

"It's a blessing. I can help you with your dress tonight. If we don't finish, there's always tomorrow."

"I liked canned meat. Easier doesn't mean better." Luke paused, his fork in mid-air, a hunk of ham hanging from it. "Annie, you'll need to deliver your desserts tomorrow. Don't you have a big order for the Millers' birthday party?"

Annie seemed to concentrate on a serving of stewed tomatoes on her plate. "Everything is ready. I just need to deliver it."

"Mark can go with you. He can help carry things into their house."

Mark's chest puffed up. "I could drive the wagon, too."

Emma saw a touch of sadness in Annie's eyes, but her sister smiled at Mark. "That would be nice. I'm glad to have your company."

Emma nudged her with an elbow, hoping Leah didn't notice. Annie shook her head and pushed potatoes around with a fork. Finally she put a small piece in her mouth. Emma nudged again and tilted her head toward Luke.

Annie swallowed. She glanced at Luke, then away. "I was thinking, bruder. With the produce stand shut down for the winter we have less money coming in right now. It might be a good time for me to get a job in Bliss Creek." Her cheeks reddened to the color of apples. "Just until spring."

Emma stepped on Annie's toe. *Go on!*

Annie glared at her. Emma glared back. She glanced at Luke. His frown didn't bode well. Annie dropped her fork, picked it up. Still, she didn't elaborate. Emma shook her head and dove in. "Home Town Restaurant has an opening for a cook. I saw the sign in the window when I went into town for school supplies."

Luke's frown deepened. Leah wiggled next to him, her lips pressed together in a thin line. She sniffed. "How could you consider working in the restaurant? They have electrical appliances. They play music all day over loudspeakers. Tourists from Wichita and Emporia come to town to look for Amish furniture and eat there. The Weavers are nice Englisch folks, but they would expect you to use the dishwasher and the electric stove. I don't think they make a lot of that food. It comes frozen." Leah wound down, finally out of breath. She inhaled before anyone else could speak. "Much too worldly."

"I go to Englisch people's houses every day," Catherine pointed out. "They have TVs and radios and electric stoves."

"None of which you use." Luke's stern stare made Emma glad he was talking to Catherine and not her. He sounded so much like Daed. "Your agreement with Daed was that you would do nothing in those houses that you would not do here at home. That agreement still stands even though…"

His voice faltered for a second. Emma wanted to finish the sentence for him, but she didn't dare. He cleared his throat. "Even though Daed is gone."

"They're at work when I come to clean." Catherine's words tumbled on top of each other. Luke was making her nervous. "Everything is turned off. I don't turn anything on. Besides, after the wedding, I'm done. I've already given them notice."

"*Gut.*"

"Annie could do the same thing at the restaurant." Emma kept her tone respectful. "She could make the salads and do the preparations before the food is cooked. She could make breads and desserts here and take them to the restaurant. With Catherine getting married, we'll not have her income."

Luke cut himself another slice of ham. He carefully chopped it into smaller pieces without speaking. Emma had to loosen her grip on her own fork. She wanted to say more, but she knew better. If Luke didn't want to talk about it anymore, the conversation was over.

"We'll also have one less person to feed and clothe." He took a bite, chewed, and swallowed. "And one less person to help with the chores. Annie will have more to do here. As will you, Emma. The answer is no."

That was it. *No.* Emma sneaked a peek at Annie. She had her eyes on her slice of bread, carefully buttering it, but her downcast face told the story. At least they'd tried. Maybe Luke did know best. He'd been right about Josiah.

"No restaurant, but I heard Sadie Plank has been looking for someone to help her part-time at the bakery since John passed." Luke leaned back in his chair and took a long swallow from his glass of water. "It's not preparing full meals like you want, but Sadie's Plain folk, and she'll keep an eye on you."

Leah didn't look happy. "All those Englisch folks go into the bakery."

"That's why the bakery is able to stay in business." Luke held up his glass. Catherine filled it with more water. "Our women folk make our baked goods. We don't need to buy them. Besides, it's only until Annie marries."

"You're right." Leah bowed her head. "It's just that it won't be long now until the baby comes."

So that's what she was worried about. Emma hurried to assure her—and Luke. "We'll all be here to help when the baby comes. I'm sure Catherine will still want to help. Don't you worry. Even the twins will help."

"Yes, yes!" Mary and Lillie crowed in unison. "We want to take care of the baby."

Leah gave Emma a grateful smile and went back to her corn on the cob.

"In the meantime, I'll speak with Sadie about Annie coming to work for her." Luke stood. "Finish up now. Then finish your chores. Bedtime will come before you know it."

The conversation was over. Emma grinned at Annie. It wasn't exactly what her sister wanted, but it would allow her to contribute more to the family while enjoying her love of cooking. And if Sadie agreed to the arrangement, Annie would be spending more time in town with more opportunities to run into the young men who went to the harness shop or the blacksmith shop, the feed store, and the hardware store.

It was all very good.

After the dishes were washed and the kitchen spotless, Emma worked her way through a pile of mending, finishing just as the sun began to sink beyond the horizon. She stuck the needle in the pin cushion and stretched her arms over her head. Annie and Catherine had laid out the cloth for the wedding dress and were cutting the pieces. It would be beautiful. They seemed engrossed in their work, so Emma lifted her skirt a little and ran up the stairs. She had a few minutes before bedtime.

Carl's sixth letter was dated about three months after he left home. It was the longest letter yet, a page filled with his familiar spidery cursive. Emma took a deep breath. She glanced at the door. Her sisters would be coming to bed any minute.

Dear Emma,

    I'm working in a huge hardware store now. It's what they call a megastore. Which just means it's very big. You could get lost in here. Makes the hardware store in Bliss Creek look like someone's storage shed. I work in the garden section. I help people with all their lawn and garden needs, as my boss likes to put it. Pretty funny, isn't it? I'm keeping close to nature in my own way, I guess. I had to read up on fertilizers and what flowers and trees grow best here. The customers work so hard to make a pretty little green space on the tiny patch of land where their houses sit when there are great wide open spaces in the country all around their town, if they would only get away from their jobs and their commitments for a while.

    People are nice, though. They're happy when they think about planting things in the earth, digging around with their hands. Getting dirty. They don't think of it as work. It's a hobby. For some it's a way of making their houses worth more money. Isn't that strange? Landscaping, they call it. I hope you find this as interesting and odd as I do. I explore, and you get to know all about it without being exposed yourself. The safe way. Do you want to be safe? Or do you long sometimes for more? I never asked you. I wish I had. I didn't want to lead you away from your faith. If I asked you now, would you come here? Would you leave everything and everyone for me? I'll never know because I didn't ask. It's one of the things I think about at night when the noise of the city keeps me awake.

    Next month I start classes at the community college. I only have the time and the money for two: English and Algebra. The advisor called them core classes. I call them playing catch-up. I need to learn a lot to know what the other students do. Now that I'm out here I see how little we really learn in our one-room schools with our old textbooks. As a teacher, does that bother you? Maybe you'll answer my letter, just to tell me how wrong I am. Anything would be better than this silence. I like the people I work with, but I haven't made any friends yet. With time,

I think. I hope. Even if I do, I'll still write to you. I don't know if I will have the courage to send the letters, but I'll write them anyway. They make me feel connected to you.

With all my heart,
Carl

Emma clutched the page to her chest and rocked for a second. He had a way with words—written words. Silvery words. That's what Aenti Louise would call them. If he really loved her that much, why did it take him four years to come back? She wanted to ask him that question, yet she didn't want to know the answer. Maybe the answer was in the last letter, written almost three years later. She reached for it.

Annie's high-pitched laughter sounded on the stairs. Emma whipped the letters under the pillow with the others. By the time Annie and Catherine tumbled into the room, still laughing and talking, Emma stood by the row of hooks on the wall, holding her nightgown. "You two sure are silly tonight."

Annie pranced across the room and snatched her nightgown from its hook. "That's because there's romance in the air."

"And it causes you to act silly?" Emma couldn't help but laugh. "Silly, silly."

"Not silly. Happy." Catherine tugged off her kapp and grabbed a brush from the small stand next to the bed she shared with Annie. She let down her long, wheat-colored hair and began to brush. "Just think. A few more nights and I'll be out of this house. I'll be living in my own house with Melvin. No more cleaning other people's houses. No more Luke telling me what I can and cannot do anymore."

"Luke isn't so bad." Emma objected. The words sounded half-hearted in her ears. *Instead, Melvin will tell you what to do.* She kept that rebellious thought to herself. "He's letting Annie work at the bakery."

"When she really wants to work at the restaurant."

Emma began to brush her own hair. "After what we've been through with Josiah, I think he's right."

"Annie would never do the things Josiah did." Catherine shook her brush at Emma. "We can be around worldly people without becoming worldly. I clean Englischers' houses, but I don't try to live like they do. Look at Carl. He was among them for four years, and he's come back to be the same Plain man as before."

"I don't think—"

"There's no point in talking about it," Annie interrupted Emma. She pulled back the quilt on the bigger bed. "I'll be content with my breads and my pies and my cookies. Will you put out the lamp? My eyes won't stay open anymore, and I have so much work to do tomorrow, I want to be rested."

Emma did as her sister asked, then slipped under the covers on her narrow bunk bed. Annie was right. No sense in talking about it. But Catherine was wrong about Carl. He had been changed by his time in the city. Emma couldn't quite put her finger on it, but he was different. If he had tried to take her with him, what would she have done? Would she have said yes? The letters made life out there sound exciting. She shouldn't have begun reading them. She should return them to him.

She smacked her pillow and rolled over. The letters were a peek into a world she was better off not knowing about. She could never fill the void in his life. Nor could she be what Thomas sought in a woman like Helen. A mother of four.

Emma sniffed and closed her eyes. Better to hide from the truth. She was alone.

Chapter 36

Thomas tugged the manger from the back of his wagon. Its wooden slats looked a little worse for wear after a couple of years in storage in his barn. He would whip it into shape again once he had it in the schoolhouse. "Eli, give me a hand."

Eli scampered around to the back of the wagon. "Can I carry the backdrop?"

"It's too heavy for one person—especially one your size. Take a bale of hay and we'll come back for another load with the other men. It looks like the Schultzes are already here and that's James Doolittle's gray mare over there. And the Karbachs."

Eli grunted and groaned but managed to pull the hay bale from the wagon and start off through the knee-deep snow. Thomas smiled to himself and took the lead, the manger over his shoulder. Emma had decided on a nativity scene for this year's Christmas pageant. He liked the idea. Rebecca was in a skit about the innkeeper turning away Joseph and Mary, and Eli was in one about the magi's journey to find the baby Jesus. They had been practicing their lines and traditional Christmas hymns for days as they did their chores. The sound brightened his mood.

Inside the school, the high-pitched voices of a dozen or more women filled the room like the chatter of birds roosting in the trees in the spring. They had their sewing notions and bulky swatches of material spread over the desks. His sister Molly had both hands in a huge box sitting in the middle row. "Here it is!" She held up a long, gray robe. "Joseph's robe. Do you think it will fit Donald?"

The women laughed.

"Only if he's grown a foot this winter. John wore it two years ago, and he was the tallest boy in the class," Elizabeth pointed out. "Maybe David should be Joseph this time. He's taller."

"No, no, they've already memorized their parts." Emma took the robe from Molly. Her gaze collided with Thomas's, then bounced away. "David is one of the magi and he's very excited about that. We'll just hem the robe a bit."

Feeling like a fir tree in an apple orchard. Thomas headed for the front of the room where space had been cleared for the pageant practices. Huffing and puffing, Eli dragged the hay bale to the same spot.

"Eli, you're getting hay all over the floor." Emma bustled after them and grabbed a broom from the corner. "Let's keep the props in their place."

His face red with exertion, Eli plopped down on the bale. "Sorry, Daed needed my help."

"Indeed, I did. My apologies also, Emma."

Emma frowned and didn't meet his gaze. Trying to ignore the feeling that he'd said something wrong, Thomas pulled gloves from his hands and knelt to examine the manger.

Emma began to sweep around him, brisk, snappy swipes that blew bits of straw into the air. Thomas coughed.

"Sorry." She kept sweeping. "I can't have a mess in the school. We have to set the example for the children."

Of course. The children. "Eli, bring me my toolbox from the wagon." Thomas wiggled the slats. Too loose. The baby Jesus might fall through. "I need my hammer."

Whack. The broom collided with his ankle. "Ouch!"

"I'm sorry!" Emma's hands flew to her face. The broom slammed to the floor. "I didn't mean to hit you with the broom. I would never—"

"I'll live." Thomas dragged himself to his feet, aware of the now silent group of women watching. "I'm sure it was an accident."

"It was. Really, it was."

Their gazes locked. Thomas turned so his back faced the curious gazes of the women. "Why do I feel like I owe you the apology?" He kept his voice down, hoping the women couldn't hear. He longed for two minutes alone with Emma. "Did I do something?"

"No. You did nothing." She picked up the broom. "How was Helen's pumpkin pie?"

Aha. "I only had one piece. I was stuffed full of turkey and couldn't really appreciate it." The truth might work in his favor in this instance. "My mother's feast did me in."

Emma began sweeping again. The broom made a s*wish-swish* sound on the wooden floor. Thomas sneaked a glance over his shoulder at the women. They had gone back to their sewing, but Molly had a watchful gaze turned their direction. He stayed where he was. "I don't know how you're keeping up with Catherine's wedding in two days."

Emma didn't look up from her task. "Leah and Annie have borne the brunt of it. Both are so handy with needle and thread, and of course, Annie is a whirlwind in the kitchen. Thank goodness, it's the last wedding of the season."

"You missed a few while you were taking care of Josiah."

"'Tis a shame." She didn't sound particularly upset about the missed festivities. "But we've plenty to do between now and the New Year."

"Indeed."

Emma glanced at him and then down at the manger. The broom stopped moving. "Looks like you have plenty to do right now."

"Right. Right! Where did Eli get to, anyway?" He strode to the door, feeling like a boy who had been suspended from school. "There are a few more pieces to be brought in. I'll get the others to help."

When she didn't reply, he looked back. She had returned to her sweeping.

Her face burning, Emma propped the broom against the wall by the stove and checked to make sure it still had plenty of wood. Thomas had left the door open so they could carry in the other bales of hay and the backdrop. The cold draught of air made her shiver despite the heat from the stove. She couldn't believe she'd smacked him with the broom. It wasn't on purpose. Of course not. She shook her head.

"Why are you shaking your head? Is something wrong?"

To Emma's surprise, Helen Crouch stood next to her, her arms full of costumes. She looked from Emma to the manger and back. "It'll be fine. They just need to tighten the slats and touch up the paint a little."

"No, it's not that." Emma stuttered, flustered by the woman's knowing stare. "The men left the door open and now it's getting cold in here."

"Take these." Helen thrust the costumes into Emma's arms. "I'll shut it."

"No, no, that's fine. They're bringing in the backdrop." She ran her fingers over the rough fabric of the costume on top of the pile. Helen's oldest daughter Naomi would play Mary, Edmond served as a shepherd, and the younger girls were citizens coming to Bethlehem for the census. "These are great, Helen. You did a wonderful job."

Helen beamed. "The girls helped. My mother and my sister pitched in. We worked on them together. It was fun."

Emma touched the sleeve of Mary's robe. The costumes had been made with love. All four of Helen's children would be in the pageant. Emma enjoyed planning the plays and the songs and seeing her scholars perform, but it wasn't the same. Not the same as having her own children. "You're so blessed to have four children." It took a second to realize what she'd said. If George Crouch had lived, there would've been more children. "I'm sorry, that was a silly thing to say."

"No, I *am* blessed to have four children." Helen lifted her chin and smiled a watery smile. "I wish George could be here to see them play their small parts in the pageant. Of course we wanted more children. But it wasn't meant to be. This is God's will."

Emma could only nod, afraid to say anything more for fear of putting her foot in her mouth.

Helen held out her arms. "Do you want me to leave them here or shall we keep them at home?"

"Home for now." Emma handed them back. "They can wear them the night of the pageant, or, if it's too cold, put them on here."

The older woman nodded. She started to walk away, then stopped. When she spoke, her voice was barely a whisper. "Thomas is kind."

Startled by the change of subject, Emma groped for an adequate answer. "I'm sure he is."

"That's why he came to my house for pie." She ducked her head like a teenage girl. "He was too kind to say no."

"Helen—"

"I thought you should know." Helen waved her hand. "Don't worry about it."

She trotted away, one of the costumes trailing on the floor after her.

Chapter 37

E mma stuck another pin in Catherine's apron and smoothed the material of her skirt. Her sister looked good in the traditional blue of the wedding dress. Except that Catherine looked unusually pale today. Her silly high spirits of the previous week had disappeared. Her eyes and the tip of her nose were red, as if she'd been crying. Tears of happiness? Or was she nervous? She hadn't said two words while dressing. Emma took a step back and surveyed her work. "There. You look very nice."

Bertha, Catherine's attendant, cocked her head. She brushed a loose strand of hair from Catherine's shoulder. "Emma's right. Like a bride."

Catherine twisted her hands in front of her. "I'm glad you were able to get Minnie Stahl to take your scholars today." She sniffed and wiped at her nose with a wrinkled handkerchief. "I didn't want to...go through this...without you."

Go through it? Catherine sounded like she was about to have an operation or be sent on a long journey through the desert. "I wouldn't have missed it for anything." Emma made her tone reassuring. "My scholars can spare me for one day."

The door opened with a squeak, and Leah stuck her head in. "You should see the barn. It's full. Everyone is here. Are you ready?"

Catherine's hands fluttered to her cheeks. Bright red spots stood out in stark relief against her white skin. She picked up a small rectangular mirror and peered into it. The mirror shook in her hand. She patted her kapp. "I feel sick." She dropped the mirror on the bed. "I'm not ready. I'm not ready!"

The panic in her voice sent a wave of uncertainty through Emma. It sounded so much like the hysteria that day behind the chicken coop. She exchanged a glance with Bertha, who raised her eyebrows, but said nothing. Emma gave Catherine a quick hug. "It's just pre-wedding jitters. You'll be fine. Melvin is waiting for you."

"No. I can't. I can't. I've changed my mind." Catherine plopped onto the bed and put her face in her hands. "Don't make me go out there."

"Get up right now." Leah stormed into the room. She yanked on Catherine's arm. "You'll not do this. You've made a commitment to that young man. His family is out there. Our family is waiting. People have traveled here from Ohio, from Pennsylvania. The bishop is out there. The whole community expects a wedding today, and you're going to give it to them."

Catherine teetered, then sank to the floor. "I'm so sorry. I've done something horrible. I should never have said yes. I thought I could do it, but I can't."

Leah put both hands on her hips. "Emma, get Luke."

Emma hesitated. She didn't want to leave her sister at Leah's mercy. If Catherine had doubts, surely it was better to halt the wedding now rather than suffer a lifetime of marriage to the wrong man. "Catherine, what is it? Is it second thoughts about Melvin? Or are you sick?"

"Melvin's a nice man." Her hands over her face muffled the words. "He deserves someone who loves him."

"And you deserve the same." Emma knelt and rubbed Catherine's shoulder. "Are you saying you don't love him?"

"Not enough to marry him." Catherine raised her tear-stained face. "I thought I could do it, but I can't. I wanted a new start. I wanted...my own children to occupy me instead of cleaning up after other people's children. But it won't work, not with Melvin."

"It's just cold feet." Leah insisted. "Emma, get Luke. Now!"

Emma rose. "Leah, please—"

"It's for Luke to decide."

Emma squeezed Catherine's shoulder one last time, grabbed her coat, and scurried out to the barn. It had been transformed into its prayer meeting set-up. They'd spent hours cleaning the floor, rearranging the farm equipment, and setting up the benches. The men were already gathered on their side and the women on the other, quietly chatting. She swallowed against the lump in her throat. How could Catherine do this? After everything the family had been through. Why didn't she say something sooner?

It didn't matter. Her sister couldn't marry someone to escape from what her life had become since Daed and Mudder's accident. Greeting several women, she slipped through the aisles until she saw Luke talking with a knot of men near the front row of benches. One of them was Bishop Kelp.

She took a deep breath and smoothed her skirt with damp palms. She waved her hand, trying to get her brother's attention. It took several seconds, but finally Luke's gaze traveled in her direction. He said something to the bishop, then strode toward her.

"Why are you interrupting a conversation with the bishop?"

The barely tapped down anger stung Emma. She wouldn't interrupt if it weren't an emergency. Luke knew that. She leaned closer to her brother. "Leah needs you."

A look of alarm spread across his face. "The baby? Is it time for the baby?"

"No! No, it's…" She glanced at Helen Crouch's father and Bishop Kelp, still standing a few feet away. They had looks of mild curiosity on their faces. She leaned closer to Luke. "Please, just come."

Luke nodded at the men and proceeded toward the door. Once they were outside he turned to Emma. "What is this about?"

"It's Catherine. She—" Emma waited for the Hersberger family to pass. "She's changed her mind."

A look of fury so intense it caused Emma to take a step back infused Luke's face. He whirled and marched toward the house.

"Luke, wait!" Emma trotted after him, hampered by her long skirt and the drifts of snow. Her breath came in quick, white puffs. "She's confused. With everything that has happened—"

Luke didn't slow until he had his hand on the door. "She'll not shame this family. These people have been very good to us. They've taken care of us, supported us. Melvin Dodd's family helped with Josiah's hospital bills. Before that, they helped rebuild the barn."

"They don't expect Catherine to marry their son in exchange for their good will." Emma couldn't believe she had the courage to argue. "They'll want him to be happy."

Luke's face darkened. "Neither do they expect to be embarrassed and shamed in front of the entire community."

He stalked into the house, forcing Emma to run after him. He didn't even pause to knock at Catherine's door. He jerked it open and barged in. Catherine still sat hunched on the floor. Bertha crouched at her side, trying to comfort her friend. Leah simply glowered over them. She started talking immediately. "The silly girl says she can't marry him."

"She's not silly." Emma rushed to defend her sister. "She's not herself—"

"You hush." Luke's fierce tone silenced Emma. He turned to Catherine. "You will not act like this. You made a commitment when the bans were announced at the prayer service. You will honor that commitment."

Catherine's mouth opened and closed. Her gaze circled the room. She began to wail. "I want Mudder. I want Mudder." Her hands tore at her kapp. She ripped it off and threw it to the floor. "I need my mudder."

The anguish in those words pierced the carefully knitted, almost healed wounds on Emma's own heart. She sank to the floor and gathered her sister in her arms. Together they rocked back and forth, sobbing. After a few seconds, Emma managed to look up. "Luke, please, please!"

His face like a stone, only his lips moved. "I'll speak to the bishop. He'll have the final word."

He stalked from the room, Leah right behind him. Catherine went limp in Emma's arms. Her ragged breathing filled the room. Emma held on tighter. Her sister needed help. None would come from Luke and Leah. "Bertha, get Aenti Louise. She'll know what to do. And Annie. Catherine needs her sisters."

Her face wet with tears, Bertha rushed from the room, leaving Emma alone with Catherine. "It's all right. It'll be all right."

The familiar words echoed in the room, mocking her. How many times had she said them before? Yet, here they were again.

Chapter 38

Emma tried to flatten herself against the wall. She wanted to make herself small so the men wouldn't notice she stood near the living room door. They congregated, silent, waiting, their faces somber. She let her gaze drop to the floor. She couldn't bear the look on Melvin Dodd's whiskerless face. Embarrassment, shame, and anger mingled with hurt.

"I want to see her." Melvin folded his skinny arms against his Sunday suit. "I want to talk to Catherine myself."

Luke started to speak. Bishop Kelp held up a hand. "No. You have every right to wish to confront her directly, but she's not well. She's resting in her room. When she has come to her senses, I'll meet with you both."

Come to her senses. Emma bit her lower lip to keep from speaking. Luke's warning gaze pinned her to the wall. He jerked his head toward the door. She turned and slipped from the room. Her brother was right. Her time would be better spent checking on her sister. She moved into the hallway, intent on getting up the stairs without speaking to anyone.

"Emma!"

One hand on the banister, she turned at the soft, high voice calling her name. Miriam rushed toward her, her hands fluttering in the air.

"Is it true? Josiah says the wedding is off. Everyone is standing around out there, waiting, wondering."

Josiah and Miriam had been talking. Emma only had a split second to savor that thought. She had no idea the two were on speaking terms. It was a small wonder in the midst of so much turmoil. Still, Josiah shouldn't have said anything about Catherine and Melvin. "The bishop will come out in a minute to talk to everyone."

"Then it's true." Miriam's brown eyes widened. Her hand flew to her mouth. She let it drop. "Is Catherine sick? Did something come between them? What happened?"

Emma sat down on the stairs, her legs suddenly too weak to hold her. Miriam squeezed in next to her. "I'm sorry. It's not my place to ask about this. I'll wait for the bishop."

"It's all right." Hot tears burned Emma's eyes. She willed them not to fall. "I'm sad for her and for Melvin." She patted Miriam's arm. "And for you. I told Bertha to make sure she seated you and Josiah together."

Miriam flushed. "Don't worry about me. Josiah said he'd see me at the singing later this week."

"So you're talking."

"He hasn't shone a flashlight in my window yet, but yes, we're talking."

A step forward for Josiah. He really did mean to reclaim his place in the community. Emma would be relieved if it weren't for this new setback with Catherine. They couldn't seem to all get on the path together in that neat, organized pattern that her parents had always maintained. "Good, that's good. I'm happy for you."

The hallway filled with Melvin's family. They clustered around him, silent, their faces grim. Melvin's gaze crossed with Emma's. She opened her mouth to say she was sorry, but he looked away. The group marched through the door without a word.

"Poor Melvin."

They spoke at the same time.

Miriam's hand squeezed Emma's. "Poor Catherine."

Emma stood. "I have to go to her."

Miriam scooted from the step. "I'd better get back to the barn. My parents will be looking for me."

Emma trudged up the stairs, wishing her parents were out there looking for her. Cold wrapped itself around her heart like a northern wind on a January day. *See God, this is why it's so hard to forgive. Because the consequences of that farmer's actions go on and on. They never stop. Seven months now and we're still in pain. Please, God, make the pain go away. Heal our hearts.*

She peeked through the door to her bedroom. Aenti Louise sat on the bed, her short legs sticking straight out. She had Catherine's head on her lap and she stroked her hair. Catherine seemed to be asleep. Aenti Louise put a finger to her lips.

"Can I do anything?" Emma whispered.

"Pray."

Emma nodded. As she wandered aimlessly through the house, she lifted Catherine and Melvin up to the Lord. She lifted her family up, praying for continued healing. After a few minutes, she sighed and headed toward the kitchen. She didn't want to be in the barn when the bishop made his announcement. She didn't want to see the shocked faces of her neighbors, friends, and family. The aroma of goulash and roast cooking that had been so tantalizing earlier made her put her hand to her mouth as nausea swept over her.

Someone should make sure the food didn't burn. Emma forced herself toward the kitchen door. The sound of pots and pans clanging together told her someone had beat her to the task. She found Annie scrubbing a pot so hard the washrag flew from her hand and landed on the floor.

Emma stooped and picked it up. "Careful, you'll rub a hole in that pot."

Annie barely looked up. "I knew she never recovered from seeing the accident. I knew it and I didn't say anything." She plunged the pot into the rinse water, making a tiny tidal wave in the tub. "She pretended to be so happy, but she came home from her outings with Melvin and cried herself to sleep. I should've said something."

"Catherine chose her path, and there's nothing you could've done to change that." Emma pulled the pot out and let it drip for a moment before laying it on the drain. "She fooled us. She fooled herself into believing she was healed. We all share in the blame for not getting her help."

"What do you think Luke will do now?"

Emma cringed at the possibilities. "I don't know. He's very angry."

"No one will have her now." Sadness bloomed in Annie's voice as she bent over a dirty skillet. "Not with the shame she's brought on herself."

"Any man would be afraid of having her change her mind again."

Annie dropped the skillet in the water and leaned against the tub for a second. She glanced around the room. "What will we do with all the food?"

"Our guests came here expecting to be fed. We'll feed them, I reckon."

"I hope so, or a lot of food will go bad." Annie tucked a wisp of runaway hair under her kapp with wrinkled, hot water-reddened fingers. "There's no way all this will fit into that little gas refrigerator."

Emma's stomach rocked at the thought of eating. "What they don't eat, we send home with them."

Leah marched into the kitchen, her face a dark scowl. "You'd best get out to the barn now. The bishop is fixing to start the service."

"But there's no wedding—"

"No, but everyone has gathered for a service. Some have come a long way. These are unusual circumstances, so the bishop has asked Deacon Pierce to speak a few words about the commitment of marriage and the sin of breaking that commitment."

"Did he say what he'll do about Catherine?" Annie laid the washrag on the edge of the tub. "Is she…is she to be punished?"

"I don't remember this ever happening before." Leah rubbed glassy eyes with both hands. "Your brother is beside himself."

"How can he be upset with Catherine, instead of worried about her?" Emma resisted the urge to throw the towel at her sister-in-law. This wasn't Leah's fault. "She's in trouble. She's not right in her head."

Leah dropped her hands. "Your brother is no fool. Don't you think he knows that?" Her voice faltered. "He's heartbroken. That's why he's so angry."

Emma clutched the dishtowel to her chest. She wanted to lift it to her face and hide behind it. Luke was heartbroken. He might be the head of this house now, but he was still her brother. "I'm sorry, Leah," she whispered. "What will he do?"

"Whatever the bishop tells him to do." Leah gripped the back of a chair. She lowered her head and inhaled. "We must go now."

"Are you all right?"

Leah raised her head. "I'm fine. Go."

Her heart a stone in her chest, Emma followed Annie and Leah from the house to the barn. Everyone turned their direction when they entered. Emma kept her head down, but she felt the gazes on her like the barbed sting of dozens of bees piercing the tender skin on the back of her neck. She slid onto the bench next to her cousins and Aunt Sophie.

"Where's Catherine?" Aunt Sophie whispered. "Is she all right?"

Leah raised a finger to her lips. "Bishop Kelp will explain."

Aunt Sophie gave Emma a sad look of commiseration and squeezed her hand. Swallowing hard, Emma squeezed back. She dared to look around. All gazes were forward. She closed her eyes for a second. *God, help Catherine. Help us all.*

Chapter 39

E mma pushed through the glass-plated double doors at Plank's Pies and Pastry Shop. A bell dinged, a cheery welcoming sound after the dreary, sunless sky and icy wind outside. A wave of warm air enveloped her. She inhaled and her mouth watered at the aroma of baking cookies. The spicy scent hinted at gingersnaps. A knot of customers clustered in front of the display cases that held a dozen kinds of pie, along with cakes, and an array of freshly baked breads that would tempt even the strictest dieting Englischer. The Englisch women always seemed to talk about dieting. Even when they were skin and bone. Even when they were buying two dozen chocolate chip cookies or a pound cake.

Refusing to let her gaze linger on the goodies, Emma marched past them. One of the advantages of having a sister who loved to bake was that the items that weren't too expensive to make at home were all available by simply asking. Her trip to the bakery involved a different mission. She needed to talk to Annie about Catherine. Their sister had shut down so completely she barely spoke. She never smiled, let alone laughed. They had to do something. They had to convince Luke to get her help instead of alternating between ignoring the problem and being angry about Catherine's behavior.

"Emma. Emma, dear!"

The sound of her name being called in a tinkling, high-pitched voice jolted her from her reverie. Mrs. Jenson, her face twisted in a smirk that surely intended to pass as a smile, rushed toward Emma, her daughter and another lady in tow. "Hello, dear, I simply had to stop you. How is poor Catherine?"

The lady made it sound like Catherine had a terminal disease and might die any second. Emma opened her mouth, then shut it. Catherine had left the house that morning to go to the Jensons to clean, as she always did on Saturdays. Twice a week, Tuesdays and Saturdays. At least that's where she said she was going when Luke questioned her at the breakfast table. Was Mrs. Jenson fishing for gossip? She would get none from Emma.

"My sister is well." She carefully let the sentence dangle.

"Well? Really? That's good, then maybe she'll return to her housecleaning duties." Mrs. Jenson pursed her thin lips and wrinkled her nose as if she'd just smelled a piece of spoiled meat. Her penciled eyebrows arched. "We're trying to make allowances for her erratic behavior. After all, she's been through so much."

"Erratic—"

"You know, since she called off the wedding, she hasn't been coming regularly. She says she's sick." Mrs. Jenson patted Emma's shoulder with a hand weighted down by three enormous, sparkling rings. "We do a lot of entertaining, and I need the floors to be absolutely spotless, you know?"

Sick? If Catherine wasn't going to the Jensons's house, where did she go when she left home? Emma worked to keep the worry off her face. "I'm sorry if you've been inconvenienced in any way."

"Oh, don't let it worry you, dear." Mrs. Jenson tossed shiny blonde curls—they'd been brown the last time Emma saw her—over her shoulder. "I can always find someone else if she doesn't get better."

"I'm sure she—"

"Mrs. Jenson, your packages are ready," Annie broke in. The sharp jerk of her head and narrowed eyes sent a message loud and clear to Emma. *Hush up.* "That will be fourteen thirty-two with tax."

"My, my, that's a lot for cookies and bread, but they're worth every penny." Mrs. Jenson's sugary sweet tone gave Emma a toothache. The lady sashayed—there was no other word for it—on her high heels back to the counter. "My Gerald just can't live without those peanut butter macadamia nut cookies, and the French bread will be lovely with the spaghetti this evening."

Annie nodded and smiled. Emma didn't know how she did it. Her sister's expression never wavered. Emma would have been tempted to suggest Mr. Jenson would like cookies baked by his wife much more, and her efforts would save him a few hours of hard labor to earn money wasted on buying them at the bakery. Of course, if everyone did that it would put Sadie Plank's bakery out of business, and Annie would be out of a job. Emma came around to her sister's way of thinking and plastered a smile on her face. "Enjoy your baked goods."

Mrs. Jenson shooed her daughter and friend out the door. As soon as the bell dinged, Emma whirled and slapped her hands on the glass countertop. "What is she talking about? Where did Catherine go this morning, if not to clean that lady's house?"

Annie peeled Emma's fingers from the glass. She grabbed a rag and wiped off the counter. "Fingerprints, schweschder!"

Who could think of fingerprints at a time like this? Annie was stalling. Emma put her hands on her hips. "What? Tell me."

Before Annie could answer, Sadie trudged through the door that led from the backroom, carrying a twenty-five-pound bag of flour over her shoulders. "Emma, so nice of you to drop by. How are you?" She dumped the bag next to Annie's prep area and dusted her hands off. "Have a cookie. You look much too thin."

She grabbed a cookie from the cooling rack and held it out. Emma took it. When Sadie made no move to continue with her work, Emma dutifully took a bite and chewed. The warm chocolate chip cookie melted in her mouth.

"Delicious." Emma caught Annie's grin. Sadie loved for people to praise her baking. Even when it was Annie who'd done the baking. "The best I've tasted in a while."

"*Gut. Gut.*" Sadie surveyed the supplies. "I'll bring up more sugar, too. Oh, and David will come in at noon to spell you for lunch, Annie. Don't let him hold you up with his endless patter about this and that and nothing."

Sadie's snippy tone notwithstanding, Emma knew the woman doted on her son. His cancer was still in remission, but she never stopped worrying about it. He wasn't well enough to work at the family farm yet, so he helped at the bakery. Instead of answering, Annie busied herself with a huge measuring cup. Sadie didn't seem to notice. She kept a running commentary going about David's propensity to chatter until she disappeared into the backroom.

Emma studied her sister's bent head. "Annie, what's going on? Your face is the color of pickled beets."

"Hmmm? Nothing. It's just hot in here with the ovens on."

"Annie! Why did the mention of David's name make you look like you just came in from working in the fields in the hot sun all day?"

"What are you talking about?" Annie made a big show of cutting butter into flour, an innocent expression anchored on her face. "I'm just baking."

"You like David." Emma tried the idea on for size. David was one of Josiah's closest friends. They'd all gone to school together, played together, laughed together. He was a year older than Annie, but his cancer had kept him from his rumspringa and courting. He was in remission, but for how long? "Has he said anything to you? Is he interested?"

"Don't be silly." Annie stirred so hard, she tossed plumes of flour about that hung in the air, and then landed on her hands and sleeves in a powdery dust. "Besides, we're talking about Catherine, not me."

"Right. What about Catherine?" Emma tucked her concerns away for the time being. Catherine's situation took precedence at the moment. Emma felt as if she kept pouring buckets of water on a grass fire only to have another one pop up a few feet away. "What happened?"

"You can't tell Luke." A scared look scampered across Annie's face. "Promise me."

"Tell Luke what?" Emma couldn't make any promises, not without knowing first. Annie knew that. "What is Catherine doing?"

"I'm not sure, but I saw her coming out of Doctor Miller's office yesterday." Annie handed Emma another cookie—this one oatmeal raisin—then selected one for herself. "When I waved at her, she pretended not to see me. I was late opening the bakery so I didn't have time to go after her."

Emma chewed and thought for a moment. "Did you ask her about it last night?"

"Of course I did." Annie laid her cookie on the counter without taking a bite and brushed flour from her dress. "She said she was picking up a prescription for Mrs. Calloway."

"So she picked up a prescription. That makes sense."

"Why did she pretend she didn't see me, then?" Annie's scrunched-up eyebrows and wrinkled nose gave her an almost comical look. "And why would Mrs. Calloway send her cleaning girl to pick up a prescription? She has a car. She drives. She always comes to town while Catherine cleans. It takes much longer for Catherine to do errands in a buggy."

The door dinged and another gaggle of customers swarmed in. The bakery always did well on Saturday mornings when many of the Englischers did their shopping. Emma stepped out of the way and concentrated on the last bite of her cookie. Why indeed? What was Catherine doing at Doctor Miller's that she didn't want Annie to know about?

The cookie turned to sand in Emma's mouth. If it involved Doctor Miller, it couldn't be anything good. "I'll see you at home," she called to her sister, who waved and went back to a lady trying to decide between Deitsch chocolate and carrot cake.

Emma pushed through the door and stood on the sidewalk, torn over what to do next. Catherine was eighteen, legally an adult. Doctor Miller would never talk to her about her sister's medical care. Maybe she should try to find Catherine. Where would she hide all day? Maybe she had returned home by now. Resolute, Emma turned and ran smack into a woman carrying two large paper bags of groceries that obscured her face. A head of lettuce hit the ground and rolled. Canned goods scattered.

"I'm so sorry, I should've been looking where I was going." Emma knelt to gather up oranges escaping in all directions. "I'm really sorry."

"It's all right. Don't worry about it, honey." Emma looked up at the high voice she'd heard only once before. Mr. Cramer's wife. She knelt next to Emma, scooped up the head of lettuce, and stuffed it back in the bag. Her eyes were puffy and red behind wire rimmed glasses that made them look huge. "I'm sure you have a lot on your mind."

Mrs. Cramer looked like the one with a lot on her mind. "Are you all right?" Emma handed her the oranges. "You look...upset."

The lady frowned. She grabbed a can of peas and popped it in the bag and then heaved herself to her feet. "I'm fine. It's my husband I'm worried about."

Emma stood as well. "Something's wrong with Mr. Cramer?" He was such a big, strapping man. He looked the picture of health—something that Emma couldn't help but resent. "I'm sorry to hear that."

"It's not physical, mind you." Mrs. Cramer leaned toward Emma, her tone dropping to a whisper. "His heart is broken over what he's done to you poor things. He feels a terrible guilt for having taken your parents from you. It breaks my heart to see him suffer so."

Mr. Cramer suffered from a broken heart. Just like Catherine.

Emma fought back tears. She'd been so focused on her own pain and the suffering of her family, she'd been blind to what this tragedy could do to the one who caused it. "Is there any way we can help?"

"No, no, you've done plenty by being so forgiving." Mrs. Cramer's smile didn't reach her eyes. She hoisted the grocery bags into her arms with a grunt and straightened. "He just has to learn to forgive himself."

He couldn't forgive himself. Emma understood that feeling, but she had her hands full with Catherine's problems and school. How could she help the man who killed her parents?

"Take care now, dear." Her shoulders slumped, Mrs. Cramer started to walk away. "Tell your brother my husband meant every word of what he said when he came by the house the day of the funeral," she called over her shoulder. "He wants to help with the farm work. Just name the time, and he'll be there."

Emma hung her head in shame. She could barely get the words out. "Yes, ma'am."

The words she needed to say stayed buried in her throat. *I forgive him.*

Chapter 40

Aware of the avid gazes of her entire family, Emma forced a smile as she held out the ceramic serving bowl filled with slips of paper to Catherine. Her sister pulled her shawl tighter around her thin arms. She hesitated, her gaze stuck somewhere over Emma's shoulder. Despite the warmth of the fire and the pungent aroma of the evergreen garlands on the mantel, Emma still felt the chill brought on by the absence of two people during this holiday season.

Mudder loved Christmas. She made every holiday special with her girlish enthusiasm for making homemade cards to send to family who'd moved away and their Englisch friends, cooking sweets, and making small gifts for each of her children. Emma now stood in her place and the shoes seemed far too big to fill.

"Pick one." Trying to catch Catherine's gaze, Emma made her tone encouraging. "'Tis the season of giving."

Her pale face averted, Catherine stuck trembling fingers in the bowl and pulled out a name. She managed to avoid eye contact. She'd also refused to talk to Emma about where she'd gone on Saturday when she was supposed to be cleaning house. When Emma confronted her about it, she simply walked away. She dropped the paper in her lap without looking at the name and turned to stare out the living room window at the snow-covered fields.

Emma moved on to Josiah. She refused to let tension with her sister spoil this Christmas tradition. She hadn't told Luke about her conversation with Mrs. Jenson. If things didn't improve, she would go to him after Christmas. They needed the spirit of Christmas to pick them up and carry them through the end of this year. A new year would bring a new beginning. Catherine would get better. Emma forced herself to smile at Josiah. "Pick your name. Remember, we're making our gifts this year. Nothing store bought." Money was too tight for store bought. Made with love represented the holiday better anyway. "Everyone will have so much fun making presents."

"But I wanted gel pens and a coloring book." Lillie pouted from her seat on the rug by the fireplace. "Or a tea set for my dolly."

"And I wanted skates." Mary chimed in. "I'm old enough to skate on the pond all by myself now."

Emma doubted that, but she understood the girls' disappointment. Gifts were rare in Plain households. Birthdays and Christmas. This year there was no money to be had for store bought, but that just meant the gifts they would receive from each other would be much more special. "Count your blessings." She fixed them with a stern stare. "You have brothers and sisters who are good at making things. Sewing. Carpentry. Drawing. Painting. I think you'll have a nice surprise on Christmas morning."

"You can have my old skates." Mark sat cross-legged on the throw-rug next to Lillie. He propped his hands under his chin, looking very pleased with himself. Emma wanted to laugh. Being he was ten and a boy, his feet were twice as big as his little sister's. "My feet are too big for them. You'll have to share them with Lillie."

"And I have lots of gel pens you can use," William piped up. Luke's boys liked to tag along after their young uncle and do whatever he did. Even when it came to being generous with their pesky girl aunts. "Aenti Louise gave them to me for my birthday."

Appeased, Lillie grinned and stuck her hand in the bowl. After she looked at the name she'd drawn, she clapped her hands and popped up on her feet. "I got—"

Emma held up a hand. "No, no! Don't tell. It's a secret."

"I forgot." Lillie sank back on the rug. "Can I tell Mary?"

Emma pretended to consider. "That's no fun. The idea is for it to be a secret from everyone until Christmas day." She turned to Mark. "And now you."

He wrinkled his freckled nose and selected his slip. "I guess there's no way to make a rifle at home."

Emma patted his arm. At ten, he was old enough to hunt with his older brothers and cousins. "Fortunately, we have enough of those around here to share."

"That's right." Josiah squatted next to his little brother and elbowed him. "It's not too late to hunt turkey or deer. If you want, you can go with me, Mark."

Mark ducked his head, obviously pleased. Emma loved the generous feelings the Christmas season brought out in everyone. She offered the bowl to Annie. "Now you."

Annie was staring at Catherine. Emma followed her gaze. Catherine had rolled her piece of paper into a tiny tube. She seemed to be contemplating something far, far away. "Are you all right, Catherine?"

Catherine jumped at the sound of her name. "I have to make a kneeling confession in front of the entire community." She stood. "I have to admit to the sin of lying to Melvin about loving him and ask to be forgiven. I don't think I'll ever be all right."

Luke made a *humph* sound deep in his throat. "The idea of confession is to be forgiven and then move on. The sin is not only forgiven, but forgotten."

"Melvin won't forget. He'll try very hard to forgive, but it'll be impossible for him to forget." Catherine smoothed her apron with hands. "Likewise with his sisters and brothers and parents. They're right not to forget."

Her face listless, she shuffled from the room. Emma started to go after her. Luke's voice stopped her. "No, Emma. Drawing names for Christmas gifts is a family tradition. She'll not ruin that with her self-pity and hysteria."

Hysteria. Emma swallowed a retort. Catherine didn't eat. She barely slept. Her behavior posed no threat of hysteria. It seemed that all the emotion and energy had drained from her, leaving a shell of a person with no life left. Emma held the bowl out to Luke. "Your turn, then."

Luke's expression said he knew what she was thinking and ignoring it. His fingers rummaged through the remaining slips. He took a quick look at the one he drew. His lips curved into a small smile. Whose name had he drawn? If not Leah, one of his boys. They were the only ones who made him smile anymore.

Emma waited until everyone else drew their names and then extracted the remaining scrap of paper. Leah. So Luke hadn't drawn her name. Emma swallowed the desire to sigh. She must tame the discontent that bucked inside her like a horse that needed to be broken. The season of giving demanded a generous spirit. She should be happy to give to her sister-in-law. She would sew a stack of cloth diapers for her. There was plenty of birdseye diaper material left in Mudder's chest. If there was time, she could make Leah a new cape. Something for her, something for the baby, it was really a double-draw.

"That's it. Everyone has their name. Have fun with your gifts." Luke slapped his hands on his knees and then stood. "Work to be done. Off to school, the rest of you."

The children raced up the stairs for their coats. Annie swept from the room, murmuring something about mopping floors. Emma gathered up her satchel and her lunchbox. "Have you thought about what you'll call the baby?"

Luke shrugged on his heavy coat. "We've talked a bit, but nothing for sure."

"Do you want a girl?" She hadn't ever thought to ask before. As the birth of the baby grew closer, she began to think less of the extra work of another child whom she would not call daughter and more of the joy of holding a newborn. "Since you have two boys already?"

"We'll take whatever God gives us." He stomped toward the backdoor. "But boys are more help in the fields."

Emma sneaked a glance at Leah. What did her sister-in-law think of Luke's attitude?

Leah tilted her head, her forehead wrinkled. "He's right." She winced and rubbed her belly. "I should start the bread dough. Annie and I have to do the mopping and the laundry Catherine didn't get done last week."

Maybe Luke was right, but women did all the cooking, cleaning, and sewing so that boys could help in the field. Somehow the thought gave Emma comfort. Each had their jobs, their roles, their places. There was security in that. "When I get home tonight, I'll help with whatever doesn't get done today."

"Catherine should do it." Leah's words floated on the air as she lumbered toward the kitchen. "You're not helping her by coddling her."

"She works hard cleaning houses all week." Leah couldn't know that Catherine had been missing days of work. Not until Emma figured out what she was really doing. "She needs a little time to rest and catch up."

She didn't hear Leah's response. Just as well. She didn't want to argue. They wouldn't agree on Catherine or anything else.

"Emma, Melvin Dodd is on the porch!" Annie's excited screech could surely be heard on that very porch. She pulled down the green shade that covered the window. "What do you think he wants?"

More drama. Too much for so early in the day. "If you open the door, I'm sure he'll tell us."

Annie did as instructed. Melvin ducked past her without waiting for an invitation to enter. "I'm here to see Catherine."

He looked as ill at ease as Emma felt. She clutched her satchel, unsure what to say. Would Catherine want to see him? Should she? "I'm not sure, I mean, I don't think..." Her face burned with embarrassment. "Are you sure..."

He removed his hat and rolled the brim in his hands. "I have to talk to her before the Sunday service. Please."

"Didn't the bishop tell you that Catherine will make her apologies at the service next Sunday?"

"I don't want her apologies." His lips quivered. His jaw clenched and he sucked in air through his nose. "I want to talk to her. I haven't been allowed to tell her how I feel. If I could just talk to her for a few minutes, I know I could...change...her mind."

Emma fought the desire to pat his shoulder. He looked so young and so hurt. He really cared for Catherine. Emma knew how it felt to be rejected so publicly. Carl hadn't abandoned her on their wedding day, but his leaving set many tongues to wagging about what she might have done to cause him to flee.

She sank into the rocking chair, her satchel in her lap. "Catherine is very confused right now. She's not in her right mind. The accident affected her."

"I know. We talked about it a lot. The buggy rides helped her. I drove and she talked and I listened. She was getting better." Melvin seemed to be trying to convince himself as well as Emma. "This is a little setback, but it's not over. She doesn't need to confess. We can still get married."

The anguish in his voice made pain vibrate inside Emma like a lightning rod that quivered and hummed, setting waves rippling through her body in a sickening onslaught. It sounded so familiar. Felt so familiar. "I'm sorry, Melvin, but Catherine's sick. She can't marry you."

"Why can't I talk to her?"

"You can."

Startled, Emma looked up. Catherine slipped down the stairs, the tread of her feet—bare in the middle of winter—so light, she didn't make a sound. "Catherine, I don't think you—"

"He deserves an explanation, face-to-face."

Melvin rose, his hat in his hands. "Catherine, you look...they said you were ill, but I didn't realize...have you seen a doctor?"

"I'm better." Her face had an odd, almost serene, look on it. "It's a relief to be able to look you in the eye and say this."

She paused at the bottom of the stairs. "I'm sorry, Melvin, so sorry." Her face crumpled for a second, then smoothed. "You deserve a wife who loves you."

Emma whipped from the chair and backed toward the kitchen. "I should go." Should she leave them alone? The bishop hadn't specifically said they couldn't speak before the confession. "Catherine, will you be all right?"

"I'm fine." She tottered toward the center of the room. "Sit down, Melvin."

Emma slipped away. She couldn't be late for school and she didn't want to be there when Melvin lost his last bit of hope.

Chapter 41

Emma rolled over for the fourth time. She'd never had trouble sleeping before. Loneliness lay on her like a heavy, suffocating blanket. She sat up. The regular pattern of her sisters' breathing assured her both were asleep. Annie had nodded off the second her head hit the pillow. Catherine had tossed and turned a good deal longer. Now and then, she whimpered and sighed, but her eyes remained closed.

Despite all her resolve to leave the past in the past and be happy with her lot, Emma had to know. Catherine's public rejection of Melvin had brought everything back to the surface. How could people say they loved you one minute, and run away the next? Why was it so important to Carl that she read his letters? What difference would they make?

She had to know or she would never be able to move beyond it. Emma tugged her stash of letters from under her pillow and took the lantern into the hallway where she paused to light it. The shadows of the flames made strange, jittery shapes on the wall. Jumpy like her. Shivering, she sat down on the top step and undid the ribbon with clumsy fingers. She'd waited long enough, ignored it long enough. She had to know.

She studied the dates on the envelopes again. Three years. For three and a half years, Carl hadn't written a word. Or if he had, he'd chosen not to give her those letters. What made him finally decide to write again? Only months before he returned to Bliss Creek, he'd written to her. Then he'd decided to come home. She slipped the last letter from its envelope and smoothed open the page. Carl's familiar spidery cursive filled it.

> *Dear Emma,*
>
> *I've thought about writing you again so many times. But I couldn't. I knew it wouldn't be right. You must wonder what happened to me. I didn't fall off the face of the earth. I didn't perish in the fiery flames of hell. God didn't strike me down with a bolt of lightning from a stormy sky. No. You see, God has a sense of humor. I met someone. At the church I told you about. Someone special.*

Nausea in the pit of her stomach forced Emma to stop reading. She dropped the pages in her lap. Her palms were damp, and her face felt hot. She sucked in air and tried to breathe. She shouldn't be reading someone's private thoughts like this. A man's private thoughts at that.

Carl should never have given her these letters. He'd met someone out there in the world. Someone he liked enough to stay out there. But he had come back after four years. Something happened. Something big enough to make him want to come home. Despite the ache in her throat and the roiling of her stomach, Emma picked up the letter. She had to know what happened to make him come home.

> *Her name is Karen Johnson. She's a school teacher, like you. Funny, huh? I told you God has a sense of humor. You probably don't want to hear all the details, but the thing is, it's important. Because of her, I understand love now. At least, I think I do. I understand my limitations. I understand how Plain I really am. I thought I could enter this world and start working, going to school, listening to music, watching TV, driving, and that would make me like them. I could become one of them.*
>
> *It doesn't work that way. I'm not one of them. I'm one of you. I dated Karen for over a year. She taught me to dance.*

*She took me to see old movies. She cooked for me. She taught
me to barbecue steaks on a grill and make homemade French
fries. We had fun.*

Emma struggled to swallow the burgeoning lump in her throat.
She doubled over and rocked against the pain. In her mind's eye, she
could see it. Carl in blue jeans and a white T-shirt, driving a fancy
automobile with a woman named Karen in the passenger seat. Emma
couldn't know what she looked like, but she would wear jeans, too,
and sneakers, and have hair with curls that bounced on her shoulders.
Maybe she liked to wear rings on her fingers and hoops on her ears.
And lipstick. Surely, she made her lips red.

Emma crumpled up the letter and tried to stuff it in the envelope.
It wouldn't go. The edge of the paper sliced her finger in a tiny paper
cut. She sniffed hard and wiped at the unwelcome tears. There was no
reason for this to hurt her now. She'd gotten over this abandonment
long ago. What good reason could Carl have for giving her these
letters? What point could he be making? He and this Karen had dated
for a year. That accounted for only a third of the time in which he had
ceased to write letters.

Emma watched the shadows of her lantern's flame dance on the
wall. She tugged her robe tighter around her shoulders. Determined,
she smoothed the paper.

*I fell in love. I don't say this to hurt you, Emma. I want
you to understand what happened. We spent all our free time
together. I met her family. Her father is a doctor, her mother a
homemaker. Karen has a brother who is in the military, serving overseas. Yes, it's a different world, but one I thought I
wanted to be a part of. After a year, we got married.*

Emma gasped. For a second, it seemed too dark to see the words.
They blurred on the page. Yet pain seared each word on her heart
and mind. Her fingers tightened on the paper. Her gaze raced ahead,
wanting to read, wanting to know, yet not believing.

I got carried away with the feelings and so I did it. I asked her to marry me. She said yes. The wedding was on a June day. Yes, a summer day. No waiting until the harvest is in and getting married when everyone else does. It was a special day. I felt happy. As happy as I could ever remember being. I thought I had finally become who I was supposed to be. But I was just fooling myself. I wish I could talk to you. You're so smart and wise, teacher. You could tell me what to do.

Marrying an Englischer was a terrible mistake. It was a mistake to think I could forget my other life. I asked Karen to come back to Bliss Creek with me, but she said that's no life for her. Or our baby.

Yes, there will be a baby in the fall. I can't find it in me to be happy. A child who will be raised in this world of fast food and video games. A baby who might grow up to serve in the military. Karen doesn't understand. I don't know what to do. I can't stay and I can't go. If only I could talk to you.

I'm coming home. I know you'll understand.

With all my heart,
Carl

Tears hot on her cheeks, Emma crumpled the letter and let it drop into her lap. He had a child. She fought to still her hands enough to smooth the paper, fold it, and stuff it back in its envelope. She couldn't seem to swallow the knot in her throat. She blotted at the tears with her sleeve.

Carl had a baby, one he'd never seen. While he was here, chopping wood, harvesting wheat, hunting, and trying to court Emma, his wife was having a baby. The baby Emma so badly wanted. What kind of man did that? Wooed one woman while leaving another alone to have his baby?

A man who ran away from his responsibilities.

Sadness gave way to a sizzling anger. He'd done this not only to her, but to a woman named Karen. Karen had given birth to a child alone. Emma could imagine the anger, hurt, and the fear. And that devastating sense of abandonment. Emma understood the feeling of abandonment. She did not understand Carl. Nothing he could say or do would make her understand. Only in his small, cowardly mind, did any of this make sense.

"What are you doing?"

Emma jumped. She clasped the envelope to her chest and craned around to see Leah standing barefoot in the hallway. Her long chestnut hair hung loose around her shoulders. "Why are you sitting out here in the middle of the night?"

"I couldn't sleep," Emma stuttered. She cleared her throat. Leaving the lantern on the floor in hopes that Leah wouldn't notice her tear-streaked face and red eyes, she gathered the rest of the letters and stood. "Why are you up?"

Leah's gaze fastened on the papers. She pursed her lips. "Indigestion. The light of dawn comes early, and you have to teach tomorrow. And make the final preparations for the pageant. Christmas is only two days away."

"Yes, I know." Emma didn't need Leah to remind her of her duties. She grabbed the lantern. "Goodnight."

She scurried past her sister-in-law before Leah could inquire about the letters.

"What were you reading?"

Too late. "Just some old letters." She kept moving. "I think I can sleep now. Good-night."

She dashed into the bedroom and shut the door behind her. Her stomach heaving, she bent over and fought nausea. A baby. The baby she wanted. Carl had not only abandoned her, but chosen to make a family with another. How could she forgive that? How? *God, don't ask me to forgive.*

"*Ach!*" Annie rolled over and shielded her eyes from the light with one hand. "Sleeping!"

Emma extinguished the flame. She crawled into bed, wrapped her arms around a pillow, and stared into the darkness. Carl should never have put her in this position. Now she would have to tell the bishop. She'd have to tell Luke. Let him tell the bishop.

Carl was a married man with a family, posing as a faithful Amish person. Tears slipped down the sides of her face into her hair. She longed to confront him. To know why he thought giving her those letters was a good thing. Why hadn't he told her the truth from the beginning? She could never be with a man already married in the eyes of God. He knew that.

His actions were unforgiveable.

Chapter 42

Wind whistled in the eaves of the schoolhouse. Emma peered through the window. Beautiful, icy designs glistening on the panes made it difficult to see anything. She breathed on the glass and used her sleeve to wipe a clear spot. Two more buggies had stopped on the road. *Gut.* Families were coming despite the threat of more snow on top of the two feet that fell the previous day. The children had practiced hard for the pageant. They also cleaned the classroom, mopped the floor, and moved all the desks to make room for the benches. They would have one small moment in front of their parents and families. It only happened once a year and everyone had such a good time. It would be a shame to miss it.

She added a few pieces of wood to the stove. The familiar, comforting smell of burning pine seemed to have a warming effect on her. Even with its belly blazing, the stove couldn't heat the entire room, of course, not with that northern wind howling through the cracks and crevices of the building. She held out her hands and concentrated on the heat, trying not to think about the one thing that refused to leave her mind. Carl and his letters. Not one second alone had presented itself in the last two days. Between the preparations for the pageant and for the Christmas visiting, she was never alone. Never had an opportunity to seek him out and confront him.

Now that she wanted Carl to come to the house after the others went to bed, he had failed to appear and she had lain awake in bed, tossing and turning, anger coursing through her. She wanted to tell Luke, to tell the bishop, but first she had to talk to Carl. Nervous anticipation filled her. He would attend the pageant to see his nieces and nephews perform. But here was not the place for the conversation she wanted—needed—to have.

The door flew open and Luke stomped through it, Leah and the children right behind him. Catherine and Annie brought up the rear. They both carried casseroles for the meal to be served after the performance. Catherine's nervous scan of the room told Emma her sister feared running into the Dodd family. The Dodds likely wouldn't attend the pageant, though, since three of their youngest were down with the flu. Emma should probably share that information with her sister. She started forward. Aenti Louise stepped out from behind Leah.

Her mission forgotten, Emma rushed over to her. Aenti Louise almost never got out anymore. Only on special occasions. "Aenti, I'm so glad you came." Emma wrapped her in a hug that Aenti Louise returned with equal fervor. "Get warm by the fire. Did you come in Josiah's sleigh?"

"I did. What a ride!" Her wrinkled face red and glowing, the older woman used clawed fingers to undo her wool bonnet. "I couldn't miss this. Lillie and Mary's first Christmas pageant."

Their first pageant and their parents wouldn't be here. That's what Aenti Louise was thinking. No one would say it aloud, but everyone wanted to make this a special day for the youngest Shirack children. "Come, sit on the front row where you'll be able to see."

"Close the door!" Luke yelled at Josiah and Mark, who lagged behind talking to the Glick boys. Luke tromped across the room to the stove. He stuck both hands so close to the red-hot top he was in danger of searing the fingers of his gloves. "Do you need more wood before everyone gets here?"

"Jah, that would be good." An unfamiliar wave of happiness ran through Emma. No matter what else happened, her family rallied for something they knew was important to their sister. If it could just hold off from snowing until the end of the evening. She took Leah's spaghetti casserole from her and placed it on the tables they had set up along one wall. "I'm so glad you could come. The children have worked so hard. Is it snowing yet?"

Leah grimaced and held her belly with both hands. "No." Her response sounded more like a grunt. Her breathing ragged, she plopped down on the closest bench. "But it looks like it will any minute."

"Are you all right?" Emma set the cake down. "Should you be here?"

"I want to see William present his poem." Leah grimaced. "It's just indigestion. I always have it during the last month. With both boys, it was bad. I wonder if that means it's another boy."

Aenti Louise changed spots so she could sit next to Leah. "I expect we'll know soon enough." Her feet barely touched the floor. "The baby has dropped. I can tell by the way you walk."

Feeling left out of the conversation, Emma wished she knew about these things. She had no experience with having babies. She was old enough to remember when Mark, Lillie, and Mary were born, but she'd been kept in the background most of the time. She had only a vague understanding of what went on. What little she knew had been startling and amazing. Mudder never spoke of it. Now Emma kept silent, hoping to learn more so that some day she would be prepared for her own baby's birth. Someday. *God, please.*

"Then why do I still have such indigestion?" Leah went on. She wasn't complaining. She sounded like she really wanted to know. "The baby shouldn't be pressing on my stomach as much."

"Big baby." Aenti Louise patted Leah's belly with a proprietary air. "Have you made arrangements with the midwife?"

"Yes. If the weather allows, we'll go to the clinic when the time comes."

"And if it doesn't?"

Leah shrugged. "Joseph was born without her help. I'm sure we'll manage."

The door opened. Helen Crouch's brood traipsed in, bringing with them a gust of cold air, ending the conversation. Thomas and his family flowed in right behind the Crouches. Emma stopped in her tracks. She took a deep breath and went to welcome them.

Thomas smiled. "Merry Christmas."

She inclined her head. "Merry Christmas." She couldn't help herself. Her gaze slid over to Helen, who was directing the placement of a pecan pie and a plate loaded with brownies on the table.

"We didn't come together." Thomas sidled closer. "By chance, we arrived at the same time."

"No need to explain." Emma took a step back and felt the heat of the stove singe her hands held behind her back.

"Apparently there is—"

"No, there's not. I…" She shut her mouth. She had no business chastising Thomas when she was so thoroughly embroiled in Carl's mess. "I'm sure you've been working hard."

"As you have with the wedding and the pageant." Thomas rubbed his hands over the stove. "I'm sorry about Catherine."

"Me, too."

Thomas leaned closer. "We have to talk—"

The door opened and a fresh wave of families flowed in, bringing more icy wind with them. Whatever Thomas planned to say died on his lips.

Carl and his sister and her children were among the new arrivals. Thomas's expression didn't change, but he moved away. With each step, Emma felt a greater distance that had nothing to do with geography.

She whirled and busied herself putting more wood on the fire. It roared. Carl would see her face and know. Know that she knew his dark secret. She couldn't confront him now, not with the pageant about to start. She gazed around the room, counting children. Everyone had arrived. Avoiding eye contact with Carl, she trudged to the front. "Children, children!" She clapped her hands together. The noise quieted. "Gather round. Quickly, now."

They crowded behind the sheets they had rigged from one corner to another to make a "backstage" area. Everyone wore his or her costume as instructed. "Quiet now!" Except for two or three of the little ones, the children's whispers subsided. Emma put a finger to her lips. The offenders were silenced.

Butterflies unexpectedly dove and spun in her stomach. She stood in front of a classroom every day, but this was different. A group that included nearly all the men of her community faced her on the other side of the sheet. She swallowed hard, took a deep breath, and slipped out from behind the sheet. The faces in the audience were friendly and expectant. Everyone enjoyed this one time a year when their children were allowed to shine. Emma's nerves calmed.

"Welcome to our Christmas Pageant," she said. "The children are very glad you could come. I present our pageant."

That concluded Emma's duties. The children would handle the rest. Giggles floated from behind the sheet. She held up one corner and fixed her scholars huddled in the corner with a stare. The giggles subsided. "Donald!" she whispered. "Now."

His homemade beard slightly askew, Joseph tromped onto the "stage." Mary waddled behind him with a pillow under her flowing robe. "Are we almost there, Joseph?" Naomi's voice held a whine so real, Emma hid a smile behind her free hand.

Joseph stumbled over the hem of his robe and nearly fell. Mary grabbed his arm and her pillow fell to the floor. "Oh, my." She swooped down and stuffed it back in place. Amused smiles assured Emma that no one in the audience minded the misstep.

Things moved quickly after that. The hymns were beautiful and even the little ones seemed to remember all the words they'd so carefully practiced. The skit with the innkeeper drew lots of laughter, and everyone clapped after William recited the little poem he'd written himself about the baby Jesus.

The children were halfway through the final hymn, "O Little Town of Bethlehem," when a sound that was half groan, half shriek overcame their rowdy rendition that included two new verses they'd written themselves. Emma let go of the sheet and rushed forward.

Leah rose from her seat on the front bench. She clutched at her stomach and took two steps forward. "I'm sorry," she whispered. "The baby's coming. Now."

With a groan, she sank to the floor.

Chapter 43

E mma squeezed through the crush of people surrounding Leah in the center of the classroom. Annie, Catherine, Josiah, Mark, even the twins, formed the innermost semicircle around the spot where their sister-in-law huddled on the wooden floor, her arms clasped to her big belly. Trying to ignore their stricken faces, Emma knelt next to Leah and put a hand on her shoulder. Leah gasped and started to rock. Emma looked up at Luke, who held back his two squirming boys with both hands. William was crying and Joseph looked close to tears. "What do we do?"

His face frozen in consternation, Luke didn't answer. Aenti Louise elbowed him. "Luke? Your wife needs you."

Letting go of the boys, he jolted away from the sharp elbow. "I know, I know."

Joseph ran to his mother. "Mudder, get up. It's time to go!"

Emma tugged him away. "Go to Josiah. He'll take you home. Your mudder will be right behind you."

She nodded at her brother, who grabbed both boys by the suspenders and backed them away, their little arms flailing. "Out of the way, boys. Little ones must stay out of the way."

Luke put both hands under Leah's arms and tugged. "We need to get her up. Get her in the buggy. I'll take her to the clinic."

"No, no, it's too far! Take me home! The pain's worse this time. It's coming faster." Leah panted. Sweat shone on her face, and she clutched at her middle. "I'm sorry about the pageant."

"Don't you worry about it for one minute!" Emma squeezed her hand. "Babies come when they're ready. There's no stopping them."

She sounded like she knew what she was talking about. How she wished she did. "What do you think, Aenti?"

"I need to take a look at her before we decide. We don't want to have this baby in a buggy halfway between here and home." Aenti Louise clucked and fanned her stubby fingers in the air. "Everyone, the pageant is over. It's time to go. Take some food with you. Not the dish you brought. We'll call it a recipe exchange, and then we'll call it a night."

"I want to stay!" Annie began. "I can help."

"Me, too." Catherine chimed in. "We can—"

"Go home!" Aenti Louise shook a finger at the girls. "Your job is to take care of the little ones. Get them home. Put them to bed. Then get things ready. We'll be along shortly."

Neither Annie nor Catherine looked happy, but they each grabbed a twin's hand and joined the knot of people putting on their coats and moving quietly toward the door.

"Need any help?" Sadie Plank called out as she tied a woolen bonnet over her kapp. "I can stay."

"We're fine." Aenti Louise called back. "You should get home before the snow comes."

Luke didn't look fine. His face constricted with fear, he put his arm around his wife's shoulders. "We need to get her to the clinic."

"Let me take a look and then we'll have a better idea how much time we have." Aenti Louise patted Leah's damp cheek. "You're doing fine. This is as good a place as any. We've got a fire, we can use coats to keep you warm. Check to see if you have any string, Emma, in case we need it, and scissors. If you have more of those sheets like the one you have hanging there, we can use those."

Emma turned and nearly ran into Carl. He shifted from one foot to the other. "Can I do something to help?"

"Go home." She brushed past him. "You can help by going home."

His face reddened as if she'd slapped him. "You read the last letter."

"Not now, Carl. Go home." Let him read all he wanted into that statement. She wanted him to go home. To his wife and baby, if Karen would still have him. "We'll talk later."

Head down, she dashed to the storage cabinet where she kept all her supplies. Thomas stepped into her path. "May I help by taking your brothers and sisters home?"

"What about Eli and Rebecca?"

"They've already gone with Daed and Mudder." His hands tightened around the hat in his hands. "I want to help you."

His gentle tone unnerved her. Suddenly tearful, she nodded. "Ask Josiah how many he can get in the sleigh. I'm sure he would welcome splitting them up."

He slapped the hat on his head. "Done."

Emma grabbed the supplies she needed and hurtled across the room. Between Luke and Aenti Louise, they'd managed to help Leah to the "backstage" corner. Leah's clamped teeth and stranglehold on Luke's arm told Emma her sister-in-law suffered in the throes of another contraction. Again she thought of how it was when Mudder had Lillie and Mary. Emma had been so frightened, but Mudder kept saying everything was as it should be. All that pain to bring a life into the world. And for Mudder, two new lives. Bountiful, she had called it.

Emma handed the supplies to Aenti Louise, who barely looked up. "All right. All of you. Outside the sheets."

His face strained with reluctance and worry, Luke did as she ordered. Aenti Louise let the sheet drop. Luke strode away. A moan from behind the sheet sent him rocketing back toward it.

"She's done this before, remember?" Emma slipped between him and the hanging sheets. He stopped. "So has Aenti Louise, many, many times. Leah will be fine."

After a few minutes, Aenti Louise brushed the sheet aside. Her wizened face concerned, she wiped her bent fingers on the washrag Emma had given her.

"Well, how is she? Do we move her?" Luke towered over his aunt. "Is the baby coming now?"

"Hush, a minute, will you?" Aenti Louise's eyes narrowed. She paced about for a brief moment. "The baby's not going to come on its own. It's breech."

Emma didn't know that term, but Aenti Louise's expression said it wasn't good. "What does that mean?"

"The baby's feet are first, instead of its head."

"What do we do?"

"Not we, dearie. A doctor. A doctor knows how to turn the baby." Aenti Louise snatched her coat from the hook on the wall. "Bank the fire. Let's go. Luke, help us get her in the buggy. We'll move her to your house. Then you go into town and get Doctor Miller. Quickly now!"

Emma did as she was told, but Luke stood frozen in the middle of the room. "Can he help her at home, or do we need an ambulance?"

Emma hated the look of terror on her brother's face. He'd been through so much.

"The bishop's house is in the opposite direction. We'll lose too much time going to his house to call." Aenti Louise tapped a finger on her cheek, her eyes narrowed. "Better to get Doctor Miller. His house is on the edge of town. Babies are born breech all the time. They just need a little more help. And so does the mother. If he thinks Leah needs to go to the hospital in Wichita, he'll make that call. Now, let's go. We're wasting time."

The ride home in the backseat of the buggy, holding Leah's hand, seemed unreal. Darkness had fallen. The trees cast shadows on white crests of snow that glittered in the moonlight. No one spoke. The only sounds were the horse's snorts, the crunch of the wheels against the snow, and Leah's occasional half-suppressed groans. She tried so hard to be brave, but the bones in Emma's fingers felt as if they would break in the stranglehold of her grip. Inhaling the scent of pine, Emma breathed through the pain. It seemed the least she could do.

Luke snapped the reins. The buggy lurched forward as they picked up speed. "Slow down!" Aenti Louise grabbed the seat and hung on. "I'd like to get your wife and baby there in one piece, if you please."

The buggy slowed on the curve that led to the final stretch of road and their house. Emma breathed a sigh of relief. Home was better. They had pots and pans for heating water, lots of blankets, a nice bed, and all the baby things. Catherine and Annie would be there to help. A thought hit her like a boulder in a landslide, hurtling from above. She leaned close to her sister-in-law. "If it takes very long coming, your baby will be born on Christmas Day!"

Leah gripped her hand so hard Emma gritted her teeth to keep from crying out. "A new beginning. Child of God." She gasped. "Maybe that's why it hurts so much. Joy in the pain."

Emma leaned closer to Luke's broad back. "Hurry," she whispered. The buggy jolted forward.

Lights bore down on them. "Is that Josiah? Why is he headed out again?" Luke pulled on the reins. "Who is that?"

"It's me. Thomas." Thomas shielded his eyes from Luke's headlights with his hand. "I can't find Rebecca."

Chapter 44

E mma couldn't see Thomas's expression in the harsh glare of the battery-operated headlights, but the fear in his hoarse voice reverberated between the side-by-side buggies. Leah moaned, shifted, and dropped Emma's hand. Her breathing became even more ragged. Emma tried to focus on Thomas's form, dark against the brilliant light. "I thought you said Rebecca went home with your mother and father."

"It was a misunderstanding. They left, thinking she was with me." The words came out jerky as if Thomas had to corral them one at a time. "If she's not with you, she must still be at the school. You didn't see her?"

"If we had, we would've brought her home with us." Aenti Louise's tart tone said she didn't like wasting breath on stating the obvious. "You'd better get to the school and look for her. Emma, you go with him and open up the building. If she's wandering about outside, you'll need to warm her by the fire. Stoke it while Thomas searches for her. I'll send Josiah after you, just in case you need to start a bigger search. Luke will go to Bliss Creek to fetch the doctor."

Leave it to Aenti Louise to take charge in an emergency. She was the only woman in the Shirack clan who could get away with it. The chaos in Emma's mind subsided. She patted Leah's hand one last time, then switched buggies. Thomas had his buggy in motion the second she stepped in. She jolted back, her arms flapped like a wild turkey. The door slapped shut and she plopped into the seat.

"Sorry." He snapped the reins again. "I'm…sorry."

"It's all right. You must be worried sick." Emma grabbed the door and held on tight. "Go as fast as you can without throwing me into the road."

"It does no good to worry." His harsh tone belied the words. He pulled up on the reins and the buggy slowed a little. "Worry is a sin."

"You sound like Luke."

"Your brother is a wise man."

"Right now he's a worried man."

Thomas's laugh sounded broken, but it still qualified as a laugh. She took refuge in the welcome sound. "What do you think happened? What does Eli say?"

"He says he didn't see her after she played her part in the skit. He was too busy horsing around with the boys to pay any attention to his little sister."

"It's not Eli's fault. He's eight. He was just doing what boys do."

"He has the responsibility of looking after her when I'm doing other things."

"What were you doing? Talking to Helen?" The words slipped out before Emma could stop them. Contrition filled her immediately. The last thing Thomas needed right now was recrimination. Especially from her. "I didn't mean that. I don't know what's wrong with me."

Despite all that must be going through his mind at that moment, Thomas managed a fleeting smile. "You're jealous. That's a good sign."

"I am not jealous." Emma stopped for a second. She gripped the arm of the seat tighter. "We'll talk about this another time."

"Yes. We will."

❦

Nothing.

Thomas saw nothing of Rebecca along the dark, shadow-pitted road that led to the school. Barren tree branches whipped and danced along the edges, casting bizarre shadows in the light of slivers of moonlight that came and went as clouds scudded overhead. The thought of her walking alone in the dark in the frigid cold of night ripped a hole in his heart.

Why hadn't he talked to both children about staying in one place if they were ever separated? Because he never expected it to happen. They were always together. Rare were the moments when family didn't surround them. He'd made sure of that since Joanna's death.

Now, his gaze set upon another woman, he'd lost sight of the need for vigilance. Guilt and remorse stuck together like stone and mortar inside him. With the evening sun long gone, the temperatures would continue to dive. If Rebecca were wandering around lost, she wouldn't last long. *God, please don't let that be the case. Give her refuge. Take me to her.*

Thomas turned off the headlights so his eyes would adjust to the dark. He scanned the roadside. "Do you see anything on that side?"

Emma shook her head. "Nothing. Slow down. We have to keep looking."

He tugged on the reins, and the horse slowed to a walk. Thomas strained to hear. The only sounds were his ragged breathing, Emma's light and quick, and an occasional hoot of an owl. A wet snowflake smacked him in the eye. Another brushed his cheek. Snow. The snowstorm that had been threatening all afternoon announced itself with a few icy early arrivals.

"No. No! Rebecca, where are you?" Calling to her in the thick of the night in the middle of the road seemed all the more desperate. "Answer me, daughter!"

Emma touched his coat sleeve. Her hand withdrew. He wanted it back, but he didn't dare say so. Even in a moment so fraught with emotion, decorum had to be maintained. He would never do anything to place her in a position that could be disrespected. Her features were hidden by the dark and her thick, woolen bonnet, but her breathing came more rapidly. "We'll find her." Hope and faith cloaked the words. "You know we will. Surely, she's between here and the school."

"I'm trying to hope that she thought to stay at the school, knowing

I would realize my mistake and come for her." He clucked and slapped the reins. The horse picked up its pace again. "But Rebecca is always so sure she's all grown-up. She wouldn't think twice about starting out on her own. She's independent."

"She's smart and you've taught her well."

"Not about this I didn't. I didn't tell her." He clamped his mouth shut for a few seconds, afraid an unmanly sob would slip out. "She's only six years old, after all."

They rode in silence. Thomas worked to regain his composure. When he was sure no emotion would escape with the words, he posed the question. "Did you look to see that everyone was gone before you locked up the building?"

Emma brushed wet flakes from her lap with gloved fingers. "I'm sorry. I don't remember." Her voice cracked. "I can't remember even if I locked the door. Sometimes I don't. But I was so wrapped up in helping with Leah, I don't even remember what I did."

"If she was outside and everyone left, she could still get into the building." A small ray of hope. "That's good."

"I'm just not sure."

"You didn't know."

They were silent then for the remaining mile, except to call her name now and again. His heart pounding harder than when he plowed the land behind a team of horses, Thomas flapped the reins. They were getting closer.

The schoolhouse came into view. The windows were dark, forlorn. Nothing indicated that a bright, busy-as-a-bee six-year-old occupied it. He bit his upper lip to keep from crying out. *God, You have Joanna. Please don't take Rebecca just because I failed to watch over her.*

He replayed the sudden end of the pageant and Leah's distress. He'd been focused on Emma, more concerned about helping her than keeping track of his own little girl. He bowed his head.

"It's not your fault."

"She's my child, my responsibility. Instead of watching over her, I was watching you."

"And now you think you're being punished?" Incredulity filled her voice. "That's not the God we worship, Thomas."

She was right. He sucked in air and exhaled, willing the emotions to flee in the face of a greater faith. *God, forgive me for my lack of faith. I give this up to You.* "We'll find her."

He drew back on the reins and brought the buggy to an abrupt halt. Emma hopped out and ran up the steps. Thomas grabbed a flashlight and followed. She fumbled for the knob. The door opened. She hadn't locked it. Such were the Plain ways. What they had, they shared, so they thought little of leaving doors unlocked. Thomas stayed close behind her, even though he knew in his heart Rebecca couldn't be inside. As grownup as she liked to believe she was, she still feared the dark. She would've lit the lamp.

Emma lit it now. The flames made shadows that danced across the walls as the lamp swung slightly in her hand. She held it up high. "Rebecca?"

"She's not here."

"Try the outhouse, then." Emma slapped the lamp on a desk and moved toward the stove. "I'll build up the fire. We'll need to get her warm after we find her."

"You stay here. Wait for the others. Josiah should be close behind with any other men he's gathering."

"You'll not go alone."

They glared at each other. Emma grabbed wood from the pile and stoked the glowing embers in the stove's belly. When she turned her face was set. She reminded Thomas so much of her Aunt Louise. Strong will ran through the Shirack women. As a wife, she would be a handful. She brushed her hands together briskly. "Let's not waste time. I won't get in your way, and I won't slow you down. You wanted to help me. Now, let me help you."

The lump in his throat didn't allow Thomas to respond. He nodded.

Together, they hurried down the steps. He snagged a second flashlight from the buggy and handed it to her. He took the boys' outhouse, Emma, the girls'. Nothing.

"Where can she be?" Frustration filled Thomas. "Rebecca! Rebecca, come out now!"

As if this were a simple game of hide-and-go-seek.

Snowflakes glittered in the glow of the flashlight. The snow fell in a thick blanket. It would obscure any tracks she might have left. He trained the light in front of him and searched the ground. Many shoes and boots had crossed paths here with the marks left by the wheels of the buggies. Nothing helpful. "The snow will cover her tracks. We have to hurry!"

"Did you ask her friends?" Emma picked up her skirt slightly, revealing sturdy boots. Her pace increased. "Did they go outside after Leah interrupted the pageant?"

"Everything happened very quickly. They didn't have time to go too far before your aunt told everyone to go home." Thomas stopped long enough to grab his rifle from backseat of the buggy. Gratitude seeped through him that providence had kept him from putting it away after the hunting trip earlier in the week. "I didn't know she was lost until I got to Mudder's house. Eli told her Rebecca was with me. That boy... sometimes...he doesn't think. He just figured if she wasn't with him, she had to be with me."

"He's a child." Emma puffed as she scurried to keep up with his pace. "Why do you have that rifle? Why do we need it?"

"I've been out hunting several times in the last two months. I keep seeing coyotes—or signs of coyotes. The snow has brought them in closer to the farm." He stopped and searched the ground again. One set of small tracks moving away from the school. "We've lost chickens, a calf, even a piglet. It's best to keep the rifle handy."

For the first time, Emma looked frightened. Thomas slowed. "Are you sure you don't want to wait at the school?"

"No."

The light picked up small, even boot tracks in the road. They veered off toward the edge and then into the deeper snow that led to a dark stand of trees. "Rebecca? Rebecca!" No answer. Just the sound of his voice echoing in the silence. "Why would she leave the road?"

Emma's response was a breathless shake of her head. They threaded their way through the trees, the combined light of their flashlights illuminating the thick darkness several yards in front of them.

Emma gasped as she plowed forward. "Surely she went back to the road."

The wind whipping up flurries of snow around him, Thomas squatted for a closer look at the tracks. What he saw made him close his eyes for a second. Animal tracks curved around the small footprints—most likely those of a little girl.

"Unless something drove her deeper into the trees. Something that scared her." Panic twisted his tongue, making the words come out in a stutter. "Something that scared her more than the dark."

Chapter 45

"Daed! Help me! Someone help me!"

Thomas stopped moving.

His daughter's high-pitched scream filled his head, blotting out everything else. The trees, the snow wet on his face, the icy north wind, the black night sky, the entire rest of the world disappeared from his periphery. "Rebecca! Where are you?"

"*Daed!*"

Flashlight held high, Thomas stumbled forward. He whipped the light back and forth, desperate to see. Trees and more trees. Nothing but trees, their branches dipping and dancing in the wind. And Rebecca's terrified voice beyond the reach of the light.

Panic sent him careening forward. "Rebecca, are you all right?"

"Slow down! You'll fall," Emma shouted. "It won't do any good to break your neck. We've got her."

Got her? Not yet. She was close, but still too far away. He couldn't see her or protect her from whatever threat compelled her to scream for her father in the dark. "Rebecca, keep talking. I need to hear your voice so that I can come to you!"

"Daed, Daed, the coyote!"

Dread weighted down his legs. So heavy. They were so heavy. They wanted to topple under him. Instead, he plowed through the snow, forcing himself to put one foot in front of the other, faster and faster. "Don't move, Rebecca, don't run. Stay still."

"It chased me, Daed, but now I can't see it." Her whimpers filled the air, the sound like a sharp blade under his fingernails. "I can't see where it went."

"Keep talking, I'm almost there. I'm coming to get you." Thomas let his momentum carry him down a slope toward the stream where he'd seen the coyote before Thanksgiving. Now ice and snow covered the waterway, making it possible to cross it on foot. "I'm coming. Don't move. Be still. I'm almost there."

"I'm not moving. I'm being still." Her childish voice served as a beacon in the dark. "I'm being brave, aren't I?"

"You're doing fine. I'm almost there. Then we'll talk about why you never leave a building to walk home in the dark alone." Panting, Thomas hurled himself toward her voice. The toe of his boot caught on a gnarly root. He flailed for a second and down he went, face first into the snow.

The flashlight, its beam rocking crazily, disappeared into the bank of snow. The rifle slid in the opposite direction. He rolled and rolled until he smacked against a fir tree. His head hit the trunk.

Darkness swallowed him whole.

❧

"Thomas! *Ach,* Thomas! Get up!" Emma shook his arm. He didn't move. She shoved her hands under his arms and tried to lift him to a sitting position. His head lolled to the side. She laid him back in the snow and patted his face. "You need to get up. We have to get to Rebecca."

"Who is that? Who's that talking? Daed, are you still coming?" The little girl's voice echoed with fearful uncertainty in the darkness. "Are you there?"

Her hands shaking, Emma shone her flashlight on Thomas's face. Blood dripped from a cut on his forehead. His eyes were closed. She put a palm on his chest. It heaved. He still breathed. "Wake up, Thomas, wake up! Rebecca needs you!"

Rebecca's sobbing intensified. Desperate, Emma whirled and searched the snow with the flashlight. There. The rifle. She swooped down and grabbed it. "I'll be right back. I promise." His still form didn't move.

Her heart clanging against her ribcage, she trotted toward the sound of Rebecca's sobs. The stand of trees opened into a clearing. Emma edged forward, flashlight in one hand, rifle in the other. A few more yards and the flashlight picked up the white of her face. The girl crouched behind a fallen tree trunk. "There you are." Emma swung the flashlight across the expanse of open space. Nothing that looked threatening. Nothing moved. "Are you hurt?"

"Where's my daed?" Rebecca's hiccupping sobs slowed. She pushed away from the trunk. "I heard his voice. Then it stopped."

"He's waiting for you nearby. He hurt his head so I came ahead."

"He's hurt?" Rebecca's voice rose. "Is he...is he dead?"

Emma's heart broke. It would be Rebecca's first thought. Having had a mother die. "He's not dead. He's alive. Just got a bump on his head." She needed to get Rebecca's mind off Thomas and get her out of here before another coyote came upon them. "We need to go to him."

"I hurt my ankle. I wanted to walk home so Daed wouldn't have to come get me and be worried." Rebecca hobbled toward her. "But I saw the coyote and it scared me so I ran into the woods. Then I twisted my ankle, and I couldn't run anymore."

"I don't see the coyote now. Maybe you scared him away." Emma hugged the girl close. Rebecca's hands and face were icy cold. Her skin had a white, frozen feel to it that scared Emma. "We need to get you home. You're so cold."

"I don't feel cold anymore." Rebecca rubbed her mittens together. "My fingers and toes don't even hurt anymore. But my tummy does."

Frostbite? Emma wondered if she had the strength to carry a six-year-old back to the fire. "Let's get to the schoolhouse, and I'll make you some hot tea."

"What if the coyote's out there? He had big teeth and growled really loud." Rebecca shuddered in Emma's arms. "I didn't like him very much. I liked the white owl I saw outside the school better."

She raised her head. "That's why I got left behind. I didn't feel good so I went outside to the...you know...the outhouse...and I saw the owl. I wanted to get closer—"

"We'll talk about it later." Emma was certain Thomas would have plenty to say to Rebecca about her irresponsible behavior. Poor Rebecca's case of nerves over the pageant had led her to this spot. "Right now, we need to get to your father."

They started forward. A deep, hair-raising growl stopped them. Fear turned Emma's legs to pillars of stone. She couldn't raise her foot to take another step.

"It's him!" Rebecca's tiny whisper sounded like a shout in the quiet of the woods. "It's the—"

"I know. Hush." Emma pushed the girl behind her and lifted the rifle. She'd never shot another living thing in her life. "Stay behind me."

The coyote stalked deeper into the clearing. Its coat matted and dirty like an old rug, the animal stood out against the white backdrop of snow lit by the moon overhead.

Emma raised the rifle to her cheek. Her hands shook. She would never hit the animal. She didn't want to shoot it, but a child's life depended on her. "Please go away, please go away, please go away."

Another deep growl met her whispered command. The coyote crouched, its haunches tense. Yellow fangs appeared. It growled again, a sound that Emma would never forget. It took two steps toward them. Emma stumbled back, Rebecca's hands entwined in the fabric of her coat.

"Teacher..."

"Shhhhh, shhhh..."

The coyote kept coming. Emma put her finger on the trigger. She closed her eyes for a second. *God, please don't let me miss.*

Chapter 46

The blast exploded and lit up the night. Rebecca screamed. Emma jerked back. The recoil sent pain ricocheting through her shoulder, neck, and back. She hung on to the rifle as she staggered, her boots sliding in the wet snow. Had she hit it? Or missed? She peered at the animal. Whimpering, a painful, high sound, it crawled toward her on its haunches, teeth bared. Hit. Gorge rose in her throat. *God, I'm sorry. I had no choice.*

The smell of gunpowder and smoke thick in her nostrils, Emma kept a tight grip on the rifle with one hand. With the other, she grabbed Rebecca and threw her to the ground, then covered her with her body. *Oh, God, please, please. Don't make me shoot it again.*

The coyote stopped moving. Its body dropped, mouth open in a horrible grimace.

"Emma! Emma! Rebecca! Are you all right?" Josiah's voice, a welcome sound in the fearful aftermath, rang out. "It's me, Josiah. Don't shoot me!"

"Here, we're here." She peeked over Rebecca's head. The coyote sprawled in the snow, still not moving. The teeth looked no less frightening in death than in life. She breathed. "We're fine."

A light flared and danced in the clearing. She shielded her eyes. A rifle in one hand, Josiah came into view. His steps were slow, tentative.

Kelly Irvin

Thomas hobbled along behind him, one hand to his head. Josiah edged toward her. "Rifle down?"

"It's down."

"We heard a shot," Josiah squatted next to Emma. "Are you all right?"

Before Emma could answer, Rebecca dragged herself up. She moaned, leaned over, and heaved at Josiah's feet. "I don't feel so good." She coughed and wiped her mouth with the back of her coat sleeve. "My tummy hurts."

Josiah scooted back so fast, he fell and landed on his behind. "Whoa, girl, too much excitement?"

Ignoring him, Emma patted Rebecca's shoulder. "No wonder. Being chased by a coyote! I don't feel so good myself."

Thomas hobbled toward them. "Rebecca! Rebecca!"

Rebecca broke away from Emma. *"Daed!"* She limped toward the middle of the clearing where Thomas stopped. "Daed, the coyote, I think it's dead!"

She stumbled and fell to her knees. "I can't feel my feet." She sounded surprised. "My ankle doesn't hurt anymore."

Thomas worked to get to her. His limp was every bit as bad as hers. He staggered to within reach, then dropped to his knees in the snow. His arm went around his daughter, but his pain-filled gaze fixed on Emma. "Danki." His hoarse voice held tightly tethered emotion. "Danki."

"It's a wonder I hit him, my hands were shaking so badly." Emma tottered toward them. "Let me help you up. We need to get you both to the school."

"Home. I want to go home!" Rebecca whimpered. "I'm tired."

"The school's closer."

"I'll carry her." Josiah hoisted Rebecca into his arms. "Whew, girl, you don't smell so good. Emma, you help Thomas."

Josiah seemed unaware of the powerful emotion those words produced in Emma. Did Thomas notice? Did he feel the same way? She didn't dare ask, not in front of her brother.

Thomas held out a hand. "Help me up?"

Maybe he'd given her the answer, in his own, simple way. A lump the size of Kansas in her throat, Emma tugged him to his feet.

No one spoke, their energy drained by the sheer effort to make progress against a north wind that whipped the snow flurries like tiny pinpricks in their frozen faces. Emma picked her foot up, set it down. *One more step. One more step. One more step.*

Emma fought the urge to wail when the schoolhouse finally came into view. They staggered up the steps and through the door. Josiah deposited Rebecca on the floor close to the fire. "Are you sure you're only six?" He tugged her coat up around her chin. "You're pretty heavy."

"I don't feel good." She rolled on her side and tucked her knees up toward her stomach. "I might have to…"

"I'll get the blankets from the sleigh." Josiah darted toward the door.

If her face weren't frozen Emma might have smiled at her brother's queasiness. She slapped the kettle on the stove and opened its door long enough to poke at the wood. The blazing heat seared her face. It felt good. She couldn't quit shaking.

"Here." Josiah thrust the blankets at her. Her bruised shoulder ached when she reached out to accept them. Josiah didn't immediately let go. "You look peaked. Are you sick, too?"

She took the blankets from him. "I'm fine."

"Good. I'll round up the other men and send them home. It's getting late."

"You don't know anything about Leah and the baby?"

"Aenti Louise had Catherine and Annie heating water and getting out more quilts when I left. They were all in Leah's bedroom. I could hear her moaning." He ducked his head, but Emma saw the worry on his face. "Luke was probably already half way to Bliss Creek. He lit out on the horse like somebody was chasing him."

Not somebody, but the thought that his baby was in jeopardy. And his Leah. "Go home now, in case they need you."

"What about you?"

"We'll get Rebecca warmed up and then we'll be right behind you."

"I'm not sure it's right that I should leave you alone with Thomas."

Josiah jerked his head toward him. Thomas knelt next to Rebecca, rubbing her feet, his big, calloused hands dark against her white toes. "What will Luke think?"

"Luke has his own problems right now. Thomas is hurt and Rebecca is sick. My virtue is safe." Using a potholder, Emma poured water over a tea bag and set the kettle back on the stove. She picked up a bottle of honey. "Can you stop at Thomas's house and let his parents know Rebecca's been found? I think he should take her to our house since the doctor will be there. They'll be worried if he doesn't bring her home."

"I'll take care of it." Josiah grinned. "Good shot, by the way. You can come hunting with me anytime."

"I think I'll leave the hunting to the men." Emma couldn't control the shudder that shook her body. She added honey to the tea, letting its rich, sweet scent calm her. "Better hurry. Thomas's parents will be worried."

Josiah headed for the door. After he opened it, he looked back. "See you at home as quickly as possible."

He sounded so much like Luke, Emma almost smiled. Almost. "Go."

"Going!"

He slapped on his gloves and disappeared through the door.

Emma focused on her two patients. Thomas had his hand on Rebecca's forehead. "She's burning up." He leaned back on his haunches. "She needs a doctor."

So it wasn't excitement from the pageant that made Rebecca feel sick. Emma handed him the tea. "This will warm you. Rebecca might not be able to keep it down. The Dodd children had the flu this week so she's been exposed to it. All the children have. That may account for the fever and the vomiting." She brushed hair from Rebecca's damp, warm face. "Luke is bringing Doctor Miller to our house right now. We should get her there."

"Bank the fire." Thomas struggled to his feet. Tea slopped on his hand. He didn't seem to notice. "I'll get her into the buggy."

"I can carry her."

"You? You barely weigh more than a sparrow yourself."

"I'm more like a mother hen than a sparrow. I can help you. Just give me a minute and we'll do it together."

"I like the sound of that." His voice cracked. "The together part."

"We'll see." She touched Rebecca's fevered forehead again. She felt so hot. The little girl moaned. Fear rippled through Emma. "We need to get her home."

Home. Help.

Chapter 47

E mma rushed down the hallway toward Luke and Leah's bedroom. Thomas was taking care of Rebecca. Someone needed to take care of him, with his bleeding head and injured hip. The doctor must look at them both. Soon. Surely the baby had arrived by now. She slowed, taking in the tableau in front of her. Annie sat on the hallway floor, her back against the wall, hands over her ears, a look of desperation on her face. Luke paced in front of the closed door. Emma halted a few feet away. "Where's Doctor Miller? Isn't the baby here yet? We found Rebecca, but she's sick. She needs him. And Thomas fell. He hurt his hip."

Annie threw her hands up in the air. "I don't know if the baby is here or not. They asked for more water and more towels and then sent me away." She wrapped her arms around her bent knees. "I heard a baby cry, but Leah's still yelling. If the baby is here, why is she still yelling?"

"Doctor Miller's hurting her," Luke muttered. His hair stuck up all over his head like he'd been pulling on it and the bottom of his shirt had snagged on his suspenders, leaving it half in and half out. "He's hurting her. I should've gone for the midwife."

"Aenti Louise is a midwife." Emma hurried over to Luke. "If she says Leah needs a doctor for this breech birthing, then that's what she needs. Doctor Miller's helping, not hurting."

He shook his head. "It's never taken this long before. The boys were quick."

"They must not have been breech." Emma remembered another night like this. Six years ago. Lillie and Mary. Lillie came first, according to Mudder. She was a little bigger and a little stronger than her younger sister Mary, who came five minutes later. "You don't think…"

"Think what?"

"Twins. It could be twins. Leah has twin brothers. Twins happen in both our families. Maybe that's it."

"Two babies?" Annie screeched and slapped her hands to her cheeks. "Two babies? Do you think?"

Luke stopped pacing. Stunned surprise replaced the exhausted look on his face. "Twins?" He pulled on his suspenders and let them snap against his chest. "You think it could be?"

"It could be!" Reenergized by the thought, Emma knocked on the door, two quick raps. "I hope Aenti Louise can take care of Leah for a few minutes—"

Squalls poured from the bedroom. Loud and strong even through the closed door.

Luke stopped pacing.

Emma dropped her hand. Doctor Miller and Aenti Louise might be very busy right now. But Rebecca needed help. "I don't know what to do. Rebecca has a high fever and she's vomiting."

A creaking sound made her turn back. The door had opened. Aenti Louise stuck her head out. "Where are those towels?"

"Here!" Catherine streaked down the hall, a stack in her arms. Aenti Louise held out her hands and Catherine reached in front of Emma. "Here's everything we have left that's clean."

"Aenti, Rebecca needs help. Can you—"

"Doctor Miller has done the hard part here, what with delivering twins and all." She cackled like a satisfied mother bird. "I'll send him out. Luke, you best get up to the attic for the other cradle."

Aenti Louise shut the door in Emma's face.

Twins. Double the trouble, double the joy. Emma glanced at Luke.

He had a silly look on his face. "The attic. Twins. Boys or girls? She didn't say if they're boys or girls." The grin disappeared. "She didn't say if they were healthy."

"She wouldn't have been standing there talking to us if they weren't." Emma couldn't contain a small chuckle. Luke looked so different from the stern head of the family he'd become since the accident. "She wouldn't be sending Doctor Miller out if they weren't. Maybe you'd better sit down."

Luke leaned against the wall and slid down until he sat, legs sprawled in front of him. "Maybe you're right."

Doctor Miller slipped from Leah's room. "Where's Rebecca?"

Emma led the way to Mary and Lillie's room. She'd moved them to her own room, too embarrassed to think of Thomas passing through that doorway. Nor could he be separated from his child. Now he leaned over Rebecca, a wet washrag in one hand.

"How is she?" Emma's whisper barely pierced the silence. "I've brought Doctor Miller."

"The same." He laid the washcloth on her forehead. "Burning up."

Doctor Miller set his bag on the bed. "Rebecca, dear, you've grown since you came in with that sore throat. Let's take a look. Emma, why don't you give us a few minutes?"

"No." Thomas held up a hand. "She can stay. If you don't mind, I'd like her to stay."

Doctor Miller's examination was quick. He laid his stethoscope in his bag and pulled off his gloves. "We've had a bad strain of the flu racing through town for the last week. Looks like Rebecca has it. We need to get her fever down." Frowning, he glanced from Thomas to Emma. "I can give her tamiflu, but we also need to immerse her in lukewarm water—not cold, warm. I know you don't have hot running water, but—"

"We'll heat water and add it to the tub where we take our baths." Emma moved toward the door as she talked. "If you'll bring her downstairs in a few minutes, I'll hook up the hose and get the water running."

She ran down the stairs, not waiting to see if they followed. Despite exhaustion that seeped into her bones, making them heavier than she could ever have imagined, she whipped through the house to the laundry room. She grabbed the hose from its hook and attached one end to the faucet, then ran it over to the tub that doubled for laundry and baths.

"Can I help?' Annie stood in the doorway, her hands twisted together in front of her. "What can I do?"

"Put the pots and pans back on the stove—start heating water. The doctor says we need to put Rebecca in lukewarm water to bring her fever down."

"More hot water!" Annie whirled and trotted into the kitchen. "We can both carry."

Without talking they worked side by side, carrying the pans of hot water to the tub, letting it mix with the cold water until it reached a temperature Emma felt Rebecca could tolerate. "Go tell them to bring her down. Tell them to hurry before the water starts to cool."

Within minutes, Annie was back. Doctor Miller carried Rebecca, wrapped in a blanket that trailed after him. Thomas hobbled along behind him.

"Give her to me." Emma took the girl from the doctor's arms. Rebecca laid her head on Emma's shoulder. Emma nodded at the men. "You'd best wait in the kitchen."

Doctor Miller opened his mouth, but Thomas spoke first. "I'll put more wood on the fire so it won't be cold when you bring her out. We'll be right there, if you—if she needs anything."

Looking reluctant, Doctor Miller stepped out with Thomas. Emma quickly undressed Rebecca, keeping the blanket tucked around her as much as possible. She tested the water, not cold, but not hot. "Here we go, Rebecca. You didn't know it was bath night, did you?"

She gently lowered her into the water. Rebecca's sudden intake of air told Emma her fever made the water seem colder than it was. "I don't like this," she whimpered. "I want to get out."

"It's just for a little while." Emma eased onto a stool next to the tub and began to trail water over Rebecca's shoulders and pat her face with wet hands. "Doesn't that feel good? Don't you feel a little better?"

Rebecca sighed. "I guess. A little."

"It's nice, isn't it? You just relax and I'll wash you up a little, how about that?"

Rebecca's eyelids drooped. "I'm really tired. I might want to go to sleep."

The medicine Doctor Miller had given was finally having an effect. Emma continued to smooth the water over the girl's shoulders and neck, over and over again, until her arms ached. She touched Rebecca's forehead. Cooler? Maybe. So was the water. "I think we're done here."

She lifted Rebecca from the tub, dried her off as quickly as possible, and tugged one of Annie's old flannel nightgowns on her. "It's too big, but the twins' clothes are too little, so we'll just have to make do."

Rebecca didn't answer. Her soft, regular breathing said she'd already slipped off to sleep. A deep sense of relief rolled over Emma. Rebecca would be all right. She hugged the girl to her chest. Emotion threatened to choke her. Thomas's child would survive, and she'd helped make that possible. They were forever yoked by the experience.

She sniffed and wiped at her face with the back of one free hand. This must be what being a mother felt like.

⁂

Thomas waited for Emma to go in front of him before he hobbled up the stairs. He wanted to say something, but the knot in his throat wouldn't allow it. She looked like she might drop any second, yet she bustled in the room, fluffing pillows and adding a quilt to the twins' bed. It had been nice of her to offer their room, moving them to hers. She knew he couldn't be with her there and he had to be with Rebecca right now.

Doctor Miller did another examination after laying Rebecca on the bed. "Looks like we've got it under control. Nothing to do now but keep her hydrated until it runs its course." His sober gaze encompassed both of them. "In other words, give her plenty of fluids, water, and juice if she can keep it down. Give her ibuprofen for the fever. If it spikes again, stick her back in the tub and call me—come get me. Immediately."

Thomas tried to take it all in. Fear and fatigue muddled his brain. Unsure how much he would remember, he longed for a pencil and paper to write the instructions down. "What about her fingers and toes?"

"You got her inside in the nick of time. Keep an eye on them, but they'll be fine."

Doctor Miller stuck out his arm until his sleeve rode up enough that a wristwatch showed. "It's been a long night. Gonna be even longer for y'all, I'm sure. I better go check on those babies before I go."

"Babies?" Thomas tore his thoughts away from Rebecca for a second. Maybe his hearing had been affected by the fall. "There's more than one?"

"Yep." Doctor Miller smiled broadly. "Two healthy little girls. I should've known when Luke said the baby was breech. That can signal a multiple birth."

Nodding, Thomas barely heard the words. His mind flew back to his daughter. His baby girl. "So we do nothing more for Rebecca right now?"

"Now all you can do is wait for it to pass. Let her sleep. Keep a close eye on her." The doctor shoved his glasses up his nose with one finger. "Most of my patients get through this flu pretty well, but it's rough on some of them."

Thomas didn't want to wait. He wanted her better now. A doctor should be able to do more.

Waiting reminded him of Joanna's last days. Waiting for her to get better, knowing she was going to die.

He hated waiting.

Chapter 48

Emma watched the emotions whirling across Thomas's face as he hovered near Rebecca's bed, trying to hang on to Doctor Miller's instructions. Exhaustion etched itself around his eyes, worry around his mouth. Their evening stumbling around in the dark looking for his daughter had left its mark. Inside and out, from the looks of his face. He looked as if he were holding himself upright by sheer force of will. The slash on his forehead looked dark and angry against his fair skin. She switched her gaze to Doctor Miller. "Before you go back to the babies, what about Thomas? Do you think you should look at his forehead?"

"It's fine." Scowling, Thomas waved a hand. "Just a little scratch."

Doctor Miller peered through glasses perched on the end of his nose. "Hmm, Emma is right. That's more than a scratch. A few stitches are in order." He pointed to a single straight-back chair situated between the room's two windows. "Sit there. Emma, you can help me with my supplies. I'll need more light. Do you have another lantern?"

Grateful to be of use, Emma did as he asked. She handed the doctor items as he requested them. She wondered if this were what it felt like to be a nurse. The image of the bloody, dead coyote assailed her. She wanted nothing to do with blood. She bit her lip until the pain made her stop. "He hurt his leg, too, Doctor."

"Aha. When were you going to tell me about that?" Doctor Miller snipped a thread and dropped the scissors in the basin Emma held. "Give it up, Mr. Brennaman."

Glaring at Emma, Thomas growled and then explained the tumble he'd taken by the stream.

"Emma, I think maybe you should wait outside now." Doctor Miller cancelled out Thomas's glare with a kindly smile. "I'll want to take a quick look at that hip."

Emma slipped out. Silence reigned. She peeked in her bedroom. Annie and Catherine had finally gone to bed, the twins sandwiched between them in a tight, snug row. In the boys' room snoring wafted from Mark's bed. The younger boys didn't move. Everyone was down for the night, except Josiah, who nodded at her from a chair in the corner where he sat peeling off his socks. She withdrew and continued down the hallway. Not a sound came from Leah and Luke's room. Emma longed to see the babies. She wanted to hold them and inhale their sweet, baby smell. *Patience.*

Her head aching more with each step, she plodded down the stairs. Despite being tired, she twitched with nervous energy. She sat. Stood. Began to pace the floor.

Finally, after what seemed like hours, Doctor Miller clattered down the stairs. Behind him, Thomas hobbled more slowly.

"I checked on the babies. Your aunt has everything under control. If anything changes with Rebecca, give me a call—I mean come get me. Especially if the fever doesn't come down tomorrow." Doctor Miller set his bag on the table and tugged on his gloves. "Right now, I'm going home to get some sleep. The missus has probably forgotten what I look like."

"How much do I owe you for a home visit?" Thomas grasped the banister with one hand, a look of pain on his face.

The doctor waved his hand. "I was already here, but you can stop by my office sometime next week and settle up for the rest." He slapped a furry cap on his bald head. "No hurry."

Emma showed him to the door. A gust of damp wind rattled the eaves until she managed to get it closed again. She faced Thomas. "How's Rebecca?"

"No change."

"I'll make coffee." She rubbed gritty eyes. "What did the doctor say about your leg?"

"Pulled a muscle. Bruised it. Nothing's broken. It'll be fine in a few days." He limped to the chair closest to the fireplace, sat, and held his hands out to the flames. "Is Josiah back yet?"

"Yes, he came in a few minutes ago. Everything is fine. All the children are down for the night."

When he didn't respond, Emma went to the kitchen and put fresh coffee in the filter and set the metal coffeepot over the flame on the gas stove. Just the aroma of the brewing coffee revived her. She watched the coffee percolate in the clear knob on the lid, half mesmerized. She might be sleeping, standing up. The even sound calmed her nerves and gave her time to gather her wits. She'd killed a coyote and helped save Rebecca. She was now the aunt of newborn twins. All in one night. She set out the mugs. Familiar routine grounded her. She poured the steaming liquid and let the scent roll over her.

Carrying the mugs, she returned to the front room, pleased to realize her hands didn't shake. She didn't spill a drop. Thomas slouched in the chair, chin down, eyes closed. Emma set the coffee on the table and watched him sleep for a few seconds. His guard down, he looked so much younger.

He straightened and opened his eyes. "I want to thank you again." He looked up, his brown eyes dark with emotion. "You saved her."

He stood and hobbled until he was within arm's length. "I know you didn't want to shoot that animal, but you saved my daughter's life."

"I wasn't afraid to shoot it. I was afraid I would miss," Emma whispered. Her heart leapt in her chest, each beat painful. "Then what would I have done?"

"You didn't miss." His hand came up as if to touch her. She stopped breathing. The hand dropped. "God was with you."

"We should check on Rebecca." She handed him the mug. Now her

TO LOVE AND TO CHERISH

301

hand shook. His fingers wrapped around the mug, brushing against hers. She couldn't take her gaze from his. "After you drink your coffee."

"Jah, you're right." He backed away and sat down again. "I know it's a long time until the wedding season, but I want to ask you to marry me. When the times comes."

"Because of tonight?" The room spun around her. Emma plopped down in the rocking chair. "Because I shot the coyote? Because I took care of Rebecca?"

"No. Yes. No, it's…because…" He ducked his head. "You know why."

She closed her eyes and savored the unmistakable emotion in his voice. Then cold reality darkened the light that had shone all around her. Thomas didn't know about Carl and the letters. Would he still want her, knowing how close she'd come to going back to a man who'd left his wife for her? What would he think when he knew that Carl had a wife and child and yet pursued Emma?

"Will you marry me?" The harsh rasp of his voice said everything rode on her response. "I need an answer."

She cleared her throat and forced herself to meet his gaze. "I have unfinished business."

He flinched as if she'd slapped him. "Carl?"

"Yes."

He set the mug on the end table and stood. "Then I have my answer."

"No! No. I just need to talk to him first."

He crossed his arms. "About what?"

"It's between him and me." Emma placed her mug on the end table. "But it's not what you think."

"If there's something between you and him, there can be nothing between you and me." Pain flickered in his eyes, and then disappeared. His features hardened. "I take back my earlier question."

"Don't do that."

"I'm trying to make this easier for you." He limped away until he stood near the fireplace. The air seemed colder in the space he left behind. "You share something with Carl."

"No. Only a past." A past that had wormed itself into her present and now her future. If only she could make it go away. "What is past is past."

"Then what do you have to talk about?"

If she told Thomas, would he understand? Or take back his question forever? "He's done something—something unforgivable."

"Nothing is unforgivable. Tell me what it is."

"I can't. If I do, you'll have to…you'll have to do something about it."

"Like what? Tell the bishop?"

"Yes."

"So you should tell the bishop."

"I want to give him a chance to do it himself. If he doesn't, I will."

"If you feel the need to protect him, then I have my answer." His face stony, Thomas turned his back on her and held his hands close to the flames. "Just don't let him bring you down with him."

"No, Thomas, please. I'm not protecting—"

"Look what we have here."

Emma's attempt to make things right was lost in the delighted sound of Aenti Louise's voice. She whirled to see her aunt coming down the stairs, a tiny bundle in her arms. Luke descended behind her, a second bundle gripped as if it might shatter. He had that loopy grin on his face again. She rushed to the stairs. "How are they?"

"See for yourself!" Aenti Louise held out her bundle. "Meet Esther."

"Esther. What a beautiful name." Emma started to hold out her arms. She wanted to gather the little bundle against her chest. No. She'd been exposed to the flu repeatedly over the last two weeks. "I shouldn't get too close. The doctor says Rebecca has the flu."

Esther's tiny red face scrunched up. She opened her mouth and wailed. For a little thing, she had a mighty fine set of lungs. "Oh my goodness, you're fine."

Aunt Louise backed away, concern on her wizened face. "You're right. Best not get too close. There'll be plenty of time for that later."

"Jah, Leah will need everyone's help." Still grinning, Luke held up his bundle. "This is Martha."

"She's beautiful." Tears trickled down Emma's face. She brushed them away. Tears of joy mixed with tears of pain. Thomas didn't understand. She knew who she wanted to be with. To have and to hold forever. As soon as her unfinished business with Carl was done, she would show Thomas how much she cared for him. "I don't know why I'm crying. Tired, I guess."

"In awe, maybe."

Thomas's voice made her turn. "Can you believe it? More twins."

Thomas shrugged. "They run in your families." The anger was gone from his face, replaced by a sadness that broke her heart. His eyes were black with emotion. "Merry Christmas."

Emma sank onto the bottom step. She'd completely forgotten. "Merry Christmas."

"I'd better get back to my girl." He brushed past her and limped up the stairs without looking back.

Chapter 49

Christmas morning dawned so crisp and clear, it hurt to breathe the ice-cold air when Emma went out to sweep off the front porch. Still, it helped brush away some of the cobwebs in her brain. She went back inside and trudged up the stairs to the room now occupied by Rebecca. After only a few hours of sleep grabbed under a quilt, she felt as if she were sleepwalking. Rebecca had slept in fits and starts, crying out with dreams that sounded horrible. Thomas had finally insisted Emma try to get some sleep. Her own dreams had been troubled.

She knocked lightly to give Thomas warning, and then poked her head in the door. She needn't have worried. Thomas sat in a chair next to the bed, reading an old copy of *The Budget*. Rebecca still slept. Thomas looked over the top of his reading glasses. "Good morning."

Not warm, not cold. Like an acquaintance. So be it—for now. "Good morning." Emma tiptoed across the floor and touched Rebecca's forehead. Still warm, but not as bad as the previous evening. She breathed a tiny prayer. Rebecca opened her eyes. "Teacher! Am I dreaming? What are you doing in my bedroom?" She wiggled, stretched, and looked around. "This isn't my room." She sagged against her pillow. "Daed?"

Thomas folded the newspaper and laid it aside. "You were sick, so we brought you to the Shiracks's house to see the doctor."

"I remember now. I took a bath. I don't like baths. It's Christmas!" Rebecca threw back her quilts. "My present for you is at Groosmammi's!"

"Whoa, whoa." Emma caught her arm. "You're sick. You'll not be galloping about until your fever is gone, and that's going to take a while."

Thomas stood. "We'll go home. My mother will be worried. We can take care of Rebecca at her house."

"Not without breakfast." Her heart hammering in her chest, Emma stood her ground under his cool gaze. "She needs to eat. You heard what the doctor said."

Frowning, he smoothed his beard. "We'll eat. Then we'll go."

"Thomas." Emma stopped. "Rebecca, your father and I'll step outside for a moment. You stay under the covers until I bring you some hot tea, toast, and jam."

In the hallway, Emma gathered up her last remaining remnants of courage. "There's nothing between Carl and me."

Thomas's gaze bore into her. She was certain he could read every word written on her scarred heart. "Then promise to marry me. When the time comes, marry me."

The words melted the icy cold around her heart. "I want to."

"You want to or you will?"

"I need to untangle myself from this mess with Carl." She refused to lower her gaze under his ferocious stare. "It's the…it's the honorable thing to do."

"Still Carl."

The disappointment in those two words sliced through her with all the searing pain of a fresh wound.

At first Emma thought he might simply walk away. Instead, after a long second, Thomas inched closer. She could smell his soap, clean and fresh. His dark head, hair unruly from a night of fretting, dropped. His gaze settled on her hands clasped tightly in front of her. After a second, his fingers moved to trace the veins on the back of her hand. A touch so warm and gentle it made her think of a leaf floating on a soft, spring breeze. Of its own volition, her whole body leaned toward that touch. He fixed her with a sad smile. "Sweet Emma. You always want to do the right thing, don't you?"

"Jah." She could only manage that one syllable. Everything in her told her to throw caution to the wind. Let go of old fears. Let go. "Jah."

His gaze lifted until his dark eyes enveloped her. Her whole body began to shake. His Adam's apple bobbed. He cleared his throat. "Do what you need to do, but come back to me, Emma."

"Soon."

His hand dropped. He brushed past her, so close she might have reached out and caught his arm, kept him close. Emma already felt the void. She touched the place on her hand where his fingers had lingered. The breathless fluttering in her chest reminded her to inhale. "Thomas."

Hand on the knob, he looked back. "I'll wait. When you're ready, come find me."

He entered the bedroom and closed the door behind him. Emma stood still, unable to move. Nothing in her past prepared her for the onslaught of emotions that wrapped themselves around her head to toe like a tangled, knotted rope. She needed to sit quietly and undo each knot, each tangle. Quietly. Quickly. It was the only way she could have what she so desperately wanted.

She knew now what that was.

Chapter 50

The devotions were done, the presents opened, and the meal served. Emma smoothed the pretty material of the new dress Annie had made for her. It was a beautiful green color. She stood in the living room and reveled in the quiet for a second. After the adventures of the night before, everyone was napping. Tomorrow would be a day of visiting, but today was one of prayerful devotions. They had so many blessings with the new babies and Rebecca's safe return. Thomas had taken her home immediately after breakfast without another word or another look at Emma. His coldness had invaded her heart, making it hard to concentrate on the devotions. She had to show him she loved him, but first she had to be free to do it.

Emma grabbed her coat from its hook. Somehow she had to get to the Freiling farm without drawing attention to her absence from the house. With everyone napping, now was the time. She had to act or she would be party to Carl's actions. Either Carl told the bishop, or she would have to do it. On trembling legs, she teetered down the stairs.

"Where are you off to?" Leah came out on the landing above, a sleeping baby in each arm. Dark circles ringed her eyes. "It's bitter cold out there."

"I need to stretch my legs. I'm too wound up to nap." Emma cringed inwardly. It wasn't a lie. She couldn't nap, knowing what she knew about Carl. Knowing that it stood between her and Thomas. "I won't be long. I just need a breath of fresh air. When I come back, I'll watch the babies and you can rest."

"You didn't get much sleep last night, either." Leah winced and shifted the babies in her arms. Neither stirred. "Be quick about your walk, though. Luke doesn't like for you to go too far on your own."

"I won't be long," she promised. "Believe me, I'm about to run out of steam any second."

It only took her a few minutes to hitch the horse to the buggy and slip from the barn. When she pulled onto the road that led to the Freiling house, Emma tugged on the reins and brought the buggy to a halt. She let the north wind cool her burning face as she contemplated what to say. What would she say if Carl's parents saw her? Visiting on Christmas Day. Tomorrow would be the day for visiting. They would surely tell Luke of her appearance at their door.

She clucked and shook the reins. It didn't matter. She had no choice. The thought of a little baby who still hadn't been held by his father spurred her. The road was short. She arrived sooner than she wanted. She pulled on the reins, surveying the scene. Would she have to go to the door? What if Solomon Freiling answered her knock?

To her relief, Carl came into sight almost immediately. He trudged across the porch carrying a load of firewood. When he saw her buggy, he stopped.

"You're here." He clomped down the steps. "I was meaning to come talk to you after you had some time to calm down a little."

Calm down a little? He sounded so pleased and relieved to see her. Emma gritted her teeth to hold back the ungracious words that threatened to tumble from her mouth. How could he be so self-deceiving to think she would accept his advances once she knew of his marriage to the Englisch woman? She swallowed the bitter words of recrimination. She would not stoop to his level. With a steady calm she didn't feel, Emma slipped from the buggy and tied the reins to the hitching post. "I came to talk to you. For the last time."

His pleased smile died. "I knew it. You finished the letters."

"I did."

Their gazes battled.

"You were the one person I thought would understand—"

"If you thought I would understand, why did you tell me in a letter? Why not tell me face-to-face?" Once she opened her mouth, she couldn't stop herself. The words rushed out in a torrent she couldn't contain. "Because you're a coward and a liar?"

"I'm not a coward or a liar."

"Do you remember when you first came to see me that day when I was hanging clothes on the line?"

He nodded.

For a second Emma could feel the warm heat of summer on her face and smell the soap they used to wash the clothes. "You said you'd done nothing that shamed you or me." She'd wanted to believe him so much. "You lied."

"I made mistakes, but I'm not ashamed. I learned from those mistakes. You have to forgive me." His voice thickened. "A coward wouldn't have said anything at all. I wanted time to win you back first. I thought the letters would help you understand what I went through—"

"Learned? At what cost to your wife and child?" The audacity of his claim made her want to laugh, but the ability seemed to elude her. "Understand? Forgive? You're married to another woman. You have a baby."

"You understand why I went. You can understand why I had to come back."

"No. I don't."

"You understand wanting more than this life offers. You told me you can't understand not giving our children a better education, more education. You can't understand not giving them a teacher who knows more than basic reading, writing, and arithmetic. You understand not being able to live up to impossible standards, like being forced to forgive the man who killed your parents."

"Do I wish I could do more with book learning? Yes. But I understand that our way of life depends on practical knowledge far more than anything we'll find in books." Like the whirlwind of emotion inside, the fierce northern wind threatened to bowl Emma over. She hung on to her bonnet with both hands even as she tried to control her bitter anger. "As for forgiveness, I pray for it every day."

"But not for me? I thought surely someone you once professed to love would be included in that group that you would want to forgive."

"You're married to another. You have a child." Emma clamped her mouth shut. Her voice had begun to rise. Standing in front of Carl's house was no place for this conversation. "Walk with me."

"Yes, that would be better." He dropped the wood in a haphazard pile next to the steps. "Daed and Mudder are napping. The barn is empty and you need to get out of this cold wind."

He was concerned for her comfort. She would be alone in the barn with a married man. She hesitated. If Thomas found out, he'd never ask her the important question again. Yet, the circumstances demanded she do this. "Only for a minute."

Long enough to say what she had to say.

The air in the barn felt almost warm after the frigid gale outside. She inhaled the familiar, comforting smells of hay, feed, and manure. She faced Carl. His expression said he dreaded what came next. So did she. "How could you abandon her? Abandon your child?"

"I had to do what was best."

"For whom?" The horses that occupied the long row of stalls behind them reared their heads. One snorted as if to share in the anxiety Emma's voice carried. "Not you or me or anyone involved in this. You courted me as if you had the right to court a woman. You made me doubt my feelings for another man who offered me the possibility of a life I dream of having."

"You could have that life. Say the word and I'll divorce Karen."

The words battered Emma and bruised her heart. "I'll never be your wife. Never. Do you understand that? You are married to another. You vowed to love and honor another for the rest of your life."

The horses nickered again. Carl strode to the stalls. His back to Emma, he smoothed the mare's forelock. "Do you really think I should abandon my faith for an Englischer?"

"You abandoned your faith when you left Bliss Creek. You didn't meet your wife until later. Don't blame her for it."

"I thought you would see that the most important thing is to come back to the Plain ways."

"If that were what you are doing, then I might agree, but that's a question for the bishop. If you really plan to stay, you need to tell him what you've done."

"I can't tell him. He'll send me away."

"If you don't, I will." She clasped her cold hands to her chest. "Don't make me do that. Stand up and be a man. Admit your sin of omission. You abandoned me a long time ago. I forgive you for that. Give Karen a chance to forgive you, too."

Even as she said the words, Emma realized they were true. She forgave Carl. The burden rolled from her shoulder. "When you hold that baby in your arms, you'll know you did the right thing. Maybe someday you'll be able to bring your wife and child here. I don't know what God's plan is for you." She moved to stand next to him at the horse's stall. "But I know you'll never find out if you don't go back. Run, Carl, run to your future, not away from it."

He turned to face her. His jaw worked. "I can't."

"You can. You have until the end of the week. Then I'll tell the bishop."

He shook his head. "I never expected you to be so unforgiving."

"You're forgiven, Carl. By me. But that's not what matters now. You need a much greater forgiveness. Don't you understand that?"

He ducked his head like a little boy. A little boy who needed to grow up. "Yes."

"Good. Good-bye, Carl."

She rushed toward the door, anxious to get away from his noisy, ragged breathing. She shoved it open and collided with Solomon Freiling. "I'm so sorry!" She staggered back, mortified at the shocked expression on his face. "I didn't see you there."

"No, you didn't." The older man's gaze traveled to his son, who stood, not moving in the middle of the barn. "What's going on here?"

"We needed to talk." Carl's voice held none of the emotion of the previous moment. "I have a problem I must solve, and Emma was helping me. Now it's done. Now I need to talk to you and Mudder."

"I was just leaving." Her face burning, Emma squeezed past Solomon and trotted across the snow-covered drive. She fought the urge to break into a run. The snow crunched under her feet, but she could still hear Solomon questioning Carl. Her cheeks blazed. He would surely bring it up to Luke that she'd been alone in the barn with his son. Surely, Carl would tell his father the truth.

Or maybe not. Truth wasn't a virtue he seemed to relish.

Emma turned the buggy toward home. She clucked and shook the reins. It wasn't far, but the cold seeped into her bones as the sun started to drop on the horizon. She urged the horse to pick up speed. Another buggy came into view. As it moved closer, Emma peered at the driver. Who was out in this weather on Christmas Day? Catherine. Catherine, who had been so quiet all morning and then rushed to her room after the noon meal, pleading exhaustion. Now there were two of them out and about when they should be resting. Emma's heart lodged in her throat. Did Catherine have an equally pressing errand to run—one that couldn't wait?

She pulled even with her sister. "Where are you going? It'll be dark soon."

Catherine pulled up on the reins to keep an impatient horse in line. Her eyes were red rimmed to match her red nose. Emma looked closer. It was more than the cold. Catherine had been crying. "Catherine?"

Her sister sighed. Tears trickled down her cheeks. She opened her mouth. A sob came out.

"Catherine—"

"I just want you to know that…that I love you." Her voice quivered. "No matter what happens, remember that."

"What are you talking about? Is something going on?" The Shiracks, like other Plain folks, weren't ones to talk about emotion. It was understood. "You sound…you sound like you're saying good-bye."

"There's something you should know." Catherine gave her a sideways glance, then studied the horizon. "You're not going to like it. No one will."

"Tell me. Just tell me."

"Doctor Miller has been driving me into Wichita to see the psychologist." Catherine said the words quickly, letting them run together in her obvious desire to get them all out. "Twice a week."

"*Ach*, Catherine, what have you done? Without telling Luke!" So that's where she'd been when she was supposed to be cleaning houses. What a web of lies she'd woven. Emma could see her brother's disappointed, furious face already. He would worry that people would find out. Catherine with mental problems that needed treatment in Wichita. "He'll be so angry. I don't know what he'll do."

"I'm eighteen. I don't need his permission." Catherine's tart tone said that fact gave her great satisfaction. "This isn't about Luke or our family. Or what people will think. It's about me. I know it's hard for you to understand. I needed help. Help no one was willing to let me get. I was drowning. I wanted to die. I thought about it all the time."

"I'm so sorry." Hot tears warmed Emma's face, but her heart could feel only cold dread at what was coming. "I tried to be a good sister."

"You are a good sister." Catherine sighed. "But that's not enough. Don't you see? Aenti Louise's stories are not enough. I needed real help."

"So you went to Doctor Miller."

"Not on purpose. I was in town, getting cleaning supplies, when I saw him at the grocery store." Her voice faltered. "He saw it in my face. He was so kind. He stopped and asked me if I was all right."

She wiped at tears with the back of her glove. "I couldn't lie. I burst into tears right there in the soap aisle. It was awful, shameful. He took me aside, and he asked me to let him help me."

"So you did."

"At first, I was too scared. But then I knew if I didn't, something horrible was going to happen. So I went to his office. It was like he threw me a rope in the middle of a lake. I came up for air just when my lungs were about to burst."

They sat in silence for a while. The horses whinnied at each other and their heads nodded as if they too were having a conversation, but one much more amiable.

Emma rubbed her woolen mittens on her cheeks, trying to warm them. The material scratched at her face, but she welcomed relief from the numbness that threatened to overcome her. "What did the doctor in Wichita say?"

"A lot!" Catherine's face lit up for the first time that day. "I like her. She's nice and she's funny and she doesn't see anything wrong with me feeling bad. She's says I have a right to be upset. My parents died in front of me—"

"Nobody thinks you shouldn't feel bad." Sudden anger whipped through Emma. "We all feel bad. It was horrible for everyone."

"But you've moved on and you don't understand why I can't! You think I should be able to say 'mind over matter' and be done with it. My faith in God should be enough. It's enough for you."

"That's not true!" Emma contemplated setting the buggy in motion. She no longer wanted to have this conversation. Something held her back. The knowledge that she should try to convince her sister to turn from the path she'd chosen. Yet, a niggling, small voice in her head said *no. No.* Catherine had done what she needed to do to save herself. "I struggle with my faith, too. But without it, I'd be lost."

"I'm not abandoning my faith. It's stronger than ever. God will be with me on my new journey." Catherine threw up her hands. "Can't you see that? God is everywhere. And he is faithful, even when I'm weak."

"I know. I'm selfish." Emma couldn't stop the tears from falling. The sun, a fiery red ball, began to dip behind the horizon. Soon it would be dark. "Family is everything."

"Yes, it is." Catherine wiped at her face again. "But sometimes it's not enough."

Fear raced through Emma. Not again. She couldn't go through this again. Everyone kept leaving her. "Don't go."

"I have to go."

Emma had just gotten Josiah back. Her family was complete—minus two very important people whom she could never get back. A sob wracked Emma. "Please don't do this."

"I spoke to the bishop—"

"You spoke to Bishop Kelp?" Emma couldn't begin to imagine. "Without Luke knowing? All by yourself? When?"

"A few minutes ago. I couldn't wait any longer. We met in his barn. He was...firm. He says I must go immediately. He will speak to Luke this evening. The bishop knows it's what I want."

"What else do you want?"

"I've decided to study psychology. I want to know why I suffer like this. I want to help other people who suffer from depression and post-traumatic stress disorder."

"You'd leave your family and everything you know for that?"

"What I'm doing will help other people. I feel called to help. This is the only way I can do it. If there were another way I would take it, but our community doesn't allow that. I understand it and I accept it."

Catherine wrapped the reins around her hands and laid them in her lap. "I know it's impossible for you to understand." Her voice dropped to a tearful whisper. "And I'm sorry it hurts you. I'm not like Carl. I'm not running away. I'm running toward something. A future that has meaning. Doctor Baker ran some tests. She says I'm smart and I feel things more deeply than most people. She's says I'll make a good psychologist."

Running toward something. Exactly what Emma had told Carl to do. "How? How will you do this?"

"One day at a time."

That was no answer. How would Catherine manage?

As if she'd peeked into Emma's mind, Catherine went on. "Each time I was paid for cleaning, I set aside a portion and saved it. I needed to have something that was my own. I needed a plan, a plan that involved being able to leave. It was the only thing that kept me from falling apart completely. Can you understand that?"

Emma nodded. She couldn't speak, not without sobbing. She swallowed and closed her eyes against the setting sun. When she thought her voice would hold steady, she spoke. "I understand, but I'm scared for you. The world out there is frightening."

Her sister hopped down from her buggy and covered the small space between them. She enveloped Emma in a hug. "I'm scared, too."

"Then maybe you shouldn't go."

"I'm scared to go, but I'm more scared of staying."

"We won't be able to talk to you or see you ever again. Unless you change your mind."

"I know." Sadness etched lines on Catherine's face. Her eyes stained red as she patted Emma's shoulder. "I know, sweet Emma. I'll miss you, but you need to do something for me. You need to run toward something, too. Whatever it is that matters to you, run toward it."

Emma's throat ached with the effort not to break down. "I promise," she whispered.

They hugged again, Emma didn't want to let go, but Catherine pushed away. "I have to go. Doctor Miller is waiting."

"Now? You're going now? On Christmas Day? What about your things?"

"It's my present to myself. Doctor Miller is taking me to Wichita tomorrow morning." Catherine pointed at the bag on the floorboard. "It's not as if I have much that is my own, schweschder."

A small bag of clothes. That was it. All she was taking with her. "Catherine—"

"Bye!"

Catherine whirled and mounted her buggy. She sat up straight, reins lifted, facing her future. Emma already felt left behind. "Catherine!"

"Send Josiah for the buggy," Catherine called back. "It'll be parked in front of Doctor Miller's home on Willow Street."

"I will. Good-bye!"

"Remember, Emma, run toward it."

Emma sat in the middle of the road, watching the buggy until it disappeared from sight. Run toward it. She clucked and snapped the reins. Toward him. If Catherine had the courage, so did she.

Chapter 51

H er breath coming in white puffs that immediately disappeared, Emma slipped and slid along the path the Karbachs had shoveled from their house to the area behind the barn where the buggies parked after the prayer service. Thomas was no longer with the men who chatted around the picnic tables inside. Maybe he'd already left. Her heart clenched at the thought. Or maybe she could still catch him at his buggy.

Picking up her pace, she licked her chapped lips and wiped at her runny nose with the handkerchief she clutched in her gloved hands. What a time to catch a cold. Leah blamed it on Emma running around outside on Christmas Eve and then again on Christmas Day. It didn't matter. She'd do it all again, if need be. The only drawback remained that she still couldn't hold the sweet new babies, which meant more work for Annie and the twins.

The icy air burned Emma's nose and made her lungs ache. Leah had suggested she stay home from the service, but Emma couldn't do that. If she did, she had no idea when she would get the next opportunity to see Thomas. To speak to him. As it was, with the serving of the food and the washing of the dishes afterwards and Leah's watchful gaze, Emma may have missed him. Since Catherine's departure, it seemed Luke and Leah both had been watching them all with eagle eyes. Determined eyes. Determined not to let it happen again.

Three days had passed since Luke announced at the kitchen table he'd heard that Carl had left again. He'd seen Solomon Freiling at the feed store. Something in Luke's stern gaze suggested Solomon had shared a story about her Christmas Day visit to the Freiling barn. But Luke asked no questions and she offered no comment. Even Annie remained silent on the subject. Not something Annie did often. There was nothing to say. Simple as that.

Time to move forward. That meant convincing Thomas she loved him and wanted to spend the rest of her life with him. Emma glanced across the road to the neighboring field. The children were making an enormous snowman. They whooped and laughed and carried on the way only children could. Eli and Rebecca were in the thick if it. That meant Thomas hadn't left yet. She hadn't missed him.

God, please let me talk to him today. She couldn't bear the suspense. Would he understand? Would he pose that all-important question again? She had to know. No more waiting around. No more beating around the bush.

She slowed at the corner of the barn, knowing the buggies were parked just on the other side. Her stomach rocked. The moment had arrived. Hand on her heart, she peeked around the corner. There stood Thomas, hitching his horse. *Thank You, God.*

She started to step out. Her boots seemed frozen to the ground. What if he had moved on? Helen Crouch had served his plate, her face all smiles, just a few hours ago. What if he'd stricken Emma from his heart? What if he'd decided to court another? No, he'd said he would wait. Thomas was nothing if not a man of his word. She set one foot in front of the other. *Step. Step. Step.*

Thomas checked the bit in the horse's mouth, then smoothed a gloved hand across her long, graceful neck. Emma shivered.

"It's getting colder. Time to be getting on home, I reckon." Thomas spoke to the horse, whose head dipped in acquiescence. The horse pranced and whinnied. Thomas tugged on the harness. "What's the big hurry? Wait until I call the children. You'll be in a nice warm barn soon enough."

Emma couldn't help but smile. Thomas talked to the horses just the way Daed had done. She preferred conversations with the dog that lazed on their porch most summer evenings. Her fear melted. This was Thomas. The man with whom she wanted to spend the rest of her life. She took a deep breath of air so cold her teeth hurt and slipped out into the open.

Thomas tightened the harness. Time to go home. They'd lingered far longer than usual over the meal served after the last prayer service of the old year. He enjoyed the conversation with the other men about hunting and what the spring planting season would bring. Since they did no work on Sunday, there was no need to rush home. The children would be worn out, though, from the endless games they'd played in the snow. It looked like they were in the final stages of building an over-sized snowman complete with someone's Sunday hat. Patches—so named by Eli and Rebecca after much debate—snorted and pranced, making it difficult to finish the job. "Easy, there, stand still, girl." He patted her rump. "We're almost ready."

"Talking to the horse?"

Startled, Thomas looked up to see Emma standing near the buggy. He surveyed the area. They were alone among the buggies. He forced himself to meet her gaze. "Yes, we were just discussing the weather."

She patted her nose with a hankie and smiled. Her nose was bright red and her eyes sparkled in the cold air. "Sometimes animals make better conversation than people, I expect."

"I'm sorry about Catherine."

Emma's smile faded. "She's in God's hands."

"Indeed."

"Did you hear Carl's gone, too?"

"Yes. Shamefully, the gossipers among us have linked their names."

The thought made Thomas feel queasy. "Going away at almost exactly the same time didn't help their causes much."

"Have people nothing better to talk about?"

"Better they should sew those lips shut and leave them that way." Thomas bent over the buggy's wheel, not wanting her to see his face. "Why did Carl go? I'm not asking out of idle curiosity. I thought he'd made a firm commitment to the Plain life."

"I know you would never gossip." Footsteps told him she'd moved closer. "Could you look at me?"

He forced himself to raise his head. Her cheeks were red, but her expression remained determined. "He left because he needed to go back. He had a life and responsibilities he'd abandoned. People who needed him."

So Carl had stayed true to his colors. Abandoning those who loved him. "He ran away from someone not once, but twice?"

"Yes."

Thomas had to ask the question, even if he didn't get the answer he wanted. He was no coward. "And what does that mean for you?"

"I sent him away. He came here for me, and I sent him away. Do you understand that?" Her chin lifted. Her gaze met his. He saw no hesitation now, only a ferocity that set his heart pounding. She took a step closer. "It's time for me to run, too, but I'm not running away from anything. I'm running toward what I want."

Thomas couldn't rip his gaze from her beautiful face. Her fair skin and blue eyes mesmerized him. His heart ached for her. She hadn't said no when he asked her to marry him. Nor had she said yes. "I should get the children," he said. "They'll be worn out from playing in the snow and building that snowman. I'm hoping that's not Eli's hat on its head." He clamped his mouth shut and started walking toward the field. Why was he nattering like an old woman? "It's time for us to go."

"Thomas, wait!"

Despite having every intention of leaving, he stopped moving. Even his heart ceased to beat, or so it seemed.

"Yes."

Yes. To him? Thomas found it hard to believe. He'd managed to convince himself that she would never be his. That he would learn to live without her. "Yes?"

"Yes, I'll be your wife, if the offer still stands. I know it's a long time until November and a lot can happen, but I know I won't change my mind—"

His heart started again. In fact, it pounded so hard Thomas feared he would drop in his tracks. Instead, he covered the half dozen feet between them in two strides. He grabbed Emma by the waist, hoisted her in the air, and kissed her hard. Her arms came up and wrapped around his neck. She felt warm and soft, just as he had imagined, despite every attempt to keep those thoughts at bay. Her lips simply received his at first, but when he started to move away, they sought his with an urgency that made it almost impossible to stop. Knowing nothing more would be proper, he forced himself to break away. Their gazes intertwined. Her breath was sweet on his face and her tremulous smile lit the space around him. Her face suddenly pink, she dropped her forehead to his shoulder, hiding her face.

"Oh, Thomas," she whispered, her voice muffled against his coat. "I can't breathe."

"Look at me and I'll help you." She raised her head, her expression delighted, as if she knew what was coming. He kissed her again, even more deeply. He'd waited so long. Tradition dictated that more waiting was in store for them, but knowing they would be husband and wife before the new year ended made the thought easier to accept. He ended the kiss even though he wanted it to never be over. "How's that?"

She laughed, high and breathless. "Better."

He held her in a hug for a few seconds more. Finally, with deep regret, he dropped her to her feet. Her cheeks rosy, she staggered and the hankie fell to the ground. He caught her hand, certain she would fall.

"I'm sorry." Flustered, he let go of her and stumbled back, stammering the words in a rushed mishmash. "That won't happen again. I promise."

"Never?" Her arms out as if to catch her balance, she grinned. She raised one to her face and her fingers touched her bottom lip. "What a shame. I hope you don't catch my cold."

Leave it to her to tease at a time like this. Life with Emma would never be dull. "Until you're my wife. Then I reserve the right to kiss you every day."

"I reserve the right to kiss you back."

He picked up the sodden hankie with two fingers and handed it back to her. "By the way, it would be worth it."

She accepted his offering, her face puzzled. "What would?"

"Catching a cold. I could always ask you to nurse me back to health." Aware that he was smiling like a fool, Thomas counted on his shaking fingers. "January, February, March, April, May, June, July, August, September, October. Ten months. It'll be a long year, won't it?"

Her eyes shining, Emma leaned into his space. "I plan to enjoy every single minute of it."

He leaned into her space. They weren't touching, but it felt as if their hands were clasped in a tight embrace, one that could never be broken. "Promise?"

"Promise."

Epilogue

The beef and noodle casserole balanced in one hand, Emma climbed down from the buggy, walked past the green pickup truck parked in the driveway, and trudged up the snow-covered steps. Before she knocked, she turned and looked back at Luke. He smiled and nodded. She faced the screen door and knocked, a hard, quick rap. It rattled against an inner door painted a bright blue.

A dog began to bark inside, but the door didn't open. She inhaled and tried to be patient. The frantic barking got louder. "Hush, stop it!" Mr. Cramer's voice boomed, even through the thick wooden door. "Sit!"

Finally, the door opened. Mr. Cramer put one hand on the frame and peered out. White stubble covered his craggy chin and one loop of his overall straps was undone. His long-sleeved undershirt had a brown stain on it. "Miss Shirack." He couldn't look more surprised if she had been a bear foraging on his front porch. "Is something wrong?"

"We understand you're still in mourning. So are we." Forcing a smile, Emma held up the casserole. "So we wanted to share some food with you in honor of our parents."

Mr. Cramer's face crumpled. He hung his head. "How can you…" His voice broke. "I don't understand how you can…"

"You're forgiven, Mr. Cramer." Emma glanced out at Luke. A sad smile on his face, he hopped from the buggy and started up the steps toward them. "We all are."

Discussion Questions

1. At the beginning of *To Love and to Cherish*, Emma's Amish faith demands that she forgive Mr. Cramer for the accident that caused the death of her own parents. She finds it almost impossible to forgive him. Has there ever been an instance in your life when someone did something "unforgiveable"? Were you able to forgive? How did you go about it?

2. Eventually Emma learns that Carl has abandoned not only his wife, but a child. She's caught between believing he should retain his Amish faith, forsaking the world, and knowing he must return to his obligations as a husband and a father. Do you think it was more important for him to return to his wife and child or to remain in his community of faith? Why?

3. Emma worries about Josiah; Luke tells her worrying is a sin. Thomas tells her the same thing. The Amish believe that worrying shows a lack of faith. What is the scriptural basis for this belief? How do you keep from worrying about situations you can't control or change?

4. The Amish also believe God has a plan for each one of His children. When something bad happens, they accept it as part of God's plan. Do you agree? What steps have you taken to discern

His plan for you? How do you deal with events in your life that are difficult to understand in light of God's love for you?

5. When Catherine is unable to overcome the devastation of seeing her parents killed, Aenti Louise takes her for a walk on the farm. Aenti Louise says she feels God's presence in the breeze, the warm sun, and rustling of the leaves on the trees. Where do you feel closest to God? Why?

6. Aenti Louise says God understands the anger and hurt we feel at the loss of a loved one because His Son died. Have you ever been angry with God? How did you overcome that anger?

7. At the last moment, Catherine backs out of the wedding because she realizes she intended to marry for the wrong reasons. Did she do the right thing, even though it caused terrible pain and hurt for Melvin? Have you ever done something for the wrong reasons, only to have it backfire? How did you reconcile the pain you caused with doing the right thing? How does God reconcile your actions?

8. After his parents' funeral, Josiah can't accept the loss of his parents as God's will for him and his brothers and sisters. Do you ever have difficulty accepting God's will for you?

9. Josiah recites the verse, "This is the day which the Lord hath made; we will rejoice and be glad in it," to Emma. He asks her, "how's that working out for you?" On difficult days, how do you find the joy of the Lord?

10. Aenti Louise reminds Emma and Catherine of the story of Jacob wrestling with the angel of the Lord all night long until the angel touches his hip and makes him lame. He could've done that at any time, but he waits until Jacob is exhausted. Aenti Louise says that was because God wanted Jacob to know who was in control. Do you ever wrestle with God over who is in control of your life? How do you give up control to the Lord?

Kelly Irvin is a Kansas native and has been writing professionally for twenty-five years. She and her husband, Tim, make their home in Texas. They have two children, three cats, and tank full of fish. A public relations professional, Kelly is also the author of two romantic suspense novels and writes short stories in her spare time.

To learn more about her work,
visit www.kellyirvin.com

To learn more about books by Kelly Irvin or
to read sample chapters, log on to our website:

www.harvesthousepublishers.com

HARVEST HOUSE PUBLISHERS

EUGENE, OREGON

More Great Amish Books from Harvest House Publishers...

THE HOMESTYLE AMISH KITCHEN COOKBOOK

Straight from the heart of Amish life, this indispensable guide to hearty, home-cooked meals is filled with hundreds of recipes for favorites such as Scrapple, Amish Friendship Bread, Potato Rivvel Soup, Snitz Pie, and Graham "Nuts" Cereal. "Amish Kitchen Wisdom" sections highlight fascinating tidbits about the Plain lifestyle.

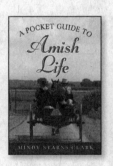

A POCKET GUIDE TO AMISH LIFE

Full of fun and fresh facts about the Amish people, who abide by an often-misunderstood faith and unique culture, this handy-sized guide covers a wide variety of topics, such as: beliefs and values, clothing and transportation, courtship and marriage, shunning and discipline, teens and *rumspringa*, and education and work.

THE AMISH MIDWIFE

Adopted as a child, nurse midwife Lexie Jaeger learns the true meaning of the Pennsylvania Dutch word *demut*, which means "to let be," as she reaches out to her birth family and changes from a woman who wants to control everything to a woman who depends on God.

THE AMISH NANNY

Amish-raised Ada Rupp is at a crossroads. It's time to make a commitment to the faith and join the church, especially if she wants a future with the handsome Amish widower Will Gundy, but a young Mennonite scholar named Daniel also tugs at her heart. Which path will she choose?

❦ The Adams County Trilogy ❧

REBECCA'S PROMISE

Rebecca Keim has declared her love to John Miller and agreed to become his wife. But she's haunted by memories of a long ago love—and a promise made and a ring given. Is that memory just a fantasy come back to destroy the beautiful present...or was it real?

REBECCA'S RETURN

Where will Rebecca Keim find happiness? In Wheat Ridge with John, the man she has agreed to marry? Or should she stake her future on the memory that persists...and the ring she's never forgotten? Does God have a perfect will for Rebecca—and if so, how can she know that will?

REBECCA'S CHOICE

When Rebecca goes to Milroy to attend her beloved teacher's funeral, her fiancé, John, receives a mysterious letter accusing her of plotting to marry for money. Soon Rebecca learns of her large inheritance with the condition that she must marry an Amish man. Will John believe her motives are pure?